CRASH

J. L. Harvey

LEIGH PUBLISHING

ISBN-13: 978-1-8380841-2-7

BY THE SAME AUTHOR

DOMINOES (2020),
available on Amazon in paperback and Kindle edition.

CONTENTS

ACKNOWLEDGEMENTS

Thanks again to the encouragement of my friends – Sue, Lynne and Trish – who offered sound critical advice and some thoughtful editing. And to my extended family for their interest and patience when I'm writing and keep telling them about my progress. Thanks also to my publishing team for their support and guidance.

'Nothing is ever lost … Nothing that can't be found.'
'Sometimes you just have to do what you can and try to live with it.'

– Stephen King, *The Dead Zone.*

Chapter 1

Glass splinters   sudden as gunfire

Fragments bursting through sharp air

Grinding metal buckles

Then a jarring

lurching

rolling over and over

Unstoppable.

A second lasts forever

Death in an instant

What the fuck

*

I smell it all first. That unmistakeable smell of hospital. As though the air is thick and chloroformed, embalming the patients – I must be one – as we lie, I imagine, in serried rows waiting to be administered to. I sense the bandages, tight round my head and some hard structure on one arm. There is a plastic tube touching my cheek. Impossible to open my eyes, the lids weighted down, my head so heavy, it can't be moved. Or turned. I don't even want to try...

I wake to a deafening pounding in my ears. It reverberates round my skull and I pray for it to stop. I need to speak, to ask for help but it is beyond me. Words are totally beyond me.

It is then that fear wells up, a surge of terror, and I know I'm in deep shit.

Something has happened to put me here — some awful accident — but I have no idea what. I can't remember a thing.

I can hear, though. The rhythmic clicking of a machine. A faint buzz and the swish of a door opening and closing. Footsteps, rubber soles, measured steps passing. Not once, a number of times. The steady hum of what I think is fluorescent lighting above me.

I feel cocooned. Which should be comforting, safe. But it isn't. More like being entombed.

The panic rises again, but I try to reason my way out of it. If I'm in a hospital, I'm being looked after. I've heard they put you in a coma if you have brain damage, so perhaps that's what this is — why I can't open my eyes or speak. No-one ever tells you how scary it is when you can hear what's going on but can't communicate, do they? I've read about 'locked-in syndrome', which I've always thought was the most terrifying state to end up in. Better to be 'locked-out'. Totally.

Someone touches the plastic tube. Professional hands adjusting something. I want to tell them to be careful, that I can feel. That I can hear.

And then I can. Hear. A voice that sounds familiar and I know it's Carrie. After all our years together, I'm not likely to forget that. And she sounds… what? Angry?

'I'm sure he should be conscious by now. It's been four days.'

Four days! God, must have been a hell of an accident. Was I mugged? Was I driving and lost the plot? Did I fall off a ladder?

'It can sometimes take well over a week.' A stranger's voice. The nurse. 'Or longer, in some cases. The consultant discussed the results of the CT scan with you, didn't she?'

'Well, discussed isn't quite the right word. I was being told. I gather, anyway, it's inconclusive. And I didn't really understand this Glasgow Coma Scale. A number doesn't mean much to me. I need to know if his condition has improved. What the prognosis is.'

No reply.

'Will she be back in the hospital tonight?'

'I'll find out for you.'

A sigh, Carrie frustrated, clothes making a rustling noise as she moves. Perhaps crossing her legs and folding her arms. A typical stance when she's annoyed.

I try to hold on but I fall into blackness again. Floating, released.

And then the furious whisper which shatters the calm and sends alarm chasing into my head.

'And what were you doing all the way out there? Where had you been? You were meant to be in the city, for God's sake, not halfway to Chester. Wake up, damn you, and tell me what's going on.'

My whole body is on Red Alert. She is furious with *me*, not the consultant. She wants me to wake up and explain myself so she can vent her fury and find out… what? I'm suddenly glad I'm flat on my back and out of it, unable to answer questions for which I *have* no answer.

What had I been doing? Where on earth had I been? I'd obviously lied, but why?

I try to concentrate, searching for some mental image that would make sense of all this, but nothing comes. I do the old trick of telling my brain to switch off for a bit, hoping some scrap of memory will hit me a few minutes later. But nothing does.

The pain in my arm cuts through me, so agonising it seems to be the only part of me that exists. And my ribcage is gripping me in a vice. Had I moved? Am I capable of movement? And then, like a ministering angel, someone brings relief – a sharp prick and I breathe and melt away…

The sand is warm under my feet and the evening sky is streaked with orange and red, reflected in the sea near the horizon. We walk, all the time in the world to talk and stay close. No-one else in sight. I am happy. You can't see the last stretch of the beach from here, not in the fading light, anyway, and it looks never-

ending as it curves along the front. Some lamps, spaced evenly, skirt the road above and there's the occasional sound of a car cruising along, no-one in a hurry. The tide is out so we could choose to walk anywhere but we pick the dry sand midway between the road and the surf, which I can just hear lapping gently even this far away. The air is still, not a breath of wind. This is how it should be. Peaceful. Just being with the one person you love. We hold hands and match our steps, heading towards the far end of the bay...

I feel my eyelids flutter in an involuntary tremor and know my brain is awake. I have no idea whether I've been dreaming or remembering, but the images stay in my head and I'm sure it has something to do with a real moment. Something in my past. I read once that dreams are rarely pleasant because when we sleep, we try to deal with all the difficult stuff of the day – like a sort of mental work-out – and I usually dream of moments of crisis – nothing to do with actual happenings, but scary as hell –falling down a cavernous hole, being on the wrong train, losing all my teeth (what's *that* about, for God's sake?). So my picture of the beach and the feeling of being uplifted, of being *happy* (how often can we say that about a day, or even a moment?), I am more convinced it's something that actually happened to me. Whatever… it was special…

I was lucky once.

I sense a quiet in the room. Carrie isn't here. The relief is enormous. Her anger is more than I can take at the moment. Formidable. That's Carrie. A force to be reckoned with. And I don't have the will or the power to deal with whatever she's going to throw at me. Call me a coward if you like but I have to be on guard. I'm making it sound like a battleground – if I could smile, I would – but marriages can be combative as well as companionable.

And I have no bloody answers for her.

An ambulance siren shrieks through the air then dies suddenly. Probably how I arrived here – paramedics rushing me into the operating theatre, doctors testing reflexes, machines pumping and bleeping. OK, so I've watched too many hospital dramas. Well, just let's hope this turns out to have a positive ending.

So what happened? Must have crashed the car. Must have been somewhere I wasn't supposed to be. But for the life of me, I can't make sense of it. The last thing I remember was having breakfast at home, drinking strong coffee and eating toast, skimming through the front page of the Guardian, but that could have been weeks ago, not days.

Hardly a pointer to the main event.

Memory's a funny thing. You can remember some bits of your childhood with amazing clarity – getting a miniature fort for Christmas, running into a pan of porridge and the blistering pain, first dive into a freezing lido in Colwyn Bay – so long ago they should have been forgotten. And yet when you're an adult, you so often struggle to recall details. You can't think what you were doing at Christmas four years ago or in the summer when you were twenty-seven. And that trip to Amsterdam? When was that? I read somewhere that the moments that stay with you are when your emotions are singularly intense, no inhibitions, just raw fear, or joy, or shock – the essence of us under all the superficial trappings of living.

Well, it'd be nice to have that working now.

So I try to concentrate on what I *can* remember.

Well, I know Carrie's my wife... we live in a small village near... God knows where! The name escapes me. And I'm certain I work outside. But...

I give up. Basic facts elude me – anyway, they don't give any real sense of me. They're not who I am. And it's exhausting. Funny how I sense that in the shadows, there's something else more important. Something vague yet ever-present which holds the key to all this.

Hidden from me.

Somewhere in the blanks.

'And how are you tonight, Alex?' A male voice, jolly – professionally jolly and this isn't really a question. I can't answer, after all.

'Just checking all these machines and then I'll make you comfortable. It's time to settle everyone down for the night. Tomorrow's a new day. Don't you worry. We'll have you up in no time.'

The rustle of material, fingers touching my face, a tapping sound, the bed sheet too tight over my chest, like an iron band. I am drowning and no-one seems to notice. Fighting to reach the surface but too weak to claw my way up. How long can I hold my breath?

'There you are.' He talks as though he knows me. I want him gone.

And then he is.

It is at that moment, alone and helpless, long past understanding what state I am in, whether I'll ever come out of this, that a sense of pure dread sweeps through me, consuming me with a ferocity I could not have experienced before. Because I'd surely remember. I am falling into the depths again and nothing is going to save me... nothing can...

I push a wheelbarrow filled with soil. It is so heavy, my back is bowed. I come to a narrow bridge with stone walls hemming me in and I start to move slowly across. But behind me I hear an engine, a car coming closer and closer, trailing me. It comes so close I smell the heat of it, feel the vibration of it. It revs and harries me. It is not going to wait patiently till I'm across. It is going to mow me down. I know this but I can't move any faster. I must keep going, keep pushing this wheelbarrow over the bridge...

Chapter 2

Carrie pulled off her muddy boots and threw them onto the tiled floor. The kitchen was in such a mess, a bit more mud wouldn't make any difference. She felt angry and tearful, but mostly angry. She'd asked Jack to clear up the dishes and he hadn't even made an appearance yet. You'd think in the circumstances he'd move himself and give her some help. Four nights in the relatives' room at the hospital, half-awake expecting to be called to Alex's bedside, had left her ragged and grouchy. She was never good without sleep.

And she couldn't just leave all the horses to Steph – she was only meant to be part-time and was doing far more hours than she should at the moment. But some jobs had to be done whatever else came up. You have a commitment when you take on fifteen liveries. Whatever else is going on, the horses have to be put out in the big field and the four paddocks each day (even though it was now May, some owners insisted on having them in overnight), straw in the stables, water buckets filled, hay nets, lessons to schedule… God, it was hard work in the normal run of things, but this awful accident had thrown everything to pot.

'Jack!' She opened the kitchen door, nearly tripping over the dog and yelled again. 'Could you please get up and help? It's past eight and I need to be back at the hospital.'

No sound of movement.

'Jack!'

She hadn't managed to see the consultant yesterday and she was determined to corner her today. Waiting in the corridor outside the ICU for forty-five minutes, only to be told there'd been an emergency that *had* to be dealt with, had done nothing for her fretful state of mind! Well, fair enough, these things happen. But that was yesterday. This morning, she'd get some answers, one way or another.

I'm becoming a strident, demanding woman, she thought. *I can hear myself. Trying to keep control and failing. And I'm furious with Alex, furious with everyone. Truth is I'm scared. He might never come out of this coma. He might be brain-damaged and not be the Alex I know anymore. It's OK quoting percentages and possibilities at me and reassuring me he'll recover gradually. Nothing's certain.*

The phone rang. She'd already rung the hospital so she guessed who it would be.

'Yes, Joe.'

'Is there any change? I waited up last night thinking you'd ring.'

'Well, I would have but couldn't get hold of the consultant so I'd nothing new to tell you. I'll see her today.'

'Do you want me to come with you? I could meet you there. When I ring the ICU, they don't give me much.'

'No. I'll get hold of this doctor and report back. He's still unconscious, that I do know. No change. Go this evening when Jack leaves. That'll be best.' She moved over towards the hob and switched the kettle on, wanting to get off the phone. 'Joe.'

'Yes?'

'I wouldn't say too much to your parents yet. I've played it down. They're worried enough and until I know something definite, they'll be more anxious than they are now. Your dad's not too good as it is.'

'OK. They were saying they wanted to come and see for themselves but I put them off,' he said, sounding tired. 'The sight of him lying there with all that paraphernalia was bad enough for me, so I know what it would do to *them*. Let me know as soon as you talk to someone.'

'I will.' Carrie leant against the kitchen units and closed her eyes. It was all getting on top of her, one thing after another to deal with –

the police, the insurance company, Alex's work, friends wanting updates…

Jack put his head round the kitchen door.

'Who was that?'

She could feel the irritation rising in her chest. He hadn't even changed out of his pyjamas.

'Your Uncle Joe.' She gave him a meaningful look. 'You need to get dressed, Jack, now. Go out to the barn for me and offer to help Steph. She could do with bringing some feed bags out of the truck.'

He muttered something she couldn't hear and it was just enough to tip her over. 'Christ, Jack. We're in a crisis here and you're not shaping yourself.' (Wasn't that her mother's mantra when she was growing up? Before she left them for the charming George. Carrie, at twelve, had hoped she'd never have to hear those words barked at her again but they still resonated like a slap – *Shape yourself, girl.* There was never an option but to do just that!)

Jack nodded slowly. Then made the mistake of frowning as he turned to leave.

Carrie gritted her teeth. 'For heaven's sake, get dressed and help out. And while you're at it, take on some responsibility. You're not a kid anymore.' God! She was beginning to *sound* like her mother now, sharp and demanding, that scathing tone that always got her back up. So she said, more kindly, 'And Jack, could you please take Sam down the field when you go? He hasn't been out yet.'

It was pointless starting a row when everyone was under such strain. But he was so laid back about everything – it always infuriated her.

'Yes, OK.'

Carrie saw how dejected he looked and began to feel guilty. She was too hard on him. and she knew it. She forced a smile and put her hand out in a conciliatory gesture. 'After lunch I'll run you back to see your father.'

He hesitated at the door. 'Yes, sure. How was he last night?'

'The same. Just the same.' She put two slices of bread in the toaster. 'Do you want some?'

'No. I'll get dressed first.' He nodded thoughtfully, pulling up his pyjama trousers and looking as though he was about to say something.

'What?'

'I don't go to the pub till six, so I can spend the afternoon with him. I'll take some CDs in and play them to him. They say music helps.'

'Jack, it's a nice idea, but you have to get permission from Nurse Graham. There are other patients in the ICU and it might disturb them.'

'OK, I'll do that. It's worth asking though.'

She raised her eyebrows and gave a wry smile. 'Go carefully. They might freak out at your taste in music.'

'Yeah. They might.' He grinned and she thought then what a charming boy he could be, how his face changed when he wasn't in a huff or shutting her out. There'd been too much of that lately.

'Must change my clothes and get going.' She bolted down the toast and the tea, feeling all the time that if she didn't hurry, something would happen at the hospital and she'd be too late. For what, she wasn't sure. 'Don't leave Steph to do it all on her own.'

'I won't.' His voice rose and she knew by repeating herself, she'd annoyed him.

'See you later.'

When she climbed into the car thirty minutes later and started the engine, she felt relieved to be on her way. Driving was therapeutic, eyes focussed on the road, all the actions so automatic it gave her time to think. Time to go over the days before the accident… again… searching for something, some clue, as to what made him crash when no other vehicle was involved (with the roads 'in good condition', the police had told her), and why he was miles from where he said he'd be.

Why he'd lied about that evening.

On the Tuesday, after the phone call and after that frantic first night, in shock and terrified he was going to die, she'd had no suspicious thoughts in her head. No thoughts other than – *Please let him live*. Until she'd asked his boss, Adrian, who'd rushed to the hospital as soon as he'd heard, whether Alex had been heading for a site. Had he been called out? Had there been some emergency he'd needed to deal with? Adrian had looked perplexed. No, there was no work in that area. He'd seen Alex that afternoon before he left about five o'clock and nothing had been said about the evening. It was then Carrie had become guarded, wary about going on with that conversation. She felt vulnerable and caught out. She was quite clear about what Alex had told her when he left on that Monday evening. Remembered every word. He was driving into central Manchester for a meeting with an architect.

And if he'd crashed on Oxford Street or Wilmslow Road, she wouldn't have questioned it. But not miles from there, on some by-road off the M56, for God's sake.

And she was certain now, convinced, there would be no simple explanation for it. He wasn't there by chance. He was there for a reason. He was going to – or coming from – somewhere with a purpose. What had been so important to him that he needed to go at break-neck speed?

Nothing made sense to her. It was baffling but more than that. Frustrating. How could she get to the bottom of this when she couldn't ask him outright? And it might be weeks, months before that was possible. She noticed her hands were gripping the steering wheel with such intensity, her knuckles had gone white. *Come on, think,* she said to herself. What in the days before the accident had they done, talked about? Was there something she should have noticed? Perhaps not, because most of the week had been leading up to the barbecue for Lucy's birthday on the Saturday so her mind had been on that. She furrowed her brow, trying to piece it together, but it was like being asked by the police to recall where you were on a certain night and you can't for the life of you give an exact account. Days just run into days and you're not expecting you'll ever be asked.

Well, I'm the one asking now and I need answers.

Start with the village supper the weekend before – music and a quiz, Bring your own wine. Alex hadn't fancied going, but she'd persuaded him to show some community spirit and in the end it had turned out to be quite fun. And he was fine then. It always came as a pleasant surprise to her how people warmed to him. There was something about his natural expression, open and interested, a way of listening as though he really cared – he could get anyone talking away as though he'd been their friend for life. He was socially at ease, that was it, much more than she was.

OK, then Sunday, it rained. They read the papers, had lunch, made phone calls to his parents and Lucy, watched TV in the evening. Nothing unusual there.

And then work. She'd had her hands full, organising deliveries of feed, mending and creosoting some fencing, tending to a lame horse and calming an anxious owner, keeping an eye on the blacksmith (she really must hire some extra help to cover afternoons). All this on top of everything else. A quick visit to Lucy's flat in Withington one evening to go over the arrangements and pick up glasses from Belling's Wines on the way home.. Alex had his usual ten-hour day but at least it was all local, no visits to any sites further afield which would have meant spending a couple of nights away, as often happened. They'd started preparing for the party on the Friday evening, sorting the garden out, cleaning the barbecue, putting up the lights and then Saturday, buying steaks and sausages and hamburgers from the local butcher, picking up the birthday cake (no presents this time; they'd already given Lucy a fairly large cheque after her divorce three months ago. Making a new start was proving expensive and not so easy. Carrie had a shrewd idea that underneath that brash exterior Lucy was not so sure now she'd done the right thing. Danny still wasn't quite out of the picture). She'd talked a bit about that to Alex but he'd shrugged. *'She's twenty-four and made her decision. It's not for us to interfere.'* So… what else? Just brief, unimportant conversations… whether the house needed painting… a film they both wanted to see… another fruitless conversation about Jack working at the pub in the evenings, not doing a 'proper job'. She knew she'd harped on about that too many times lately.

It was all ordinary, everyday, mundane.

She crunched the gears as she took the roundabout in the wrong lane, and someone hooted their horn at her. 'Oh, get lost!' she muttered. A bit of road rage was all she needed at the moment.

Then there was the barbecue.

It had gone well, she thought. A good evening, with most of the guests, people they knew fairly well. Some close neighbours, including Mary from next door, who'd lost her husband last year and Carrie had kept meaning to ask her for dinner months ago, and Colin from the village; some old friends from the cricket club; one of Alex's work colleagues and his wife; Meryl and Bill; Steph had brought along her husband, who farmed a couple of miles up the road; Alex's parents came late and left early, his dad sitting on the terrace by the end of the night looking tired; Jack had invited two rather interesting types from the pub (colourful, was the word that came to mind), who ate for England and were gone by eight o'clock and last of all (literally, she had a bad habit of always being late for everything), Lucy, dressed to the nines, with three rather stunning-looking girls, one from her exercise class – Zumba was it? – and the others, apparently worked with her in HR. And of course, Joe and Anna, the girls on their best behaviour and that poor little boy Aaron, going haywire as usual, knocking things over. He was desperate to see the dog and kept shouting for him but no-one seemed to mind. They all knew how difficult the situation could be.

Anyway, it was a real mixed bunch, but everyone seemed to mingle quite happily and the atmosphere was relaxed, easy. Carrie was a born organiser and she'd planned everything down to the last detail, preparing the salads and baked potatoes and rice dishes earlier on, meringues and fruit tarts and cheese laid out already so she didn't have to do a great deal all evening other than refill glasses and announce when the food was ready. Only a few guests were left by ten o'clock, sitting in garden chairs under the decorative lanterns strung in the trees and taking in the last of the day's fading light. Jack had left with Lucy and her friends to go to a club in Stockport, so she could finish off her birthday in her own style. After all the heartache of a year ago, she seemed determined to show she could 'move on', if that awful phrase meant anything!

And most of Sunday had been spent clearing up. Was Alex a bit quiet then? Just tired, perhaps. But so was she. She'd had no desire to talk.

And Monday? He'd come home to change his clothes and left about six thirty. Where for, it turned out, she didn't know.

This was futile, she thought, turning the wheel sharply to pull into the hospital car park, which already looked full. She wasn't getting anywhere with this stupid diary of events. She'd have to just stop now. Anyway, there were more imminent issues to worry about. And this was a problem she couldn't solve or share right at this moment. She only wished the one person she could have unburdened herself to hadn't died long ago – her father might have been bluff and unemotional but he was full of common sense. He would have kept her grounded, helped her find a way through. Not by telling her what to do, that wasn't his way, but by listening and making her use her own resources.

Well, those resources felt inadequate now.

She drove slowly up and down the lanes three times before she found a spot and edged into the space, hoping she wasn't too far away from the ticket machine. To stay for most of the day cost six pounds every time and she wondered how people managed if they had someone to visit long term.

She hurried through the parked cars to the main entrance and took the lift to the ICU, pressed the buzzer to the right of the door, exactly as she'd done on the days before, and gave her name. Once she'd been let in, she used the gel dispenser to disinfect her hands. The procedures alone made her pulse race.

'How is he?' She needed to ask the vital question before she reached him.

The nurse was already turning away. 'There's been no change, Mrs. Taylor. I believe the consultant's going to talk to you later today.'

There was something very intimidating about Intensive Care – white and green and sterile, normal sounds of a busy ward absent and in their stead, the steady whirr of machines, the flashing monitor screens beeping steadily above each bed, the pumping of the ventilators and the faint rustling the nurses made as they moved down the ward. The patients lying atrophied in prone positions, no flicker of movement, wires attached to more machines, drips and snaking tubes.

And blinds over all the windows, closing out the sky.

It made Carrie's blood run cold.

She took a deep breath as she approached Alex's bed. She sat down and put her hand over his, careful not to dislodge the taped cannula and tubing, and tried not to look up at the machines keeping him alive. Instead she fixed her eyes on his face. So odd that he had a healthy colour. There was some grazing and purple bruising on his forehead and right eyebrow below the heavy bandaging but otherwise his skin was unmarked. He looked peaceful.

She wished she knew more about head injuries. She'd spent hours the night before searching the internet for information on comas (just what you're not meant to do, of course) and there was so much conflicting, confusing information and advice. But one report made sense to her: *Talk to the patient as though they can hear you. Tell them about your day. Anything that might register in their mind and prompt some response.*

So, here goes, she thought. I'll probably bore him to death, but at least he won't be able to tell me to shut up. Or you never know, perhaps he will.

Chapter 3

Jack stood in the shower, letting the water cascade over his head, the force of it making him shut his eyes. For a few minutes, he was glad to block everything out – frightening thoughts, pictures that cluttered his mind, demanding voices. He struggled to get the image of his dad lying in that bed out of his mind. All those tubes and machines keeping him alive. It looked so hopeless. Whatever the doctors said, there didn't seem to be any sign that his dad was coming out of this. There was nothing more nerve-shattering than seeing someone so full of life reduced to a shell – which is what it seemed like to Jack. Empty, nothing there but a body. The person inside it had gone. He'd read about people being like this for months, years – was it called a vegetative state or something? His dad would hate that, he really would. And all the times he'd told *him* to be careful when he drove.

God, what a disaster!

It didn't help that his mother didn't think he cared enough! Just because he wasn't running around like a headless chicken didn't mean he wasn't as scared as she was. He knew people dealt with stress in different ways but they were all meant to stick together, weren't they? It was only Uncle Joe who was any comfort at all. And Anna. When Jack had gone round to their house the next day, they'd been realistic, that was fine, but encouraging as well. Calm. It didn't feel like it did at home.

His mother didn't seem to think he'd grown up. He was twenty-two, for Pete's sake, not some wayward child who needed reminding how to behave. He wanted to say to her, 'Hey, hold on here, *I'm* affected by this situation as much as you are.' He'd already had Lucy doing her elder-sister bit, going on about supporting Mum and taking on some of the jobs around the house. Then this morning! Of course he'd go out and help Steph without being asked! She hadn't given him a chance. Just started on at him before he could say anything.

He climbed out of the shower, rubbed his hair dry. Not often he got angry but the idea that he was pretty useless in any situation annoyed him now. Perhaps it was being the youngest, he thought. And living at home. Not exactly his choice, but there you go. He'd really tried to find a job, something that didn't bore him to death and would be going somewhere, but it wasn't easy. His parents didn't realise how different it was in their day – plenty of jobs, bought their own house by the time they were thirty. There'd been a lot about it on the news recently and how his age group were called the Boomerang Generation. Well, he didn't quite fit into that. He hadn't ever left home to come back. The apprenticeship he'd had such hopes for ended after six months, the stint in a call centre was more than he could take (God, it was awful!) and the temporary labouring work – well, that's what it turned out to be – temporary. So he'd ended up at the village pub and was surprised how much he enjoyed that, even though it only paid pocket money. But it wasn't what his mother saw as 'a real job'. And although his dad had been more encouraging, the sort of advice he'd offered wasn't really much help: *Try and find something you're interested in and go from there.* But he wasn't sure *what* he was interested in.

He'd never been good at exams, lacked the ability to concentrate on goals he wasn't sure he could achieve. And he'd always been a daydreamer. *'The boy has his head in the clouds'* was how one teacher put it and he supposed that was true of him even now to some extent. But it was hard to change into someone else. He really wished he could.

And it wasn't just exams, studying, the whole academic thing. It had all come to a head before GCSEs and there was far more to it than the work. It had been a difficult time. Well, more than just difficult. He didn't like to remember just what life had been like for him at fifteen. Better not to think about it. But he'd come through it all in the end. His dad had been bloody great then. Now *he* had to be there for *him*.

He went across the landing and got some clothes out of the wardrobe, pulling a t-shirt over his head. No good looking too far ahead. It was too frightening. Yet he couldn't stop thinking that this might be a permanent state. But other than searching the internet for answers, what did he really know? Very little about the amount of damage a blow to the head like this did to your brain. The car was a write-off, so it must have been some crash. And it had been days since it happened and there was no sign of his dad improving. How many hours had he already sat at the bedside, watching intently for the flicker of an eye, holding his breath to listen for a sound that might be a word, but nothing. Just a terrible stillness, as though life had drained away. Waiting. And waiting. It was a relief to leave the ward and try to forget the whole distressing scene, but the picture of someone he'd always thought of as invincible lying there, so inert, so *lifeless* kept coming back to him. It was like something out of a horror film. Alien and frightening.

He called to Sam, who padded slowly across the tiled floor to the back door and lowered himself over the step into the garden.

'Take your time, old boy.'

The dog trundled on at his own pace, rolling his hips in a disjointed waddle as he walked. Ten years old and getting too fat, but, a typical Labrador, he loved his food, hoovering the floor for any scrap he could find. A bit late to put him on a diet now.

The day was warm and there had been so little rain the ground was cracked and hard. Jack could feel the ruts through his trainers as he walked. At the side of the garden, he opened the gate and passed through the yard with its assortment of trailers and horse boxes and containers, and a large stone mounting block. Then he turned towards the barn and the indoor school, almost hidden by tall trees, their tops swaying in the breeze. He could hear whinnying from the first paddock and knew the turning-out had already been done. Still, there must be some other jobs he was capable of.

He liked Steph. She was comfortable to be with. Made you feel better. Five foot three and sturdily built, a round, kindly face and a straightforward way of talking, usually in platitudes, it was fair to say, but she saw the good in everyone. She never seemed to stop from the minute she arrived at work and that was after all the stuff she had to do on the farm before she set off as well as looking after two young kids. Yet she never seemed stressed, taking everything in her stride. And Jack liked the fact that she was always calm around the horses. He'd never dare say so, but she coped far better when the pressure built up than his mother.

She was filling water buckets when he was close enough to speak.

'I'll do that, Steph. You can leave me with the easy jobs. Ones I can't get wrong.'

She straightened up and smiled. 'Thanks but you don't have to. I can get it all done by eleven.' She studied his face for a moment. 'Any change?'

'No.' He shrugged his shoulders. 'Mum should have seen the consultant yesterday, but they're busy all the time; hard to get hold of. I'm going in later. I'll know more then.'

'Well, you might be surprised. He could come round before the end of the day.' Jack knew this optimism was meant to make him feel better, but it sounded like pie in the sky to him. She didn't seem put off by his dubious expression. 'You read about people being in a coma for weeks and they come out of it. Gradually, perhaps, but...' She rubbed her hands on her jeans to clean them. She was running out of positive things to say, falling silent as she concentrated on aiming the hose at the next bucket.

'Did you get that job you went after? The one in the timber yard?

CRASH

You said the interview went well.'

He pulled a face. 'Haven't heard. And the more I think about it, I was too vague in some of my answers. I should have done some research, found out about what they produced beside planks of wood and who the customers were. I don't think I'll get it.'

'You always put yourself down, Jack. You're far brighter than you think.'

He laughed and looked round to see where Sam had gone. 'With a sister like Lucy, you know where you are in the brains department. She's the bright one. Look at the job she's got. And the money she's earning.'

'Well, money isn't everything.'

'No, but it certainly helps.'

Steph nodded her head slowly as though she was thinking something profound. 'Things don't always go well for a while and then they do. You'll see.'

She turned off the water and looped the hose round its metal peg.

'Come on. If you want, you can muck Bruno's stable out. He'll need fresh straw.'

They split the chores between them, with Jack doing most of the heavy jobs and finishing long before Steph's time was up. They were both red in the face from the physical effort they'd put in and the rising heat. As a final gesture, Jack promised to brush the yard.

'I'll be back at five.' She was already climbing onto her bike. 'Tell your mother not to worry.'

He wandered over to the paddock fence, with Sam panting behind him trying to keep up. He loved this place. By the trough, some pigeons were pecking away at the dusty earth searching for seeds with sharp, jerky strokes. And in the distance, he could hear the rumble of a tractor making its laborious way up Holly Bank. He leant his elbows on the wooden rail and looked over the field towards the far hedge. There was something soothing about watching horses grazing on a summer's day, he thought. Heads down, they picked their way across the grass in their own time, moving steadily from one patch to the next, contentedly eating. Part of the herd. No ears pricked anticipating danger. Just chomping away, with the occasional shake of the head to ward off flies. Nothing to disturb the peace.

He remembered when they moved here, he must have been thirteen. No longer surrounded by houses in the middle of a town, it seemed like another world, not just a few miles out in the Cheshire countryside. It didn't take very long for him to settle in, happy to follow the footpaths and roam through the woods, unlike Lucy who'd had to leave her friends behind at the secondary school and kept insisting she was being held a prisoner and was going to escape the first chance she got.

And this morning, he wanted nothing more than to stay in the outdoors. He didn't want to go back to the house. It seemed empty without his dad which was silly really because on a normal week, there were so many hours in a day when he wasn't at home. But this wasn't a normal week. Everything had suddenly been turned upside down. And when it was just him and his mother alone – it didn't matter whether they were eating a take-away or reading or waiting for news – it was as though she was looking to him for some response to a question that hadn't been asked, as though she expected him to take some decisive action and it was beyond him. He didn't know how to deal with it. He didn't know how to deal with her... expectations. They were just so different; she was all energy and action and he... dithered, he decided.

The mucking out and feeding up hadn't helped the headache he'd woken up with, the payback from last night when he'd had a few beers after the pub closed. He never drank when he was working – Benny disapproved of that sort of thing anyway – but once the customers had gone, he sat for a while with Leo, who deliberately kept the topics away from illness and comas, and relaxed for half an hour. Leo was an oddball but funny, a wry sense of humour and a cynical way of looking at life that made him the perfect barman. God only knew what age he was, anything between thirty and forty, hair streaked with grey which matched the stubble on his chin, a gold bangle on his wrist and always the same chinos that he never seemed to change. Where he'd originally come from, where his family was, no-one ever asked. If he was going to open up to anyone, it would be Jack. But he never did.

They'd sat at the bar, Leo's turn to lock up, and he seemed in no hurry to go home. 'So…' he said, 'you went on to some night spot after the barbecue? In all that female company!' He swung back in his chair, cradling his glass of rum and club soda and tilting his head as though expecting an interesting bit of gossip.

Jack wasn't going to be drawn but he couldn't help smiling. 'You're fishing. I'm not going to tell you anything.'

'That means there's something to tell.' Leo raised an eyebrow. 'She was attractive, I'll give you that. Well, they all were. Your sister certainly has some classy friends.'

Jack took a swig of his beer and put the glass down on the table. 'I'm not being drawn, Leo. Some things you don't talk about.'

'Ah, understood. Makes me think, though. If you're so prissy all of a sudden, then there's plenty to hide.' He nodded, knowingly. 'Perhaps I'm wrong, but I thought you were keeping an eye on the one in the white dress. You know – dark hair, amazing eyes. Or was she a bit old for you?'

Jack shrugged and hoped he appeared indifferent. 'Fran, you mean. Well yes, older, but not that much. Anyway, she's Lucy's friend, not mine.' And then because he was trying to cover up, he said too much. 'And the bar we went on to was for all ages…'

Leo sniffed. 'Ah!' He gave Jack a long look. 'I thought you didn't go around with your sister. You've always said she mixes with bull-shitters and name-droppers! Did she actually invite you?'

'Well, not exactly. Her friend did. Sort of.' He flushed,

remembering. 'The barbecue finished far too early and I wasn't going to bed at ten o'clock on a Saturday night...'

'No, that wouldn't do.'

Leo waited.

'Look, they were *all* really nice. And that girl you thought I fancied, she's way out of my league. She might have been friendly and all that, but nothing's going to come of it.'

'And she's called, you say...?'

'Fran. She's called Fran. Really nice, but...'

'I heard you. She's out of your league.'

And boy, she was, thought Jack. He'd noticed her at the barbecue the minute she'd come across the patio into the garden – self-assured, no need to make an entrance or put on a show, unlike the other two girls with Lucy who were laughing too loudly, raising their voices. She seemed separate from them, held back a bit, not shy, just steady away, taking everything in. She'd stood for a moment, looking round at the groups below her, quite still, tall and slim, elegant in a white dress that showed off her tan, an expression on her face that gave nothing away.

Jack had taken in every detail – shining black hair that curved round her face, eyes framed by incredible dark lashes, a straight nose, a detached look on her face. Even the way she stood, how she turned her head, the way she held her drink looked elegant to him. He had to remember to move away and pass some plates to his grandparents, who weren't mixing too well, and chat with them about the latest episode of '*Line of Duty*' and the cost of holidays in Spain.

By the time he'd made sure Ernst the foreign language student, who was another part-timer at the pub, and Leo, had been looked after, he'd lost sight of her. He'd headed back towards the house and suddenly, there she was by the rose trellis, still standing a bit apart sipping a Pimm's. She had a serious expression on her face and her gaze – those eyes so blue you couldn't help staring – seemed to be puzzled. As though she wasn't quite part of this.

Lucy seemed to have abandoned her.

'Hi, I'm Jack. Can I get you anything?'

She turned her attention to him and smiled briefly. 'Lucy's brother. Of course.'

'You've heard terrible things about me, I'll bet.'

'No.' She took a sip of her drink, then raised her head and looked directly at him. 'I've just realised that's who you must be. I'm Fran.' She held out her hand. 'I've been trying to work out who everyone is. I'd no idea it'd be a family do. Not quite like this.' She looked round at the guests, small groups chattering away, familiar with each other, her gaze resting on people's faces as though working something out. Then she seemed to remember that Jack was standing in front of her. 'I've only known Lucy for a couple of weeks but she insisted I came to her birthday party. We do an exercise class together.'

'Lucy can be very persuasive. That's the nice way of saying it. You've been bulldozed is what you mean.' He'd meant it to be funny but she didn't react. 'Steaks are nearly ready and there's salad stuff laid out in the kitchen. Just help yourself in about ten minutes…'

He sensed she wasn't listening. She seemed preoccupied with her own thoughts, concentrating on something over his shoulder. He didn't know how to go on. It was an awkward moment, nothing to say and embarrassment filled the gap. He didn't want to make a fool of himself so he pretended he had something urgent to do and hurried away.

But later in the evening, after the party, things became easier…

The ping from his mobile brought him back to earth. He fumbled to pull it free from where he'd jammed it into his pocket. He'd allowed himself to drift and lose all sense of time. He needed to concentrate on the important stuff today. Looking down at the screen, he saw a message from the dentist reminding him of an appointment that afternoon at 2.30. Well that'd have to be cancelled.

He called to Sam, cajoling him to walk a bit faster on the way back to the house, determined to 'shape himself', as his mother so aptly put it. He would do the washing up and tidy the living room. That'd be some sort of help.

Chapter 4

I can sense it's morning. Early. There's a quiet bustle about the ward, stealthy movement and low voices. A wakening up. It's a comfort to know I'm still alive. I'm in pain, but that's good, something that anchors me to the real world. And today, the real world seems nearer. Beyond my reach perhaps, but as though if I could just stretch up far enough, I could touch it.

It's strange what you imagine. I mean, when you read in the newspapers about this situation – whatever my situation actually is – you think to yourself, it must be all darkness, a sort of solid night, a nothing. But it isn't. There are shades and depths and *differences*. I haven't the faintest idea how the brain works but it seems to function all on its own, even when it should have shut down. It seems to store all sorts of memories you thought you'd lost and then loses ones you need.

My mind might be working after a fashion, but my body is anchored down with stones. It's held in place, bound tightly, swathed like an Egyptian mummy. An object. A thing. No use to me if it can't move.

'Now Alex, how are we this morning?'

Here we go again! The two of us having a one-sided conversation about the state of my health.

*So, how **are** we this morning, lying in a bed, immobile and losing the plot, Alex! Haven't you got something to say about that?*

No, I bloody haven't. I've nothing to say and I hope you're not going to be all jovial about it. It's wearing thin!

And then suddenly, there's a flicker of light, a strobe catching me unawares and I look up and see a face. Not clearly. It's mottled and pale like an Impressionist painting, fringed round the edges and made up of blotches. And it wavers, as though it's trying to take on form and exactness. It's gone in an instant and I will it to come back, to show me that my eyes really do have the ability to see.

But no. The moment's gone. And this amazing feat is unnoticed. There is no corresponding shriek of eureka, no call for the whole nursing staff to witness this wonder, not even an intake of breath.

What was that nurse doing when I opened my eyes? Studying the bloody machines and forgetting that a human being was attached to them? For heaven's sake, his job is to notice things. Look for signs of life. Not tinker with tubes and switches and miss vital changes going on in front of his nose.

Yes, I know what I sound like, churlish and disagreeable, and I don't think that's how I am normally. But frustration is eating away at me, this awful inability to communicate in any way, this closing down of all the channels, all the senses we take for granted. I have as much chance of reaching out as a goldfish swimming round in a bowl, the only hope being that someone will eventually see that conditions aren't great.

Time seems to have its own agenda – it has little meaning for me in my dormant state – so I have no idea how many minutes or hours have passed since I opened my eyes for that brief moment. But I'm sure now, it's later in the day. The sounds are more distinct. I read somewhere that if you lose one of your senses, the others become more acute and I'd go along with that. Hearing's become my lifeline. It gives me some idea of what's going on, where the day's up to and most of all, a link, however tenuous, with those familiar voices trying to haul me out of this nightmare.

A buzzer vibrates and it's the ward door opening, the seal broken on this vacuum of sterile air, quickly shushed closed again to protect us all from germs. Protect us from the outside world.

We are kept safe, concentrating on something more important. Staying alive.

And then, as suddenly as before, the light penetrates my eyelids in the way the sun filters through the curtains in the early morning, and I am aware of trembling colour. And shapes – a bluish line where the wall meets the ceiling, an arc of a lamp, the top of a monitor. OK, not quite in focus, but they're real.

Funny how memories jump into your mind from nowhere, often from so far back you've long ago packed them away in storage. But just now, a short story we read in school flashed into my head. I'm fairly certain it was an exam text and at first, we all thought, *This is going to be so boring – a boy swimming through an underground tunnel. So what?* Hardly what we'd have picked if we'd had a choice. But it got us in the end. The boy becomes fascinated by the local youths who dive into this water hole and resurface quite a way out to sea. To make it, you'd have to hold your breath for minutes and he has to build up his time under water before he can attempt it. And he only just makes it. The bit I remember is the euphoria he feels when he finally manages to reach the far end of the tunnel and breaks the surface of the water, lungs bursting, to take in great gulps of air. The moment when he's so close to dying and life's given back to him.

That's how I feel now. Giddy with the escape from the cavernous hole. Relief, after those strange hallucinating hours at the simple act of seeing. But of course it isn't simple, is it? Hell, I'm just grateful to resume a bit of normal service, to be *allowed* to have one of my faculties back which I thought might be gone forever.

There's some confusion now round my bed and low voices sounding urgent, a new presence I feel close by, attention centred on me. Then the command: '*Open your eyes, Alex.*' Then, '*Can you do that? Just open your eyes.*'

I know I must obey, must show them what I *can* do. Can't be hard, for heaven's sake. I've managed it twice. I strain to lift my lids, heavy as lead, but some perverse force is fighting against the involuntary action that will prove I'm still in here, the *me* that they think has left the building. And I fail. I hear someone say that I haven't yet reached the 'minimally conscious state' they had anticipated and something about 'time'.

Then all is quiet. Except one of the machines has changed its rhythm, the one I've got used to hearing. It sounds as though it's missing a beat. Like a defective heart. Hope it's not mine.

A chair scrapes the floor by my bed.

'Dad.'

The voice is quiet but insistent.

'Dad, can you hear me? I'm holding your good hand.' I can feel the warmth of his skin. 'If you can hear me, squeeze my fingers. That's all you have to do... I've looked this up on Google, you can answer me by squeezing my hand... you've opened your eyes once so you're coming round, I know it.'

Ah, Jack, you were always the one who saved one-legged frogs and rain-soaked bees and cried in *'The Lion King'* and every Disney film that had an animal in it. Hopeless! We always agreed that on a desert island, you'd be the perfect companion, undemanding and stoical, but in the cut-throat world of business you wouldn't survive. Well, I'm not *in* some tower block wanting financial advice. I'm not in any situation I ever thought I'd be and I'm bloody glad you're the one who's with me now. It's taught me one thing, never make judgements about how your children are going to turn out. Or how you *want* them to turn out. They have some say in it.

'Dad.'

And I try desperately to tighten my fingers in some response and I suppose I must have made them move because he grips my hand, too tightly and I can hear his breathing quicken.

'Great. I got that. You can hear me, even if you can't do much.' He shifts his chair closer to the bed. 'Well it'll come. I'm not going to call that nurse in yet. We'll just try and work together. Better if they don't badger you... Next time you open your eyes, you'll see my face... might be a bit of a shock, I forgot to shave, but at least it'll be a face you know.'

Thank God, a real conversation. Well, a monologue. But at least it's a part of life I recognise. He chatters on: his shift at the pub last night, the call from Joe, emptying the coarse mix into the bins for the horses, one of the kitchen lights on the blink, Sam eating the birds' bread... trivial bits of information I would have nodded my head at over the morning cup of coffee, only half-listening, mind already somewhere else. But not now. My mind is focussed, gleaning every scrap, every detail, grateful for this rope he's throwing me.

'And Mum's going to be back at four, so she'll tell you more about what's going on... and what Uncle Joe said... you're only allowed close family in here so even if other people wanted to visit you, they can't, but everyone has been asking after you and how you're doing... they ring all the time...'

Well, that's nice. Or it would be. But I can just imagine what they're saying. That it was an accident waiting to happen – I always drive too fast... that I'm inclined to walk through life as though some Guardian Angel is looking after me. And this time – what a surprise – He was looking the other way.

To be fair, that sounds more like my alter ego than anyone I know.

See, I'm talking to myself and giving me what-for before Carrie starts, which as soon as I open my eyes, she will. And I must deserve it. It's just that I can't defend myself if I don't know the crime I've committed. Why can I remember some things so clearly – in 3D almost – but have no idea how I got into this state? It's bad enough wrecking my body, but if my mind's shot, if this is irreparable...

I am looking at the side of Jack's head. It's floating oddly, shifting slightly, but it's him and my eyes are open. He's staring at something,

31

perhaps one of the machines behind me and doesn't notice, so I blink to make sure I *can* blink. It must have made the slightest sound and he turns, a smile spreading across his face, mouth half-open in surprise. And joy. I feel like crying.

Something catches in his throat and his voice is barely above a whisper. 'You've done it. Dad. Brilliant. You can see me, can't you! This isn't a fluke, I know it. Take it slowly.' He leans over me. As hard as I try to make my throat work and think I've managed the word *Sorry,* I know it's trapped. Just as I am. Jack presses his fingers into my palm again. 'God, you've given us all such a fright. Should I call the nurse now?'

I have nothing to say. Of course, I haven't. I feel like a mechanical doll, one that can only come to life a bit at a time. But never mind. It'll do for now. One bit's actually working again.

I am more aware than ever how constrained I am. But that's perhaps just as well. If I *could* move any part of me, I'm sure all these pieces of equipment would snake off, leaving me an amorphous splodge found later in the middle of the mattress, like flotsam washed up by the tide.

But too much is going on now. A nurse, not the one who tries to jolly me, side-lines Jack and has found a torch which she shines into each eye, pushing my lids up, not carefully enough, I can tell you, to get a better look. And there's another person, a doctor I think, hovering over me from the right. So close I can smell his breath. And questions, questions… *Can you hear me? Blink for me. Can you do that? Press your finger on my hand. Try making a sound.*

Christ, this is going to be hard work.

I can see what is straight ahead of me but to the right and left, it's cloudy, smudged, so I can't do all the doctor asks. He has a strange-looking metal tube with an eye piece hanging from his neck on a cord, but he doesn't use it. He keeps on asking me questions, gently, it's true, but it's no good him going on and on. There's a limit and

I've reached it.

He turns to the nurse. 'Too early to do a Visual Field Test.'

Yes, it bloody well is. I have no idea what a Visual Field Test is but it sounds strenuous and I'm not up to it.

I can feel the bed sheets smooth against my toes and it occurs to me that I never even considered that I might be paralysed. You would have thought that would be the thing I'd have dreaded most, but I was too busy worrying about how my brain was working, the part of me that makes me who I am. That seems to have blotted out all other concerns.

They think I need quiet and rest now, thank heavens, and the interrogation stops. They move out of my line of sight and I don't know whether Jack is still there. I want to look to my left but it's just a blur. And it is Carrie who appears above me, face strained, eyes wide and alarmed, but she's trying to smile and talk in an encouraging voice, as though I'm a child who's been lost in the park and then found against all hope by the swings.

'Oh, Alex, what a relief! You've no idea. Just to know you're awake. If you can open your eyes, the rest will come. I can't tell you how worried we've been. All of us.'

And a tear falls onto my cheek.

Carrie is crying.

I look at her troubled face and if I could have expressed amazement, I would have. Carrie never cries. Well, not in a long time. Her gaze is fixed on my face for so long, it seems as though she can see into my soul.

'I love you,' she says and touches her lips against mine. Very carefully. She doesn't want to disturb the tube that lies across my cheek. I'm in a delicate state, everything hanging in a fine balance and no-one wants to send me back to the nether regions from where I might, or might not, return.

Another tear falls and I see her anguish. The lines round her mouth are marked and the skin has reddened on her neck. I mirror her anxiety for a second but I am incapable of feeling anything else. Certainly anything that requires an effort. My eyes close.

I am too tired.

*

The song comes to me when I am on the verge of either waking or sleeping. I'm not sure which. A twilight time, anyway. It's old, this song, and the voice is melodic and sweet, reminiscent of the big band era before the war, when the vocalist would stand centre-front holding the microphone and looking out over the dance floor. She takes it slow and easy, the melody carrying the words in lazy, sad sweeps, so that you know you couldn't have one without the other. And it makes me want to weep…

I thought of you last night,
I thought of you and thought of you
Until the morning light...

I have a strange certainty that I only heard it recently. From some film soundtrack that was trying to capture the mood of a bygone era. The name of the film or who was in it? That's gone, but the song has stayed with me. And it's haunted me before. I can't say why. Except there's something in its yearning that's in me too.

If I recover my memory, perhaps I'll find out what I've lost. Or who.

It might be better never to know.

Chapter 5

As Carrie closed the front door, her mobile buzzed in her pocket and she wanted to ignore it. But in the wake of the last few days that was the last thing she should do. It could be the hospital… No, she could see from the screen it was Meryl and so let it go to Voicemail.

She needed time to think what to say. No good kidding herself, she'd made things awkward between them, been too sharp, too dismissive and that wasn't the way to behave when someone only wanted to help. Although she wasn't going to apologise, at least she could smooth things over. They'd known each other a long time.

It was two days ago when the stress had robbed her of sleep and her temper was frayed. And eight o'clock in the morning wasn't the best time for anyone to pay a visit. She'd heard a car draw onto the drive and hurried to the bedroom window to see who was going to be ringing the bell any time now. She immediately recognised the grey Audi, and there was Meryl, a bunch of flowers in her hand heading up the drive.

As much as Carrie appreciated the concern, she didn't appreciate the intrusion. Especially this early in the morning, when she was still wrapped in a towel and when a few minutes ago, she'd been shocked at the pale face looking back at her in the mirror. She seemed to have aged ten years. The exhaustion was etched into her skin.

Anyway, she had nothing new to report – just two days of waiting and watching, worn out with long hours at the hospital, no sleep and endless phone calls and worry. What could she say to anyone?

She sighed and rubbed her forehead, shouting, 'Just a minute,' when she heard the doorbell. Hastily pulling on a T-shirt and jeans, she ran down the stairs barefoot, no time to brush her teeth or comb her hair which frizzed out in a wide halo.

Under normal circumstances, she was fond of Meryl, having the occasional lunch, going shopping, a weekend trip to London once or twice. But this situation was on a different level. They weren't exactly close, not in any comfortable, intimate way, perhaps Carrie never wanted that in a friend, but they'd known each other for a number of years, ever since Lucy and her daughter had been in the same class at secondary school. Meryl and her husband, the established villagers, had taken her and the family under their wing when they moved here, introduced her to people, looked after her at functions when Alex was away, helped with business contacts. Meryl had certainly made it easier for them to settle in. So meeting up at regular intervals had become a habit. They found each other agreeable company and useful allies when it came to coping with village factions.

But what made their friendship edgy at times was Carrie's perception that some sort of competition was being played out between them. Perhaps it had something to do with Meryl's sophisticated manner, her air of entitlement. Perhaps she didn't mean to be condescending. But she played a game of one-upmanship, name-dropping and having political opinions that Carrie found a bit extreme; Alex said there was a simpler term for it – Meryl was a snob. Maybe it was all for effect to show she wasn't thrown by Carrie's affluent upbringing (she'd soon found out about her childhood, the boarding school education, the horses, the skiing in Europe). And, as Carrie had opened the door that morning and fresh flowers had been pressed into her hands, it wasn't the first time she'd felt she was wearing a mask, wary of letting Meryl know too much.

Anyway, she wasn't quite ready for *any* visitors, not even ones with good intentions wishing her well. She didn't like sympathy and the last thing she wanted to seem was needy. It was important to appear composed, able to cope with anything. It was the way she'd been brought up. How her father hated 'silly women' who flapped and crumbled and went to pieces when faced with the slightest obstacle! She could hear him saying, *You put on a 'good face', whatever life throws at you.* So she'd always prided herself on proving to him she was strong, self-sufficient. And there was something about the present dire situation that made it important to be worthy of that legacy.

As though it really mattered in the whole scheme of things, she thought now. Except... she couldn't help making the comparison between herself, dishevelled, pale and weary-eyed and Meryl standing in front of her – Meryl, who always looked as though she were about to do a fashion shoot, with her beautifully made-up face, crisp white shirt and tailored trousers and neat blonde hair. But in a way, this was just vanity. Who cared what she looked like!

Carrie had ushered her into the kitchen, switched on the kettle and given an apologetic shrug that wasn't quite genuine. 'Sorry, no cake. I just haven't had the time.'

'Don't be silly. I only called over to see if I could do anything today.' Meryl drew her chair closer to the kitchen table and put out a comforting hand. She closed her eyes briefly and shook her head. 'Must be so difficult when you need to be at the hospital all the time.'

Carrie poured the boiling water over the coffee grains in two china mugs and added milk.

'Well, Steph's doing most of the work. And everyone on the yard – you know, the owners – have been doing their bit. Good job it's the summer. We're managing.'

'At least I could get you some shopping. I'm going into Stockport later, so it's no trouble.' Meryl had managed to shift her chair so that Sam couldn't lie on her feet or get hairs on her trousers.

'No, we're fine, honestly. It's just a matter of waiting. No-one can do anything really, until we know where this is going.'

Meryl nodded. Neither spoke, as though all had been said that needed saying. But Carrie had the uneasy feeling that her friend had come for something more than bringing flowers. That pause was just a bit too long. And Meryl was fiddling with her collar and looking up at Carrie as though something was on her mind but she didn't know how to start.

'Carrie, I don't know whether this is helpful... but I've been thinking about it for a few days, and honestly I didn't know whether it was worth mentioning.'

'What's that?' She frowned, not caring to hear what was coming. *Another theory? More 'coma' stories with amazing outcomes?* The trouble was, everyone 'Googled' these days!

Meryl placed her elbows on the table. 'It might be nothing at all. And I know they've ruled out any sort of seizure or fit that could have made him lose control of the car. I know that's what they've said.' She pressed her lips together. 'But I thought...'

'Thought what, Meryl? For heaven's sake, they're the experts.'

'I know. I know. I wasn't questioning that.' Meryl looked out through the kitchen window as though trying to find the right words. 'It was something I noticed before... before the accident. Something I noticed at the barbecue on the Saturday night. If you remember, we arrived a bit after everyone and I wasn't drinking because I was driving so perhaps I was more observant than most.'

Carrie let out a puff of annoyance and stared hard at her. *Get on with it, whatever it is for God's sake.*

'I thought – and I said so to Bill – I thought that Alex didn't look quite right. Not his normal self. He looked, well, strained, you know... preoccupied... as though there was something bothering him. Or perhaps he was sickening for something. And we wondered afterwards whether that might have caused him to...'

'No, no.' Carrie cut her off. She knew she sounded sharp but she couldn't hide her irritation. 'Listen, Meryl, I would have noticed if there'd been something worrying him. He was perfectly all right that night.' She found she was on her feet, tired of it all and exasperated.

'Don't you think I've been over everything in that last week? Over everything on that day? Every *bit* of it. He was fine, just busy looking after all the guests making sure it all went well. There was nothing else. If something had been bothering him, he'd have told me. I'd have noticed.'

Meryl flushed and bowed her head, apologetic, embarrassed. 'Of course you would. I'm sorry I brought it up. Please don't be upset. I'm truly sorry.'

Carrie sat down again. 'It could have been oil on the road, avoiding a cyclist, a deer running out in front of him. We just don't know yet. There's really no point adding to all the "possibles".'

'Of course. It was silly of me.' Meryl's eyes watered a little and Carrie looked away knowing she'd hurt her. 'Forget I said anything.' She hadn't touched her coffee.

And what followed was a difficult silence, only broken by the sound of the old dog panting. Meryl pushed back her chair and excused herself, she was late, she must go. It was obvious she wanted to leave the uncomfortable atmosphere behind her.

Now, Carrie climbed into her car and placed the mobile phone on the passenger seat. She should call her back. She could at least let her know things were improving. That there was a light at the end of the tunnel. *Don't be a sulker*, she told herself. So she touched the name on the screen, not bothering to listen to the Voicemail and waited.

'Meryl, thanks for ringing.'

'I left you a message. Just hoping you're all right.' A pause. 'And hoping there's been some sort of... development.'

'Actually, there has. There was a breakthrough yesterday. Alex opened his eyes. We could hardly believe it.'

'That's wonderful.' Meryl sounded elated and Carrie felt even more guilty about how she'd been the other day. 'So he's coming round at last.'

'Well, it only happened twice, but it showed he's responding and that's a huge step forward.' She hesitated, wondering how much detail she should go into. But she felt she owed Meryl, so she went on. 'Jack said he actually squeezed his hand when he spoke to him as though he knew what was being said. I must admit I was beginning to think he'd never come out of the damn coma and the whole situation would drag on for months. And when the doctors aren't prepared to tell you anything, it's even more difficult to be hopeful. They just seem frightened to commit themselves. You're left in the dark.'

'They're bound to be cautious. Wouldn't do to get your hopes up…'

'No, I suppose not.' Carrie breathed out, stretching her back against the car seat. 'Sorry about the other day, Meryl. I snapped and that isn't like me.'

'Don't worry about it. It's quite understandable when you've been through such an awful time. Just glad things are working out. I'm sure the worst is over.' Meryl's voice was warm and oddly comforting. Carrie was glad she'd rung back. 'Let me know if there's anything I can do. Anything at all.'

'I will.'

She finished the call and as she sat in the silent car, that familiar feeling of frustration swept over her.

Well, you can do plenty for me, Meryl, but you can't answer the one question that's eating away at me.

There's only one person who can do that.

She certainly wasn't going to admit that she had no knowledge of why Alex was on that particular road when he crashed. And until she understood what was going on, until he became fully conscious and could explain to her satisfaction (he'd lied, after all) she'd keep her worries and her questions to herself. This was between the two of them. Even Lucy and Jack didn't have to know anything yet.

She pushed back her hair. She wanted to be told that there was a simple explanation, that she was reading too much into it, she'd be laughing later at her foolish suspicions. But Carrie's mind was razor-sharp, she was intuitive, she sensed when things were off-kilter. She'd always believed that it was working with animals that made you sensitive to the smallest changes in mood, in behaviour. And her instinct was telling her there was something here that wasn't right.

The truth is you never really know anyone, she thought now. Not totally. However long you've been together, however well you think you know someone, there's always something that is never spoken of, never revealed. Because who is ever completely honest? You don't ever really bare your soul. There are hidden aspects of your life you could never share with anyone, some you could barely admit to yourself. She was only too aware of that. So what did that say about this marriage? Was it all based on a tissue of half-truths and untolds and growing indifference, on a fabric so flimsy the whole lot could come tumbling down? She hoped not. But she'd stopped paying attention to their life together until the crunch came and she'd been afraid she could lose him, or certainly lose the man she'd married, grown used to. How long had it been since she'd thought about her and Alex as a *couple*? A hell of a long time. They'd become an arrangement that just functioned automatically, day after day without much effort. On either side. She hadn't told him that she loved him for years until the other day in the hospital. When had that kind of intimacy stopped?

She suddenly felt so tired, her head ached and her shoulders hurt. She didn't want to think about it anymore, but the question mark over that night was causing her grief. She was usually so practical, in control, running everything. And having no satisfactory answer left her feeling hollow and anxious.

Well, it was no good just sitting here. She'd have to work it out for herself. Start looking, do some investigating, however underhand that might be. Look at his mobile phone history, computer sites he'd been on, go through his desk in the study. Snooping wasn't a nice trait but there were times when it was necessary.

Didn't she deserve to know?

She put the key in the ignition and manoeuvred the car round the drive and onto the road. There were jobs to do before she could head for the hospital. She just hoped Joe wasn't going to be there this afternoon. He was one person who she had difficulty with. Anna was fine and the children – well, everyone found Aaron a handful and she didn't know how she would have coped with *him* – and family gatherings went off OK. But Joe on his own? Beside his sick brother for hours? He was too protective of Alex, even when everything was going well, as though he was the older one who had to stand guard. She'd been aware of this from the start, even before she'd married Alex. If she made a decision or contradicted Alex, Joe would be watching, that silent gaze giving nothing away but she knew he thought her bossy and controlling, that Alex was hard done by. What he didn't understand and never had, was that in a marriage, one of you had to be practical, get things moving. If she hadn't taken the reins in this household, nothing would ever have got done. And, of course, there was an added problem. When her father died, she'd bought the house and land with his money, built up a business which probably didn't square with Joe's idea of how a partnership should work. Well tough, she couldn't change any of that. She was never going to be 'the housewife'. If he didn't like the way she and Alex led their lives then he could butt out.

She moved up a gear and joined the main road, turning on the radio and keeping her eyes firmly on the way ahead.

Lots to do.

Chapter 6

It was still warm as Jack walked down the lane to start his shift, ten minutes to spare. He was up-beat. Optimistic, which was unusual for him. But that brilliant moment when he'd felt the pressure of his dad's hand had made his day. *You can't have brain damage if you can react like that,* he reasoned, *obey an instruction, understand what's being said to you.* Things were looking up. He'd get to the hospital early tomorrow and carry on talking away, see if he could break through what he imagined was kind of like a wall. Anyway, there was hope now. A chance his dad would recover.

'The Fox and Hounds', squat and weather-worn, stood at the bottom of the hill facing onto the village green, with a wide path crossing the front entrance which led down to the river. No hounds or horses gathered on the carefully mown grass now, but you could imagine the hunt meeting there on a Boxing Day morning. There was something traditional and timeless about the look of the place. It was inevitable that the owner, Benny, had played to the gallery by hanging an old hunting scene above the bar – *The Meet*, all red coats and whips and baying hounds, the horses, straining to be off, the Master holding the stirrup cup high. Even though the restaurant area had been modernised years ago, the public bar still managed to retain some of the old character. The locals didn't like change.

Jack loved working there when it was summer. The regulars, sitting for hours, chatting across the room, swopping titbits of local news and arguing about the political state of the country, long on prejudice and short on facts; families out for a special treat, eating at the rectangular tables in the lower part of the dining area; and later in the evening, the garden crowded with groups of youngsters his own age, all a bit wild and too loud but good natured and funny. It was just what he needed after the strained atmosphere of home at the moment, his mother on edge, sharp in every comment she made, always seeming to expect too much from him. Or, at least, expecting more than Jack could give... and the phone jangling urgently, frightening them both in case this was bad news.

He just wished he had more to take his mind off it all. He wished he could find a job, well the right job for him, anyway. There must be something he could do. Something practical. Not in an office, he'd decided. Not in some soulless building where you were cut off from the outside world shifting papers around. But when he did searches online, it was qualifications that seemed to stump him. All he had to offer was six GCSEs and half a college course at the local Tech. He was beginning to think he'd have to go back to studying but the idea didn't appeal to him at all.

He let his mind wander as he walked that same familiar route he used to take past the pub then up Wild Duck lane to school where academically he never quite made it. Sporty, yes, that let him fit in to some extent. Not a bad football player. But just not clever enough. Told often, *'You're a bright lad. These results are way below what you're capable of'* or, *'If you don't pull your socks up, you won't get any qualifications...'* Well, here I am at twenty-two, he thought. Exactly as predicted. He'd felt bewildered when the final year came and everyone else seemed to know where they were going, what subjects to pick at A level, having such confidence in the route they were going to take. Particularly Grace, she'd always wanted to teach – and to go away to study, away from this 'graveyard' she called the village. He'd registered at the local technical college with half an idea to do something with computers and media, but knew after two weeks that this was going nowhere. It took him that first year struggling away with the course before he plucked up the nerve to tell his parents that it just wasn't for him.

'Well, what *is* for you, Jack?' His mother had turned from cooking the dinner that evening and stood, a hand on her hip. 'What *do* you want from life? You're nearly eighteen and you're treading water. Tell me you've *some* idea about what the next move is, because you never take my advice.'

He'd murmured something meaningless then remained silent. He had no defence. His mother was right, of course she was, and his mind was a total blank when it came to offering suggestions. He was stumped.

The consolation was that although any kind of academic work wasn't for him, at least in the last couple of years before everyone went away to study, he'd made some good friends. Yes, they'd gone off to university now or left to take up jobs in the cities, but they came back to see their families and then it was like old times – the same jokes, the same quirky memories that could be shared, a language which belonged to the few. And one of his closest friends was coming back next weekend for his parents' wedding anniversary, so that'd be good, another party of sorts, but… Jack screwed up his face at the thought of it… Grace might be there. He'd heard she was thinking of coming back from Doncaster when the school term ended and, surprise, surprise, she'd been looking at flats in Didsbury which was just too close. It was a situation that could be dealt with at a distance, that was easy, bumping into each other on the main street every three months or so and exchanging mindless platitudes. But back to live? How would he deal with that?

He kicked at a stone as he walked. Perhaps he always dodged issues he didn't want to face. Perhaps he was inclined to let things slide rather than having confrontations. He was like his dad in that. They avoided rows if they could. Until they were pushed too far. He'd seen his dad angry a few times, then it was cold and steely. Using words like a stealthy weapon. You wouldn't want to push him further.

Jack was the first one to arrive. Benny had left the door on the latch, so he had time to get the bar ready for the early drinkers. It was always slow at the start of the evening, but there were the two or three regulars who set the clock by the pub's evening opening times and turned up as soon as the door was unlocked. It was probably more like home to them than their real homes. At least there was company here.

Leo joined him a few minutes later, rinsing glasses and looking over at Jack, a sardonic smile on his face. 'Did you get the message?'

'What message? No.'

'The CD's playing up. It's jumping. Benny wants it fixing and that's what you're good at.'

Jack sighed. 'Don't know why we bother. No-one listens to it anyway.'

'It provides atmosphere. Ambience. Benny likes to think we're in a wine bar in a London mews. Just humour him.'

Jack was glad to be doing something and as the night went on and the pub grew busier, he felt more and more comfortable with himself. As he always did in this place. It was that feeling of being useful, he thought. The more you focussed on what other people wanted, the more your own worries slipped into the back of your mind. Old Barry sitting at the bar, doddery and rheumy-eyed, the same shirt worn day after day with half his dinner spotted down his front. Nothing ever changed – he liked to have the next pint ready just before he'd finished the current one; liked to chat about cricket; about the sixties; about his latest battle with the district nurse. And the two farmers still in their work clothes and heavy boots, who always sat on the long bench outside the front door and ordered two ciders and ham toasties most nights before heading home. And the young couple, just moved into the village, who drank Coke and were looking for someone to fix the fencing round their garden…

Other people's lives fascinated Jack. They were all different, of course, but each one was made up of stories that followed on, continued, to form a complete history. As though on a path that must be taken. As though everything was predestined. Listening as he did, he'd come to the conclusion that you set off certain of where you were going and then gradually realised that you didn't have the power to change course. It had all been mapped out for you. Even when you thought you had a choice...

'Over here, son. Another half and a white wine.'

It was good to be busy. Surrounded by people. And, when asked, he could say, yes, his dad was 'coming round' (such an odd phrase, as though he'd be at the door any minute) and it was good to hear the comments about him – 'such a nice bloke', 'no airs and graces', 'always has the time to chat' and the heartfelt optimism about his recovery. They were sure he'd make it... he was young enough... doctors can do wonders and so on. Never mind that they had none of the facts, it was all speculation, but the concern was genuine and the words were in stark contrast to the hospital's po-faced prognoses that week. Better to look up and be optimistic, he thought, than be full of gloom.

Later, when he got home, he sat in the kitchen for a while, the house quiet around him. At least the dog was happy to see him back, tail thumping against the chair leg. His mother had gone to bed but she'd left the light on in the hall and a cheese sandwich wrapped in cling film on the table. He went to the fridge and poured himself a glass of milk, then sat back in his chair.

He'd tried not to think about Lucy's birthday because he was having pipe-dreams; he knew that's what they were. But however hard he tried, he couldn't get Fran out of his mind. No good telling himself she was out of his league... far too good-looking, quite a bit older than he was, more worldly. She wouldn't ever take him seriously. That was a given. And you try to put yourself off fancying someone like that, but... well, the rules of common sense just don't apply. Your head doesn't listen. Or is it your heart?

What did he recall about the early part of that evening? Nothing that had any importance. Just mundane stuff, handing out plates, filling glasses, finding extra forks, making sure Leo and Ernst were looked after and not feeling like spare parts. But from the moment Fran entered the garden and they'd had a brief chat, if you could call it that, it was as though he'd come alive; he was on tenterhooks, unable to concentrate on anything but her. A brief conversation, not really even that, and he was caught. It was as though he had a sixth sense. Always aware of who she was talking to, where she was standing, as though he could see through the back of his head. *Don't leave early,* he kept saying to himself. *Wait till I've finished doing the dutiful son bit and then we can really talk.* And part of him could see how ridiculous this was. He didn't know her. They'd spoken a few words, that was all.

As the guests started to leave, he could see that Lucy and her friends were heading for the back garden gate, Lucy waving a farewell to her mother who was picking up paper plates and napkins off the wooden bench. He made up the ground as fast and as casually as he could and called after them. 'Hey Sis. Are you going on somewhere?'

He could see the irritation in the way she straightened her back and knew what she was thinking – *God, the annoying younger brother cashing in.* She looked over her shoulder in that dismissive way she had when she was with her friends and didn't answer straight away.

One of the girls (Rachel, he found out later) caught Lucy's arm. 'Hold on. Jack wants to join us. Come on, we can fit him in the car.'

'Hardly.' Lucy puffed out her cheeks, pretending to look sympathetic. 'Sorry Jack, there's only room for two in the back…'

'We can squeeze him in. No-one's going to see at this time of night. Sod the insurance.' It was obviously Rachel's car.

His sister shrugged her shoulders and they climbed into the red Kia parked in the back lane, Lucy claiming the front seat and Jack squeezed in the back between Fran and the other girl, whose name he hadn't caught.

'You probably won't like it, Jack,' said Lucy, not even turning her head. 'It gets really crowded, lots of noise and a fight to get a drink. But…'

He felt, rather than saw Fran smiling slightly beside him. 'Might not be my kind of thing either.' And he felt grateful that she was there. And that she'd sort of stood up for him.

By the time they'd hit the main road through Stockport, turning off towards Didsbury, the girls were chatting over his head, the conversation so alien to him it was as though they were speaking in code. All he could think of was Fran's leg pressed against his and the warmth of her arm on his skin, every sense heightened to such a degree, he felt light-headed. She was much quieter than the others, didn't really join in the banter or seem as familiar with their latest escapades. He was glad of that.

He cleared his throat and raised his voice over the chatter. 'Where are we going?'

Lucy was giving instructions. 'Just keep straight on, Rachel,' she said. 'Past the Parrs Wood Leisure Centre, down towards the tennis club and then turn right.'

They pulled up on a residential street beside what once must have been a pub, but the name had gone and the frontage and doorway were now lit up with what seemed like hundreds of coloured bulbs. Music throbbed out from the building and the place was buzzing. Groups stood around in the forecourt, some sitting on the low walls, smoking and drinking from plastic cups, some shouting and play-fighting, one scantily-dressed girl lying on a bench, her arm drooping to the floor, a couple dancing on the flagstones and the music pumping out into the night was deafeningly loud. It was such an unlikely spot for a club to be, thought Jack, surrounded by suburban houses. You'd have to know about it to find it. Well, obviously plenty of people did.

'Looks interesting, doesn't it?' said Lucy, unbuckling her seat belt and, stretching her long legs, almost leapt from the car. Jack and Fran followed the others more slowly, as though being led into a den of iniquity and exchanged rueful smiles as they approached the doorway.

'Don't know whether "interesting" is quite the right word,' said Fran, tripping on a broken step. 'More like "decadent". It's a wonder the houses round about don't complain.'

'It's been a pub so they're probably used to noise.' Jack put out his hand to steady her but she quickened her step to avoid it.

'Well,' she said, over her shoulder, 'I'll have one drink to be sociable and then get a taxi home. Don't think I could manage more than half an hour of this.'

The others had made it to the far end of the room to a long wooden, make-shift bar, with bottles and glasses covering the surface; three harassed-looking lads were trying to cope with the impatient demands of too many punters.

'I'll bet it doesn't have a licence.' Jack could see it would take ages to get a drink. 'We'll probably be raided!'

He felt stupid and young standing next to her and overawed, somehow. He couldn't be himself. There was something about her he couldn't quite figure out. He was fairly certain she was only there because she *had* to be She seemed to be holding herself apart and looking at it all – looking at him – with the sort of tolerant indulgence you'd show to a child. He felt annoyed. Unreasonably, he knew. She might at least be pleasant company for the next half hour as it was clear they'd been abandoned by the others.

He had to do something. Say something. 'I'll get you a drink and we can sit outside, if you want. Quieter there.'

'Not much.' She stood just inside the doorway. 'OK. I'll have a white wine please. Any'll do.'

And she left him to struggle to the front of the queue, which wasn't really a queue, just a mass of bodies leaning over the counter, waving at the barmen. It took minutes before he could get noticed and even then he had to shout his order.

Carrying the drinks, one in each hand, he manoeuvred through the crowd into the cool night air and looked around for where she might be sitting. He couldn't see her at first, but the white dress caught his eye and he edged his way to join her on a low wall adjoining the side street.

The wine was in a cheap thick glass and she wrinkled her nose as she looked down at it. 'Doesn't look too appetising, does it?'

'No.' Jack sat beside her. 'A rip-off and not even cold. Sorry.'

'Not your fault.' She took a sip. 'It's not too bad actually. And, anyway, I've drunk enough at your house already.'

Jack nodded. 'Same here. It doesn't take much to knock me sideways.' There was a pause he didn't know how to fill. Fran sat quietly, balancing her drink against her thigh, a thoughtful look on her face. Taking everything in. He was happy just to sit beside her. As though she was his date. Which, of course, she wasn't.

'There was a good mix at the barbecue, I thought,' she said, after a while. 'Many of them were obviously your parents' friends.'

'Yes, well, family friends really. Neighbours. We've lived there a while so most of them know each other. I'd invited two people I work with from the pub so they weren't part of the usual crowd.' He looked across at her. 'I hadn't met the two girls Lucy brought with her before.'

'Neither had I.' She brushed at her dress. 'And I don't really know Lucy well. We're in an exercise class together but only got talking a couple of weeks ago.'

'Did Lucy bulldoze you into coming?'

She laughed. 'Sort of.' Then her expression grew serious and she looked away. 'In hindsight I shouldn't have come. I was a little lost.'

'Well, you didn't look it. You came across as confident and... aloof.'

'Aloof?' She frowned, as though considering this. 'The last word I'd use to describe me.'

'Sorry, it wasn't meant as an insult. But you seemed to be by yourself quite a bit – sort of choosing to be. Have I got that wrong?'

'No. I suppose you haven't got that wrong.'

'My mother's idea of a small party usually turns out to be something else. She always goes overboard. It can be a bit intimidating. I can understand how you felt. I *know* everyone and even *I* find it a bit daunting.'

'In what way?'

'Well.' He thought about it. 'Demanding, I suppose. You have to be on your best behaviour, keep going round making sure everyone's looked after – you don't enjoy it yourself. I run out of things to say. Funny, at the pub where I work I don't have a problem, but… well, I'm not really good at small talk.'

Fran studied him for a moment. 'You're not a bit like Lucy, are you?'

'No, not a bit.' He shook his head. 'Is that a bad thing?'

She smiled. 'No. Different doesn't mean good or bad.'

They fell into a more comfortable silence as they watched the comings and goings in front of them. Jack liked the fact that she didn't bother with small talk, either. Better to say nothing than churn out platitudes. In fact, he liked everything about her. He began to hope the evening would keep going till the early hours.

So he wasn't ready for how quickly she pulled her mobile out of her bag and called for a taxi. 'It'll take a good fifteen minutes,' she said. 'Not too long to wait. I'll have time to finish my drink. Need to be up early in the morning.'

It sounded like an excuse to get away and he felt disappointed. It seemed as though she was brushing him off and of course, he'd no right to expect anything else. Still…

'Seriously. It's an early start. I'm in a conservation group in Hazel Grove – just a small group – we clean up ditches and streams, mend fences and lay stone paths.' She was looking at him, her eyes kind and sympathetic now, as though she realised he was hurt. 'You know, environmental do-gooders. It's our day to go out to Marple to restore a footpath there. And we're starting at 8.30.'

He perked up. 'Sounds really worthwhile. Wish I'd done something like that instead of just worrying about earning some money all the time.'

'We choose Sundays so that everyone can get there. It's team work so I can't let them down.' Fran put her drink on top of the wall and pulled a face. 'This stuff really doesn't get any better.'

'Is it every Sunday?'

'No, once a month. But we do evenings sometimes as well. Had quite a coup last week. Got ourselves an article in the local paper with a large photograph, and that sort of publicity lets people know what we do and it encourages them to volunteer.'

'Sounds a lot more noble than working in a pub,' said Jack. 'It's OK but I'm still trying to find out what I'd like to do long term.'

She smiled. Such a warm smile. 'You're young. Don't worry so much. It'll find you.'

'Wish it would hurry up.'

A horn sounded from a black cab that had drawn into the kerb. Early.

Fran stood up and so did he, hoping she'd offer him a lift but there was no way he could ask. And she could live miles away from his neck of the woods. He couldn't think of what to say; he just knew he must have had a silly look on his face because she touched his arm, gently and gave him a brief kiss on the cheek. 'Say goodbye to the others, would you?' and she was gone.

Chapter 7

*I*t's frightening, this bewildering lack of focus.
Sometimes I have no idea where I am.

And yet I sense something is changing. There are differences I can't fully understand..

I know one day must pass into another, into night, the dim lights, the shadows, the sudden noises...... but it is a confusion of hours.... of trying to grasp moments...

I am in half worlds, one so nearly waking, the other oblivion. Darkness at my feet as I slip into the abyss. Then lights flash and my head explodes.

It seems to be a purgatory I can't escape from and I'm struggling, wishing I was back in dreams again. It was more peaceful there.

But now...

I lose control. I surface and there's shouting and arms flailing then a voice, hard and clipped, tells me off. 'You must be quiet. You need to lie still so that you can recover.' And less comforting, 'This is not good enough.' For what, I think, when I'm writhing in a hot, exhausted state, iron bands pinning me down? Not good enough for who? I fight (if that's what they think this is) when I am trying to breathe, trying to cut free from the nightmare... I am trying to break the spell.

I don't know how many days actually pass, but they do. I know because some of the tubes have gone (although the cannula is still strapped to the back of my hand) and I am '*maintaining vital signs*'.

The voices talk over me.

What exactly are my 'vital signs'?

Anyway, I mustn't knock it. I am responding. More often now, I am conscious of my visitors, not perhaps in any sequence, but their presence is felt. Carrie, not asking questions, just uttering comforting words; lovely Jack, who never demands anything from me for which I am grateful almost to tears; Lucy, I can smell her perfume before she reaches the bed; and Joe, who sits close and grips my good arm as though I will drift away and never come back.

And the doctors. I am being examined constantly as though I am some rare new species in a botanical lab, and that's OK.

Except for the headaches. They aren't OK. They attack me when I'm least prepared. And I'm not capable of telling anyone. Not coherently anyway, only garbled sounds. The words are just beyond me, refusing to come out of hiding. And I can't concentrate long enough for them to show up.

But one thing strikes me constantly. And it seems odd for someone who never thought about himself in any physical sense, other than stretching an aching back or checking on a sprained ankle. I am aware of every tiny movement and fluctuation going on in my body and it absorbs me: the pulse throbbing in my neck, the sensation that is oddly unfamiliar in my fingertips. I count my breaths. I am conscious of being able to swallow – whoever thinks about that? And my body, heavy, inert, holding me still.

I have become a mere organism.

Does all this make sense?

'Alex, it's Joe?' He's holding my hand, fingers rough against mine. 'If you can, open your eyes.'

I open them for a brief moment and they close again of their own accord. It takes strength and willpower to respond to all these commands and I'm not quite there yet. If I drift, I can create my own world, even though I'm never sure what is real and what is fantasy. But it's more comfortable than…

'Come on.' I can hear the frustration in Joe's voice. You can't spend your whole childhood with someone and not get exactly how they feel and how they're going to react. He's determined to 'pull me through'. So like him. Two years younger, and yet, for some reason, he's always been the one who ended up the leader. Brighter, more energetic and determined, the golden boy my parents pinned their hopes on. And I understood. He was always worth it.

He's talking away, memories dredged up from long ago. Trying to reach me. 'The park, you must remember the park up the road. Where we used to take our bikes and crash through the trees down the bank to the stream. And that annoying little jerk who told the park keeper so we got into trouble at home. You just kept dumb and I had to make up all sorts of excuses so Dad wouldn't hit the roof. He confiscated the bikes for a while. So we went into Beaver Road and decided to ruin the football game that the Harris kids always played after school...'

A picture comes into my mind. And the words fight their way through... 'The girl... broke a window...'

Joe's grip gets tighter, a vice on my wrist now. He must have made sense of the sounds I'm making. 'Yes, yes... she did. Kicked the ball right over the high wall into Mr. Parry's garden. She was fierce, that girl, scared of nothing, and she could really play. Better than the boys.'

He pauses, waiting expectantly. I can hear him breathing.

'We always seemed to be in trouble,' he goes on, laughing a little to himself. 'You can blame me. I think I was the ringleader. I could never stay still, could I?'

I open my eyes. His face is close, cheeks flushed, wisps of hair standing on end. It's so good to see him. So reassuring and familiar. I am not lost in a world I don't understand any more. Joe is Joe and he's my lifeline to the past and somehow, in a way, to the future. I feel such gratitude.

'Hi,' he says. The smile warms me through and I try to smile back. 'Good to know you're still in there.'

'I'm in there,' I manage and hope he understands the words which don't come out quite as I intended. It's as though my tongue is in the way. Messing things up.

He tells me, or perhaps reminds me, of the time he dived into the swimming baths at Colwyn Bay and the life guard had to fish him out, me standing paralysed on the side, not even shouting for help. And the disastrous afternoon when ink splattered all over the newly decorated dining room as we were doing our homework, or pretending to. We'd been given fountain pens by an aunt one Christmas – such a mistake!

It's good just to take it all in and rebuild what I'd been in danger of losing. A crazy relief that I can actually recreate the scenes he's describing in my mind, pictures so clear it amazes me.

Thank you, Joe.

*

And things keep getting better in every way.

I improve. Faster than I could have hoped. I am moved out of ICU into a two-bedded room, with me the only occupant, near the nurses' station. Still monitored, still sleeping a lot, some confusion at times but much more aware. The dressings round my head don't feel as though I'm in some sort of medieval animal trap now, although my right arm makes movement difficult – the plaster is heavy. Headaches come and go but not as frequently and they're less violent. The physiotherapy seems to be about four times a day but I need it. My legs feel like lead and don't obey what my brain is trying to tell them, but it'll come. So they say.

The bit that's scary is this blank before and after the accident. And worse, the blank that's the accident itself. The last thing I remember is eating breakfast – and I've worked out that was a week, perhaps more before the crash – and then nothing till I realised I was in a hospital bed. Where's it all gone? And will it come back? There's probably no-one who can answer that.

The light from the high window hurts my eyes at first but it's good to see the sky. I keep being told the weather's '*nice*' but it looks cloudy to me. Not that it matters. I'd appreciate any weather just to be outside. Breathe the open air, smell the grass, feel wind on my face. I should be grateful I'm alive, I tell myself, and able to speak and eat real food at last (well, it's *almost* real food – slop, mostly) and my sense of taste is coming back.

It's the night time I like best. The quiet, the hushed sounds, the lowered voices of the nurses who sit outside my room at their desk, young faces lit in a pool of light from a lamp, whispers and stifled laughter. Until the buzz of a patient's bell sets them in motion, swift and alert again.

The night offers me a solitude I treasure, long hours ahead when I can just *be*, with no anxiety that I'll fail to do what I am asked to do. There's peace. Funny saying that when a hospital is full of drama and fear for so many. But in the darkness, I am wrapped in a false sense of security that I believe in. And I feel I can face whatever's coming.

In the end, I fall asleep and, much too early before I'm ready, morning arrives. Some change in noise and pace has woken me. It's five thirty. And it all begins again... all kinds of rituals ahead, exercises and tests and visits. In between – long stretches of boredom, I suppose. But you soon realise in a situation like this, how much human contact matters when you're vulnerable and pretty helpless. A bond grows with those who look after you and I know how thankful I am for... well, not for how *efficient* they all are... it's more for the chat and the smiles and the humour. They share something of themselves with you.

The nurses, particularly Julie who's on today, are patient and cheerful to a degree I couldn't manage in a million years – not in a job like theirs. There's such generosity in their selflessness. What touches me most is how understanding everyone is.

Perhaps easier when they're not related to the person in the bed.

'Come on, Dad. You must remember *something*.'

Lucy is sitting beside the bed and patting the sheets flat in an annoying manner. It's teatime and Carrie has just gone home to sort out something at the yard, and I'm defenceless. She's left behind her weapon of choice to chivvy me along – our daughter. I'm not being fair here but when there's any sort of family crisis, Lucy feels the need to sort things out. A bull at the gate approach. Works at times, and not at others. Some problems are more complex than others.

I let out a sigh.

Then I look at her tired face, her uncombed hair and how she fidgets and immediately feel ashamed. I have always been aware that she deals with challenges the only way she can. She's a doer, practical and decisive and she hates feeling helpless. Which is what she's experiencing now. The situation here is beyond her reach and she's frustrated and angry. None of what's happening makes sense to her and she needs to make sense of it. She's the opposite of Jack but that doesn't mean she's uncaring. A bit selfish – aren't we all? – and at times gets tunnel vision but when the chips are down, she's there for you and you'd want her in your corner.

She lowers her voice, suddenly aware of a head turning and a pair of eyes looking across from the nurses' station. She pours some water for me from the plastic jug by the bed, finds a straw and holds the glass for me. 'Sorry. Didn't mean to hassle you. Just trying to work things out. Mum hasn't told me much and I'm worried. Because if we knew what caused you to… go off the road, say you were dazzled by headlights, or a pheasant went under the wheels, there'd be a reason for it.'

I sip the water, then try to smile and look earnest at the same time to reassure her that I'm taking her seriously. 'If I could remember, Lucy, I'd tell you… but there's nothing there.'

'Not even the minute before the car turned over?'

'I try to find a…' (What? What can't I find?) 'Lucy, I can't… It's like falling into… I've lost a whole chunk of time.' I feel quite emotional and she must see that because she puts her head down, forehead resting on my good arm.

59

'Sorry,' she mumbles. 'Don't get upset. I'm not helping you. I'll shut up.'

She lifts her head and her eyes are full of pain, mascara smudged on her cheek. 'It's been horrible to see you in such a state. Nothing ever happens to you. This is so scary.'

'I'm going to be OK,' I manage to croak.

'Gran and Grandad wanted to come and visit you but Mum put them off. Said you were only allowed one visitor at a time, so it seems hard but they'll have to wait.'

'Yes. That's best.'

She rocks a little in her chair. I don't know what to say to comfort her. She likes to be tough – to create that image anyway, and that's not who she is, really. The divorce from Danny didn't help. Never thought they were that well suited but you can't give any sort of parental advice that would be taken when someone's determined. Still, fifteen months is no time for it all to fall apart. Not sure why it did either, because Lucy was busy hiding it all and keeping us at a distance. Pride, I suppose, feeling she'd failed. And when we found out they'd broken up, Carrie decided how this whole episode should be played. Lucy must move on, find her own place, get her social life back, she'd said. It was all better behind her.

I wonder now, looking at Lucy at her most vulnerable, why we haven't put up more of a fight over what *we've* wanted over the years, instead of letting Carrie make all the big decisions? Why *I* haven't, which is fairer. It's not good enough to say it was for the sake of peace.

By the time Lucy's leaves me, I'm exhausted. I've missed my afternoon sleep and I lie on my one pillow and welcome the quiet. I can understand how a patient in hospital becomes institutionalised if they stay too long. There's a pattern to the day that makes you feel secure. I begin to have this dread of going home. All sorts of weird misgivings creep into my mind, nothing concrete… just everything about moving back into the world where I won't have the confidence to cope with being a semi-invalid, which is what I'll be for a while. The thought of getting completely back to normal isn't in my thinking. I just imagine a painful, embarrassing coming-to-terms with my inability to function, certainly not in the same way I did before the accident.

I see it all as a before and after. How I was. How I am now. God knows what state I'll be in when Adrian says '*And are you ready to go back to work?*' That's another part of the world that's beyond me. Let's hope I can remember what an abutment is!

*

I've been hoisted into a sitting position, which is a hell of an improvement. I can look at my surroundings straight on, instead of looking up and counting the light fittings and how many corners the room has. Not much to see, to be honest, but I feel more, well, normal. One small step…

*

A supper that's made up of little squares of pasta fills me with ridiculous pleasure.

Although trying to use my left hand instead of my right is proving really difficult. But never mind. It's back to basics anyway. For nearly everything. I'm like a child, looking forward to small surprises, the next meal and some attention. Must be getting better.

*

On my feet today. Well, with two strong bodies either side of me. And OK, it's only a trip down the corridor to the loo! But upright. And the words that come out of my mouth seem to be understood at last, so I'm sounding like the rest of the human race. I'm still in my small room, sheltered I suppose from what's going on beyond that half-open door, but I'm curious now when there's a noise or I hear bits of a conversation. And my thinking is more coherent. The dreams aren't, though. They're an odd mixture – hospital corridors, people I don't recognise, conversations that don't make sense, journeys on buses that never make a stop when I want them to. And the recurring one of diving head first down a dark hole in the ground, wide enough so my body never touches the sides, hurtling so fast I have trouble breathing. I plummet headlong towards the bottom, sure I'm going to die, then at the last moment jerk awake, hot and covered in sweat. I can remember these dreams in startling detail when I come to (I could recount them if anyone would listen), something I could never do before.

So it goes on. My senses have become uncomfortably acute, an obsessive awareness of the objects around me; I touch what I can reach constantly with my good hand – the glass of water, the spoon, a paper bag; I feel the texture of the sheet, the smooth plastic of the tray they pull across for my meal, the coldness of the damp cloth when they wash my arms, the odd sensation on my scalp when the dressings need changing. As though I am a conduit for every nerve in my body. As though I'm slowly coming alive.

But when I wake all alone, when the family has gone, when there is a lull in the routine of the day, usually after lunch or before they dim the lights, it is the obscure thoughts in my half-conscious state that trouble me most. I'm sure the painkillers and other medicines I'm taking are part of it, but an unsettling melancholy pervades my whole being, an underlying ache that weighs heavy and I wish I could give it substance so I could deal with it. All I know is that I'm sad and anxious and full of longing.

And I could weep.

Chapter 8

Carrie stood at the door considering the practicalities. She was sure of one thing. Alex would want somewhere quiet to recover, away from the goings-on in the rest of the household. So adapting the spare bedroom for him was the answer, but how manageable was that?

It wasn't particularly large but it caught the sun in the middle of the day, so was usually warm and bright. It was at the front of the house and, even though it looked out onto the road, this was the country; it wasn't as though there was much traffic other than the odd tractor or farm truck. And anyway, their house was at the far end of the village with nothing but fields for miles, a few farm buildings and a small cluster of cottages. There would hardly be any noise to disturb him. It would work, as long as the stairs didn't prove too much of a problem...

She couldn't quite believe he was coming home. And the responsibility of caring for him still in a delicate state played on her mind. All the instructions from the consultant seemed too much to take in. She'd jotted down notes in as much detail as she could. But her constant questions to anyone in a uniform prompted one of the nurses to reassure her she was worrying unnecessarily. *'You'll be given a discharge plan, Mrs. Taylor. It'll all be in there. No need to write lists.'* But Carrie needed to be on top of this. You never knew how things would work out. And she felt she had to satisfy other family members that everything was under control, stop them interfering – Joe would be keeping a watchful eye on how they were doing and his parents... well, they would panic at every turn. They were already asking what would happen if Alex had a relapse! That caused Carrie to grit her teeth. God, she didn't want to think about it. She wasn't a nurse. How did *she* know?

She pushed a small chest of drawers flat against the wall and brought in another bedside table from Jack's room, then fetched more pillows from the storage space above the wardrobe. At least the bed was a double from when Lucy and Danny used to stay overnight. It would do. She took a final, cursory glance around the room before shutting the door and heading downstairs. There were a few days for her to sort it.

*

She'd been up at seven, downing a bowl of cereal while still on her feet and then spent two hours getting back into her usual working routine. Steph hadn't yet arrived so she let out the three liveries who'd been in all night. As soon as they got through the gate, off they went, heels up, cantering in high-spirited loops. Then she bedded up ready for the evening. It was pleasantly warm as she set out round the edges of the fields where a light haze hovered a few feet off the ground. It would soon burn off. There hadn't been rain for most of the month and one of the paddocks had become parched. She'd have to change the grazing groups around for a week or two.

When she rounded the last hedge near the barn, she could see Steph pulling up and climbing off her bike.

'It's going to be hot,' Carrie said. 'Once this mist lifts. Bloody flies'll be a nightmare!'

Steph nodded. 'At least we aren't knee deep in flood water like this time last year.'

'True enough. Mustn't moan.'

'Alex is coming home this week, isn't he?'

'Hopefully. And I've still things to do in the house so it isn't primed like a booby trap. Difficult to know what he'll be able to manage and what he'll struggle with.'

'Before you go, I just need to check on orders.' Steph led the way to the little office space in the corner of the barn, with its old table, wooden chairs, a telephone and some shelving. On all the surfaces were catalogues, bags of samples, papers held together with bulldog clips and pieces of string and a stack of entry slips for a charity ride. A booking form for lesson times in the indoor school was tacked to the wall.

Carrie followed her in.

'If the weather stays this dry, we'll have to supplement with coarse mix and chaff,' said Steph. 'Shall I just go ahead and put in an order?'

'Yes, that's fine. They'll deliver before the weekend.'

'Carrie, I don't mean to butt in here and offer advice, but… why don't you do something for yourself for a change? Why don't you get that horse of yours in, give him a brush and a bit of love? Do you both good.'

Carrie smiled and waved her hand in a dismissive gesture. But as she stepped out into the yard, she saw him, head over the field gate, watching her. Merlin. She'd bought him three years ago, an ex-racer (he'd run under the name of Double Take – owners make some weird choices), coming tenth out of twelve runners in his last race. At eight years old, past his best. But boy, he was handsome and moved well; he seemed to float. It took Carrie just an hour to make up her mind to buy him and she never regretted it, even though the first few months had been a bit of a challenge. Perhaps, in hindsight, that was an understatement because thoroughbreds have a mind of their own.

She was about to walk on but decided, after all, Steph had a point, so she brought him into his stable and spent half an hour grooming him, oiling his feet and making a fuss of him. It was good therapy, but enough was enough.

'No riding today, boy,' she told him, rubbing his forehead. 'Back in the field for the day. Not that you care.'

She'd gone back to the house, changed out of her jeans, showered and washed her hair. She was grateful to be able to slow down for a bit after the past weeks when her feet had never seemed to touch the ground. And very soon, no dashing to the hospital and spending hours by Alex's bedside. It was OK now to spend some time on herself. She'd put on some make-up and dress in something cool. Leave sorting out the room for Alex till later.

Sitting at her dressing table, she'd studied her face in the mirror. Applied foundation and eyeliner, grey eye shadow and a bit of colour on her cheeks. Better. She smoothed oil onto her hair with her palms to take the bounce out of it.

But the result didn't have the effect she'd hoped for. She sat back. When had her forehead taken on a permanent frown, her mouth become a straight line? Even she could see she looked... stern. She'd once overheard one of the mothers at a school concert talking about her as she'd passed – 'Carrie has such a haughty manner.' Was that the impression she gave? God, what an awful indictment.

Where was the girl who'd been 'fun', 'a laugh', someone who'd have a go at anything, someone who was confident enough not to care what people thought? When had all that changed? When her father died? When the years with Alex had become unrewarding?

She remembered a time when they'd had a falling out a few years ago. Alex had gone to bed, silenced and angry, and she'd sat alone in the darkened garden, despairing and holding back angry tears, saying to herself, '*Is this all there is?*'

Is that what her face conveyed? Disenchantment?

Later, as she made her way downstairs, she found herself pausing at the closed study door. She was well aware of what she wanted to do. And it was only eleven o'clock. Plenty of time to do a quick search before she had to leave for the hospital. She pushed the door open, with an odd feeling that she shouldn't be in there. But come on. It wasn't just *his* study – they shared it, after all.

A work room, it was just big enough to have two desks, which stood against opposite walls, so that when they were both sitting at their computers, there was little conversation between them. Carrie took pride in keeping her side of the room orderly, invoices and correspondence paper-clipped and stacked in piles on the work-top, pens in a tall jar, waste basket at her feet. Organised, efficient. Alex's desk was anything but. He wasn't running a business, of course, but it was exasperating that he never kept on top of things. She ended up paying most of the household bills and generally looking after their finances because he didn't seem to care if he made a late payment or had to be reminded the phone was about to be cut off. He kept abreast of everything related to his job but he dealt with problems mostly face to face, sorting out snags and difficulties on site or at meetings. So a tidy desk wasn't important to him.

She hesitated for a moment. It wasn't right to delve into someone's private space, not even when you lived together. There were bound to be secrets, everyone had them. But this was different. This lie he'd told wasn't some small slip or something he'd forgotten to tell her. It was deliberate. This was something that could undermine everything you believed to be true. And you didn't think about your relationship after so many years of marriage. It just was. You assume you know everything about someone. But there was something she obviously *didn't* know. The reason he'd crashed. The reason he'd been driving miles away from where he should have been. And it raised a bigger question. Had she neglected something long before which should have alerted her? Put up a warning flag?

One thing was certain – she was determined to solve the mystery of where he'd been going that night. And solve it, if she could, before he came home tomorrow. His mobile had apparently been lost in the wreckage of the car, so she'd been told when his wallet and watch had been handed to her. The only way to try to understand this was to... what? ...sneak around and look into his private correspondence, the dates of meetings, his personal messages? It seemed a shabby way of going about things.

She had never gone into his computer unless he'd specifically asked her to check on his emails a couple of times when he'd been away. Well, at least she knew his password – he used it for everything from buying trousers to garden tools – *Samiseight!* Not the strongest, by any means.

She moved swiftly over to Alex's desk and bent over the computer. She was just about to power it up, when her mobile rang out from upstairs, making her start, as though she'd been caught in a criminal act. Well, they could wait. This was more important.

She pulled his chair forward and sat down at his desk, waited for the monitor to come up with '*Hello Alex.*' and tapped out the password. She was conscious of her breathing, shallow and quick. She went into Outlook and as it opened, an avalanche of emails downloaded, some going into Junk Mail, so she had to wait a minute till it all settled down. Even with the filtering, there were 243 in the Inbox. It would take her forever. She started scanning the latest ones on the left hand side of the screen. There wasn't anything that made her curious. Unsolicited offers from holiday companies, menswear firms, wine merchants, chemists; work emails – site managers, architects, suppliers, names she didn't always recognise but obviously business links. She shook her head. She'd have to look further back, the weeks before the accident. He had no truck with Facebook or other apps so there'd be nothing personal to discover on those forums. Then an idea struck her – what about other places to store information. So she went through Calendar, Maps, People, Notes.

Nothing there either.

She clicked the Power Off button and sat back.

No time to go through everything now or search all the papers and notebooks on his desk; she'd leave that for when Jack had gone to the pub for his shift. Even then, time would be against her. And her conscience. What on earth was she doing, checking up on him like this? If she could just ask him… but he had no answers, did he? What other choice did she have?

She moved over to her computer and checked if there'd been any more emails from the travel insurance company about the cancellation of their holiday to Crete. She found yesterday's, informing her that '*the matter was in hand.*' Whatever that meant!

'Carrie!'

Someone was shouting from the road, and she recognised the voice. Mary. She'd want to know how Alex was doing and never seemed to like coming to the front door, even though they'd been neighbours for years. She left her desk, closed the study door behind her and walked out into the garden.

Mary waved and leant against the gate. 'How's the old man?'

'He's coming home soon,' she called back. 'Give him a few days and he'll be glad to see you. You can read the newspaper to him.'

'Will do. Jolly good. Really pleased.' And she wandered back to her own house.

Carrie suddenly realised she'd forgotten to tell Steph that the two o'clock lesson had been cancelled. Still plenty of time though. She washed up the breakfast plates and picked up the post from the doormat, a bill from the accountant and an appeal from Greenpeace. She threw them on the kitchen table and went out the back door.

By the time she'd neared the yard, she could see from the way Steph was standing, her body held tight, shovel in hand, that things weren't going well. David seemed to be towering over her and whatever was being discussed, it had obviously turned awkward. She eyed Carrie over his shoulder then came towards her, managing to mutter as she passed, 'He's not happy. Get ready.'

Carrie put on her best smile, straightened her back and approached him.

He waited, then bowed his head slightly, courteous, a bit exaggerated with an air of disdain about it. He was an imposing man, sturdily built with a tanned face and deep-set eyes; rather handsome, she supposed. But he often wore this expression of disapproval as though ready to find fault or pick holes. He struck her as an odd mixture. Irascible at times, tetchy. Then suddenly charming, quite gracious and appreciative – depending on which side of the bed he got out of in the morning, Carrie thought. Or perhaps it depended on whether things were going his way or not. Today obviously wasn't a good day. No wonder Steph had left him to her.

He stood now, legs slightly apart as though he was about to command a regiment, immaculate in his checked riding jacket and well-fitting jodhpurs, boots polished to a high gloss.

'It's Jodie,' he said as though she would immediately understand the problem from those few words.

'Yes?' Carrie put on her '*Anything I can do to help?*' face. 'I know she's having a lesson with Sarah now.' She could hear the instructor's voice coming from the indoor school and the rhythmic sound of hooves as the pony tracked round the arena. What's he going to grouch about this time? she thought, already on the defensive before he said any more. This wasn't the first time he'd brought up issues involving Jodie – well, not with the child – it was more complicated than that. He liked things set up *his* way. He'd come to the stables a couple of months ago, bringing his thoroughbred over from Wilmslow. Not happy with the turning-out there, not enough grass. All she knew about him was that he was recently divorced, had his own business and looked after his daughter Jodie every other weekend.

Carrie had soon realised he made his own difficulties – he was determined to make Jodie, only eight years old, into a rider (and a good one) expecting far too much too soon. She'd only ridden at a local riding school, ponies that plodded along one after the other. But four weeks ago, he'd bought her a Connemara. No problem with that; usually a good children's pony, but the kid was a beginner, she needed time to gain confidence. And she was losing it fast. Here was David, an experienced horseman, someone who entered dressage competitions and local cross-country events, who should have known better, being far too ambitious for the child. When she hadn't even got the hang of basics he pushed harder, paying for extra lessons, borrowing different saddles for her to try, butting in when she was being taught.

Back off a bit, Carrie had tried to tell him. *It doesn't work that way.* Of all people he should have known that. *Just let her enjoy riding instead of all this pressure.* But no. He wasn't listening.

He stood now, a frown on his face. 'It's the pony, Carrie. He's too strong for her and I'm sorry to say, I don't think Sarah's doing a very good job.'

He always seemed to assume the manner of someone to be obeyed, she thought, and his attitude, this air of entitlement he used to browbeat others was irritating. She couldn't help wondering what his ex-wife was like. Perhaps she'd been a match for him and decided she'd been playing second fiddle for too long. Decided she'd had enough.

'Well, let's go and watch then,' said Carrie, moving slightly away from him. He wasn't going to make her cower. She knew as much about horses as he did, probably more. There was no way she'd bend to his whims and start criticising Sarah, who taught a lot of her liveries and who she trusted. 'We can go in the viewing area and if we stand back, we won't put them off.'

She strode to the side metal door of the school and opened it, with David following close behind. The dust hung in the air from the sandy floor of the arena like a gauze drawn up in front of them, blurring outlines. Carrie had watered the surface earlier but you could never dampen it down enough.

They stood in the shadows near the back wall and watched. She knew David would start talking so she turned her back slightly. She'd make up her own mind about the lesson. She didn't need him pulling her strings.

71

The grey pony trotted round, Jodie sitting, small and crouched in the saddle, legs just a little too short to get a decent grip. Her face was tense with concentration as she did her best to follow Sarah's instructions – *Keep your back straight... try not to lean forward or she'll go faster... legs quiet... soften the reins.*

Carrie could hear David making impatient noises beside her and she gave him a look she hoped would silence him. But after a few minutes, she decided it was best to leave before they were either seen or heard.

Out in the yard, he shrugged as though to say – *See? I'm right, aren't I?*

Carrie gave him a straight look. 'I think Sarah's doing a good job. Jodie's only had the pony a few weeks. They have to get used to each other.'

'That doesn't look as though it's going to happen soon.' He was determined not to give way.

'Well, there's no hurry. Have her ride in the paddock and go at her own pace. She'd relax then and start enjoying it. I know when I was a kid, my father used to let me—'

'Oh Carrie, come on, you're not getting the point. It's not working, is it?' He shook his head, impatience making his voice sharp. 'I want *you* to teach her. You know what you're doing and I trust your judgement. I'll pay more for the lessons, of course.'

She wasn't going to enter into that.

But as they walked away from the indoor school, David stopped and faced her; he moved close, too close for comfort, and put a hand on her shoulder. She tried not to flinch.

'Carrie, as a special favour.' His voice was soft and persuasive now. 'I just want what's best for Jodie.' And she saw in his eyes that he was sincere when he said that.

But his manner was all too familiar, too *intimate* and she flushed with annoyance.

'David, I've enough on my plate. I don't teach. I run a business.'

He seemed to remember the situation and dropped his hand to his side. 'Ah yes, I, sorry. How *is* your husband? It must have been a bad time for you.'

'It has been,' she said. 'Extremely difficult in every sense. He's improving gradually but when he comes out of hospital we don't know what we'll have to face. He'll obviously need a lot of care.'

Surely he'd got the message!

He took a step back. 'Of course. But you never know, in a week it might be easier. Will you think about it? I'm sure we can arrange something to suit us both.' He held eye contact deliberately and for too long but she wasn't going to be the first to blink. *You're not going to play me,* thought Carrie.

He was about to leave her, when he turned slightly. 'I came here because I'd heard such good things about you, Carrie.' He seemed to be measuring his words. 'You have an excellent reputation which is so important to hold on to in this business. I hope I'm not going to be disappointed.'

She didn't answer, well aware of the tactics he was using.

'Well, hope your situation lightens up. It can only get better.' As he walked away, he said over his shoulder, 'And I'm sure you'll do your best for Jodie – fit her in somehow.'

Carrie's eyes followed him across the yard, nettled by his last remarks and resenting that element of threat in them. She wasn't used to being dictated to and she didn't like it. Or was she reading too much into it?

She'd have to talk to Sarah and try to work something out that would satisfy everyone. But that might be easier said than done.

Chapter 9

He'd been told to take a seat and he tried to keep his hands still. He wanted to appear composed, even if it was only the girl sitting behind the computer in the outer office who'd notice how nervous he was.

What a time to be called for an interview when he desperately wanted to go to the hospital to see his dad, make sure there were no setbacks in bringing him home. Any day, they'd said. And even then, he'd need a lot of care, someone around to look after him, a shoulder to lean on (literally), help him exercise. And now this. Out of the blue.

Well, almost. He'd filled in the questionnaire online four weeks ago and forgotten about it. One of those psychological profile tests which are impossible to answer honestly:

I have more good qualities than bad ones: Not True/ Slightly True/ Moderately True/ Very True.' What on earth is Moderately True?

And another one: *'Friends see me as cooperative and agreeable.'* Of course they do. You're not going to say you're a social misfit!

A door opened and a small man, round and dressed in a brown suit beckoned him forward. 'Mr. Taylor? Come along.'

He turned, not waiting to see if Jack followed.

They sat facing each other over a wide desk. The office was badly in need of paint, its high walls a strange shade of yellow and the window smudged with dirty marks. The smell of cigarettes and coffee hung in the air. If this was the local head office, Jack thought, it didn't say much for the rest of the organisation.

'So… Jack, isn't it?

He nodded.

'I'm Sean Clarke.' He looked down at the sheets of paper on his desk. 'I'm seeing a few people, you understand. But you're local and your answers seemed OK on that questionnaire. Not that I hold much truck by these things – too American for me, but we've been taken over recently. This new chief believes in hiring that way. Young fella. New ideas.' He looked at Jack with sharp, unblinking eyes. 'You seem a pretty sociable bloke.'

Jack felt he should say something. 'Well I work part-time in the village pub and I enjoy mixing with the regulars there.' Mr. Clarke was obviously waiting for more. 'I've had a few jobs, but what I like most is dealing with people, helping people…'

'You'd be doing that. Our slogan is *"Make every customer a happy customer"*. And you have to be prepared to help the numpties. Some haven't a clue what they want or where to find it. So you have to know where everything is. You'd get a week's training before you start.'

Again, he stared at Jack, as though he could read his thoughts. 'What do you know about agricultural merchants?'

'Well.' At least this time, Jack had done a bit of research. 'I've been to Parsons a number of times. My mother runs a livery stables, so we're always needing feed and power tools, fencing, stuff like that. I know you have a wide range of products…' (he was sounding like a salesman) 'and they're always very helpful and really know their stuff in our local branch. I get how important it is to look after people.'

'Exactly.' Mr. Clarke managed a smile. 'So you know there's machinery, a garden section, a café, clothing… quite a lot to get your head round.' He drummed his fingers on his desk and sat, staring at Jack as though weighing him up. 'OK, start Monday. Six months trial and main office will discuss salary with you when you've signed the agreement. We'll check your references but I'm sure they'll be fine.' He half rose and extended his hand. 'Welcome to Parsons. Make us all proud.'

By the time Jack was outside the front entrance and taking a deep breath, it was beginning to sink in. He'd got it. What happened to the others Mr. Clarke said he was 'seeing'? Not that it mattered now. He'd be earning and at least it would involve some variety and it wasn't in an office. And he could still keep some of his shifts at the pub. He felt elated. He knew his mother wouldn't see it as a step on the ladder to higher things but that was too bad. He needed to work and get some independence, perhaps enough to rent a place in the village or further out. Even a bedsit would be a start.

He looked at his watch. One o'clock. He'd have to move fast to get to the hospital. He'd promised to be there at two and anyway, he wanted to give his dad the good news.

He drove off in a hurry, slowing down as he approached the 30 sign and changed gear as he entered the main street. Suddenly, a figure was jumping off the pavement, arms waving madly and yelling his name and then pointing to a spot further down the road where he could park outside the Spar. Terry, of course. Shit! Jack had missed the party at his parents' house, the anniversary thing, and he hadn't let them know. He should have rung them, if not before, at least afterwards.

Terry had run along the pavement to catch up and now pulled open the car door and threw himself into the passenger seat. He never seemed to change or look any older, hair flopping over his forehead and eyes that always had the look of a basset hound, large and droopy, and full of hope. He punched Jack on the shoulder. 'You missed it, you old bugger.'

'God, Terry, I'm so sorry. Everything's been upside down and I can't honestly say I forgot. I just couldn't quite face it. And then it was too late to ring on the day, and afterwards… well…'

'Ah, that's all right. Quite understand. Not the same without you, though. I was looking forward to catching up.' He leant his back against the door. 'You OK? Mum told me about what happened. Must have been grim.'

'Well, it still is, really. But things are looking up. He's out of the coma and they're talking about letting him home in the next few days. Long way to go I suppose, but at least he'll be with us.' Jack paused. 'And... I've got a job at Parsons. Start Monday. Well, training starts Monday but at least I'll be earning and doing something I might enjoy.'

'Brilliant. Though I still think you should have carried on at college. You're bloody bright.'

Jack shrugged. He didn't want the shine taken off his good news. 'And how're you doing? Still with the finance people?'

'Yes. Don't really enjoy it to be honest.' Terry had lost his flippant tone. 'It's a bit of a slog. Same old, same old. I'm just bored and it's not what I went to uni for. I'm just not using my brain. And I owe bloody thousands. Things don't always work out how you think they're going to.'

'No,' Jack nodded. 'But at least you're in a city. With a bit of life. It's pretty dead here.'

'Suppose. And I might get to reach the next grade by the time I'm 40.' He grinned. He was always the one who looked on the bright side. 'I took two days' holiday to make it a long weekend, so if you're about, we could go to the pub tonight.'

'I'm doing a shift, but yeah. Can work something out.' He glanced at the digital clock on the dashboard. 'Need to move though. Going to the hospital and I won't make it by two at this rate.'

'Right, mate. Of course.' Terry's hand was on the door handle. 'Oh, by the way, Grace was asking after you.'

Jack felt sick. 'When?'

'Well, she came to the do at the house, didn't she? I knew she would. Think she sort of expected you to be there.'

Jack looked straight ahead not wanting to be reminded of the past. Certainly not this bit of it anyway. 'And?'

He shrugged. 'That's all. Wanted to know if I'd seen you. How you were. She's got a job in a school in Alderley Edge I think, or somewhere near there. Needs to find a place to live.'

'Just hope she doesn't find anywhere near here.'

'Jack, that's stupid. You can't just brush off parts of your life as though they didn't exist.' A sly smile crossed his face. 'She looked damned good, I know that.'

'*You* take her out then.' Jack could feel the blood rushing to his head. 'Drop it, Terry. And if you want a drink tonight, don't talk to me about Grace.'

'OK, OK, keep your hair on.' He opened the door. 'Eight o'clock.' And then bent down to give Jack a comical wave through the car window.

Jack breathed out slowly, annoyed that he'd got uptight. For heaven's sake, it was no big deal. They'd been eighteen when it all went pear-shaped and you grow up. But you don't always forget. Funny how teenage years can be so painful. Well, 'funny' perhaps isn't the word.

He turned the key in the ignition. Don't start getting excited about things that happened ages ago, he told himself. Leave it… Looking in the rear-view mirror, he saw the Poynton bus trundling towards him and waited for it to pass before pulling out.

He'd left himself short of time and was late reaching the hospital, dashing up the main corridor and just missing the lift as the doors closed. Taking the stairs two at a time, he could feel the sweat creating prickles under his hair. He stripped off his anorak as he reached the right floor, his whole body overheated from the run. It didn't help that it was like a sauna in the hospital. He slowed down as he reached the ward, thankful his dad was out of Intensive Care, as though a bridge had been crossed back to the living. The Sister recognised him as he pushed past an empty gurney, jarring his hip, and waved him on to the open door of number six.

'Hi.' He tried to catch his breath. It was good to see his dad sitting in a chair, still bandaged and looking thin but so different from the mummified body lying in that high, sterile bed, kept alive by machines, unaware of the world around him. 'Thought you'd be reading the latest best-seller by now.'

'I'm just about on my feet and managing to pee. Both quite an achievement.' He gave a weary smile and reached for the glass of water on the nearby table.

Jack couldn't help noticing how his dad's hand shook with the effort and seemed to have difficulty keeping his head steady. 'They've left you on your own in here, then.' He sat down on the empty bed. 'Good to see you sitting in a chair. Though perhaps you need a shave – don't think I've ever seen you with stubble. It makes you look like someone out of *Narcos*.' He could hear how he was burbling on – nervous, that was why. He so wanted to see the old spark of humour, the quick response like in the old days. He wanted everything back to how it used to be. 'Sorry I didn't bring you anything.' He waited a moment. 'Just come from an interview. At Parsons. You know, the farm merchants.'

'And?'

'Got it.' He grinned at the pleased expression on his dad's face. 'Start next week. I honestly thought the bloke would stall, give me a load of waffle and then say he'd let me know. He'd started talking about seeing other people and then suddenly, it was weird, he told me the job was mine. I was in shock. Didn't really ask about salary… that won't please Mum…'

'Good for you.'

'There's training to start with. And I can still do shifts at the pub so I'll be bringing in more money…' He could see his dad's eyes losing focus and wondered whether he should go on. 'Have they told you when you can come home?'

'A few days. They have to do some sort of assessment – a plan…' He stopped as though trying to think it through, trying to find the right words. He was in his own dressing gown now but it seemed too big for him, hanging round his shoulders. There was something disconnected about him. Jack couldn't quite put his finger on it, but it unnerved him.

'Have you got a headache?' he asked.

'A bit.' His dad rubbed at the skin below the bandages. 'These'll come off soon. Trouble is, Jack, I think I'm all right, then I'm not. Can't explain. It's as though I'm on a wave in the sea, down and then up... everything moving... and I have to wait to clear my head.'

Jack moved towards him. Strange to be the one doing the comforting after all those years of it being the other way round. He made a gesture as though to pat his dad's good arm then pulled back. He didn't want to make this odd change in the relationship permanent.

'It'll take time.' What a bloody cliché! Surely he could do better than that. He was relieved to hear a trolley being wheeled up the corridor and the sound of plates and cutlery rattling, cheerful voices. Tea was on the way. He could help with that.

Something practical he could do.

He thought back to all the times his father had come home after a long day, something purposeful about him from the world of work, from outside the ordinariness of his own day at school, a strength and confidence in his voice, in his movements. He was successful. Someone to emulate. Jack had seen him as invincible long before he understood the word, certain that it would always be like this.

The illusion of safety.

All gone now.

When the tea had been put on the bedside tray, he cut up the sandwiches into tiny strips and handed them to his dad one by one, trying not to see the shake of the hand and the slowness of the chewing. It all seemed to take so long. Then a young nurse put her head round the door.

'We need to sort your dad out in a minute.' She smiled. 'Would you wait outside? You can sit in the corridor if you like. Or the coffee shop's open downstairs.'

'Thanks. I'll go and get a coffee. Be fifteen minutes.'

'No hurry. He's not going anywhere.'

The little café was tucked away, one side of the main corridor on the ground floor. Jack realised he was actually quite hungry and ordered a cheese bap, which he carried to an empty table nearest to the entrance. His mother might decide to arrive at any minute and he didn't want her to catch him having a moment of respite. But just as he was about to start eating, he saw Lucy coming through the sliding doors. For a guilty moment, he had the urge to pretend he hadn't noticed her. But she saw him first.

'This is what you get up to when you're meant to be visiting,' she said, her voice loud enough to be carried to an old woman sitting nearby, who looked up, puzzled, as though she'd been woken from sleep.

'The nurses are just "sorting Dad out" – whatever that means,' he said. 'So I'm having a five-minute break. I didn't have any lunch.'

'Only kidding. Don't be so defensive.' She flopped down in the chair opposite as though she'd just finished a twelve-hour stretch in a sweat shop. Jack wished she wasn't always so dramatic, so full on.

'How is he?'

'Weak.' Such an odd word to use for his dad, but it was true. 'Sitting in a chair, drinking tea, but struggling to cope with even the most basic things. He trembles and his balance is dodgy. Loses his train of thought…'

'I suppose it's not surprising,' said Lucy with a shake of her head. 'He won't be back to normal for weeks, at least. I've been reading up about comas and how it affects you afterwards – not that all brain injuries are the same – but often, you need physio for months and feel tired out. And some never regain their memory. Ever.'

'Well that's not Dad. He remembered loads of things when I was talking to him yesterday. About us when we were kids, about Joe and things that happened last year…'

'But he hasn't remembered the accident.' Lucy spoke slowly, making circles with her finger in the sugar that was spilt on the table. 'He can't remember anything about the week before it happened or the day he crashed.'

'So?'

'Nothing. I'm just saying. What do I know?' She shrugged her shoulders. 'Perhaps it'll all come back to him. Suddenly, when he's back home with familiar things around him.'

Jack sighed. 'Let's just wait and see. A Google search doesn't turn you into a neurosurgeon, Lucy. We're all guessing.'

Lucy stood up, annoyed. 'I know that! Eat your sandwich.' Then, she smiled in a way he didn't like. Something was coming. 'I was going to give you some news that would cheer you up.'

What made him think of Fran?

'Are you going to give it me now? Or let me guess?' He knew the more he seemed interested, the more she'd play her game.

'Well.' She strung out the word. 'Someone found you really interesting the other night.' He looked down, pretending to ignore her. 'The night of my birthday? You came with us to that club? Rachel thought you were *really* nice. Good looking, "sweet" was the word she used. I *thought* she kept looking in the rear-view mirror when she drove us back, but… takes all sorts. I can give you her mobile number, if you want.'

Jack felt a rush of disappointment and shook his head. 'No thanks. I'll pick my own girlfriends if that's OK with you.'

'Only trying to help. You haven't been out with anyone for a while, have you! Thought I was doing you a favour, but never mind.' Then, as she got up from the table, brushing down her coat as she stood up, she paused and gave him a knowing look.

'Ah, that's it, is it? You spent a lot of time outside in the moonlight with Fran. I remember now.' She waited for his reaction.

'Don't tell me you've set your sights on *her*.'

'Course not.' But something in his face had given him away.

'Jack, don't get any ideas there. One, she's got a boyfriend. And two, you'd end up her toy boy. She's over thirty, you idiot.'

Jack put down his sandwich. He'd lost his appetite and could only glare at his sister with what he hoped was enough ferocity to shut her up.

'Go and see Dad. He'll be on his own. I'll be up in a minute.'

She left him, knowing she'd scored. Typical elder sister, he thought. Well, he wasn't going to listen to any of it. He'd decided exactly what he was going to do. And sometimes, you have to follow your instincts.

Sometimes, you just have to take a chance.

Chapter 10

I am home. As I'm being wheeled through the front door and into the hall, my eyes fill up and my throat tightens. Strange, this, for someone who usually keeps their emotions in check. But I'm beyond caring.

And the house itself is like an old friend, familiar and welcoming.

It has a feeling all its own. Everything recognised, particular – the shape of a room, the light reflected from a window, the sound when the back door shuts or someone climbs the stairs, the odour of coffee from the kitchen. And the photographs of course, on the bookshelves and lining the walls, mementos in colour, capturing the past.

Do I recognise the blue curtains in the lounge, the soft oversized cushions on the sofa, the ceramic plate by the front door where we hang the car keys? Of course I do. There's something about the collectibles built into the fabric of a house that allow us to sink back into our place again, even when we've been away a long time.

Though for me, well, I can only count my absence in days but they're days of indescribable length, lost in oblivion. A disappearing act. And my brain has to readjust, account for itself. I'm being melodramatic, I know. Imagining myself as the protagonist in a play, one that could have ended in tragedy. That's not how it's turned out and I don't like myself for going along with the 'gallant man of the moment' I'm being made to feel.

'You came through it, Alex. Bravo.'

'You're doing so well.'

'One day at a time – that's the ticket.'

A hero. Welcome back.

I certainly don't deserve any of it. After all, I brought this on myself. I crashed the car into a tree, no-one else involved, so the authorities tell me. The police and the insurance investigators have trampled over the tarmac, the verges, studied surface conditions, the weather, the possibility of another speeding vehicle with some nutter at the wheel. And there is no evidence that this was anything other than my fault.

No way have I been found innocent! Far from it.

In fact, after that visit from DI Johnson before I was discharged, I'm left as wary as hell. I'm being treated with kid gloves at the moment, but that won't last. Not when I'm back on my feet and have a chance of remembering what happened. Christ, I could have killed someone, gone head-on into a passing car, bowled over into a garden. Ironic, isn't it, that I've only ever had one speeding ticket two years ago – the full extent of my driving offences. And now this.

The detective came to see me on the last but one day in the hospital. All cleared with the consultant so I was as ready as I could be, sitting by the bed, feeling oddly anxious. God knows why. I had nothing to hide. Had I?

He'd knocked gently on my door, a small man casually dressed in sports jacket and navy chinos, looking nothing like a policeman. He introduced himself and then pulled up a chair like a regular visitor, facing me at eye level; better than him standing over me, I thought. He waited a few moments before he spoke.

'So, you're a lucky man.'

I didn't know how to answer that, so I just nodded.

He went on. 'We cleared this visit with your doctors and you knew I was coming to verify some facts about the crash.' It wasn't a question. 'We just need to establish what actually happened, but I realise there'll be some difficulties here because you have amnesia. Is that correct?'

'Well.' I frowned. That word hadn't been used. 'I can't remember

85

anything about the accident, or the days before it… it's a blank. Although my long-term memory seems to be OK. To be honest, I don't really understand the mechanics of the brain well enough to explain.'

He smiled encouragingly. 'Neither do I. But some questions need to be asked before we write this off as just "one of those things".'

Is he humouring me? I feel like a teenager returning home after a night on the tiles who can't account for his movements. He pulls out a notebook from his pocket and opens it up at a page fastened down with a clip.

'You were on the A533. Just off the M56.'

'So I'm told.'

'But apparently, your plans had been to drive to the city.'

I said nothing.

'You have no knowledge of why you were on that particular road?'

'No.'

'You have no idea of your speed that night?'

'I have no idea of *anything* that night. I wish I had.' I was getting tired and I could hear the irritation in my voice. 'Look, I wish I could help you. I wish I could answer all these questions myself. But I can't.'

DI Johnson looked uncomfortable. 'I realise this is difficult for you. But there's one point we need clearing up.'

'Which is?'

He paused. 'Whether you were stressed, in a state of anxiety, unable to cope… you were driving over 70 miles an hour on a country road – we know that from the evidence at the crash site, the tyre marks, the final landing place of the car…'

'What are you trying to say?' I felt a flutter of fear.

His gaze was unwavering. 'Sir, were you trying to kill yourself?'

Christ!

I stared at him, so shocked I couldn't speak. I wanted to say *I bloody hope not,* but I couldn't even manage that. It was as though my mind wouldn't let me deny something I couldn't prove or disprove. I was in the dock and I hadn't the capacity to refute the accusation. Because how the hell could I know for certain that I hadn't had a death wish?

DI Johnson waited, watching my face with a look that gave nothing away. He wasn't judging me. He just wanted the information he'd come for and I couldn't help him. I had no idea whether this line of questioning was linked to the insurance company and liability, but I didn't think so.

I found my voice, determined to hit this idea on the head whatever I might discover later, if I ever did. 'That isn't the way I am, Detective. I'm an optimist, I work through problems. I've never ever wanted a way out like that. I honestly don't think I meant to injure myself in any way.'

What else could I say?

He nodded slowly, pursing his lips, and got up. A few more questions and he'd gone – *sorry to take up your time, sorry to intrude,* etc. etc. But that visit left me with more worries than I already had to start with.

But for now, I tell myself to stop probing. If my memory of it all comes back, fine. If it doesn't, there's sod all I can do about it. I'm home. Carrie pushing the wheelchair into the kitchen. (I'd protested I was quite capable of walking, but the hospital had rules for patients needing aftercare. I could fall and break the other arm! Finish myself off nicely!) So I accept the inevitable. But I hate this vulnerable state I find myself in.

'Do you want a cup of tea?' Carrie is being so solicitous, so *caring.* Not her usual brisk self.

'Prefer a vodka.' Humour might restore the balance.

'On your medication? Not likely.' That sounds more like her.

'You're going to follow the rules. Rest, physio, doing as you're told. That'll be a first.'

'I thought I *always* did as I was told.'

'You pretend to.' She comes round the chair to look straight at me and smiles. I thought, as I haven't done for a long time, what an amazing face she has, high cheek bones, those eyes full of a fierce intelligence, the wild curly hair, bleached almost white from the summer sun. There's a different Carrie when the hard edges are erased. The Carrie I fell in love with.

It seems so long ago.

But as I watch her moving round the kitchen, quick and efficient in every way, I think about the first time I saw her. I was eighteen, waiting for my A level results, riding my bike aimlessly round the country roads, dreading the steep bank I'd have to climb in another mile. It was early August, I remember, a Saturday, and the weather had been good for two weeks. No rain, which was unusual in our neck of the woods – we always seemed to have rain, especially when the exams were over and we got our freedom at last. And now I think about it, there's a certain irony in how, if it hadn't been for an accident, well, a near accident, we probably wouldn't have met that first time.

Life going full circle.

That day, the road ahead of me clear, my feet resting on the pedals, I let the momentum carry me forward. No good thinking about Results Day. Nothing I could do about it now. It was in the lap of the gods, as people say when they have to trust fate. I rounded a corner and suddenly woke up to the clattering of hooves on the road ahead. A grey horse was coming towards me moving at a pretty fast pace. As it grew closer, I could see the girl on board having to use all her strength to keep a tight hold on the reins, the horse turning its rump sideways every so often and ducking its head. She was sitting tight, elbows out, talking to it loudly enough for me to hear. The damned thing looked out of control so I kept a wary eye on it as they drew level. At that moment, the horse, eyes wild, froth spewing from its mouth, swerved sideways into the middle of the road. I panicked and slid into the overgrown hedgerow to save myself. I only just managed to keep upright.

'Sorry,' the girl was shouting over her shoulder. 'Are you all right?'

But she was already yards down the road and there was no way she could have helped me, even if I'd been a mangled wreck.

Bloody animal, I was saying to myself as I steadied myself, arms scratched and one side of my hair snagged with brambles. *Shouldn't be on the road.*

And then, as I was brushing myself down, I heard the sound of pounding hooves coming back. *Not satisfied with one attempt at trampling me to death, she was going to have another go.*

I turned and saw the horse still prancing about, knees up and neck arched. The girl, amazingly was smiling, almost laughing and shaking her head. 'Really sorry. He can be a bit naughty when he's not been out.'

What on earth could I say to that? 'Naughty' seemed a bit of an understatement to me.

The horse was still twirling in circles. 'I'm from the house up the road,' she went on. 'If you're hurt, I'll meet you back there and I can get you a drink and some hot water to clean up if you need it.'

I was going to give a short-tempered answer to that idea, then I stopped and took a breath. Even under a riding hat, with not a trace of make-up and pulling a face at the antics of her horse, I could see she was nice looking. It didn't take me long to make up my mind. I wasn't going to let *this* chance go by.

'Well,' I'd climbed off my bike and tried to look annoyed, 'you certainly owe me.'

She pulled a serious face. 'I do. Give me fifteen minutes and sit on the wall at the house called Greenacres about a mile up there on the left-hand side.' She gestured with her head as a way of pointing. At least she didn't let go of the reins. That was some comfort.

'I will,' I said, then added, 'just don't bring that mad animal any nearer. I want to live.'

She laughed. God, she was pretty.

So I cycled what I thought was about a mile and came across a long, low wall. It bordered an orchard and beyond that I could see a paddock and fences and the side of a large house. The name '*Greenacres*' was carved into the stone gateposts.

I was impressed. Shouldn't have been because we lived very comfortably in a nice semi-detached with four bedrooms and a decent sized garden and I hadn't ever thought money mattered. You were who you were, not who your parents were – that was how we'd been brought up. But this house... I was a bit disappointed in myself, even as my jaw dropped, but hell, that girl on the horse was worth getting to know and I had nothing better to do. What the heck!

So I sat on the wall and waited.

She came back, trotting more slowly now, almost relaxed as she sat in the saddle and when she'd gone through the gates, she swung to the ground with the ease of a gymnast. She was certainly different from the girls in our 6th form. That last year, we'd spent so much time studying and revising, we could all have been the same gender – barely had time to notice each other unless it was to ask for the answer to a maths question or to borrow a protractor.

I was told to follow her and left my bike propped against the wall, hoping no-one would pinch it. She led the way over the gravel into a stable (I kept my distance) and whipped off the saddle and bridle, placing them on the ground outside before closing the half door and shoving the bolt home. The horse thrust its large grey head out and the girl patted its neck. Reward for being 'naughty', I thought sarcastically.

She turned and introduced herself. 'I'm Carrie. And you are?'

'Alex.'

'Hello. And sorry again.' But she didn't sound it, too self-assured, her tone a bit condescending. 'Do you want a drink of orange or something? It's rather hot and I know I need something cool.'

She walked to a back entrance and up some steps with railings either side and near the door, an iron contraption for pulling your boots off. Then on into a large kitchen that was like something off the TV. Pine cupboards, black shiny counters, stone slabs on the floor, even pans hanging from a wooden beam over some sort of range. She pulled a carton of fresh orange from an over-sized fridge, poured some into two glasses and handed one to me.

'Hope that's enough of an apology, Alex. You weren't hurt, were you?'

'No. I wanted to make you feel guilty. The horse didn't touch me.' I grinned and looked round. 'How many people live here?'

'Just me and my father. Plus two dogs and three horses – well one is a little Shetland that's retired now. Used to be my pony when I was little.'

I didn't like to ask about her mother. I remember thinking it seemed a huge house for just two people.

'You don't go to the Grammar then,' I said, which was stating the obvious. 'I'd have seen you there.'

'No.' She wiped her lip against her sleeve. 'Boarding school in York. My mother left six years ago, so it seemed best all round.' She sounded as though she was giving the practised response. 'Would you like some cake? Mrs. Symmonds always bakes for the weekends.'

Mrs. Symmonds? Do they have a housekeeper? I felt out of my depth. I put the glass down on the counter. 'No... thanks. I've recovered. I'll see what other adventures are waiting for me down the road.'

She laughed again. It made me feel good and I wanted to escape before I made a hash of things. If I left now, perhaps I could return. But as I moved towards the back steps, a voice, deep and commanding made me stop in my tracks.

'And who's this, Carrie?'

Her father had entered the kitchen and stood, head a little to one side, one eyebrow raised, expecting an answer. Or at least, to be introduced. As though I was someone who must at least show their credentials. He was a big man, broad shoulders, tall with white hair. He seemed to me quite formally dressed in a sports jacket and some sort of club tie. Made me wonder what he wore on weekdays! But what I noticed most that first time I met him was the way he carried himself – like a soldier, straight-backed, head held high. I suppose *imposing* is the word I would use now. A man of substance in every way.

He waited, his steady gaze directed at me.

Carrie shrugged. 'Nobody. He was just going.'

I felt annoyed that she'd dismissed me so rudely. So I stepped forward.

'Alex Taylor, sir. Carrie's horse and my bike came to blows on the road and she invited me for a drink and a clean-up.'

He nodded then came towards me offering his hand, which seemed to smother mine as we shook. He turned to his daughter.

'You must be more careful, Carrie. If you aren't in control on the highway, you're liable for any accident you cause. Are you sure you're all right, Alex?'

'Oh, Daddy. What a fuss. Of course he's all right. I was just being... kind.'

And that was the sum total of our first meeting. We didn't see each other again for, it must have been three years. By then, we'd both taken our first steps into the world of work. And I suppose you couldn't have found two people who were less alike. But you can't always explain what attracts you to someone. It just happens. I was in freefall, 'madly' in love (what a good way of describing it) and no inner voice would tell me otherwise. Funny how such desire can lose all its intensity. Or is it that when we're young, we expect too much?

The cup of tea is placed in my good hand and I allow it to cool a little, balancing it carefully on the arm of the wheelchair. Sam has been allowed into the kitchen and he lies close to my feet, head down, snuffling as he breathes. Carrie is offering suggestions about what we could have for dinner, and decides on fish pie, easy to eat and something to 'build me up.' And before she starts preparing the meal, I am glad to be pushed into the sitting room, to be by myself, with the news channel on the television.

I try to concentrate but keep drifting off.

Perhaps I am tired in more ways than one.

Chapter 11

This was crazy! She had even knocked on the bedroom door instead of walking straight in. As though he were some relative on a visit. But it seemed strange to have him back home, yet not waking up beside him. It somehow made the day begin with a false start.

He was already up, sitting on the edge of the bed in his pyjamas, half-turning when he heard her.

'Sorry, I was letting you sleep in,' she said, not knowing why she was apologising. 'I'll open the curtains. It's going to be a nice day.'

She glanced cautiously at his face, trying to catch from his expression what mood he might be in. But he just looked blank, withdrawn. This wasn't going to be easy, she thought. It was a bit like treading on egg shells. But what did she expect from the first few days at home? Nothing miraculous, that was for sure.

She waited until he nodded.

'Come on then, I'll help you have a shower.' She put on a bright smile, feeling like a nurse on duty. The whole situation was awkward. It wasn't in her nature to pander to anyone, least of all members of her own family. And here she was at her most attentive, mollycoddling him – totally against type. Well, there are times when we all have to adjust. 'I've got some clothes out for you. We should be able to get that polo shirt over the plaster.'

He sat, staring ahead as though he was puzzling over something.

'I'm having weird dreams.'

She sat down beside him. 'That's common after a head injury, surely.'

'I'm driving on a high road in India I think, with this town below me. There are people in the car who are trying to help me find the place I'm looking for. I know it lies at the bottom of this jumble of shacks and gardens but I only have a vague memory of exactly where.' He stopped for a moment, staring past her, recalling it in pieces. 'I should phone to say I'm late but I can't work out how to get through, can't press the right buttons. The only way to settle it is to get out of the car and climb through a hole in some railings and start down this steep path, the sort where you could break your neck and it's getting dark...'

Carrie could only stare at him. 'And... did you find what you were looking for?'

'No. I woke up.'

She couldn't help letting out a laugh, gasping and shaking her head. 'Alex, that's the most you've told me in a year.'

He had a wry smile on his face. 'Well, it was so real. When I woke up, my heart was going like a hammer.'

'Did you recognise where you were?'

'No. It was like a shanty town you see on the news where people live on top of one another in dreadful conditions. But it was so real.'

Carrie didn't know what to say. Her experience of frightening dreams was a healthy blank. She never remembered anything when she woke up. But she couldn't quite let it go. It was obviously troubling him.

'Do you always remember these dreams in such detail?'

'Often, now. But not quite like that.'

'Well, when you're dressed, we'll find a good psychiatrist for you.' She rubbed his back and felt the sigh run through his body. 'Stop worrying. This is all quite normal. You don't just get over something like you've been through in five minutes. It'll take time.' She nearly added, *and some peace and quiet,* but knew he wouldn't get that today.

She helped him up and walked him to the bathroom. At least

they'd removed the bandages from his head, and replaced them with a dressing, although the edge of a row of stitches could still be seen, a black line crawling down to his eyebrow. Without his hair falling over his forehead, he looked older. Almost fragile. Not a word she'd ever have used before the accident.

There's an odd intimacy about helping someone do something as basic as wash themselves, she thought. Embarrassing almost, as though you should back off and give them some privacy, some dignity. But it couldn't be helped. At least he managed to shave after a fashion with his left hand, which was something. After they'd struggled to pull on his clothes and socks without hurting any of the sore parts of his body, they sat for a while letting him get his breath, saying nothing.

Eventually, she reached over and cupped his left hand in hers. She wasn't sure he'd want to hear what she had to say. 'Hope you're feeling up to it, Alex – really sorry if you aren't – but you're going to have visitors this afternoon. Joe's bringing your parents over.' She paused. 'They wanted to come yesterday but I told them you were worn out and needed more time to settle back in. Thought that was the best thing to say. But I couldn't really put them off any longer.'

'Of course you couldn't. That's OK.'

'And there's one more thing.' She shook her head in disbelief. 'Guess what arrived yesterday! The insurance company delivered a brand new Volvo for you to use *"in the meantime"*, they said. It'll just have to sit there. They've no idea.'

It'd be a long time before he had any need of that.

Carrie pulled him gently to his feet and hoped she could hold his weight on the stairs. She found herself constantly watching his face for changes, for indications that any moment, he might blow a fuse. Or sink into depression. She'd had enough information about irrational behaviour and mood swings after a head injury to be ready for anything. And she'd seen how he could change suddenly in hospital from quiet and compliant to fury. She needed to remember, even though at times he seemed perfectly calm and lucid, this wasn't the old, even-tempered Alex who took everything in his stride. This was a familiar stranger.

How odd it all was.

Slowly, they made their way downstairs to the hall (she'd shut Sam out in the garden – one less obstacle to trip over) and he sat down carefully on a kitchen chair. There were some '*Get Well*' cards on the table, already opened and she gathered them up, leafing through them. 'Joe can read these to you when he comes. Lots of lovely comments.'

At last he smiled. That same lazy smile. 'Nice to know you've been missed.'

'Even Colin from the cricket club rang to say, could he come. I told him to wait for now. Never understood how you came to belong to a club like that when you've never even played cricket.'

He gave a small laugh, then winced as though his body was objecting to the sudden movement. But he seemed more like his old self. 'Ah, that's how villages work. You're accepted anywhere if you buy the first round.'

She felt her body relax, relieved that he still had his sense of humour. Surely it was going to be all right? He was still Alex. The man in that hospital bed, the confused man who seemed completely lost was part of some past nightmare.

She so wanted to believe that. They'd get back to living their normal life without the drama, the heartache, the awful fear.

She just hoped she wasn't being too optimistic.

And so the day began, with Carrie tip-toeing round him doing all the everyday jobs slowly, trying to make as little noise as possible, all those jobs that she usually rushed through before going down to the yard, or shopping or heading for Manchester.

Funny to think what our lives are really based on, she thought.

Something you don't recognise until the whole rhythm is shattered. The ordinary habitual interactions and activities that hold a family together don't seem particularly important – you're not aware of the supportive structure that keeps you steady until some crisis hits you. Then those everyday rituals – making breakfast, washing clothes, walking the dog, listening to each other's news – have a new significance. You're desperate to get the shape back into your day, something you're used to.

Carrie was aware this routine helped her from thinking about what might have been. The frightening possibility of Alex still in a debilitated state... Alex losing the fight altogether. It was a great comfort now tending to his needs, making sure he took his medication, bringing him a drink, helping him walk.

But there was one aspect of this whole business she couldn't let go. She had to know the truth. *Had* to. And this determination, this cussedness, was so deeply ingrained in her character that she wasn't able to give up. Even though she wasn't happy about how she'd gone about it. It wasn't '*playing with a straight bat*', as her father would have put it. It didn't put her in a good light. At least she had the honesty to feel shame, looking for clues in such an underhand way. It certainly hadn't brought answers. Just more questions.

So she'd gone ahead raiding his 'private' side of the office – well, it felt like a raid – rifling through papers and notebooks. Jack had only just left for the pub when she'd entered the study and closed the door. She looked at the mess on the desk and sighed, hoping she could replace everything in just the right sort of muddle that wouldn't give her away. She'd try and be methodical, starting with what was on top of the desk, then looking through the drawers. God, he hadn't done any sort of clearing up in years.

Nothing from the recent stuff that lay near the computer; nothing more interesting than a bill for a boiler repair he'd obviously forgotten about and a formal invitation card to a Brent Construction dinner with 'Ring GH' scrawled in ballpoint over the front of it. She began on the first drawer right, pens, headed writing paper, envelopes; second drawer down, a Michael Rowbotham paperback, ink cartridges, a box of labels, a memory stick; and so on...

...until she came to the bottom drawer left. All sorts of seemingly pointless junk in there. *Why don't some people ever think to have a clear-out?* she thought irritably. She pulled out a sheaf of papers and leaflets and scribbled notes and started to look through them all, fairly certain now that there was no hope of finding anything significant. What was she looking for anyway? An ultimatum from a debt collector? A love letter? An incriminating newspaper cutting?

This was stupid.

And then, just as she was about to shove the whole pile back into the drawer, a piece of card fell to the carpet. She picked it up, curious. It was a ticket stub from 2010, the elongated type that looked like the ones you're given for the theatre, a bit worn at the edges. And printed in black: CASABLANCA, Runcorn Arts Centre, The Brindley. £9. She turned it over to see if there was something written on the reverse, but no. Nothing. It wasn't a film she'd ever seen, only heard of and she looked now at the ticket and wondered whether it had any significance. Of course when Alex was away, he might well go to the cinema on his own, but... odd to stow it away for years, if that's what had happened. Perhaps it hadn't been kept at all. Perhaps it had just got shoved in a drawer and forgotten.

She breathed in, frowning, not sure what to think. She stood looking down at his desk for a moment, then came to the decision that she was trying too hard to find something significant and was ending up creating a mystery out of nothing.

But still...

By the time the light was fading in the room and shadows were making it difficult to see clearly, she put everything back in place, closed the drawer and went into the kitchen. She lifted a bottle of

Muscadet out of the fridge, pulled down a wine glass from the rack and poured herself a large drink.

Come on, she told herself, *it's nothing. This isn't like you. Imagining things, for God's sake, based on nothing more than… what? Some lack of communication on Alex's part. Why is this bugging you so?*

And that, she couldn't answer. She just had this feeling that there was something more, some threat that she was incapable of seeing that lay just beneath the surface. It was only an instinct, a forewarning. Identified, she could deal with it… more difficult was this nebulous doubt that nagged at her.

It was one o'clock when Joe knocked on the door, opening it without waiting for Carrie to answer and ushered his parents into the hall. She came out of the sitting room to take the flowers from Alex's mother and give her a perfunctory kiss. If Carrie had to describe her in-laws, Hazel and Bob, she'd have said they were 'nice' people. Pleasant, but not on her wavelength and never had been. They had brought up two clever boys who hadn't needed much guidance, it seemed, letting them go their own way in a close family unit that didn't demand a great deal in the way of expectations and a little surprised when their offspring forged healthy careers for themselves. But they weren't interesting. That was the honest truth. They watched *The Antiques Road Show* and *Britain's Got Talent* and cookery programmes and bored Carrie with anecdotes; they didn't read books or go to the theatre; they lived in a bubble of media trivia. And although she tried to hide her indifference, she suspected they knew how she felt. Joe certainly did. She was sure he believed it was her father's money, her private education, her world of horses and privilege that in his eyes made her a snob. But he hadn't got it right. Being different didn't make you a snob. He just didn't understand her at all.

She only realised how touchy people could be about family after a Sunday lunch at Alex's house, arranged specially to be introduced to his parents. It was a couple of months after they'd met up again. Alex had come back home, a civil engineering degree under his belt and a job on a waterworks with a well-established firm and things between them were getting more serious. Steady, as his mother had called it, on that day. 'Are you going steady?' for heaven's sake.

She hadn't been sure what to expect but Alex was keen for her to go.

She and her father never ate at midday. It had long been established that eating in the evening was much more pleasant, more civilised. And for her, there was lunch and there was dinner, a distinct difference. At lunch you might have salad and a sandwich… or soup. But this turned out to be another sort of meal altogether.

It was the full works – a side of beef, roast potatoes, three types of vegetables, plated up and proudly presented with all the trimmings and a huge apple pie with custard to finish. Carrie had only managed to eat half of it.

After they'd left the house and climbed into Alex's old car, she'd sensed how quiet he'd become. OK, so it hadn't gone down well but there was nothing she'd done to embarrass him, if that was the way this was going.

'What is it?' she asked. Not exactly – she demanded.

'You could have made more of an effort,' he said, jamming his foot down on the clutch and yanking the car into gear. They drove in silence.

'I'm sorry I couldn't finish all the food. It was just too much. You can't blame me for that.'

He pulled into the side of the road, leaving the engine running and turned to face her. 'Carrie, they went to a lot of trouble to welcome you. To make you feel at home. And you…'

'I what?'

'You were cold, you didn't take any interest in the conversation, you barely answered one question.'

'Oh, Alex. I can't explain.' She looked down at her lap. 'It's just difficult when people try too hard...'

His face was like thunder. She'd never seen him show anger, ever, but she was seeing it now. He gripped the steering wheel until his knuckles went white. He looked straight ahead through the windscreen and clenched his teeth so tightly it distorted his words. 'There are rules, here, Carrie, and you've just broken them. One is – you *never* criticise someone's parents, their family. It's about respect. It works both ways. I would never say a word about your father, exactly because he *is* your father. If you don't understand that, then...'

He left the rest unsaid. But she knew then that she could only push Alex so far. Easy going as he always seemed, there were certain values he held dear, certain loyalties that ran deep. It taught her a lesson for the years that followed.

Now as Joe and her in-laws hurried into the sitting room to see Alex, all she could do was offer them her best effort, which was never going to be enough – a pretence at hospitality, scones and a cup of tea.

And leave them to hear all about the accident from the injured victim.

Chapter 12

As Jack reached the turn-off to the towpath, the sun was already heating up the car even though he'd had the windows down. He parked and headed down the dirt track, tall hedgerows lining the way. Tiny flies swarmed round his head. He followed the directions he'd been given and hoped they hadn't already started. It was Sunday so the traffic had been light, but it had taken him longer than he'd anticipated – he was never good at calculating journey times and it was already nine thirty.

Pushing through the last clump of overgrown weeds and long grass, he reached the towpath at last, the waterway slow-moving and calm below. Canals had always fascinated him. As a kid, he'd followed a series on children's TV about a family who lived on a barge which was pulled between locks by a huge shire horse plodding along the bank. It looked a wonderful life. The family were always together – not much choice, really! And even the children worked at all sorts of jobs to get them upstream. Not that he was ever sure where they were heading or if they ever got there. But he'd had a romantic view of living on a canal ever since.

Of course, that wasn't the reason he was here. This was Fran's group of volunteers. It hadn't taken much searching to find them on the internet – The Hazel Grove Conservation Group, undergrowth clearance, woodlands and footpath maintenance, fencing – and it was easy to get inducted by filling in a form and taking one phone call. But now, he felt unsure. Going ahead with this was a bit more difficult than merely thinking about it. He hoped she'd be pleased to see him. That she wouldn't be annoyed. But anyway, too late now; he was here, ready to help, well-prepared in his stout boots and denim jacket with a pair of thick gloves in his rucksack. Even a packed lunch.

He stepped round the sign which warned the public of **'Conservation work in progress'**, and waited, feeling awkward, for someone to notice him. There were about ten workers, some bending low or on their hands and knees scraping away at the bedraggled path, some chopping and clipping back hedges. There was a rank smell in the air of vegetation rotting in the warmth and a strong whiff of something like garlic.

He stood, hoping someone would look up and come over. Eventually a man in a Hi Vis tabard started walking towards him, an enquiring expression on his face.

Jack held out his hand. 'Jack Taylor. Your new recruit?'

'Of course. Didn't expect you to come this week, but that's great. We need all the help we can get.' The man took off his right glove, gripping Jack's arm at the elbow in welcome and smiled. He was stooped and his hair stood on end, dressed in a checked shirt, lumber jacket and cord trousers which were already covered in earthy dust round the ankles. 'I'm Tom. Officially the Task Leader but no-one bothers with hierarchy. It's all about covering ourselves for Health and Safety.' He looked approvingly at Jack's clothing. 'You seem to be fully prepared.'

'Well, I read up on the instructions you sent. So I hope I haven't missed anything.'

'You're fine.' Tom looked behind him at the workers. 'Come and meet some people. I'll get you a fork and you can start over by that edge of the towpath. This time of year, it all gets so overgrown and there's always rubbish caught up in the long grass. Lots of cans and plastic. Bags are over there to collect all the waste. You'll soon get the hang of it.'

He strode towards the other workers, Jack following close behind not knowing quite how to feel. Nervous, that was a given. Because he was so unsure of his reception. But it wasn't as though he was butting in on a private gathering. Anyone could join, he thought defensively. Still, he had no idea how Fran would react when she saw him. Pleased that he'd taken up on a good idea? Or irritated that he'd intruded onto her turf?

Perhaps this wasn't such a good idea.

She was kneeling on the ground, her shirt loose over her jeans, concentrating on tackling a thorny bush with shears. Crouched low, her hair falling over her face, she didn't hear them approach until they were standing over her. He waited anxiously to catch her expression when she looked up. Well, there was certainly surprise! Then her face seemed to freeze, her eyelids lowering and her mouth tightening a little. She stood up slowly.

Tom introduced them. 'Fran, meet Jack, our new starter.'

It was as though time was suspended for an awful, long moment and then she wiped one glove on her trousers and nodded her head. 'We've already met, Tom.' Another pause. 'Hello Jack.'

Tom looked surprised. 'Ah, so it's you we have to thank for spreading the word, Fran. You didn't say you'd done some recruiting for us.' He laughed a bit too heartily. 'Well done – just what we need. I'll do the honours, take him round to meet everyone, get him cracking then you can get together later. Have a chat over the lunch break.'

Jack turned away. He hadn't missed any of it. Particularly not the tone Tom had used when he was talking to her which seemed to him more than just friendly. Was this the 'boyfriend' that Lucy had referred to, then? A bit old for her, he'd have thought, but then, what did he know about who she'd like? Suddenly, he felt foolish and naïve and was glad to be getting on with work that would absorb him for an hour or two and not have to face her.

But inevitably, tools were downed at twelve thirty and they all sat round to retrieve their lunch boxes and open bottles of pop and flasks of tea. Fran sat on the far side of the group, having a conversation with a stout woman in a straw hat. She kept her head bowed slightly, listening intently and not looking up. They were too far away for Jack to catch anything of what they were saying. After half an hour of a break, some pushed themselves up to return to work and Jack thought she was going to ignore him, which was worse somehow, than if she'd been angry. But finally, she moved over to where he was sitting and lowered herself down on the grass.

Jack didn't quite know where to look. By now he wished he'd never come, never put himself in this embarrassing situation. Slowly, he packed away a half-eaten sandwich in some tinfoil and put it back in his rucksack.

'So,' she said in a voice that he could only describe as neutral. 'What on earth made you join this? You didn't say you were interested in conservation.'

'Well, I wasn't.' He dared a sideways glance at her. 'Not until you told me about what you did that night after the party. And it got me thinking – how I'd really like to help. Seemed such a positive thing to do. People chucking litter and making a mess of the countryside always annoys me.' He was sounding like a nerd, even though what he was saying was true. 'I hope you don't mind me joining.'

'I could hardly object, could I? It's open to anyone.'

She sat, wiping specks of grass off her sleeves and then struggled to take off one shoe, upending it and shaking a tiny stone onto the ground. 'Lucy told me your father had a bad car accident and was in hospital. He was in a coma, she said.'

'He was.'

'But he's come round now?'

'Yes. He's a lot better. Still not right, but nothing like the mess he was after the crash. Lucky to be alive, really.'

She tilted her head slightly. 'That must have been frightening.'

'It was awful.'

'And he's going to be all right?' She looked at him in that direct way she had, so perceptive, eyes amazingly blue, that he couldn't find any words for a moment.

'A coma can have after-effects, so really, they're not sure. Depends on a lot of things.' He gathered his wits about him and thought he'd better add some details. He was glad for something to tell her to prolong the conversation. 'It lasted five days. We really had no idea when he'd come out of it and those five days were... long. He was in Intensive Care, and we talked and talked to him hoping he could hear. Then he squeezed my hand and it was quite a moment...' He could feel his eyes filling up and stopped.

Fran put her hand on his arm. 'I bet it was. And what about now?'

'He's home, which is great. Not brilliant on his feet, but his mind's pretty sharp. And that was the thing we dreaded because of the head wound, that he'd have brain damage. But he seems good. Except...' He pulled a face.

'What?' She looked at him sharply.

'Well, he can't remember anything about the accident. Nothing before either. It's as though it's all wiped like a computer, no memory of why he crashed, why he was on that particular road. He hasn't got any memory either, of the weeks leading up to it.'

'Do the doctors say it'll come back?'

He looked at her, so close, her head bent towards him, dark hair shining in the sun. She was just... perfect. Like the Ed Sheeran song, he thought. It was the only word that would do.

He took a deep breath and concentrated on a coherent reply. 'They've no idea. Sometimes it does. He'll go to the hospital for more scans and tests over the next few months but for the moment, he seems as good as we could have hoped. He's pretty fit so he stands a fair chance of getting back to normal. It's my mother who's more stressed out.'

Fran said nothing more, just looked across the water to the other bank where some kids were tagging each other and laughing. Jack fell silent as well but he couldn't help watching her. To him, she always seemed distant, wrapped up in her own world somehow. A part of her she'd never share with anyone. Was that the attraction? He'd no idea. She was just so unlike anyone he'd ever met. But to be fair, he'd had such limited experience. Living in a small village didn't give you much chance to socialise with lots of different people. He'd only had one serious relationship and that hadn't turned out too well. Not in the end, anyway. Grace had made him wary of getting involved with anyone else.

Tom was already hacking at some thistles with a small scythe and looking across at them so they stood up and picked up their tools, prepared to start again. The progress was methodical and slow but they were making some headway at last. Looking back over the shorn pathway later in the afternoon, Jack felt a sense of achievement at how tidy and well-ordered it looked, eleven black bin bags of rubbish stacked neatly to one side. The heat had become intense, burning his neck and he realised he'd forgotten to put on any sun block. Too late now. They carried on cutting and hacking away, too tired for much talking until three thirty when Tom decided enough was enough.

'OK, everyone. Get yourselves a drink – orange juice and water over there – and head off home. Really good work. Rob, you OK to take the bags to the tip tomorrow? Everyone, keep an eye on the website for the next location but don't feel you have to come every time. There are always others who can do their bit.' He looked over at Fran. 'Ready?'

There were obviously pre-arranged lifts among some of them and Jack walked along beside a small girl called Molly, who laughed at his sunburnt face. 'You be glad it wasn't raining,' she said. 'It usually is.' As he reached his car, he looked round for Fran and saw she was standing by Tom's Jeep about to climb in. Looking over, she lifted her hand in a kind of wave and smiled.

It was enough for now, he told himself as he drove home. She'd accepted him being there without any questions and at least they'd had some sort of conversation. But in a way, he was disappointed. This wasn't how he'd imagined meeting her again. It all seemed to be going nowhere. And when he was thinking straight, he knew this would probably be the outcome. For one thing, he had no right to expect anything. And she probably saw him as a mere boy, her friend's young brother. Anyway, if someone wasn't attracted to you, there wasn't much you could do. He was old enough to realise that.

So why had he formed such an attachment to someone he hardly knew? Was he just trying to fill a void in his boring life with some dream he couldn't possibly attain? It was hard to admit, even to himself. It might be OK when you were sixteen.

Not at twenty-two.

He pulled into the drive just as Lucy was pulling out in her battered open-topped Mazda. As they drew alongside, she called out. 'Hi, little brother. Mum tells me you've been doing "good works". What brought that on?'

Jack shrugged and smiled. He only hoped she didn't know that Fran had anything to do with conservation. 'Oh, you know. Community spirit and all that.'

'Good for you,' she said, no irony in her tone.

Well, she didn't know then! Let's hope it stays that way.

She jerked her head towards where the Volvo was parked in front of the garage. 'Have you seen the fancy car they've left for Dad? It'll be ages before Mum lets him loose in that.' Then her expression became serious. 'He seems much more himself. Don't you think?'

'Yes, he's doing really well. Aren't you staying for dinner?'

'No. Work to do. I've got to write a report before tomorrow. See you.'

Jack climbed out of the car, quickening his step as he entered the house. There was a different atmosphere now his dad was home, more natural, even if he did spend a lot of time sleeping.

He took a shower, washed the dust out of his hair and put on fresh clothes. His dad was sitting in the garden, enjoying the late afternoon sun with the Sunday newspaper in his lap, the dog sprawled at his feet. He was miles away, looking out over the expanse of fields beyond the stone wall, a glass of fruit juice untouched on the round metal table in front of him.

Jack put a hand on his shoulder so as not to startle him and sat down on one of the chairs. There was a comfortable silence between them that didn't need to be broken, a shared quiet that Jack appreciated after the physical efforts of the day.

It was some minutes before his dad spoke.

'Dinner's in the oven apparently. Your mother's gone down to the barn, she won't be long.' He looked over at Jack. 'How did it go?'

'Good. We were clearing a towpath on the canal. It was hard work, scrabbling on our hands and knees a lot of the time, but it looked really good when we'd finished. Certainly worth doing.'

His dad gave him that smile, warm and encouraging, which usually made him feel better about himself. But today somehow, it didn't help. He was so tired of this debilitating sense of inadequacy that descended on him whenever he didn't come up to the mark. Which was happening again, pretty often lately.

The need to confide in someone, to share this anxiety that he mustn't let build up, was overwhelming. He wanted to be reassured, told it would pass, whatever…

And why it should have been his father he felt he could open up to, well, he'd always been there for him. And he'd listen. He knew there'd be an understanding, no awkward questions asked. No judgement, he supposed.

'Dad,' he began, then stopped. He put his hand up to his mouth. Was he being selfish? This probably wasn't the right time.

His father looked at him expectantly, waiting. 'Come on. Something's up. Say it. You sorted me out, now it's my turn.'

Jack half shut his eyes and launched in. 'I know this sounds… as though I'm going backwards. But I feel…' It was difficult to put into words… 'I just feel I don't fit in anywhere. Other people seem so easy with themselves.' He paused again. 'When you were young, when you were my age, did you ever feel you weren't like other people, that you were always on the edge…?' He shook his head. 'It's not easy to explain.'

His father looked over at him, a solemn expression on his face. 'Jack, never mind when I was younger, I *always* feel I don't fit in. Anyone who's got a sensitive bone in their body and is capable of *thinking* must feel that at times. And those who seem confident, breezing through life, never worrying – well, it's an act everyone puts on to keep going, to keep the outside world from seeing how bloody vulnerable we all are. As you get older you make a better job of covering up but if you're honest, there's self-doubt an awful lot of the time and it's hard. You just learn to deal with it.'

Jack nodded slowly. He hadn't quite expected this amount of honesty. It was oddly comforting in one way but not in another.

'You always seem so easy with people. And you've got a job that earns good money, a career…'

'Yes, I know what you're saying. That might be how *you* see me. But these aren't as important as you think. Believe me, Jack, you have qualities I'd give my right arm for. You're kind and honest and care about others, really care, particularly for anyone vulnerable. And you act on it.'

Jack flushed and looked down, awkward, pleased. 'But it doesn't…'

'Look. Everyone has hang-ups of some sort or another. I might appear confident but I sometimes look around at a social do, some gathering of business people or at a formal dinner and think – what have I got in common with these people? Nothing. And all I want to do is go home, climb into bed with a good book and not pretend.

There are very few people you'd pick as friends anyway. Only a few. So in the end, you have to *like* who you are, warts and all.'

Jack let out a gasping laugh. Surprised. Oddly relieved. 'Blimey. I'd no idea.'

His dad gave a rueful smile. 'No, just as well. I'm one of the great pretenders. Don't let anybody else into my secret. I'd be embarrassed.'

'It's between you and me.' Jack breathed in, close to tears. 'And... thanks. It's helped.'

'Well, don't think life is always that lonely. If you have the luck to meet someone who thinks like you do, shares your values, someone you can be totally honest with, then... you've a chance that'll save you. But you have to be very lucky.'

A shout from the kitchen made them both start. They looked at each other, the shared moment broken. Jack helped his father to his feet and they left the peace of the garden, now full of shadows as the sky grew darker, to go indoors.

Chapter 13

I'm sitting at the French windows, raindrops pattering against the glass the only sound. A sudden shower has ended a spell of really warm weather and the garden is a blur of waving trees and shuddering bushes. It's a nice feeling, sheltered inside when the elements are doing their worst outside. Certainly beats staring at a hospital ceiling.

I've been trying to read but having one arm in plaster makes holding the book difficult, so I've given up. It's also difficult to concentrate for any length of time. Not only do my eyes ache and my head thumps, my back's decided to join in. Hardly unexpected considering the pounding my body's taken and it doesn't help that I'm sitting for so long in one position.

But hell, I'm improving! The wheelchair's gone back for someone with a greater need than me. The nurse, Alia, has been three times, checked me over, filled in all the notes in triplicate to satisfy the bureaucrats who demand every box is ticked and told me that was it – she was leaving me in the care of my own GP. The hospital would look after my head (stitches to come out in a few days), remove my plaster at the appropriate time and the physio department would help restore my limbs to their original state. Hopefully. So at least this was *'the road to recovery'* as Alia put it cheerfully, leaving me to take the rest of the journey without her help.

I think it's called flying solo.

Sam, my constant companion, eyes me hoping for another biscuit but he's unlucky. His weight is making him as dodgy on his legs as I am, so no more treats.

Three o'clock in the afternoon is a strange time to be doing nothing when you're so used to spending your days working. There aren't any problems to sort out or calls from colleagues insisting you pull solutions out of a hat. No demanding people to argue with or new starters needing everything explained twice. It should make me feel at peace, gently whiling away the hours and it often does. But sometimes, unwelcome thoughts stir themselves, muddying the waters. They make me aware that any minute, probably before I'm ready, I'll be hurled into the madding crowd again.

I'm sure this divided state of mind is because of Adrian's visit. As my boss, he wants me fit again. I've worked for Belmont since I left university so they're going to look after me. And Adrian means well. Don't they *always* say that when what they *really* mean is, yes, he might mean well, but he has his own agenda. And Adrian has his own agenda, the underlying gist being: *Have as much time off as you need… but don't take too long about it because you've left a gaping hole and we're losing money.*

Well, he's a director of the company so his priorities aren't the same as mine. It's not a huge outfit and he has to answer to the rest of the Board.

Anyway, it was good to see him. Although I could tell he was shocked at the sight of me. Understandable really. Even now, my head looks as though Frankenstein's done a bad job stitching me up. And I'm thin. Everywhere. It's worse in my face; my eyes look too big and the skin seems to be stretched too tightly over my cheek bones. Perhaps I look a bit out of it, too – the painkillers leave me a bit spaced for about an hour after I've taken them. Still alive though! And still able to function! But not quite ready to work!

'How's the wounded soldier!' Adrian was always inclined to be hearty. He sat in the easy chair opposite me, smiling, rubbing his hands together. I don't think he knew what to say.

'On the mend, thanks. Lucky to be here.'

'Yes, you are. Not good news at the beginning. Got in contact with the hospital as soon as I heard. And Carrie kept me well informed.' He averted his gaze, a give-away when you're about to lie. 'You've made a better recovery than I thought you would. Luckily, you've kept yourself pretty fit and a broken arm soon heals.' Then realising he'd perhaps been a bit too flippant, he leaned forward, elbows on his knees. 'You're not to worry about anything. We'll get by without you, keep things going till you're ready.'

And then he went on to talk about the tender for the bridge in Bury, the water treatment contract which had overrun and was costing thousands every day, the brickies who were complaining about working conditions on the silo job, the portacabins that hadn't arrived... and so it went on.

By the time he left, with a cheery, '*You can always come back gradually, perhaps two days a week, but absolutely no hurry,*' I was ready to throw him out. That is, if I hadn't stopped listening. And if I'd had the strength.

Christ!

But then Colin comes and restores my faith in human nature.

He's been at the cricket club forever, or it seems that way. He's like a village elder, wise with an authority that's earned, respected by everyone, even the teenage loose cannons and the odd rough necks. He's like a sort of mythical Indian chieftain who's seen it all and has most of the answers. Difficult to explain, this aura around him. And I've never even heard him raise his voice. But there you are.

He's straight out of '*This Farming Life.*' Everything about him embodies the outdoors – the weather-beaten face, the solid build, the comfortable well-worn country clothes, the ambling walk. And the faint whiff of straw and animals.

As he takes off his boots and shakes the rain off his coat at the front door, I hear him saying hello to Sam who's lumbered up to greet him.

'Brought you a sandwich,' he calls. 'D'you want a cup of tea to go with it?'

115

'Yes, great.' I can hear cupboard doors opening. 'Can you find everything?'

'Give me a minute.'

He brings it all in on a tray then settles himself into a chair without saying anything. He's one of the few people I know who smokes but he won't light up in here. Carrie would go mad if she smelt tobacco and he knows the house rules.

He doesn't ask how I am. He waits, settling down, slurping his tea.

'How's the team doing?' I ask.

He considers this. 'They could do better. We've got two lads coming up who can hit for England and a girl who can bowl, but some of the older members don't like letting go. They're past it but you can't tell them that.'

I nod. I chew on the sandwich. He's cut the bread so thick, it's taking me all my time to tear through the crust.

'Saw your Jack at the pub last night,' he says. 'A good lad.'

'Yes, he is.' It's nice to hear. 'He likes it down there.'

I give up on the sandwich and half of it drops onto the carpet. 'Sorry, my coordination's shot.' Sam is there in an instant, hoovering up the crusts. Shows how fast he can move when he wants to. 'They've prescribed these tablets that help with the pain, but they seem to affect my balance. I need them though. Especially when I go to bed.'

'And do they work?'

'Yes, sort of. I have weird dreams though and when I wake up, my heart's hammering away and it takes a few minutes to calm down. Then I'm sitting up the rest of the night afraid to go back to sleep.' I stop, suddenly quite emotional and my voice cracks. 'To be honest, I'm floundering a bit.' Colin sits quietly, waiting. 'It's as though I'm changed in some way. Since the accident...'

Here I am. Just days after being the shoulder to cry on for Jack, trying to help him see he's not on his own and I'm off-loading all *my* worries in the same way. Wanting answers from someone I trust, I suppose. Not that I don't trust Carrie. I do. But she wouldn't understand. She expects me to cope, I think, whatever the circumstances. So I keep feelings hidden because talking about them would end up with crossed wires.

Colin's expression is steady, patient. So I go on.

'I don't know… it's as though I'm trying to find my feet and there's no firm ground to walk on. A bit like being in limbo. Does that sound… queer to you?'

'It sounds like what you'd expect after smashing your head and spending days in the dark.' He clamps his mouth shut as though this was the only answer.

'I think if I could just understand what happened… remember…'

He shakes his head. 'Could be you're thinking too much. You're trying to puzzle it all out – everything that's happened and why – and that sometimes needs to come in its own good time.' He pats Sam's head with an old man's hand. 'If you concentrated on something else, it might help. Settle your mind, help you build up your strength. Some hobby that'd occupy you.'

I think about it. What did I do with my spare time before this? I don't play golf or tennis, go fishing or ride a bike. Work has always occupied so many hours of the day, and often weekends, there never seemed time for anything that required a regular commitment. I've let the job consume me, I suppose, that's civil engineering for you – long hours and long distances, weeks away from home and call-outs when things go wrong. It hasn't left me much free time. Having a family takes over as well. You ferry kids around, watch football matches and netball games, walk the dog, go out for meals, help out in the village, but you don't have that luxury of hours to yourself. I do things, yes – I read a lot and love films, always have done, but they aren't hobbies, are they? They're escapes.

I lean back and don't even try to pick up the cup of tea. Bound to drop that.

'Isn't there anything you can think of you'd enjoy?'

'Honestly, no. I suppose I've been a bit of a workaholic. Not intentionally. At the beginning there was no money for extras; we were in our early twenties with two young kids. And the work's always been demanding. You have to give your all to get on. And Carrie wasn't working. It was only when her father died we had money – I say, *we*, but it's her money. It meant we were able to move here and Carrie could do something she'd always wanted, have her own yard. But then my job got bigger, more demanding…'

I can hear myself rambling, saying far more than's been asked for. That's what Colin does, he seems to draw you out. He's too good a listener.

'Sorry.' I shrug an apology and smile to show him I'm all right really. 'Got carried away. You didn't ask me for my life story. But,' I try again to put my finger on what the problem is, 'I suppose what I'm trying to say is, I don't have any good ideas about now, the future… about anything.'

He makes a grunting sound and pats my knee, an awkward gesture but full of kindness. 'Join the club, Alex. None of us has answers. Most of us try to avoid asking the questions.'

We talk about the July fete and the fund for the church roof (we all contribute to maintaining that and the surrounding walls and the village hall, bits of which seem to be in constant need of repair) before Colin gets to his feet, straightening his back slowly to ease himself into standing position.

'How about I come up tomorrow and we take a walk down the village? If we make it to the green, we can sit on the bench and put the world to rights.'

'Sounds good. I need to get walking and you can always carry me back if I get tired.'

He gives a throaty laugh. 'We'd never make it.'

I push myself out of my chair to see him out and he lets me do it.

As he's leaving, he turns. 'Really enjoyed the barbecue, by the way. Best steak I've tasted in a good while. The birthday girl looked well considering everything.' He touched his forehead in a sort of salute. 'See you tomorrow. Eleven o'clock.'

And he's gone. But not before I experience a rush of adrenalin that courses through my whole body and in the next instant, saps me of energy so I have to grab hold of the door jamb to steady myself. I can't understand the suddenness of it or why I'm so bloody shaken.

No, more than shaken.

I feel in peril.

I've only experienced fear like this twice that I can remember. Once, when I tripped on faulty scaffolding forty feet up the side of a silo. And then when I nearly lost Sam in a swollen river.

It was years ago on a windy October day and I'd taken him for a swim as I often did. But this time, through my one stupid action, I watched as he was carried away by the current and to my mind, never to be seen again. Sam loved to swim and he was strong, so I never worried that he wouldn't find his way out of any difficulty. But this day, I tossed a stick for him and it landed mid-stream, much further out than I intended. He threw himself in and sped after it, the force of the current carrying him faster and faster downstream. The water rolled him on, just his sleek black head visible above the turbulence. Too fast, too distant. Panic set in. I began running along the bank, lurching like a drunkard over tangled grass and huge holes from where the cows had trampled the ground over the summer, trying to keep upright and shouting Sam's name, my chest tight with dread. This was all my fault and I'd never forgive myself for being so damned thoughtless.

I ran and ran until, exhausted, I slowed down in a cold sweat. I'd lost hope by then. But suddenly, I caught sight of a wet bundle shaking himself, further up the bank. All I could do was sink to my knees as he came towards me wagging his tail, looking like a drowned rat. I put my arms round his neck, his wet coat soaking my jacket and all I kept saying was, *'Sorry, Sam, so sorry.'*

And now, here I am with that same terrifying charge of electricity racing through me, that same sense of fear and shock, as though my eyes are wide open but I'm past being able to take everything in.

I stare through the open door at Colin's receding back.

Barely able to breathe, I make my way back to the couch in the sitting room and lower myself onto it. I close my eyes, confused, going over Colin's final words.

Really enjoyed the barbecue. The birthday girl looked well.

And then from nowhere, a picture forms in my mind – more than a picture, it's a whole scene being played out. It isn't imagined. It's more than that, I know.

It's real.

I'm standing at a griddle and I'm cooking. There are voices behind me. Laughter. A party in full swing and I'm feeling good. I take a swig of my beer and something spits on the barbecue. I turn my head as someone calls my name.... and I see her.

Christ, it can't be her! Dear God, it can't be her.

And of course, it is.

I'd recognise that face anywhere.

Chapter 14

S he tried to carry on with her meal but it was difficult to go on eating and struggling to make conversation as though nothing was wrong. He'd been doing so well. Enjoying his food again, reading the newspaper nearly as avidly as he used to, interested in what she had to say – well, at least making the effort – and managing most of the physio exercises even though that was hard, painful work. He was making a good recovery, she told his parents. *Getting back to normal.* And she genuinely believed it.

But now Carrie was having doubts.

Of course she'd been warned about the possibility of a relapse. The doctors in the hospital and the young GP, Dr. Harris had told her, *'in cases like this, progress wasn't always continuous – so much depended on the patient's capacity for recovery. Most probably there would be setbacks. There was no knowing whether Alex would suffer from bouts of depression or crippling headaches or episodes of intense irritation. Or he may just shut down, losing all interest in communicating with anyone.'*

But those were the worst scenarios and she hadn't wanted to think about them. No good being pessimistic and worrying about things that may never happen. So she pushed them to the back of her mind, determined to stay hopeful.

On the day before Alex was coming out of hospital, she needed some positive words to hang on to. It was the quiet time of the afternoon. Doctors had finished their rounds and the nurses were going from room to room doling out medicines from a small wheeled cart, the sound of voices just murmurs which seemed to accentuate the calm orderliness of the whole building. As though it was a well-oiled machine you could rely on not to break down and you knew

121

you were in safe hands.

So the last thing she wanted to do was listen to Joe's sombre 'advice'! But give it he must.

They'd sat on either side of Alex, making small talk, just helping while away the hours. Both repeating themselves because it wasn't a natural situation. There'd been long gaps and Alex was only responding in short sentences. He'd not had the concentration to watch the TV to catch up on the news, but although he wasn't saying much, he seemed interested when they brought him up-to-date with what the government was planning, the latest Opinion polls, the recent sports results, as they tried to keep him in touch with the goings-on in the world.

But he'd nodded off by about three o'clock and Joe had decided it was a good time to make some helpful suggestions about his treatment when he was sent home. Of course he was protective of his brother, she understood that, but he often failed to see that after twenty years of marriage, she might know more about what was best for Alex than he did. He'd never quite got that and it annoyed her.

His eyes were on his brother, who was sleeping peacefully, head resting against the back of the chair. 'I'm worried,' he said in a low voice.

'Aren't we all?' Carrie knew this was going somewhere. And she didn't want to hear it.

'It's so important that he recovers at his own pace.'

He glanced across at her and she gave him a warning look. *Do I really need advice right now?* There was a wariness, an unspoken hostility between them that was usually kept well under wraps, but both sensed it could erupt with the right provocation.

'Go on.'

'Well… when he's home, I think you need to take it very slowly, Carrie. I'm sure you don't need me to say this but you can't afford to rush things. His mental state is more of a worry than the physical injuries. We're dealing with the unknown here.'

She tried to imbue patience into her voice but her expression gave her away. 'I realise that, Joe,' she said with deliberate slowness. 'I'll be careful. I'll follow the advice from the hospital, follow all their instructions and the nurse will come in every day. We'll be fine.'

She shook her head and motioned that this conversation would be better continued outside. They both moved quietly into the corridor and shut the door behind them.

She turned towards him, testy now. 'Don't you think I've got his best interests at heart, Joe? It's going to be difficult for all of us so I don't think there's much point discussing how we're going to deal with it all until we know what we're dealing *with*.'

A porter passed them, smiling and lifting his hand in a friendly gesture as they stood in silence until he was out of hearing.

Joe spoke quickly before she could get started. 'It's just that it'll take more time…'

'I know it'll take time but on the other hand, for heaven's sake, he can't just sit in a chair and vegetate. He needs exercise and physiotherapy sessions if he's ever going to get back on his feet.'

Joe straightened his shoulders. 'I've discussed the effects of blunt force trauma with a friend of mine who works in A and E. He was saying the psychological effects can be… unpredictable. If you push him…'

'Well, no, I won't do that. But he has to have goals. Follow some sort of programme otherwise he'll never get his life back, never be able to return to his job. You'll have to trust me. I'm sure we can get the balance right.'

Carrie had already opened the door to go back into the room and Joe gave a resigned shrug. It was obvious he wasn't happy with how she'd reacted but too bad. His trouble, she thought, was that he always knew best and he could never admit that someone else's opinion might be worth considering. Anyway, whatever dire warnings he'd given her, she resented his questioning her judgement… and his tone. God, what a family! They couldn't just let her get on with it. It wasn't time to be thinking the worst when he was about to come home.

And she'd been right to be optimistic. There was no doubt about it, he *had* been doing well. She was sure that depended on keeping your eyes on the road ahead, gaining confidence, achieving small successes.

But now, glancing at him as he picked at the food on his plate, she was uneasy.

The forecast had been for one of the hottest days so far this summer and by twelve o'clock, it was 24 degrees, no wind stirring the crop fields in the distance. The garden was quiet except for the hum of bees which carried distinctly across the lawn from the flower beds. They'd be undisturbed. The ideal opportunity to sit outside and talk properly. Not just basic everyday to-and-fro stuff that skims the surface but talk that had some meaning. About how they were feeling, about each other, where they were in this marriage, perhaps discuss, if possible, what had happened. Carrie knew she'd often avoided all this emotional 'soul-baring', as she called it. It wasn't her way, not usually. But they'd both faced a life-changing situation and some things needed saying. Even if all they managed was some reassuring words that promised life *could* get back to normal.

And it was no good kidding herself – what she really wanted was to know the truth about the accident. She was no nearer getting to the bottom of it than she had been weeks ago.

So she'd set up lunch in a way she thought would help them both. Alex might find he could share something that so far had gone unsaid, it didn't matter how insignificant it seemed. Perhaps it would give her some idea of what was on his mind. Then and now.

At least it gave her a purpose instead of this drifting from day to day.

She'd made particular effort with the meal, setting the table in the garden, bringing out canvas chairs from the garage, even putting up the green umbrella which barely fluttered in the still air. She'd carried out the salad and condiments, placed chunks of walnut bread in a basket, napkins by the side plates and poured elderberry cordial in long glasses. Calling out to Alex to come and sit, she'd put the sliced marinated chicken, potato salad and peppers on each plate and waited expectantly for him to join her.

But now, any conversation she'd hoped to have was dying on its feet.

He seemed so quiet, well, more than quiet. He was in another place.

'Is it OK?' she asked.

'What?' It was as though she'd snapped her fingers and he'd woken with a start.

'The chicken.'

He put some on his fork which he held awkwardly in his left hand and nodded. 'Yes, it's good.'

Carrie buttered a piece of bread and swiped at a wasp that was hovering over the table. 'That's the only thing with eating outside. You get extra guests!'

She was trying too hard, it was all forced. Everything she said sounded false. He didn't even smile.

This was becoming unnerving.

'Alex, come on. Whatever's wrong, tell me. Please,' she said, leaning towards him and placing a hand on his thigh. 'I can't help you unless you speak up. Whatever the problem is, if you keep it locked away, it'll only get worse. Do you feel ill? Is your head hurting you? If you don't want to eat, leave it.'

He put the fork back on the plate and sat back. 'I'm all right. Bit of a headache but it's nothing. Just seem to lack energy, I suppose. Everything's an effort. Sorry if I've shut myself off. Didn't mean to.'

She waited but he wasn't going to say anymore.

'Look,' she said, 'I can understand this is difficult for you, and you have to adjust to being… well, an invalid for a while, but that'll pass.' She hesitated before daring to push a bit further. 'I've got a feeling there's something more than that. At times, you have such a sad look on your face… if it's me who's making you miserable, I'd rather know.'

His eyes widened in astonishment. 'Carrie, for heaven's sake, don't think that. I'm too wrapped up in myself at the moment and I'm sorry for being a selfish bastard. You're looking after me so well and I'm really grateful. You couldn't be doing more.' He reached for her hand and held it tightly. 'If I seem… distant, it's me, not you. Sorry, I just haven't been thinking about how that might affect you. Or Jack.'

She swallowed, relieved. 'Good. That's fine. I don't want you thinking I'm bullying you and making you do things before you're ready. Joe would never forgive me.'

'Joe?'

'Well, he wanted to be sure I let you recover slowly, at your own pace. He was afraid, I don't know, that I'd put you on the fast track. Get you running a marathon before you can walk.' She had to make light of it now, the two of them were so close.

He smiled. 'You know Joe. He takes the part of being "his brother's keeper" very seriously. He worries too much, that's all.'

It was as though peace had been restored, the atmosphere more comfortable now. They finished the meal and sat back from the table. The warm air was making Alex sleepy, she could see that. She relaxed, watching Sam investigate a rustling in the undergrowth beyond the hedge, where he suddenly disturbed a young pheasant which flapped off, showering feathers and squawking. Carrie felt the whole burden of anxiety had been lifted somewhat. Maybe she'd been losing sleep over nothing.

*

There were other matters, of course, to deal with. David, for one. She'd made a compromise. She wouldn't acknowledge that he'd won; she wasn't giving Jodie lessons, she was helping in a way she would do with any child, or adult for that matter, in need of a bit of guidance.

She'd tacked the pony up and led him into the paddock, loosening the nose band a hole so he was more comfortable. No point putting a stranglehold on the poor thing. Jodie had to learn to control him using her seat, not yanking on the reins to slow him down.

Here goes, Carrie thought, hoping David was too busy with his own horse for the next twenty minutes to stand at the fence and make the little girl nervous. It was bad enough the kid was afraid of the pony, never mind adding her father's critical eye to the mix.

She hoisted her up into the saddle and put her feet in the stirrups. Jodie sat as stiffly as she had done in Sarah's lesson and pressed her lips together, blinking rapidly. Carrie waited for her to gather the reins.

'Now,' she said, 'just relax your whole body, move side to side in the saddle to get your balance, then pat Bertie's neck to show him he's a good horse. They like praise.' Then she looked at Jodie with a serious face. 'Ready? OK, when you set off, I want you to sing.'

Jodie looked at her, wide-eyed. 'Sing?'

Carrie smiled. 'I used to take a really stroppy horse out on the roads when I was younger and I knew when a tractor came towards us, he'd bunch up and get ready to leap around. So when I saw he was scared of what was coming, I used to sing... doesn't matter what... a nursery rhyme, *Old Macdonald had a farm.* That's when he knows you're not afraid and it makes him feel safe.'

'What did you sing?' she said, already letting her body loosen up and her hands drop.

'It had to be something from *Oklahoma,* usually it was *Oh what a beautiful morning* because I could remember most of the words.'

'What if you passed someone walking? They'd hear you.'

'Who cares? The horse liked it.'

Then she told Jodie to move away and just potter round the paddock at a walk, keeping close to the rails. She called out to her. 'What are you going to sing?'

The reply came straight back. '*Dance Monkey*. Do you know it?'

'No, but I'll catch up.'

After ten minutes, they were both warbling away, Jodie horribly out of tune but she was easy in her seat. Back not straight enough and hands all wrong, but enjoying herself.

Out of the corner of her eye, Carrie saw David coming round the corner of the barn, striding out anxious in case he'd missed something. *Couldn't he have stayed away another ten minutes?* she thought crossly, then decided he'd be better seeing his daughter actually having a good time for once. No fear on her face now.

After a few minutes, watching but saying nothing by way of instruction, she called Jodie into the centre and lifted her off the saddle. 'How was that?' she asked. 'Did singing work?'

The child was smiling, wide-eyed. 'Yes, it did. It was amazing. Bertie wasn't at all afraid.'

Carrie led the pony into the stable and helped Jodie unbuckle the bridle and lift the saddle off the pony's back, ignoring David who was standing at the entrance. She was sure he'd find fault with something. He didn't begin until he'd sent the child away to make up a feed and then waited till she was out of earshot, propping his elbows on the half-door.

She looked over at him ready for the usual disapproval. 'Go on,' she said, although he hadn't spoken.

'She was sloppy and uncoordinated and didn't have much control...'

'But...?'

'She was happy. She was enjoying herself.' And then, a pause, as though being appreciative didn't come easy to him. 'Thank you, Carrie. That's just what I wanted.'

He gave her one of those rare smiles that changed his face completely. Gone was that stern autocratic look that he wore most of the time. With that smile which reached his eyes and softened every feature, he became a charming, likeable human being.

Carrie found it quite a pleasant surprise.

Chapter 15

Luckily, his first day off came on a Friday. At Parsons, the days changed each week according to a rota because they needed plenty of staff to cover Saturdays and Sundays when it was busy. At this time of year, a lot of customers were coming in looking for tools to do repairs, buying products to doctor their lawns, browsing in the garden centre and then going in the café for lunch or afternoon tea. It was full on. And training seemed to be non-existent or the policy seemed to be – *learn on the job.*

Jack had found the first four days something of a blur and by the time it got to five o'clock, he was glad to pull on his jacket and head for home. Of course, summer was the busiest time of the year for this kind of store and he found it hard to cope with the numbers of customers demanding attention and some of the requests had him flummoxed. It was all right being OK with step ladders and buckets but what did he know about sealants and masonry fittings? And he was too slow on the tills, especially when he could see four or five people in line waiting to be served. He'd have to learn fast. Luckily there was usually some old hand who came to his aid.

At least he'd felt better after Steve, the manager, had praised his handling of one customer who'd dithered over which ear protectors to buy and had finally chosen ones Jack recommended. *'You did well there,'* he'd said. *'Some people just need their minds making up for them.'* And the other lads on the shop floor who'd been there a lot longer were friendly enough. It was working out.

So now he had time to go into the Car Phone shop in Stockport and try to buy the right mobile for his dad, who'd asked him a few times over the week when his day off was. Then yesterday, he'd handed over his credit card with instructions on what he wanted – a decent mobile, don't worry too much about the cost. It baffled Jack why he should be worrying about a new phone right now. It wasn't as though the old one had been stolen and someone was ringing Singapore and totting up huge bills. The police had said it was lost in the wreckage so no-one could get their hands on it.

Anyway, who was he going to ring? He wouldn't need it for work at the moment. Probably not for quite a while.

And it was never straightforward. It always took an age buying a new phone or upgrading or getting it repaired. There were always too many decisions to make. A man in a grey suit with a metal logo hanging from a neck ribbon was there to greet him – *A new phone, please take a seat, our guru won't be long, he'll call you when he's finished with...* and so on.

Jack was in for a long wait.

An hour had passed by the time it was all done – different options, model choices, payment plans, new number – *No, I'm afraid you can't keep your old one* – everything packed into a little box and finally, papers signed (A. Taylor written on all the documents, Jack making sure the A could be confused with a J when he signed, so he wouldn't be done for forgery). Card validated. He came out of the shop, swinging the little white bag, his dad's bank balance £400 lighter.

He was walking through the Merseyway centre, its large glass roof creating a humid warmth under its dome, when he brushed against the shoulder of a girl walking towards him. She glanced sideways and stopped, grabbing his arm which made him lurch backwards, nearly losing his footing.

'Jack!'

As he turned in surprise, he was looking at not one but two girls, both staring at him, big smiles on their faces – Grace and Sylvie, close friends at school, his classmates and to be honest, the last people he wanted to see.

He managed a 'Hi!'

Sylvie broke the ice. 'Gosh, not seen you for years. What have you been doing with yourself? Are you still living at the stables? You don't look any older.'

'I think he does, Sylvie. You can't look eighteen forever,' said Grace, laughing. 'How you doing, Jack?'

She *certainly* looked older, he thought, hair cut short, pencilled eyebrows, silver hoop earrings and her shirt collar turned up for effect. He supposed it was fashionable.

'Come on, we've got to celebrate. A reunion,' said Sylvie, tucking her arm through Jack's and turning him round in the direction they'd been going. 'Too long without a good catch-up. Come to the coffee shop with us and we'll buy.'

'Well, I was just...' But that's as far as Jack got. He could see Grace smiling over at him as they walked and he didn't know how he felt about that. It was a relief in a way that they'd met suddenly and he didn't have to psych himself up for something he'd been hoping to avoid for long enough.

They settled themselves into a booth at the Bean Box and ordered coffee and three Danish Custards before Jack had a chance to join in any of the conversation.

Grace began, as he knew she would. 'People were talking at Terry's house about your dad, how he'd been in a really bad way after a car accident. How's he doing?'

'Much better. Home now and getting over it. I should think he'll be back at work soon.' Why on earth did he have to make light of it? He recognised that part of it was he didn't want Grace feeling sorry for him. She'd made it obvious when they split up that she considered him a loser, getting nowhere, going nowhere, someone without ambition or drive. Well, fair enough. But he didn't want any more sympathy for the sorry state of his life.

'Good,' she said. 'Really liked your dad. He had this dry sense of humour.'

Jack smiled. 'Well, he lost it for a while.'

Sylvie tucked into her cake, dropping flakes of pastry all over the pine table. 'The best cakes I've ever had were in that little café in the village, the Tea Shop it was called, remember? So old fashioned, it was like something out of Arnold Bennett. Lace curtains over the windows and a great glass cabinet as you walked in, with so much on display you could never make your mind up what to choose. My gran used to take me there after school and you had to '*sit like a lady*', she always said, so you didn't disturb anyone. Then they'd bring the tea out in a silver tea pot and the napkins were linen...'

Grace put up her hand. 'For heaven's sake, Sylvie, that's not catching up. That's going back to the dark ages.' She turned to Jack. 'And what are you up to these days? I know you've been working at the pub...'

'I'm at Parsons as well, full-time, so earning some money at last.' He picked up his cup noticing the coffee was already lukewarm. Grace nodded her head as though she understood what was being implied, the memories of past disagreements between them suddenly hanging in the air. He began to feel his old sense of inferiority returning just sitting across the table from her and decided it was high time he knew what her plans were. 'Didn't think you'd come back to this part of the world.'

'Well, I wasn't going to.' She looked thoughtful for a moment. 'Had a rethink before Easter. Was really enjoying the course, then they sent me to this primary school just outside the city, second term teaching practice – year 3.' And as though Jack needed an explanation, 'Seven and eight-year-olds. Anyway, this woman, Mrs. Bailey, was the student support coordinator and she kept giving me awful reviews, saying I wasn't teaching to the learning objectives, my discipline was poor, the displays weren't good enough. I was ready to give up. Even before I qualified. Then I saw a job advertised in the

Times Ed and I thought, Stockport – close to home.'

'So you've got the job?'

"Yes. Had the interview last week and looked round the school this morning. Temporary for a year. No-one gives a permanent contract to an NQT these days.'

He wasn't sure what to say. The initials threw him. 'Well, good for you. Start in September then.'

'Got to find somewhere to live first. Wilmslow is really expensive so I'll have to look further out... or further in. Shouldn't be too difficult.'

Sylvie beamed at them both. 'She'll be back where she belongs, won't you, Grace? Going to the cinema and having nights out and clubbing. It'll be like old times.'

'I have to work, Sylvie. The first few months I'm on a massive learning curve. Can't be turning up to teach, shattered.'

They began to talk about people he didn't know, books he'd never read and holidays they'd been on, Vietnam, Thailand – just places on a map to Jack, exotic and exciting but way beyond his reach. A different world. The four-year gap seemed to stretch between them, a gulf that was growing wider with everything he couldn't share. He'd go, leave them to it, glad to get this over with. He got up, said his goodbyes with a casual wave of his hand and a, '*See you around,*' hoping that wouldn't be too soon.

He'd reached the door of the café when Grace called after him.

'You've left this on the seat!' She was holding up the bag with the phone in it that he'd completely forgotten about.

'Oh, thanks.' He darted back to retrieve it and made his way out again.

Bloody hell! £400! His dad would have killed him.

*

The physiotherapy department was an oasis of calm... Through the main entrance, turn left along a corridor, a touch of a button and automatic doors swing open and you sit on comfy leather-backed chairs facing the office window in a cool, quiet waiting area. Jack watched people in pale blue coats come and go carrying folders and what looked like X-ray plates, looking efficient and purposeful. No-one in a hurry.

He'd been there nearly an hour and had passed the time reading all the posters on the walls – the house rules, the adverts for different help organisations, the exercise charts – and he could feel himself dozing off. Even the few sounds that created a background hum had become even more muted, the ringing of a telephone from behind the reception's glass screen, low voices as the staff answered calls and compared notes, the swish of the door opening and closing.

He'd nodded off.

Sensing someone standing in front of him, he woke with a start. His dad was looking down at him, eyebrows raised.

'Don't think you're meant to go to sleep in this part of the building. But... if you want to stay...'

'Sorry, Dad.' He jumped up. 'How was it?'

'Painful and exhausting if I'm honest but they seem to know what they're doing. Another session next week.'

They walked slowly back down the corridor and round the circular parking area to Jack's car. He fixed his dad's seat belt, then climbed into the driving seat and adjusted his own and drove out onto the roundabout to join the traffic on the main road.

He looked across at his dad. 'Would you like to go somewhere?' he said, as he manoeuvred into the right-hand lane to take them home. 'We've got all afternoon. And you've been stuck in the house for weeks.'

Well.' His dad had the habit of always looking round at the traffic when Jack drove as though he wasn't about to trust his judgement. 'Be careful, that Toyota's going to cut in.'

Jack laughed and shook his head. 'Christ, I've heard everything. You're *just* the one to be giving me instructions. Be a good idea if you drove, would it?'

'Well, no. I've had a broken arm. Otherwise...'

They drove on and Jack couldn't hide how pleased he was that the banter was back and it was all easy again as though they'd slotted back into a previous time.

'Go on,' he said. 'What would you like to do? Can't go to the beach 'cos it's too far and perhaps Blackpool might be a bit noisy.' There was something about Blackpool that Jack loved. As a little kid, he'd gone to see The Illuminations one September night and he'd never forgotten the wonder of it – just like Fairy Land.

He imagined his dad's withering look.

'Definitely not Blackpool. What about The Bell at Romily. You can sit outside and they used to do bloody good scotch eggs there.'

'That's a few miles out. And it's after lunch so they won't be serving now.'

'I'll pay for the petrol, you cheapskate. Put your foot down. We'll take a chance.'

They glanced across at one another with the old understanding developed over the years, all the humour, the teasing and the fondness for each other, alive in their faces.

'And you,' his dad said, 'can pay for the Cokes.'

*

Jack had been helping close the doors at the store and shutting down the tills with Gary, one of the lads who'd turned out to be good fun as well as a hard worker. Since starting the job over two weeks ago now, they'd become almost friends – one evening a quick drink at the nearby pub and a late afternoon hill climb that had left Jack aching and realising how unfit he was. They'd spent most of the time in the same section and worked well together, both getting increasingly frustrated with lazy Martin who'd been there too long and never went the extra mile for anybody. It wasn't often they had a day off together but tomorrow was a Sunday and Gary wanted Jack to try out a Climbing Centre in Liverpool.

But Sunday was the day the conservation group was repairing one of the wooden bridges on Weaver Way at Winsford.

He'd been on the website earlier in the week, setting his laptop on the bed and hesitating before he clicked the mouse to look at the schedule. There it was, dates, times, instructions – parking at the Ranger's Office on Weaver Valley road – a mile walk on level terrain and a box to tick for those willing to take part. Well, he was willing but was this such a bright idea? He already knew the answer to that. It was a stupid idea. Immature and foolish to carry on with this… infatuation. He was well aware of that from the furtive way he was behaving. He could just imagine what his parents would say. Or Lucy.

But whatever the voice of reason was telling him, he turned down Gary's offer to go climbing. The die was cast.

On that blustery Sunday morning he climbed into his car, studied the map once again and set off with the wind sending twigs and leaves hurtling onto his windscreen. Thirty-five miles. This time he'd be early.

The going was straight forward until he was nearly there and came to a turn-off with no signposts. He'd lost his bearings and was unsure whether it should be left or right, so choosing the left-hand road, the wrong one, he had to circle back to arrive at the same spot, wasting precious time. *The only way you'd know which road to take would be if you lived here,* he thought, frustrated, wrenching the wheel round. *What good's that?*

He set off again and when he reached the parking area, some cars were already there. So much for being early.

By the time he'd walked to the bridge that needed repairing, four or five of the workers were already sorting out tools and Tom was examining the weakened railings. At least the canopy of overhanging trees sheltered them from the wind. Jack climbed up the wooden steps and looked round. Was she here?

It was Rosie who greeted him with a big smile and as Tom bent down, he caught sight of Fran standing in the ditch below the bridge. She looked up and took off one glove to rub her eye. 'There are tiny black flies everywhere. Probably because the stream's just mud.' Then, as though he was an afterthought, she acknowledged him. 'Hello again.'

He couldn't make out her tone. Not particularly friendly, he was fairly sure of that.

'Hi,' he said, glancing round at the dilapidated state of the bridge. 'There seems to be a lot to do.'

Tom nodded. 'Too much for one day. We'll just have to come back to finish it.'

They set about it, pulling away the rotten parts of the railings and levering up some of the planks underfoot and throwing them into a pile on the path. The fresh lengths of wood and flooring were lying on a low cart which Tom must have hauled up from the car park.

There was very little talk, too much to get done until the flasks came out and they took a breather, Tom unwrapping some caramel shortbreads to hand round. 'Home made by my dearly beloved,' he said which made Jack think he must be married and not in a relationship with Fran at all. They had all found the work hard and sat where they could, on the grass, the steps, a tree trunk. Jack didn't look across at where Fran was sitting but eventually they made eye contact.

'How's things?' she said.

He nodded, embarrassed, dropping biscuit crumbs down his shirt. 'Fine. Started a new job so been really busy.'

'That's good.' She looked at him as though waiting for more. 'And Lucy said your dad's doing well.'

Nice that she'd remembered, he thought. 'Yes, he is. Took him to a physio session the other day and the plaster should come off his arm soon.'

In the afternoon, Jack found himself working by her side for about half an hour, happy to have some brief exchanges. By three o'clock they'd all had enough, straightening their backs and stiff knees, their faces covered in bits of grit and earth.

No-one was ready for the sudden shout of pain but they all knew trouble when they heard it. They turned as one in the direction of Jan who was holding up her arm, blood dripping down from the wrist. Tom ran over to her and yelled for the First Aid kit. It was Rosie who got there first, pouring water from a plastic bottle over the gash, squirting it with alcohol spray and ripping a sterilised pad out of its wrapper.

Jan was trying not to cry. 'My own fault,' she said. 'I took off my gloves to wipe my face and didn't put them back on again. It was a can. Lying just there. I didn't see it.' She caught her breath. 'Do you think it needs stitching?'

'We need to go to A and E,' Tom said, tying a makeshift bandage round her hand and wrist. 'I'll take you. Sunday, so might have to wait.' He looked round at the others. 'Can someone take care of the rubbish? And the cart needs to go in someone's boot. Hope it'll fit in.' As he hurried off with Jan, he called over his shoulder. 'Fran, you'll have to get a lift with someone. Sorry.'

Everyone packed up in a hurry and by the time they reached the car park, Tom's car had gone. He heard Fran say, 'Trish, could you...?'

A large woman with a red handkerchief round her neck cut her off. 'I would, Fran, but I'm going to Nantwich to meet Jeff at four. He's messaged me, wants to look at a car he's seen advertised.'

Jack tried to sound casual. 'I'll take you home, Fran. Not sure which direction you're going in, but I'm in no hurry.'

She didn't reply straight away, just walked slowly on towards the parked cars.

'It's no trouble.'

She turned and her smile seemed forced, he thought. He could never seem to judge her mood.

'Thank you. That's good of you.'

They climbed into his car and he wished he'd cleaned it up a bit, CDs and sunglasses on the front seat which he had to hurriedly move.

'It isn't far. Do you know Whitegate?'

'No,' he said, turning on the ignition. 'Don't know any of the places round here. Just guide me at each turn so I don't get lost like I did coming.'

They followed the country road, through Acton Bridge and Jack slowed down at the village sign for Whitegate, ready to be told where to stop.

'It's tiny,' he said. 'You could miss it if you blinked.'

'Yes, I suppose you could. It's a lovely place.'

'Where do you want dropping off?'

'This will do. I'm just down here.'

He looked across at some converted farm buildings set back off the road, all yellow-brown stone and arched windows and solid-looking front doors.

'God, that's nice.'

'I was lucky. They divided the barn into five small houses years ago and my brother and I joined forces and bought it for very little, really. He moved to Sheffield with work, so it's just me now.' She put her hand on the door handle ready to get out. 'Thank you for the lift.'

He sat quietly with his arms resting on the steering wheel. He had to speak up.

'Fran, if I'm annoying you by joining that group, then I won't come any more.' He couldn't look at her. 'I know you're Lucy's friend and I don't want to spoil that. I get the impression at times that I'm sort of in the way, and that's the last thing…'

She sat back in her seat. 'You're not in the way, Jack. You're really nice and I'm sorry if I've been off with you. I've had some problems recently that've got me down, I suppose. I've been moody with everyone. It isn't you. Please don't think it's anything to do with me being Lucy's friend.' He glanced at her and saw she was smiling. 'Of course I don't mind you joining in. Don't think that.'

And as Jack drove away, his spirits were high as a kite and he started to hum to himself.

Chapter 16

Fran closed the front door behind her, secured the latch and threw her backpack under the hall table where it skittered across the tiles. Then she sank to the floor, her back against solid wood, the barricade keeping all the mayhem out and hugged herself.

Christ, what an unholy mess!

If this was the plot of a film, you wouldn't believe it.

She breathed out in a long despairing sigh, no answers coming to her that were any comfort. She hadn't been ready for any of this. It was like falling overboard and being carried out to sea, desperate for someone to throw you a lifebelt. Well, some hope!

She pulled herself up and decided the best way to calm down was to go the fridge, take out the bottle of Sauvignon, get a wine glass from the shelf and have a drink. Blur the edges. And if that didn't work, have *two* drinks.

If only Jack wasn't such a nice bloke, didn't look like a wounded bloodhound when she did her best to put him off. If only he didn't have... expectations. This wasn't just complicated, it was torturous — there could only be disaster and a cruel ending unless she could think of a way out that didn't involve moving a hundred miles away to another county.

Because the problem of Jack was nothing compared to the problem of Alex.

OK, perhaps his accident had nothing to do with her. Perhaps she was putting two and two together and making five. Perhaps it was all about coincidence. He'd seen her at a family party and two days later he'd been driving too fast and careered off the road. A freak chance that put the incidents close in time, but not necessarily connected or linked in any way. Things happened like that in life. Random. Arbitrary.

But she couldn't convince herself.

She poured another glass of wine and knew she should have something to eat but she couldn't face it. The thought of preparing food seemed like too much effort. It was easier to sit, the cool stem of the glass between her fingers and wait for the alcohol to smooth her edges. Which in the end it did. She began to breathe more slowly. Outside, the day was still bright but inside, it felt like the approach of evening, the walls darkened by large patches of shadow shot through at angles with thin shafts of light.

This kitchen had always been a haven for her. It had given her comfort when work had become heavy, when relationships had fallen apart, when life at times had become an uphill struggle. It felt warm somehow with its oak beams spanning the low ceiling, a dresser along one wall painted a faded blue, an old chopping block for a table and wood carvings of geese and sheep above the book shelves. The window, which looked out onto a tiny courtyard, was set deep into the stone walls and on the sill were two small earthenware pots of herbs. But now, she just wanted to shut out the world.

She was glad to be on her own.

But as she sipped the wine she thought back to the horrible moment when she first heard he'd crashed his car, he was in Intensive Care, he might not survive. *Keep everything crossed.* That was what Lucy had said. *Keep everything crossed.*

She'd done more than that. She'd prayed in the grip of a fear that consumed her. *Don't let him die. If ever I've been guilty of forgetting You exist, please have mercy on me now and save him.* It was too many days before she learned he'd come out of the coma and been moved to a side ward, still in a bad way but things looked hopeful. Trouble with Lucy was she didn't answer her mobile half the time, and didn't return calls even if Fran left a voicemail message. She could hardly keep ringing up every five minutes. She couldn't afford to give anything away now.

But fate had already taken a hand, joining that exercise class. How on earth could she have known that Lucy Todd, the lively girl doing Zumba, the party girl who was friends with everyone in an instant, who talked openly about her recent divorce, was once Lucy Taylor? Fran didn't think twice about the fact she was called 'Lucy' – why should she? It was a common enough name. And when she was invited to a birthday barbecue, she thought, well she hadn't been going out much lately, it might be fun. And with an offer of a lift from one of Lucy's work mates, she could even have a drink. It was good to have a party to dress up for. As it happened, the two girls from Lucy's work were really nice, easy-going and friendly – a bit younger than her, a bit giddy, but what did that matter!

So she'd put on her new white dress and black wedge-heeled sandals that laced round her ankles, a vintage gold pendant and matching bracelet. And after pulling everything out of a bedroom cupboard where she'd shoved gloves and bed socks and neck-warmers, she found a small black shoulder bag to finish it off.

She was grateful to Rachel, who'd driven fifteen miles in the wrong direction to pick her up, offering to pay for petrol.

'Don't be daft. I might want you to give *me* a lift sometime.'

Fran climbed in beside her, tucking the skirt of her dress beneath her. 'Well, I'm not expecting you to drive me back. I'll get a taxi.'

As it happened, they were late arriving – Lucy was still doing her make-up when Rachel tooted the horn outside her flat – and finally as they drew up at the house, they knew it had already started from the sounds drifting on the evening air into the road, the music and voices and laughter. The gate was open and Lucy took them round the back, up the stone steps through the open French windows to the makeshift bar, with spirits of every kind, red and white wine, bottles of sparkling non-alcoholic cordial, Pimm's in a large glass jug. They helped themselves to drinks and followed Lucy into the tiered garden all decked out with fairy lights and silver ornaments dangling from trees.

There were shouts of, *'Here she is!'* and, *'Happy Birthday!'* as Lucy was swept away and hugged and fussed over. The girls stood a bit apart, looking on with patient, good-humoured smiles until she joined them again, a paper garland draped round her neck, a brightly wrapped present in one hand, her wine balanced carefully in the other. Then they settled into party mood and relaxed, teasing and winding each other up and laughing.

Except for Fran, who started to feel less at ease, suddenly aware, as you can be when thrown amongst strangers, that she didn't really know anyone, not well enough to chat to anyway, and she stood, looking round, feeling apart from it all. She sipped her Pimm's and half-wished she hadn't come. But if she refused every invitation, she'd end up a hermit!

Across the lawn, she could see wisps of smoke rising from the barbecue which stood over by the wall and caught the smell of meat cooking, thinking how much better steaks tasted when they were done over an open fire. She watched as the man with his back half-turned to the party prodded the charcoal and threw some sausages on the grid.

Looking back, there was nothing remarkable about any of it – the sort of scene played out in thousands of gardens on a thousand Saturday evenings. Just a party. Just people gathered together being sociable. And at last she'd relaxed, feeling quite content to be a spectator, lost in her own thoughts, her mind wandering a little.

Until he turned.

And over the crowded garden his eyes met hers.

A second was enough. An electric charge shot through her with such speed she couldn't do anything but stare, unbelieving.

'*It can't be!*'

And just as recognition hit home, the same thunder-struck expression froze on *his* face.

They stood motionless. The only two people at the party.

*

When you face danger she thought later, you learn to dissemble with such skill, you play your part so convincingly that no-one would ever know what you're hiding, what base deceit lies beneath the charming smile, the soft voice, the direct gaze. She took a deep breath, turned her head away and found a small woman with grey, tightly curled hair standing beside her who nodded to her.

'I'm Mary,' she said. 'The next-door neighbour. Isn't this a lovely party?'

'It is. Lucy's mother has gone to such trouble. You must know everybody here.' And so you cover your tracks, she thought. Fast. No give-away signs, no hesitations, an Oscar-winning performance and you hope you can get away with it.

But inwardly she was shaking. What a disaster!

How on earth was she going to get through the evening?

She tried to stay away from groups. Better to be on the side-lines looking on than suddenly facing a situation she couldn't handle or get out of. So it was when she was returning from the house with another glass of Pimm's (she didn't dare go on to the vodka) that she was glad she'd kept her distance. She saw Carrie – it had to be Carrie – come over to Lucy, kissing her on the cheek.

'Trust you to be late for your own party!' she heard her say. 'I'm Lucy's mother.'

A bright smile for the two girls. 'Do make sure she looks after you. Help yourself to whatever. We'll eat in about twenty minutes.'

From the steps, Fran watched her as she moved easily among the guests, elegant, confident, the perfect hostess. Dressed in beautifully tailored black jeans, grey and white checked shirt, a silver clip in her blonde hair, she was certainly stylish. So *in charge.*

Fran had always known she would be…

I can hardly just leave, she thought to herself. *Even if I could think of an excuse, I'm not even in my own car!*

What saved her was Jack. She knew immediately who he was — must be twenty-two now, tousle-haired, lean face, kind brown eyes. He came to stand in front of her, an empty tray hanging loosely in his hand. He introduced himself and asked her if he could get her anything. He seemed hesitant and eager to please, very different from Lucy. He was trying to make everyone feel at home and she liked him immediately.

But just as he was talking to her, she looked up and saw Alex standing very still by the barbecue, a pronged fork in one hand and a cloth in the other. It could have been such a ludicrous situation except for the look on his face, so inexpressibly sad.

He looked broken.

*

It was clear Lucy wasn't going to end the evening at ten o'clock. She'd obviously planned ahead, the next venue already lined up without telling any of them, somewhere with life and action. 'A *real* party,' she'd told them, giving them a knowing wink as she gathered up her bags of presents. 'You'll see.'

Fran closed her eyes in relief. *Just get me out of this bloody garden before I fall to pieces,* she thought, her face set so tightly her jaw ached. A mask of composure — that's what she'd been forced to maintain for two hours and the strain was killing her.

It was as though the evening would never end, trapped in a nightmare with no chance of escape, the threat closer at every turn. Waiting for the hammer blow you know is coming.

Fear was too small a word to describe how she felt. Dread was nearer.

How she'd avoided coming anywhere near Alex she didn't know, but somehow they'd kept well apart. Even when the food was served, he'd stayed at the barbecue and when Fran said she wasn't hungry, Rachel had insisted on fetching her a steak. God, it was painful, the whole situation some awful torment.

So when Lucy began to make a round of swift goodbyes and finally headed for Rachel's car, Fran allowed herself to breathe again. She'd survived. Just. And one thing for sure, she was never going to put herself – or Alex – in this position again. Ever.

They'd almost reached the gate leading to the road when someone called after them. Lucy kept on walking as though she hadn't heard. And for one horrible moment, Fran thought she'd somehow been caught out at the last minute, exposed in some bizarre quirk of fate that would reveal her for the imposter she was. But it was Jack who caught up with them, keen to join in.

It was when she was sitting in the back of Rachel's little car, jammed against the wheel arch, tired now with the strain of it all, that she felt her throat tighten and tears well up behind her eyes. They'd already gone some distance with Lucy giving directions, when she was overcome by such a sense of grief, she had to look out of the window at the passing pavements and street lamps to stem the flow of emotion that might undo her.

God, I've missed him, she thought. *Seven years and nothing's changed.* Strange that she'd always imagined, if they ever met again, if they were suddenly to bump into each other, it would be at an airport. Liverpool, perhaps. In the Duty Free. Wandering aimlessly as you do with time to spare before your flight's called. And they'd nod their heads at one another as though they'd been work colleagues, introduce their partners, children, whatever, hiding the shock and memories behind bland exchanges.

She'd never imagined anything like tonight.

The car lurching into the kerb brought her back with a start. And one look at Lucy's idea of a good night out was enough to fill her with alarm; the last thing she wanted at this moment was coloured lights, blaring music and noisy drinkers! Everyone spilling out of the front door of the club looked plastered!

She'd phone for a taxi as soon as she could.

But until then, she'd have to put a good face on it. Try to act as though there was nothing troubling her more than tiredness and too much alcohol.

And Jack did his very best to look after her, attentive, eager to please... and so young. He'd been determined to fetch her a drink so they could sit outside and not be crushed to death – Lucy had disappeared as soon as they'd got to the door – and he had this self-deprecating air about him that touched her. He'd even owned up to not enjoying the party much. 'I run out of things to say,' he'd admitted.

Tell me about it, she thought. *If you think* **you** *were struggling...*

At one point, she could almost hear the tenor of his father's voice in the way he directed questions at her. It was a strange moment.

They sat quietly, watching the antics going on in front of them, Jack occasionally throwing her a smile as though checking she was all right. But she'd spent enough of that evening on tenterhooks and it was time to get out of the whole situation. She reached in her bag and punched in the number of the taxi firm she always used. They'd have to come some distance to pick her up but that was too bad.

Jack glanced at her with such a sorry expression which he tried to hide, that she immediately wanted to reassure him – *it's not you, you're a nice boy, but you don't know the half of it* – so she started to gabble on about the conservation group and having to get up early and how she *had* to go.

Then just as she was leaving, she wanted her goodbye in a way, to say – have some belief in yourself, you've been so nice, give yourself time. And she bent down to gently kiss him on the cheek.

A friendly gesture.

No more than that.

What a mistake!

*

She sat in the kitchen, the same thoughts going round and round in her head till she heard the six o'clock bus rattle past. Last one of the day. She must eat something and get an early night. Work tomorrow would be hell otherwise.

But there were so many questions that couldn't be answered.

Had he thought at the party that she'd come on purpose to upset him? As though she'd turned out to be something of a stalker? Surely not.

Was the accident a result of seeing her there? Had it upset him so much? Or perhaps crashing the car had nothing to do with her and he hadn't been bothered by the whole embarrassing situation. How could she possibly know?

And of course, he wouldn't know either.

He'd lost his memory.

Chapter 17

I'm looking forward to the change. Not the most exciting trip out but I'm getting tired of trying to keep myself amused, watching television, trying to avoid work. Reaching the evening with little to show for the day. Some physio and that's certainly helped, but generally, I'm just wasting time. I've even started to play Solitaire on the computer. Then you know you've left the planet.

But most of all, I'm not ready to think about how the past has suddenly leapt into the present. It shouldn't be there. It's like a piece of a jigsaw that should fit into the picture to make it complete... but it doesn't. It's just a wayward fragment that has no place. And makes no sense.

So it's nice to climb into Dad's car at midday and be driven over to the house of my childhood, which never seems to change, and be fussed over by my mother and enjoy the cossetting. Joe is coming over this afternoon. It'll be like going back twenty-five years. Well, almost.

My dad (odd, we never call him that now – he's Bob and my mother is Nan from when Lucy was a toddler and those were the names she found easiest to pronounce, so they stuck with all of us, a habit we've never lost) well, he's cautious, drives thinking everyone else on the road is an idiot so the journey took us three quarters of an hour.

'How do you feel being in a car again?' he asks, eyes glued to the road as he crawls up to lights.

I shrug. 'I don't feel anything. It's odd. Some memories are coming back, a bit disjointed but nothing about the crash. I'm beginning to remember what it was like in the hospital, even early on but it's the nightmares mostly.'

'At least you've got rid of that plaster. Must make it easier.'

'Yes. Last week. Although it doesn't half ache. But one good thing, my hair's growing back so I'm looking human again.'

He smiles and moves so slowly on green that the car behind gives an aggressive toot to get him moving.

I can see the house needs painting and the garden is a bit overgrown but it's funny how the word 'home' still conjures up where you lived out your childhood. Even when you've had it rough, which I didn't. It's where you came from after all.

And nostalgia's a funny thing. It creates a new perspective. What I experienced, the ordinariness of it all, I now see in a totally different light. It's become a special place, a collection of pleasant memories and companionship. Secure, protective. Perhaps you just pick out the best bits, I don't know. But some homes like ours was, seem to have such a solid foundation, a stability that keeps you steady as you grow, that you never doubt its strength, its durability. You just don't question it. Joe and I had no idea how lucky we were. We certainly weren't particularly grateful in our teenage years, too busy moaning away, complaining about everything – the meals we didn't like, the boring evenings, studying, the rules we had to follow. And our parents rarely rose to the bait. They kept calm, expected good behaviour and always treated us kindly. Generously, in fact. When we stepped over the line and were brought to book, it wasn't long before we backed off and ended up feeling ashamed of ourselves. I don't know how they did it.

What helped in growing up of course, was having a brother to share it all with – and he was the one who usually took the blame for any crimes we committed. He might be two years younger, but he led the way, he was a risk-taker. We seem to have swapped personalities as adults. He's the careful, considerate husband and hands-on father to his three kids, wonderful with the youngest, Aaron, through all his difficulties and I'm certainly not a parent like that. Or the considerate

CRASH

husband. I'm not selfless and he is, concerned for others as well as family. A 'good' man – someone you're glad to have on your side.

And here we are. Home. A bay-fronted semi-detached house on a dual carriageway coming out of Manchester, no different from all the other semi-detached that stand side by side along the route. Bob brings the car to a stop on the drive and goes ahead through the front door, calling out as he holds it open for me. The smell of cooking from the kitchen fills me with a sense of déjà vu. Coming home from school or football practice, there was always something cooking, cakes or bread or chutney. Or some stew Nan had already put in the oven and always cooked for way too long; when that was on the go, Joe and I used to look at one another and roll our eyes – get ready for more soggy onions and carrots that had died in the gravy. We never dared say anything.

Today though, a special. Tuna fish pie, mashed potatoes (*'Cream in them, mind!'*), beans from the allotment and a blackberry and apple crumble. By the time Joe arrives, who's wangled the afternoon off, to finish what's left, I'm sitting in one of the high-backed chairs in the dining room, barely able to move. I hold my hand up when Nan wants me to have a chocolate.

'Good to see you eating again,' she says, as though I'd been starved for months. 'Need to build yourself up.'

'You'll be pleased to hear I'm putting on weight now. You won't be happy till I'm round and fat like I was when I was three.'

'Well, it's not good to be too thin. And you looked eighty.'

I laugh. 'Thanks. That makes me feel better!'

She bustles round, bringing out cheese and biscuits that none of us can eat, nagging Bob, even singing to herself – so nice to hear – and giving us all the details of a TV serial that none of us are able to follow. She wants to know about Jack's job, how Joe's children are doing, especially his eldest Stella, and whether her A level exams went well.

153

It's when there's a question about Aaron that a moment of hesitation changes the atmosphere, an awkwardness, a fear of saying the wrong thing.

Joe finishes his mouthful before he speaks. 'He seems a little more... settled. But then the six-week holidays come and it becomes harder to keep him on track. Anna maps things out for him day to day, but he loses concentration so quickly. You all know that.' He looks thoughtful. 'He's such a sensitive kid. Everything seems such a huge ordeal for him.'

'He's a lovely boy, Joe. Always wants to help when he comes here,' said Nan. 'I think you do wonders with him.'

'Well...'

And we all go quiet, knowing nothing we say can help ease the worry. It's all been said over the years, many times.

We move into the front room and I pick up the newspaper they always buy. Bloody rag! It never has a front page that bears any resemblance to hard news, just photos of celebrities, causes to fight for, scandals, government 'successes'. All under huge banner headlines that sensationalise and distort. I can't read it and so throw it down and Joe gives me a lopsided grin with a look – *Don't say anything* – because he knows exactly what I'm thinking.

And after a couple of hours when a lull has fallen over the afternoon, Bob dozing off in his chair, Joe decides it's time to get me some exercise. Strengthen my body, wear me out before he takes me home. So we set off.

'And we're going where?' I ask.

'Somewhere not too far and not too much for you. I thought Poynton Park.'

'Ah, good. I thought you might have me climbing Helvellyn.'

'You're not ready for that yet. Another week. Anyway,' he said, slowing down on a steep bend, 'I'll bet you'll be tired out after half an hour on the flat.'

'I'll bet I am. Are you sure you've time?'

He nods. 'Anything to bring you back to life, brother.'

So we park and begin walking. The path is sandy and even and takes us round a large expanse of lake, tall reeds bent over with the wind growing in feathery clusters near the bank, small yellow flowers almost hidden beneath. On the opposite side, huge old trees drop heavily laden branches that touch the water. And as we follow the track, it widens onto a sloping bank, with geese strutting over the grass, ponderous and greedy, jabbing at the earth.

I take it all in, gratefully. To be out in the fresh air, to be on my feet, to have Joe's easy company.

'Mum was in a good mood,' he says. 'She was pleased to see you eating and chatting away. More yourself.'

'They seemed OK, didn't they?' I want reassurance. I know the heartache I caused them and feel guilty about that.'

'Yes. Dad's a bit forgetful, but that's... his age.'

I can feel Joe is ready to say something and I glance over at him. 'What?'

'The one you should be worried about is me.' He gives a sort of laugh, apologetic. 'I thought you were going to die.'

'Christ. I know it was bad...'

'Alex, you've no idea. I sat by your bed one afternoon and you lay there so damned still. Those machines... I was counting the seconds between each breath you took. I kept thinking, this could be the end of us. And later, when I was rubbing your legs to get the blood circulating like the nurse told me to do...' He stops walking and stares up at the sky. 'You're so close when you grow up with someone, everything about them is so familiar... even the shape of...'

I don't want him to go on. 'Joe, I'm here. Alive. It doesn't even look as though there's any lasting damage.' I've already turned towards him and can't bear to see the anguish in his face. His forehead is all lines and his eyes are too bright. I'm desperate to pull

155

us back to somewhere lighter. 'We've got another forty years getting on each other's nerves, so look on the bright side, you daft bugger, and cheer up.'

I sound as though I haven't got a grain of sympathy in my body but he knows me so well, nods and sniffs and starts walking again, carefully avoiding the dark green goose droppings that litter the path.

But he's got more to say. 'I know it's none of my business, Alex...'

Here goes, I think – you can bet it's something I don't want to hear. 'Go on.'

He doesn't begin straight away. But eventually, he surprises me. 'I've been worried about you for a lot longer than a couple of months. Well, not worried but... You'd grown quiet, is the only way I can put it. Not just before the accident. I'd say from when you hit forty. You seemed to lose your drive, your interest in things, your sense of fun. I don't mean like a mid-life crisis – I don't believe in those anyway. You can have a crisis at any age. But you sort of removed yourself. I'm not explaining it very well. But I know you better than anyone I think, and there was something that changed.'

I stare at him. Of course he'd notice. However I answer this, it'll have to sound plausible. 'Well, I suppose I focused too much on the job. I'd just got a promotion and the responsibility at times weighed a bit heavy. And you start to wonder if you've made the right choices. Should you change companies, would that mean moving, you know? I was trying to keep too many balls in the air...' I can't go on. Only some of this is true but it isn't the heart of the matter.

'Well,' he says, 'you can have a good rest from work now and stop beating yourself up. Get back to enjoying life instead of wasting it earning money. There's so much more.'

Now he's said his piece, he seems happier.

We walk on, both of us relieved, I think, to leave the subject behind us. Joe leads the way but makes a sudden stop as he slides on a clump of moss and bangs into me. 'Should have put on shoes with a grip,' he says. 'In fact, I actually bought some walking boots last week. Thought I might take up hiking again. We did quite a bit of that when you came home from uni in the holidays. We even did some fell walking.'

'Yeah. We were young. Now we're two middle-aged men trundling along at a snail's pace. What it's like to be past it!'

'Speak for yourself,' he says, and the years drop away in the long-established banter. 'I think we should think seriously about getting ourselves fit. We could even buy a couple of bikes and get out on the open road.'

I laugh. 'I've only got one useful arm at the moment. Don't think "cycling" and "open road" would sound too good to Carrie.'

'No, perhaps not. But we could walk. Be good to do something together.'

I understand. He needs us to readjust so we're in touch again, without wives, without children. Just us, as it used to be. I find myself nodding in agreement. Your whole outlook changes when you face something that shatters your complacency. I know mine has. The threat shocks you into recognising the fragility of existence. You're not immortal. What a surprise!

We round the top of the lake towards the mass of trees that line the bank with their huge trunks and spreading overhang making it more difficult to navigate here and narrowing the path. We still just manage to walk side by side and I feel the moment's right to ask the questions that can only be asked of him.

I'm not sure how much to say so I'm hesitant, trying to tread carefully. 'Joe, I need some help here.'

He looks at me expectantly. 'Go on.'

'Well, my memory seems to be coming back in patches, so I'm not sure always of the sequence of events or whether what I *think* happened, actually did.' I push through a tangle of brambles which catch at my trousers then get back into step with him. 'Those few days before the accident… I can remember a bit about getting ready for the party… putting Sam's basket in the garage before the guests arrived and shutting him in – some odd people don't like dogs and anyway, he'd have eaten all the sausages!' I'm trying to sound casual when that's the last thing I feel. 'Colin came over, offering to help as I was frying the steaks and I remember getting really hot. Rolling up my sleeves. I had a glass of beer balanced on the table next to me…'

'Yes. Colin brought some bread buns over and Jack was going round seeing everyone had a drink.'

I stay silent. There must be more.

Joe begins prompting me. 'There were lights all over the garden. In the trees. Music was coming from the house, some eighties stuff, and Meryl, that friend of Carrie's, her husband was speaking very loudly about the benefits of public schooling.'

'Don't remember that. Just as well.'

Of course, I'm stalling. Waiting for my cue.

'Your next-door neighbour came in with a strawberry cake and we had a hard time keeping Aaron from diving into it before she got it into the kitchen.' He looked wistful for a moment. 'He so enjoyed that party. Normally all those people would have been too much for him but Steph was really good. She made up some sort of treasure hunt and kept him amused.'

'Some of it's still a bit of a blur.' I'm frowning, wondering what else I can say. What is it I want to hear? 'I remember it was a warm night…'

'It was. And just before we were going to eat, you were getting impatient because Lucy hadn't arrived. Then in the nick of time, she turned up with some friends.'

'Late as always.' I try to sound nonchalant. 'Was one in a white dress?'

'Yes, that's right. Good looking. Anna kept saying she had

amazing eyes.' He grinned at me. 'Not surprised you remember *her*. They all went off to a nightclub at the end.'

The images of the evening fill my head, details that had escaped me.

'But you haven't remembered the car crash?' says Joe. 'Or what could have led up to it?'

'No. Nothing about that. Or where I was going. And very little until I started to wake up in the hospital. Who knows whether it'll ever come back.'

'Don't worry about it. If it does, OK. But if it doesn't, there's not a lot you can do about it.'

We amble on, Joe happy that he's been a help, I know, not hindered by guilt or misgivings. Me? Well – plenty of guilt and misgivings.

Later I'm lying in bed in the guest room, for once not taking any pain relief, glad that I'm sleeping on my own. Shutting that door at night lets me have my own space. I'm beginning to welcome it.

I lie on my back and close my eyes and see the expression on her face when she realised whose house she was in. Who Lucy's father was. She certainly hadn't planned for *that* sort of reunion. It would have been the last thing she'd do. Not after all these years.

But that look on her lovely face, that unbelieving, stunned look when our eyes met shook me to the core. In my memory she'd always been laughing, teasing me, full of life. And here she was, probably in the last place she'd choose to be, staring at the man who'd let her down so badly, unable to do anything but act out a nightmare.

I can't forgive myself for causing her such pain a second time.

Chapter 18

Six o'clock. It's the light that's different at this time of the morning, Carrie thought; even in summer, there's dew on the grass and damp in the air that makes everything seem fresh. She could breathe. The walk down to the farm was an excuse really. Yes, she needed eggs, but Steph could have brought a dozen up when she came to work.

She'd woken two hours before and couldn't get back to sleep so climbing out of bed, leaving the house, *doing* something, was her way of giving her a purpose that didn't just involve reacting to others, being a cipher for everyone's problems and demands. She wasn't cut out for the role of 'carer'. Or for carrying the burden of everything on her shoulders when there were three of them in the house. It made her tetchy.

She wished she'd handled last night better, though. All right saying that in hindsight. But it had felt like one problem after another and by the time the phone call came from her mother, she'd had enough. She'd got to the point where she was past caring what anyone thought. Beyond caring about keeping everyone else happy.

It had been a difficult day and by the time they sat down to the evening meal – seven o'clock and Carrie past being interested in eating – she was already irritable. No-one seemed to be doing anything to help and it all landed on her shoulders. She wanted things back to normal, a routine, shared responsibility, everyone pulling their weight. And as weeks went on, she was beginning to resent her role in all this. For a start, she wanted a partner... not a dependant, which is what Alex seemed to be now.

It was an easy meal to prepare – lemon chicken in butter and parsley. An old favourite. Alex and Jack were drinking orange juice, she was on the red wine. After one glass, a nice Chilean Merlot, just what she needed, she could feel the muscles in her shoulders loosening. It began to cancel out the stress of the day. No wonder people became alcoholics, she thought.

By the time the food had been dished up, Alex was already asking Jack about the job at Parsons, taking more interest than he ever seemed to show in what she was doing. She poured herself a second glass and waited for them to move on to more general topics. *There's only so much you can say about working in a farm shop.*

'So does the manager leave you to it?' Alex was asking.

'Pretty much. There's a lot of stock to get your head round but most of the customers want fairly ordinary stuff, lawn feeder, fence panels, pet food.'

'You seem to have picked it up pretty quickly.'

'Well, it's not difficult…'

'No. ' She cut him short. She didn't seem to be able to stop herself. 'I can't imagine it would be.'

They both stopped eating and stared at her, as though to say — *What brought that on?* She shrugged and pulled a face. 'Sorry, that came out all wrong.'

Alex narrowed his eyes, paused and put down his fork. 'It certainly did.'

Jack gave an embarrassed laugh. No humour in it. 'I know it's not great as far as jobs go. But at least I'm earning. Pays twice as much as the pub. It'll do for the time being.'

Alex got up from the table, the food barely touched. 'Not hungry now, sorry.' And went into the lounge, leaving the two of them to finish their meal in silence, just the click of the cutlery on the plates. Carrie hadn't the energy, or the will, to make amends for creating an atmosphere. For heaven's sake, she was only speaking the truth. You can't *pretend* everything your kids do is wonderful. It doesn't do them any good.

Sod it! She poured herself another glass of wine.

Alex was really annoying her for pandering to Jack, building him up when that wasn't what he needed. Yes, he was a lovely boy, he was good-natured, everyone liked him but that wasn't going to get him anywhere. Both Alex and Joe were achievers, so was Lucy, and they'd always be secure in jobs that paid well and had… esteem.

She couldn't just let it lie.

She finished eating and went into the lounge, standing over Alex till he looked up from the newspaper and met her eyes. He didn't say anything. He didn't have to, his whole manner conveyed hostility. Was he waiting for her to apologise? Well, tough luck on that one.

'You're not helping him,' she said, folding her arms ready for the argument that was certainly coming.

'Oh? How's that?' His voice was steely.

'Praising him for some mediocre achievement is doing more harm than good. He's 22, he's never stuck at anything and you're making out this job is equivalent to getting a PhD.' She tried to keep her voice down, but she was annoyed. 'This job is going nowhere. Get things in perspective, Alex. If he doesn't go back to studying, get some qualification, then he's…'

She could see the anger in his eyes but didn't quite realise until too late that she'd gone too far.

'Oh, right!' He seemed to be having difficulty controlling the tremor in his voice. 'So the only way to prove you're any good is to have a doctorate or a degree! Look at the millions of people who earn a damned good living every day being practical – builders, electricians, farmers, shop managers – people we all rely on to keep the wheels turning.'

'Well, I'm not saying—'

'What *are* you saying, Carrie?' He stood up then, frowning, his eyes set. 'He's not an academic – never will be – but he'll be all right.

Because his heart's in the right place and he *wants* to work.' He was ready to move past her. 'Does a degree and a career make me happy? Of course it bloody doesn't! There's so much more to life than qualifications.'

He turned as he reached the door. 'And what about *your* qualifications? Ah yes, of course. Nearly forgot! You had a father who left you money to start your own business.' He smiled sarcastically. 'Well, we can't all be that lucky.'

Carrie stared after him, shocked and close to tears. She sat down on the sofa, shaking her head, at first unable to understand the venom in the assault. That last remark was below the belt and it wasn't like him. OK, she'd been tactless but no more than that, surely. And it wasn't as though Jack hadn't known for a long time how she felt about his lack of drive. She had cause to be a bit hard on him. Hadn't she?

And her excuse for her remark at the table, she told herself, was that she'd let her frustration spill out after a bad day. But she knew she'd spoken out of turn.

She went back into the kitchen, empty now, dirty plates on the table, a fly buzzing at the closed window, and put some coffee on, carrying it out into the garden to nurse her injured feelings. *Well, you have days like that,* she thought. From the morning, the day seemed doomed. The blacksmith had put off shoeing two horses badly in need of attention till later in the week (the owners disgruntled with *her*), a whole bale of haylage had been wrapped badly, letting in water, making it too musty to use. That went on the muck heap.

And then the ride had been a disaster. Even though the conditions were perfect.

Midday and wisps of cloud were high in a blue sky, there was barely a breeze and the ground had softened. She decided she had time to take Merlin over the bridle path at Hills and go round one field where the crop had been cut early. She set off up the road, comfortable as always in the saddle, reins held loosely in her hands, anticipating the pleasure of the hour ahead. There was something about being on a horse that made her feel complete.

But halfway along the stony path before she passed the sheep field, just as she was manoeuvring through a gate, the horse caught his rump on the metal closing bar; he jerked forward and ripped flesh in a long welt along his side. She jumped to the ground and could see immediately the damage was more than superficial. It needed stitching.

She realised she was probably more upset than the horse who stood placidly, rubbing his nose on his leg. But there was no way she could get back on him. She'd have to put the reins over his head and walk him home down the track and then along the road. It was a slow process and warm work. At least two passing drivers were concerned enough to turn down their windows and call out to her, '*Do you want any help?*' She waved them on and kept going, thankful when she could turn into her gate. She stabled him, bathed the wound, rang the vet and waited.

She leaned against the half-door and looked up at the sky. The weather was still perfect.

Her frame of mind was far from it.

And then there was David. Demanding. And interfering. Never able to keep his opinions to himself. It was just after the vet had come and gone, leaving antibiotic powders and advising box rest for a few days, when he crossed the yard, leaving Jodie pushing a barrow that was far too heavy for her.

He always walked in a purposeful way, always well-turned out, not a hair out of place and with such an air of self-confidence about him that assumed he could answer all questions, solve all problems. It was odd. His whole manner irritated Carrie yet she had to admit there were times recently when that certainty was reassuring. Especially when at home, Alex seemed unable to take any positive action about anything.

He ignored Steph, who'd come back to help Carrie hold the horse while the vet stitched the wound, shouldering her aside. And then came the advice that hadn't been asked for. 'If you want a second opinion, Carrie, my vet is Karl Westerfield and you can't get any better than that.'

You can't get any more expensive either. 'It's fine, David. There's no infection, so it'll heal; he just has to take it easy. Staying in for three days. It won't kill him.'

David nodded. But whether he was listening or not, she wasn't sure. He seemed to pull everyone and everything into his force field and didn't register any resistance. Yes, solicitous he could be. And she liked the fact that he was confident and direct. But, lately, more and more, he seemed to want to take charge. Of everything and everybody.

It made her wary.

She went to refill the water bucket from the outside tap and he followed her.

'I would have ridden with you. You've only got to say.'

She gave him her nicest smile. 'I like riding on my own. Honestly. It gives me time to think.'

He stood beside her and turned the tap off when the bucket was full.

'You're finding it tough, aren't you?'

'What?'

'Helping your husband recover,' he said, looking concerned. Whether the expression was genuine, she didn't know. 'I saw him the other day getting into a car on your drive. He didn't look very steady on his feet.'

Not much she could say to refute that. 'It'll take time, that's all.' She stood up, straightening her back. 'I'm fine. You do what you have to do. Things will get back to normal in the next few weeks. The scans show no permanent damage and he's having regular physiotherapy.'

He studied her face. 'Good. So things are easier.' He bent down and carried the bucket back over the yard. 'I was going to suggest a way of paying you back for helping Jodie. A token of my appreciation. D'you want to hear what it is?'

Carrie wasn't at all sure she did.

'Well, a friend got me tickets for a one-day event at Brampton the week after next and I'd like to invite you as my guest. Fancy lunch, champagne, or the pretend stuff – you can dress to kill… And the marquee's right next to the show-jumping ring, so we'll have a grandstand view.'

'Oh, that's really kind of you, David, but—'

'No buts. I owe you and I always pay my debts.'

He left her with a slight bow of his head, not waiting for a response. She felt steamrollered! However attractive the proposition might be, she didn't like being pressured like this. She wished he'd never come with his damned horse and his needy daughter.

But she had an idea that the man wasn't going to take 'no' for an answer.

*

And then the final straw! After the awkward evening meal and the silence that followed, after Alex had gone to his room and Jack had disappeared, probably to the pub (although it wasn't his night on), after she'd spent an hour brooding over all the things in her life she seemed to be losing control of, the house phone rang. Loud and shrill through the quiet house, nine o'clock and she'd been so wrapped up in her thoughts that she hadn't even turned the lights on or closed the French windows. The urgency of the high-pitched ringing made her jump.

She didn't even bother to look at the caller ID, just picked up the receiver and automatically recited her number.

'Carrie.' The voice was breathy and deep.

She didn't need to hear any more than her name, even though so much time had passed. There was only one person who sounded like that.

'Mother.' She waited. Whatever she said would sound insincere but she steeled herself to sound unfazed. 'How nice to hear from you. It must be three years. How are you?'

'Fine as always, Carrie. I'll never slow down, you'll be glad to hear. I'm ringing because…' a dramatic pause… 'I'd like you to come and have lunch with me at the Plaza. It's not immediate. I have to come to Manchester to sort out some legal matters and thought it best to give you plenty of warning.'

'I don't think so, Mother,' she began. 'Not much point really.'

Carrie's stomach was churning just listening to that voice. The last thing she wanted was lunch with her mother. Or any meal, for that matter. It would mean she had to confront all the hurt and confusion that was normally hidden away, all the cruel carelessness of words that should have been forgotten. Why, she thought, do we always remember painful moments of childhood with such clarity, moments that stay with you and somehow influence how you see yourself long after they should have been forgotten? She could still hear her mother telling her as she got ready for bed one night, that she was *almost pretty, but sadly, you have the hair of a witch. It's like a head full of snakes.'*

So much for her mother's dislike of curly hair!

At ten, you take it to heart.

'It'll probably be October, Carrie. I'll phone a few days before. Hope you're all well.' And she hung up. Not bothering to wait for a reply or listening – she was never good at that. The only decent thing her mother ever did was leave. Boarding school and holidays with her father were adequate compensation for her departure. More than adequate! It was a godsend.

But, however you looked at it, this hadn't been a good day – now there were two invitations, handed out within hours of each other, that Carrie felt pressured to accept.

She went out into the garden and Sam paddled towards her, looking hopeful for the habitual bedtime treat. He panted hot breath on her arm as she stroked his ears. She walked him to the gate and looked back at the house, unlit and somehow bereft of life. She'd been hoping Jack would come home before she went to bed. She could at least say something positive. The thought that she was turning into her mother was a sobering prospect.

But he hadn't come home early enough…

Now, in the early morning light before anyone was up, she wanted to be by herself. No-one to interrupt her train of thought. She knew she was feeling so resentful because some things were getting beyond her control. But, good heavens, she needed to gain perspective here. OK, so Alex wasn't exactly grabbing life with both hands and being decisive the way *she* would have been, and Jack might be a disappointment in some ways and Lucy was capable of doing another U-turn, but life didn't always turn out the way you wanted it.

So for God's sake, she told herself, *stop whinging! Just try a bit of tolerance and be kinder… to everyone.*

She reached the farm, picked up the eggs from their little homemade house by the gate, put her money in the Honesty Box and headed back up the hill.

Chapter 19

J ack was glad to be at work. He'd been sensing the build-up to a row before the evening meal last night. He could always tell the mood his mother was in from the way she moved about the kitchen or closed doors with a bang, but mostly from the set expression on her face, a way of ignoring what was around her and not making eye contact. It was unnerving, even though he knew it wouldn't last. He often wished Lucy was still at home to help bear the brunt of it, the lull (if you could call it that) before the storm. But this time, he realised he wasn't really the cause. Just the one to take the bullet. It had begun earlier in the week.

The start of it was on Tuesday and her exasperation with his dad, apparently because he'd spent too long with his head in a book when he should have been ordering meat from the farm shop to pick up later. Just as Jack was coming back in with Sam from a slow trip round the field he heard her saying, 'I ask you to do one thing…' and his dad's quiet, measured reply. He stopped short, nearly turning round again to take the dog for a longer walk but there was Sam, tongue hanging out and a look in his old eyes that said, *I've had enough*, so he thought better of it.

Then there was her reaction to finding the £400 receipt for the mobile that he'd left on top of the fridge. He should have put it in the box with the phone when he'd handed it over to his dad, but he hadn't. When she saw it, he was cutting up some fruit by the sink.

'What's this?' She was frowning at the slip of paper as if it were some dreadful school report he'd hidden from her and there was a reckoning to come. He certainly remembered those!

He didn't even look up from slicing the strawberries. 'Dad's new mobile. He gave me his card to get him one and organise a new contract. His was lost in the crash.'

'I know that,' she said, still examining the receipt, but what else she could find on such a small piece of paper, Jack hadn't the faintest idea. She hadn't finished. 'It seems very expensive. And why was he in such a hurry to buy another one?'

He shrugged. 'No idea.'

She waited for him to go on. As though he was keeping something back. 'Did he tell you to pay that much?'

'He left it to me.' He put the bowl on the table and sat down, trying to put an end to the conversation. Or was it an interrogation? Why was he getting hassle over something he'd been told to do? 'You can't get a decent one any cheaper. Not unless you go into these contracts where you don't own the phone. He wanted to buy one.'

And that's how it had been. One thing after another seemed to cause a bit of a situation and he couldn't quite see what was bugging her. When his dad had first come out of hospital, there'd been peace – a really nice atmosphere, the only important thing was making sure nothing caused problems for the 'patient', as she'd called him. *Help him to the chair, pass him the newspaper, get him a glass of lime juice.* But not now. The 'patient' had become a target. She was pissed off whether he *didn't* do anything or whether he *did* something. And Jack got the same treatment.

You just couldn't win.

So the uncomfortable atmosphere at the meal last night didn't take him by surprise. The food was good, at least. His mother said barely anything and it ended up with him and his dad talking as though they were the only two at the table. It was when he'd said the job wasn't really difficult that she'd come out with the hammer blow. Not just the words, but the icy tone – *'I can't imagine it **would** be.'* He choked on a bit of chicken and had to take a drink. Not a lot you could say to follow that. They all seemed to freeze. It was like a stopped clock. An absence of sound.

His dad was furious. He'd just got up from the table, his dinner barely started, and left the room. Jack had witnessed it before, this sudden fury from someone normally so easy going, had watched how he could flip when faced with something he found totally unacceptable, something blatantly unjust or cruel. Jack had been shocked seeing it for the first time when he was quite small. They'd been walking through the wooded edge of the park and had come across some boys playing in the bushes. It was what they were playing *with* that sent his dad into an explosive rage. They were throwing live frogs against a tree and laughing as the poor things splattered and fell. By the time his father had sprung between them, yelling in fury, the boys weren't laughing any more.

So, in a silence you could cut with a knife, the meal continued, the two left at the table studiously ignoring each other. Jack wasn't going to lift his eyes from the plate, he was horribly embarrassed and when his mother got up to follow his dad into the next room, he wanted to close his ears. But he could hear enough. Back to the old story, no qualifications, going nowhere and those awful words... *'he's never stuck at anything'.*

He wasn't going to wait for the rest . He'd bet his dad would stand up for him but he didn't want to listen to a row. He'd go out. Anywhere, down to the pub, anywhere. He'd made for the door and shut it behind him, ashamed of the tears welling up in his eyes as he headed down the hill to The Fox and Hounds. Somewhere he could feel comfortable.

But when he reached the few cars parked near the entrance, he couldn't face it. He'd have to pretend it was just a casual drop-in and the effort *that* would involve was too wearing. And Leo was so quick to notice things, he'd be guessing the full story before Jack had said more than a few words.

So he walked past the pub along the path which skirted the river, then climbed up to the high part where the local authority had tried to build a partial flood bank. It was more a gesture than a practical solution, as it wasn't likely to be tested. The river had never risen that far up to be a threat to anyone.

The evening air was warm and the sky streaked with wreaths of pink as the sun dropped towards the horizon. Off to the right, Jack could see lights from a farm house with its grain store and machinery shed and sprawling outhouses. Steph's farm. He imagined the family sitting together round the television watching some comedy programme before heading off to bed.

He climbed down to a gap in the hedge bordering the first field and pushed through, walking along a channel in the stubble where the baler had flattened the crop. He knew the place well. As a teenager, short of money, he'd helped Will with the harvesting and for a few years when they'd gone into pigs, he'd done some of the feeding. That was an eye-opener! Intelligent pigs might be, brutal if you got in their way.

By the time he'd reached the eight huge round hay bales lined up at the side of the last field, he was close enough to hear the cars going along the road and stopped in the fading light, no desire to return home yet. There was no-one around so he lowered himself onto the earth, his back against the stack and stared up at the sky.

So much better being by himself.

He needed to grow up, he decided. Stop being so bloody sensitive. It was no good feeling hurt and sorry for himself. That wouldn't get him anywhere. And thinking back over the last few weeks, he began to realise that perhaps he wasn't the only one who was struggling. Perhaps *no-one* knew where they were going.

Take Terry who'd always seemed a winner, always seemed to head upwards and onwards with such ease taking all the right steps – through school, on to university, good job in accountancy. Bingo! That sounded like success to Jack. Except when they'd met again after he'd missed the anniversary party, Terry had sounded… disillusioned. What had he said? *Things don't always work out how you think they're going to.'*

They'd been friends since Jack had arrived at the secondary school when the family had just moved out of Manchester and he hadn't known anyone in the new neighbourhood. But Terry had sort of taken him under his wing and although they weren't even in the same class, they both loved football and played every lunch time and eventually for the village boys' team, in fact spending more time together out of school than in it. Terry wasn't a show-off and he was funny, didn't let much get him down and he never seemed to notice that he was a high-flyer and Jack was… well… failing at everything except sport. The difference in their ability was never mentioned but Jack had realised long before he'd joined the comprehensive that he wasn't going to find learning easy, that he wasn't going to jump effortlessly through the hoops, that he would always fall short.

His first experience of school had taught him that. At five years old, it had all been pleasant enough but he was aware early on of the dividing lines. Even though it isn't spelt out, every child knows their place in the whole scheme of things, he thought.

He remembered his first day, entering the Victorian brick building in a district of Manchester that had long been redeveloped. A church school, small, just one class in each year – there were so few pupils it had closed some years later and been converted into a house (Jack had driven past it when he first got his car and was amazed to see it still looked like a school because the large front window with its small leaded panes of glass was still in place). But whatever the building was like – dimly lit with high ceilings and poorly heated in winter, what was good about it was the feeling of belonging. Someone usually had a brother or sister in a higher class – and Lucy had been there for two years before him, so at five, he was part of it.

The reception teacher, Miss Hardesty, was kind and cheerful and spoke very slowly. She wore long skirts that made her appear to be floating and had piled-up hair that didn't stay piled-up and red cheeks. She fascinated Jack, who listened to every word she said with as much concentration as he could muster. It seemed to him as though she'd stepped out of a picture book, a sort of fully grown rag doll.

And even though she made him feel cherished, even though he was very young, he understood where he stood in the order of things. He'd sat with three others at a table near the front, close to Miss Hardesty's desk. She'd spend extra time showing them how to form letters, how to sound out words, explain things twice; even then, when the others in the class would call out answers to *two plus four* or how to spell a word, he was still working it out. And the six children who knew everything sat at… (it was never named but everyone knew) …The Top Table.

How much does that play into your view of yourself? he thought. *Do you just measure up to what people expect of you? No, that's a get-out, really. There's more to it.* He could have done much better, tried harder but by the time he got to the comprehensive he'd switched off. History was OK but you didn't learn anything about the Second World War – he'd learned about that from watching old films with his dad. Maths was just difficult – what practical use were equations and the area of a sector? And French… don't even go there! He was wasting his time. No interest, no aptitude, no appetite for any of it. He chose to drop out.

But Terry of course had soared through the exams – nine GCSEs and on to the sixth form. The brains to study anything. Nothing stopping him. So why, when by all accounts he'd made a success of it all, did he feel discontented now?

Jack had been envious of him when, finding himself in an apprenticeship he didn't enjoy, he could see that Terry was '*going somewhere*', which is how the head had put it on Awards Day when the certificates were handed out.

By then though, Jack had already met Grace which made up for it all. Grace, who read books and did drama and loved going to the Royal Exchange and to art galleries. Serious, hard-working, always *doing* something. His total opposite. He hadn't even noticed her until study leave just before their last exams. It was June and a humid afternoon when he'd been walking across the school playing field to go swimming. He passed three girls who were studying or making a good attempt at it and she'd been lying prone on a rug, a sheaf of notes under her nose, glasses perched on top of her head. She didn't even look up but one of the others called after him. 'Hi Jack! Coming to the end-of-term do?'

A long time ago. Someone else who was *'going somewhere'.*

But there she was, the other day. A surprise in more ways than one. He'd never thought she'd come back to this neck of the woods. But even *she* had hit a stumbling block and after always doing well at anything she'd tried, she'd been made to falter and rethink. And from what Sylvie had said, she thought she was back where she belonged.

So it wasn't that simple then. He wasn't the only one who felt uncertain, unclear whether you'd chosen the right path, or not chosen at all. Whichever route you took, you couldn't expect to win all the time. And if his mother thought he was a loser then let her think it. His form tutor at school had once said to him when he was down about some bitchy remark a girl had made about him – *'You should only worry about the opinions of people who you value. The others don't matter.'*

Well, he didn't want to go into *that* too deeply.

He'd spent long enough like some social misfit with no home to go to, staring into space. He heaved himself to his feet and brushed dried soil off his trousers. It was late. He just hoped they hadn't locked him out.

And at work the next day, he was content to just be, satisfied with what he was doing at that very moment instead of wishing his life away. If this wasn't the best job in the world or the most demanding, at least he could enjoy it for now. For what it was. Not too demanding, he thought, but it was a satisfying way to spend the day.

*

When the text came through from Tom calling for an extraordinary meeting of the Conservation group on the following Wednesday night, Jack tried to quell his excitement. Fran would be there. Of course she would. He was going to miss the next Sunday session because of the work schedule at Parsons, but now he had a chance of seeing her. They were to meet in the back room of a pub up at Alderley Edge.

He arrived early enough to choose a seat on the bench that put him in the middle, a fair chance that when they were all gathered round the table, he'd be close enough to speak to her.

Eight of them eventually gathered in the room, some he hadn't met before. Tom was reassuring everyone that Rosie was fine, she'd had a tetanus jab and the stitching had just been those white strips they put on to hold the wound together and although she wasn't coming tonight, she'd sent her thanks to everyone for their concern.

OK, thought Jack. *Good.*

Five minutes to get in the drinks and bring them back to the table.

No Fran.

'I've called this meeting,' Tom began, opening his notebook and making sure everyone was listening, 'because all our tools were stolen out of my garage four days ago.' A murmur of disquiet went round the group. 'We're insured, you'll be pleased to hear, but we all need to make some decisions on the best way to replenish the stock. No good buying tools that we don't really need. And some'll have to be second hand.'

The meeting went on, with discussions that should have taken a few minutes but dragged on for two hours. Most of it was necessary, he supposed, but it was so slow. Did everyone have to have their say on every point? If Fran had been there, it would have made all the difference. But by the time they'd packed up and gone out into the car park, he felt he never wanted to attend another meeting. Why do committees always have to go round in circles, be so long-winded?

He sat in his car and knew before he turned on the ignition what he was going to do. He'd drive over to Whitegate, just pass through and see if she was there. See if a light was on in her house. Totally senseless, but he would do it anyway.

He didn't even turn the radio on as he drove through the roads, then the lanes across to her village, hardly on his way home. He didn't even kid himself about that! As he approached the converted barns, he began slowing down, just enough to look over at her house, see if she was home.

It reminded him of when he and Terry were teenagers and they'd go out on their bikes and ride along the streets of the girls they fancied. Juvenile idiocy.

He noticed a car parked at the pavement near the opening to her house, a red Astra but he didn't know whether it was hers or not. He moved out into the middle of the road to pass it and bent his head lower so he could see if there was a light on.

Yes, there was. So she'd chosen not to come to the meeting.

There wasn't much he could make of that. What on earth had he expected there would be? He'd just wasted another hour of his life he wouldn't get back.

Chapter 20

August was always a strange month. Low demand and long days waiting for September when the work force would get back to full strength. In the meantime, families were heading off to Spain and Turkey and other hot spots while they had the chance, leaving the streets and restaurants of Liverpool half empty. No-one was hiring or firing in the school holidays. So as Fran expected, all was quiet. A hiatus in what had been a busy year.

She parked the car and made her way over a small square to her office on the second floor of the grey tower block in the heart of the Commercial District. It was in a good position, the centre of business and yet she always thought she could smell the Mersey from here. And it was close enough to the docks to quickly reach some of the fancy shops that lined the quay.

She climbed the stairs and opened up her office – F.R. Recruitment Agency printed on the door glass in silver letters – and turned on the lights. It was always dark, even on a bright day and she often wondered whether the people who designed these buildings ever considered what it would be like to occupy them day after day. Still, it always pleased her to see how neat and functional her two rooms were – reception as you entered, desk centre facing the door, promotional posters and job advertisements displayed on two white screen dividers and pinned to the wall board, letters of satisfaction from clients and applicants. It conveyed an air of professional expertise and she knew how important first impressions had to be.

Beyond the reception area was her office. Pale blue carpet, a larger desk with a computer console behind it, softer lighting from two arched Scandinavian lamps and lining one wall, bookshelves that

178

reached the ceiling. Blinds, blue-grey, always lowered halfway as though inferring this was a place of privacy, which kept the outside world at bay. Just long enough to get the business done of finding the right job or discussing payments. Two chairs for the clients had been placed facing the desk at angles.

Fran picked up the post and walked across the room to check on her desk diary. Only two appointments booked in but often, people seeking jobs would just pop in on the off-chance hoping there might be something that would suit them. Then Jill, Fran's indispensable colleague and friend (what would she do without her!) would greet them in reception and help them fill in forms, or complete tests on the computer, or follow up on references. In the winter, when illnesses left firms short-staffed and they needed workers, the agency was sending out forty to fifty temps a week. A few years' hard work had paid off.

'We're getting known,' Jill had said in February when they were at their busiest and a large clothes outlet had asked for three assistants – '*Make it for an indefinite period*,' the man from Human Resources had said – with Jill convinced it could lead to permanent jobs which they could bill the company for.

'We are,' Fran had nodded. 'But that flat period in July and August always pulls us down. We'll have to see whether this year's any better.'

And it hadn't been so far.

Jill came through the office door, breathing heavily as though she'd been running. 'Someone took my favourite parking spot,' she called out to Fran as she took off her jacket. 'And then I didn't have the right change for the machine, so it's thrown out my timing for the day.'

Fran smiled and came out of her room. 'Don't know what you're panicking for. You've got all day to catch up. We're hardly busy.'

Jill nodded. 'Well, I wanted to check on Mrs. Thomas at the

printing shop. She was nervous about her first day and I think she'd be glad of a friendly phone call to reassure her.'

'She'll be fine, Jill. You can't mother them all.'

'I know. It's become a habit.'

'How about a cup of coffee before we start? I can't ring any of the clients before nine anyway and then we need to talk about you having a few days off.'

Fran went across the corridor to the kitchen and toilet which they shared with an independent book publishers, hoping they'd cleared up their cups and not left some Pot Noodle Chow Mein in the microwave. No, it was tidy. She put the kettle on, made coffee for them both and set the mugs down on Jill's desk.

'Let's go over those advertising pitches before anything else. We're going to have to make some decisions today.'

Jill pulled out various large envelopes, opened them and displayed them on her desk. 'It's a lot of money to spend for one month. I'm not sure it's worth it.'

'Neither am I. But we can't just go for the cheapest. Let's cut it down to the two best and then decide.'

By the time they'd studied the different bids and Fran had gone back to her room to make the morning phone calls to clients, checking whether the temps had arrived and were doing what they were meant to be doing, it was ten o'clock. Her first appointment wasn't till eleven thirty. She'd so much rather be busy. Better to be occupied than going over and over the same questions that were tormenting her and getting her nowhere.

Come on, until you know more there's nothing you can do about any of it. You just have to wait.

But the image of Alex standing by that barbecue kept coming into her mind.

He hadn't looked that much older. The same unruly dark hair, the weathered face, the raised eyebrows as though he was about to ask a question and, even more distinctive – the way he carried himself, relaxed, adapting to wherever he found himself, a lack of tension about him. Until that moment when he saw her.

She kept reliving with such clarity how the adrenaline rush coursed through her body when their eyes met – the same shock, the same horror at finding themselves in the most unlikely situation, his expression a mirror image of her own. Talk about frozen in time! It was a second, a mere second but it felt like a still from a film, the imprint burnt on her brain.

She noticed, of course, that his face was more lined and he looked a little heavier (she'd always thought he was too thin) but otherwise he was the same. Pretty much as she'd first seen him...

She'd been having lunch in a pub off Victoria Street, one she sometimes went to for the midday break, usually with Linda. They both worked at an insurance broker's, sitting at neighbouring desks, bored out of their minds with the tedious tasks they were asked to do and needing to get out of the place as often as they could to stay sane. The Talbot was the closest eating place that did toasted sandwiches and paninis, which is what they preferred, as well as proper meals, and it never seemed too busy if they got there early when there was enough room to grab seats near the window and chat without feeling rushed.

It was February, a Wednesday, and they were finishing their lunch, facing the bar and also the entrance when Alex entered. She had no idea who he was or what he was doing there, but he caught her attention because it was raining outside and as he came through the door, he shook his hair like a wet dog, showering water drops over one of the waitresses who was passing, carrying a plate of food.

Fran could hear him apologising, nice voice, nice smile. And that was it.

A few weeks later she was sitting alone in her usual place (Linda had to stay in the office to finish a quote that was needed for that afternoon) eating her way through a basket of mozzarella sticks and dipping sauce and in he came. He went straight to the bar, bought a beer and ordered fish and chips, which would be ten minutes, the barmaid told him. When he turned to find a place to sit, pulling off his coat, he headed for the empty bench along from her, nodding a greeting of sorts in her direction.

When he'd settled down, he'd pulled out a paperback from his jacket pocket and was immediately absorbed in it, oblivious of everything around him. Completely lost in the book. Fran, always curious, glanced over and tried to see the title but all she could make out was the author, Stephen King.

When his meal arrived he looked up and saw her staring at him.

He grinned at her as though he'd caught her out. 'Do you read Stephen King too?' he said.

She blushed. She'd been nosey and there was nothing worse than someone butting in when all you wanted to do was be left in peace and enjoy your meal. But now she had to say something in reply. 'No. The covers always looked a bit lurid to me and that put me off.'

'Ah, they didn't used to be,' he said, rolling the knife and fork out of the paper napkin. 'I think the publishers were trying to sell him like James Herbert – the master of horror and the supernatural. Did you know he designed his own book covers?'

'Who? James Herbert?'

'Yes. But the early Stephen King books weren't the same at all. They were far more subtle. You'd be a third of the way in before you realised something odd was going on. Just ordinary people and then...' He gave a melodramatic shudder. 'As a teenager I loved *Christine*. You wouldn't believe a story about a car taking control of this kid could be so real but it kept me awake at night. Tried to get my daughter to read it but she's into *The Hunger Games*.'

He stopped and looked down at his food.

'I'm sorry. I didn't mean to be rude,' said Fran. 'Please go ahead before your chips get cold. I'll keep to myself and not say another word.'

He laughed. 'No, it's nice to have company. I spend far too many lunch times eating on my own.'

She looked at him, really looked at him this time. He was about forty, dark hair that needed cutting, jacket a bit worn and no tie, but he handled himself somehow as though he had authority. He was sure of himself, understated, but there was self-assurance that wasn't an act. It was natural to him. Of course, she shouldn't have asked.

'What do you do?'

'Civil engineer. Contracts Manager. I'm here every week or so to look after the building up the road. It's one of those projects where the council want the façade to be left in place, fit in with the surrounding architecture, and the structure behind it to be made stable. That's where we come in. It mustn't fall down.'

He had a smile that was infectious, the only word to describe it, and that Mancunian accent added warmth to everything he said.

She finished her lunch and stood up, pulling the strap of her bag over her shoulder.

'Well, good luck with that. Wouldn't like to see everything collapsing into the street.'

'Neither would I. Don't give me nightmares!'

It wasn't an instant thing, she thought later. It was friendly and unthreatening and not something she thought about the next day. A pleasant conversation in a pub with a stranger – she didn't even know his name – except he didn't seem like a stranger. Not even from the start.

When she saw him again, she was leaving The Talbot with Linda and he was coming down the street. He quickened his step as he came towards them.

'Late today,' he said. 'Everything's going wrong, you wouldn't believe.'

'No sign of a collapse yet I hope,' she said.

'Not quite.' He hadn't included Linda in the exchange, but suddenly realised he should introduce himself, so he turned to her and put out his hand. An old-fashioned touch, thought Fran. Well at least he had good manners.

'Hi. I'm Alex. Your friend and I were discussing books over our lunch a while back. But we didn't get round to giving our names.'

He looked over at her expectantly.

'I'm Fran. And I did get round to searching out your favourite author. I went into Waterstones and bought an early one, *Firestarter*. I haven't finished it but I see exactly what you mean. It's good.'

He looked delighted. 'I've got plenty I could lend you.' He suddenly looked embarrassed. 'Anyway, must try and get some lunch before they decide they aren't serving past two.'

When he'd gone, Linda looked at Fran in surprise. 'Well, you're a dark horse. You didn't tell me about *him*.'

They started walking back to the office. 'Nothing to tell. He's just a nice bloke. Only spoken to him the once.'

'More than nice,' Linda said, with a knowing look. 'A bit old for you, but he's quite handsome in a crumpled sort of way.'

'Oh, Linda!' She laughed and caught her friend's arm. 'Come on. We're going to be in trouble if we don't get a move on.'

*

Fran sat at her desk now and remembering those first meetings, wondered why she hadn't seen it coming. All she'd thought then was how easy he was to talk to, that he was amusing and kind and well… interesting. And how the more she went for lunch at that regular time – not every day, of course, but once or twice a week – how she hoped he'd be there.

At the time, she'd been going through a stage in her life when the party scene, the club life, the careless relationships were beginning to pall. She had plenty of friends but it was like a merry-go-round of 'Enjoyment' and it wasn't particularly enjoyable any more. It all seemed rather superficial and at twenty-four, she wanted more than that. No idea what, but certainly a change. She'd flirted with the idea of joining a cruise ship or doing charity work in Africa, or perhaps starting her own online transcription service. The job she'd got might pay fairly well but the work was repetitive and insurance was about the dullest subject on Earth.

And Alex seemed a world away from all that. He was someone anchored in the real grown-up world with a job that sounded satisfying, doing something worthwhile, creative in a way, and she sensed he knew a lot – not just about books, but about living. He was married of course, she'd seen the ring on his finger, and that didn't concern her because this wasn't a romantic thing, was it? Her instincts told her he was safe and she was usually pretty good at making judgements about people. Her first impressions were rarely wrong.

So when he saw her again, sitting on her own waiting for her order to arrive, he came and sat beside her. Naturally. That's how it felt. It was like meeting up with an old friend. Conversation was easy, swapping tales of their week, discussing films, making each other laugh. That was the key, she thought later. He made her laugh.

Their meal over, they'd ordered coffee when he put his hand into the inside pocket of his jacket and pulled out two tickets, placing them on the table.

'Just an idea,' he'd said. 'We're finished here next week and there's a Topping Out ceremony at the site – well, not a site anymore, a beautifully constructed building…'

'Topping Out?' She'd never heard the term.

'It's when you've completed the job and you celebrate that it's done at last and you've not lost too much money with delays,' he said.

'OK.' She wondered what was coming next.

'The city bigwigs will be there and our Managing Director and there'll be drinks and a buffet… I wondered whether you and Linda would like to be my guests.'

She just looked at him, surprised and flattered.

'Don't feel you've got to come.' He was hesitant now. 'I won't be back in Liverpool now the job's done so it's my farewell gift.' He gave her a smile that touched her. Almost sad. 'Have to move on. There are other sites I've been neglecting to make sure this one got finished. Anyway, it's a week on Friday, so thought you might be able to get the afternoon off…'

'Alex, thank you. I'd love to come. I'll see if Linda can get time off too…'

Then, as they sat there chatting about other things, she realised this would be the last time they'd lunch together, the last time she'd see him. And couldn't quite understand why this left her with such an empty feeling…

A sense of time running out…

She never gave the other ticket to Linda…

'It's twenty-five past, Fran.' Jill was calling from the front office. 'Mr. Merton will be here any minute.'

She sat up straight in her chair, pulled the notebook and pen from the drawer and set her mind on the present. There was a job to be done and she'd better concentrate on the things she *could* deal with, at least for the moment.

Chapter 21

We climb the steps of the first Portacabin, it's ten o'clock and I can hear from the voices inside, there's some sort of informal meeting going on. I couldn't help casting a professional eye over the site as we drove in. It was tidy, no obvious health hazards and that meant Hendy, the chief engineer, was doing a decent job.

Adrian is ahead of me and as he pushes open the ill-fitting door, the five men inside stop talking and turn.

'Look who I've brought with me to sort you out,' he says, standing aside as I come through. And there's a cheer goes up and the men come and almost pull me in, but tentative as though I might break, careful to weigh up how fragile I am before they get too exuberant. It touches me and I'm embarrassed.

Great to be back though, even if it's just for a quick visit. It's one of my favourite sites – a medium-sized water treatment plant we're upgrading and they're a really tight bunch here – Hendy keeps them on their toes. I take it all in as though I'm back from an extended holiday. The cabin is the usual clutter of long tables covered with diagrams and drawings, mugs and plates, abandoned hard hats, rickety chairs, naked light bulbs dangling from the ceiling. And the wooden floor always covered with a layer of mud and grime from the earth outside and Hi-Vis coats hang from a hook on the door.

The oldest engineer, Rob, all whiskers and grey stubble, clasps my hand in his then drops it. 'Hope this isn't the broken one,' he says.

'Actually, it is.'

And the cabin fills with laughter, in relief, I suppose that I've still got a sense of humour. That I'm not like some zombie they must have heard about at the start. They insist I sit down even though

187

Adrian tells them I don't need cosseting but they only want to make me feel welcome.

'You know Ian Black's been doing your job, don't you?' Hendy says.

'I heard.'

'Bloody nightmare. Came every day one week to check the replacement borehole pump. Didn't just trust us to get on with it. If you don't get back soon, we might just kill him.'

I smile. Better not to make any comment on that one.

He calls for the chain boy to brew some tea in the little cubbyhole that's the makeshift kitchen and Stewart, the youngest engineer, brings out a bag of squashed cream doughnuts from under a coat that's lying across a chair back.

'Well,' I say. 'They look like the usual appetising stuff I get offered when I come here. How old are they?'

'Couple of days.' He grins, awkwardly. 'Had to hide them before they disappeared.'

And they all dive in, leaving just one for me. We sit and drink dark brown tea, they never have enough milk, and discuss the latest news and Manchester City and short-sighted referees. Only when all the joking and banter has run its course does Hendy ask, 'How long do you think you'll be off?'

The others look at me as though I'll come up with a definite answer. Which of course I can't.

'I'm hoping it'll only be another couple of months.' I try to sound positive. 'I'm in the hands of the doctors, my GP and the company doctor. But I'm hoping they'll let me come back part-time and build up gradually.'

Adrian is standing by, listening. Saying nothing. No idea what he's thinking but probably wishing I'd just get going as soon as next week.

I can see Hendy looking round at the men and deciding to break into the moment's quiet. 'Sure you don't want to look round the site? Check we're doing it right?'

'Don't think I need to do that!' I keep my voice serious. 'I'll wait till I get back then bollock you all for swinging the lead.'

And so everything seems to slot back into place. I get the sense that we're all relieved to establish some sort of normality. The parting shot, though, throws me a bit.

Rob reaches for my hand again and his voice is gruff. 'We were all knocked sideways when we were told about the crash. Gave us a hell of a fright, I can tell you. Thank God you're on your feet again.'

There are murmurs from the other men as they nod and shake their heads.

I don't want them to see how bloody moved I am by all this, so I lift my good arm in a sort of wave and turn, go down the steps and head towards Adrian's car. As he backs up and drives through the gates, we don't speak.

Enough's been said.

*

It's quiet in the house when I get back. Jack's at work and Carrie's down at the stables. I let myself in and get a sudden urge to have a drink. A real one. Forbidden, I know, but still I sneak into the dining room as though I'm being watched and open the sideboard, find a half-empty gin bottle and a tonic and pour myself a very weak one. Final touch – three large ice cubes from the fridge, then I swallow. God, that's good. Hope it doesn't make me keel over and I'm found sprawled on the carpet later with splinters of glass all over the floor.

I go into the study, place my drink carefully on my desk beside the keyboard and switch on the monitor. I tap into the firm's website and look over the recent acquisitions and check the progress of current jobs.

But I'm not really concentrating.

Of course I've worked out now why I was on that particular road when I crashed, even though I can't remember how it happened. She'd been at Lucy's party and I couldn't just leave well alone. I had to find her, talk to her, try to understand what had happened. Why she was in our garden after all this time.

What the hell was going on? That must have been in my mind. I was on that road because I was driving to the only address I knew for her, that converted barn in Whitegate she bought with her brother, in the vain hope that she still lived there. But I mustn't have made it. I wiped myself out, very nearly literally, and that would have been the end of it.

But that wasn't the end of it now.

I can't just leave everything up in the air.

I need to see her.

I think back to what Joe said as we walked round Poynton Park. About when I changed. He was right. Losing my drive was exactly how I'd felt long before the accident and he'd been perceptive enough to pick up on it. All those years ago. I *did* change and it had nothing to do with my age or my job... I went quiet because my world had turned upside down. And I was struggling to deal with it.

Later you go over everything – the hurt, the blame, the morality of it all, but when your emotions are stringing you up, overshadowing everything else, you're not thinking in those terms. You're not thinking at all. You're obeying some instinct that doesn't always know when to put the brakes on.

What I remember vividly is sitting in this pub in Liverpool at lunch time, absorbed in a book and looking up to see a girl staring at me. I'd not come to Liverpool that often before, but I'd just been promoted to Contracts Manager to oversee quite a tricky job, making a retention structure with the façade kept in situ. That was as well as looking after three other sites so I had precious little time to myself. Except at midday and I liked to go off by myself for a bit, eat lunch in peace and read my book.

When she realised I'd noticed, she flushed and I suppose I didn't want her to feel awkward, so I said the first thing that came into my head – had she read any Stephen King?

We began talking and I remember thinking what amazing eyes she had, a colour of blue that looked almost unnatural and fringed with black lashes that made them even more remarkable. Dark hair in a sort of bob, slim, dressed in a green wool dress and navy jacket, a rope bracelet on her wrist. She was young, inquisitive and funny. I liked her company, when usually I preferred my own in the middle of a hard day. By the time we got to know each other's names, I started looking for her when I visited the site, hoping she'd be sitting in the pub or walking down the street.

Just for a chat.

It wasn't anything other than that. There was too much going on in my life to think about her as more than good company for the occasional lunch. I'd been married a long time, I had two teenage kids at home and I was working long hours travelling round the North West. It was full on. It didn't need complications.

Was I kidding myself? Perhaps. You don't always recognise what's hit you until you're under the bus. I remember when we were finishing the job and sending out invitations to the Topping Out ceremony (earlier in the week, Head Office had forwarded a list of the special guests to be invited), I suddenly felt really down about it all ending. No more Liverpool… A few of the tickets had been left in a box on the ground floor of the building so I picked up two and put them in my pocket. At least it'd be a nice way of saying goodbye.

On the day, the buffet was set up, we'd hired catering staff and arranged for photographs to be taken. By 12.40 most of the guests had arrived. There were going to be speeches and toasts from our MD and the council's Planning Director, then we could all relax and eat and tell each other what a brilliant enterprise this had been.

There must have been about forty people gathered together and because of the emptiness of the building above, the voices and laughter carried noisily across the room. I found myself watching the door, wondering whether they'd come. They might have to work. No big deal.

Fifteen minutes later and the guests were turning towards the raised platform getting ready for the speeches. The servers had stopped handing out drinks. The photographer was in place.

Then she was there. Standing a little bemused, head on one side, looking round for a familiar face. Mine. And she'd come alone.

I steered my way through the crowd and managed to reach her before she took fright and fled. I needn't have worried. She looked perfectly composed. In fact, she looked wonderful… dressed just right for the occasion, a flowered dress, all blues and greens and strappy heeled sandals, heart-shaped pendant with matching earrings. She smiled when she saw me.

'They're just about to make the speeches,' I said, her closeness affecting every nerve in my body. 'I'll get you a drink once they're over.'

So we stood side by side while the council officer thanked everyone for coming, praised the excellent work done by Belmont and his satisfaction with the outcome. He went on about how important it had been to maintain the frontage in its original form for both aesthetic and historical reasons. And then it was our turn – Trevor Innes, the MD, taking all the praise as though he'd personally been in charge. But right at the end, he added that thanks must be due to the stalwart work of Michael Johns, the chief engineer, and Alex Taylor, 'our' Contracts Manager.

I indicated my response with a nod of my head and once the room had become noisy again, I grinned at Fran. 'Nice to be appreciated!' I said.

Her expression was serious. 'Yes, it really is. You're obviously good at your job. You should be proud of yourself.'

'Ah, that would be dangerous.' I was about to get her a drink, when I saw Trevor approaching. He shook my hand, more congratulations, then turned to be introduced.

'And who do you represent?' he asked her.

Fran gave him a warm smile. 'Insurance Company,' she said. 'Fran Rogers. Yes, the make-over's impressive. It's all been well done.'

He nodded and moved away to circulate and shake more hands.

I looked sideways at her and she pretended not to notice.

'What?'

'Just as well *you* answered that one. I don't even know your surname. I'd have been forced to say – here's Fran, we meet every so often in the pub for lunch, she's here for some free drinks and I thought she'd brighten up the proceedings!'

She laughed. 'Well, let's hope I can at least do that. How about that free drink, then?'

It all lasted about two hours and it was great to have her to talk to, to show her some of what we'd done with the building, explaining some of the technical stuff. Eventually, people were drifting away and we couldn't be the last to go. I'd run out of ideas to prolong the moment. It seemed so final.

We were moving through the door onto the street when she turned, opened the clasp of her shoulder bag and pulled out a slip of paper.

'Here,' she said. 'It's my mobile number and address... if ever you're passing my way. My brother and I have just bought a place in a little village about thirty miles from here. Whitegate. I know you travel around a lot and if you want a cup of tea...'

She flushed and I tried to make light of it. 'Or you want a wall building...'

'Yes, that could be useful.'

We laughed, not exactly sure of ourselves, or where we were in this but I knew we both felt it. And suddenly I could breathe again, I didn't have to let go. It was like a lifeline. Funny how you can recall a moment like this even after years have passed, that emotional high.

'Hold on.' I scrabbled in my pocket for a pen but couldn't find anything to write on. She tore her slip of paper in half.

'Here.' And I wrote down my mobile on the scrap she gave me and we swapped them over.

I watched her walk off down the street, took out my wallet and stowed her number behind my driving licence.

I spent the rest of the day trying to forget it was there.

*

And what now? Even if I needed to see *her*, she might not want to see *me*....

There's a knock at the door and the postman is standing there with a parcel that won't fit through the letter box. When he's off down the path, I look out at the hire car standing in the drive as I've done often in the past few days.

It's like temptation staring me in the face.

Who'd know if I climbed into the driving seat and took off for an hour and parked it back on the drive in the same spot!

Yeah. That's really thinking straight. This is like a teenager pinching his dad's car while he's not looking. With no licence and insurance. Clever! I've at least two months to go before the doctors are even going to consider me driving again, so all I can do is look at the bloody thing and go back indoors before I consider any more mad ideas.

When Carrie comes back from the yard after lunch, I am back at the computer pretending to do work of sorts.

'How did the site visit go?' she asks, her hand resting on my shoulder as she looks at what's on the screen.

'Good,' I say. 'The blokes seemed keen to have me back which was really nice to know. They don't have much truck with my replacement. He interferes, apparently.'

She bent lower and put her arm around my neck. 'Alex... I'm really sorry about the other night. I was grouchy and unfair. I'll talk to Jack when he'll give me the chance.'

'OK. I know it's been a strain. For you, probably more than me.'

'Well, no excuse.' She paused. 'My mother's been on the phone. Wants me to meet up.'

I'm surprised. It's been years since she showed up. 'What on earth for?'

'No idea. But I'll have to go.' Another pause. 'And Meryl and Bill are coming round for a bit of supper next Friday, just for an hour or so. They were so keen to see you...'

I turn in the chair. God, that awful pair of snobs. They really get my goat and I don't know what Carrie sees in them.

'Christ, they're the last people I want to see!' I'm exasperated that she's agreed to let them come. 'Can't you say I've had a relapse? Take them out to a pub.'

'Oh, Alex. Meryl thinks the world of you. She's been so concerned and, anyway, how many mutual friends do we have?'

I wonder how she can consider them 'mutual' when I can't stand them. But I let it ride. Not much else I can do.

This isn't the moment for another argument. I want to make sure Jack doesn't have to face any more upset. He doesn't deserve that.

Chapter 22

Grey clouds hung low in the sky after a windy night had brought down branches and leaves off the trees, scattering debris over the lawn and driveway. Carrie hoped it would at least stay dry; she was meeting Lucy to help choose a table for her flat and it would mean trawling round the Outlet Centre in Reddish but you could never tell what to expect.. The weather had been extremely odd all through July and August, one day hot and humid sapping all your energy, the next, torrential rain so the water would run off the fields and flood the country roads. If this wasn't Climate Change, she didn't know what was. Whatever! It made things difficult to plan.

Well, after the last few months, Carrie thought, you could say that about life. It didn't always run smoothly either and lately it certainly hadn't. And this feeling of being out of control was alien to her. She was usually so good at *managing* things, of being able to cope. It was how she'd been brought up. When she was upset as a child, her father would ruffle her hair, his only gesture of affection that she could ever remember and counsel her with obscure expressions – she had to *'weather the storm'* or *'stay on an even keel'*, as though she was a ship's captain. His voice was always a bit gruff on these occasions but she knew his advice was meant kindly. And his philosophy had been clear to her. Stand tall, keep your balance, stay strong.

Which is exactly what *he* had done when his wife left him, she later realised. Worked hard, organised the domestic arrangements to keep things running smoothly, looked after his only child as best he could... and made sure no-one ever questioned his ability to overcome his difficulties. There'd be no sign of distress or crying on shoulders or asking for help.

196

So, early on, Carrie had learnt to maintain that front, that restraint, whenever she'd had to deal with problems. If that made her seem hard at times, if that's how others saw her, then so be it. It was the way she was.

She'd kept her head after Alex's accident, although there'd been moments when she'd been angry and frustrated – and scared. She'd taken charge of the hospital appointments, the scans, supervised his medical needs, encouraged him to exercise. Week after week she'd tried to bolster his confidence and remain patient. Particularly draining in the face of his state of mind... his inertia. Even now, it wasn't easy. He might be improving physically, but mentally, he seemed to be giving up. His indifference was worrying.

So if she got irritated it wasn't surprising. She wasn't just running the livery yard, she was using much of her energy propping Alex up and to add to that, trying to make Jack realise that the road ahead would be bloody hard going if he couldn't support himself. And now... her mother had decided to return. Like some avenging angel, one of the Fallen Ones obviously, out to create havoc again. God, she could do without *her* coming back into her life!

But at least the day after Alex had seen his parents and had a walk with Joe, she'd thought he seemed brighter. They'd actually talked about general things and he'd asked about the horses. It was enough to make her feel more optimistic.

The time had come to stop treading on egg shells. Time, for heaven's sake, to ask him again – that one question he might now be able to answer. What could he remember.

He was sitting at the kitchen table reading the Sports Page while she prepared a salad for lunch. She glanced over at him. She wanted it to sound casual, as though it wasn't really that important. But she had to ask. She couldn't let it drop.

'Has anything come back to you, Alex?' A moment passed. 'I mean about that night.'

'I know what you mean.' He put down the paper. 'No. It's a blank.' He got up from his chair to fetch a treat from the cupboard for Sam, who was lying on the tiled floor, his front legs splayed either side of his large head. Alex bent down, putting the biscuit under his nose.

'All of it? A blank?'

'There's not much point going on about it.' He spoke as though at any moment he would lose his temper. 'I might never remember.'

Well, that's telling me. He wants me to shut up about it. He's not interested in finding out. Where's his curiosity? Why isn't he asking questions?

But then, she thought, in fairness, what could he add? If he was being honest.

So everything was again left in the air. Another afternoon and evening of silence. It was like living in a vacuum, filled not with emptiness but with unspoken words.

Looking back on those days when he lay in hospital, when she'd been obsessed with finding out where he'd been going and why, she could see how pointless struggling with such an enigma had been. On her own, she would never work any of it out.

But it was obvious something didn't add up. He'd been on the wrong road, in the wrong place, and according to what he'd told her about his plans, he'd been heading in the wrong direction.

Of course she knew what had always been at the back of her mind. Not that she would admit it at first. Or face the possibility. Too painful, too humiliating. Too much of a threat. *He was having an affair. He was on his way to see someone or on his way back. Was it something that had just started or had it been going on for a long time?*

And who was she?

Carrie couldn't answer any of it. She might be barking up the wrong tree but what other explanation was there? If there was, she'd run out of ideas.

No wonder she'd felt the need to go through his messages and notes on the computer, search through his desk. Looking for anything that might give her something concrete, something that would either put her mind at rest or mean she'd have to act. She'd found nothing except the cinema ticket which could easily be explained away – something he'd shoved in the drawer with a pile of papers and forgotten about.

But there *was* something. And perhaps it had been obvious all along and she'd missed it. Her instincts had always been good, but...

Only once before had she felt that same sense of unease about their relationship. Nothing really to go on but a recognition that she had to stay alert, that things were awry. It was some years ago, about the time Lucy was starting in the sixth form and Jack was beginning to cause them trouble. They'd been going through what she supposed could be called a rough patch. Alex had been spending a lot of time away with the job, instead of the odd one night. He'd been promoted to Contracts Manager and it meant travelling to sites further afield, so he was spending less and less time at home. Carrie felt they'd begun to lead separate lives, with her carrying most of the responsibilities.

Also at the time, she'd been working hard building up the business, expanding the facilities to include more stables and an indoor school. She was fully occupied so it wasn't an immediate realisation that things were falling apart, but one evening she'd sat down and thought about how distant they'd become.

A few weeks before the problems with Jack had come to a head, he'd arrived home late one particular night and headed for the stairs and bed, without even noticing she was sitting in the kitchen, waiting. So she called out to him.

'Alex. It's nine o'clock. Don't you want something to eat?'

He didn't come into the room, just stayed in the doorway. 'No, I'm fine. Stopped at a motorway café and had something. Knew I'd be too late for supper.'

She turned towards him and could see, not just the closed look that had been present on his face so often lately, but the exhaustion in his eyes and in the way he was standing. And a sudden jolt of fear went through her. She had no idea where it came from but something was wrong here.

'Was it Berwick today? Did it go badly? You look all-in.' She wanted to see some reaction.

He didn't quite meet her eye. 'Yes, Berwick. And it's been a long drive. So if you don't mind...'

He bowed his head slightly and went up the stairs.

She knew then that if she didn't work at this marriage, really make a supreme effort, she'd lose him. It'd all be over. Well, she wasn't going to let that happen.

And of course it didn't. Together, a few weeks later, they'd had to face bigger problems. And it took some time, but they'd got back on that 'even keel' her father so loved to talk about. Up until this accident, they'd been doing all right, as all right as any other couple after twenty-odd years. Yes, they took each other for granted but that was inevitable, wasn't it?

But now, that niggling doubt wouldn't leave her. And later on that morning, seeing Alex's new mobile on the table beside his bed, she picked it up and scrolled through the messages – three from work, two from Lucy, one from Joe.

Replacing the phone, she was careful to put it back exactly as she'd found it.

*

Carrie thought the dining room table and four chairs that Lucy had chosen looked a bit flimsy, but never mind, she didn't have to live with them. They'd be better than the hand-me-downs she'd been given by her granny. And delivery was free. So now they'd look at clothes, handbags, jewellery, all the stuff that Carrie hadn't the faintest interest in, but she knew how Lucy liked to browse.

They'd been in one of those shops where you can get anything from stuffed cats to mirrors and where you can never pass between the shelves without knocking something off its stand, when Lucy suddenly said, 'Saw Danny the other night.'

Carrie wasn't sure what to say. Was this a good or a bad thing? She decided she needed more detail before she put her foot in it. Lucy's relationship with Danny was something of a puzzle; they might be divorced but somehow they seemed loath to break the ties. Was it over or not?

Lucy moved to a display of Christmas decorations. (*In August?* thought Carrie. *How absurd is that?*) 'Aren't you going to ask me how it went?'

'OK. How did it go?' She pretended she wasn't too interested, centring her attention on putting a dangling paper monkey back on its hook.

'It was strange. Oh, Mum, it was so nice to be talking instead of arguing all the time. All we ever seemed to do before was fight. Those last months were *awful.* And now... we're friends. I'm not going to care what people say. It's my business and not theirs.' Still talking, she started to move towards the shop door. Out on the pavement, she took hold of Carrie's arm. 'What do *you* think?'

'Well...' She hesitated. It was typical of her family to think she had all the answers. Perhaps that was her fault. Perhaps she'd made too many of the decisions in the past. 'You've started a new phase in your life, Lucy. You have a good job, you're going out again. I'd be wary of starting this up again.'

Lucy unlinked her arm, annoyed. 'Oh Mum, that's like the stuff a magazine would churn. *Move on! Don't look back!* Every situation's different, surely.' She pulled a face which was the sort to end the discussion. 'I'll go steady, don't worry.'

And by the time they'd found a café and ordered tea and scones, the atmosphere was cordial again. Carrie should have kept her advice to herself, she realised. Lucy was an adult now – she'd have to make her own decisions.

As they were saying goodbye and heading out into the car park, Lucy gave her mother a hug. 'I know you're only thinking of what's best for me. But no-one really knows what's right for someone else, do they? It's easy when you're looking on. But when you're in the middle of it...'

Carrie hugged her back. 'Quite right. I shouldn't have tried to...'

'Well, I did ask you, didn't I? Serves me right if it wasn't the answer I wanted to hear. It's just that feelings don't just change.' She sighed as though the weight of the world was on her shoulders.

'No, they don't.'

'When you've been close to someone, it's really hard to get them out of your mind. Even when everything's gone wrong, you start remembering the good bits. And you want them back. Whatever social life you think I've got is a front. I've tried to get going again but, Mum, I miss him.'

And with that, she gave a small smile and waved her hand as she threaded her way through the cars.

*

Late afternoon and Carrie was standing by the rails of the paddock, watching David give Jodie a leg-up into the saddle. The little grey pony stood patiently until she'd gathered the reins, given him a kick and sent him off at walking pace. David waited a while before he backed away, opened the gate and came to join Carrie.

He seemed pleased with himself. 'See, I'm being good. Leaving her to her own devices.'

She smiled. 'Well, you're learning.'

'I have great respect for the teacher.' He inclined his head. 'I needed to leave her to it and it's certainly working.'

She couldn't quite make out whether he was mocking her or paying her a compliment. Probably both. He used that ironic tone all the time with her now, as though they had an understanding, as though they had some sort of 'friendship' which she was having trouble defining. The important thing, she decided, was Jodie, who'd changed from an anxious, nervous child to a happy one – well, happ*ier* – it couldn't be easy for the kid going from one parent to the other when, from what Carrie had begun to understand, the circumstances could be fraught. And not improving with time. The few remarks David had made about his ex-wife and the joint custody arrangement had been conveyed with a bitter edge.

She watched Jodie now as the pony went into trot, sitting in, keeping her hands down and her back straight and focussing on Bertie, not herself. Now she wasn't worried all the time, the child was showing a friendly, outgoing personality. Small for eight, with a heart-shaped face, freckles and a ponytail, she was beginning to chatter away to everyone, giving all the details of how she was caring for Bertie, whether he'd behaved himself, how clever he was. It was good to see her gaining confidence.

David leant against the railings, his eyes on his daughter. 'When did you become so involved with horses, Carrie? Born in a stable, were you?'

'Almost!' she said. She was amused how he put things, the manner of someone who had the right to know. But she'd stopped being annoyed by it. In fact, if anything, she found him rather amusing. It certainly wasn't how Steph found him – *'rude and full of self-importance'* was her view of him.

'Well?' He turned his head towards her.

She thought for a moment. 'I started riding when I was younger than Jodie. My grandfather had always kept horses and I suppose I didn't have to think about it. He bought me my first pony, we lived in an old house with land and stables, so it was part of everyday life.'

'Sounds like an idyllic childhood.'

She couldn't help giving a bitter laugh. 'Not exactly.'

He looked at her, waiting for her to go on.

She hadn't meant to fill in more detail but he had a way of waiting until she continued, waiting for her to fill in the gaps. 'My mother left when I was twelve. With George Clifford – the II, I believe – well-off, well-connected, an estate in Derbyshire. She never had to lift a finger again. They travelled. I saw very little of her until I was twenty. Not sure what she made of me by then.'

David nodded sympathetically and she knew she was revealing too much of her life to someone she didn't know very well. And didn't totally trust.

'And your father?'

She smiled. 'My father was a wonderful man. Quite tough on the outside but…'

'But…?'

She shook her head. It was enough. She motioned to where Jodie was nearing the paddock gate. 'Let's go and tell her how well she's done.'

He moved towards his daughter, but just before he reached her, he said to Carrie over his shoulder, 'And I'll show my gratitude at Brampton. Make sure you wear your best outfit.'

What a cheek, she thought, about to answer back. The arrogance of the man! She didn't know whether to be angry or laugh. But they'd reached Jodie by then and the moment to give any sort of reply had passed.

Chapter 23

The call from Lucy came while he was watching a film on Netflix in his room – a heist based on a true story that was so clever he didn't want to pause it. So it wasn't until he'd put on his PJs that he finally got round to listening to her voicemail. She hardly ever rang him. He was sure it'd be an errand he'd have to run or an instruction of some sort.

It's me, Lucy, she began as if he hadn't worked that out. *Look, I'm passing on a message but you don't have to come back to me on this. It's just that Rachel, you know the girl who thought you were 'cute' who drove us to the nightclub? Well, she's invited you to a party at her place a week on Saturday. I said you probably were doing something but anyway, I'll send you her address. It's very low key and if you're coming, bring a bottle. Bye. Oh and she said, if you want, the invite includes a friend.*

He sat back against the pillows and listened to the message again. To say he was surprised was an understatement. All sorts of thoughts clamoured in his head. But the one that was foremost was who might be there and the chance that Rachel might invite Fran. That alone was worth going for, even though he wouldn't know anyone there. A week ago, he could have taken Terry along – he was good company, he'd have mixed in and made it all easier but he wasn't home. So that idea had to go out the window. Well whatever, he'd go alone and probably end up standing against a wall clutching his drink, a wallflower... or like a drowning man. But he'd brave that sort of embarrassment for her.

And thinking back to Lucy's birthday, Jack remembered that Rachel had given Fran a lift, that was why she'd had to take a taxi home. Of course, he didn't know how *well* they knew one another.

But if *he* could be included in the guest list when Rachel had only met him once, then *she* just might be. He lay back, his hands behind his head and closed his eyes. He wished he was at least five years older with money to spare and a nice car. *Would that make any difference really? Well, it might!*

He'd been trying to put her out of his mind over the past few weeks but it only worked for a while; having to concentrate all day helped and two evening shifts at the pub, which left him tired out when he got home. But then she'd be back occupying his thoughts for days. He just didn't seem able to forget her. *Was it just infatuation, a here-today-gone-tomorrow crush that swept you along for a time then let you go? When you're in the grip of it,* he thought, *how are you to know?* He'd only had one serious relationship and it was nothing like this. That one, while it lasted had at least been something he understood. A mutual attraction, an honesty about it – well, through most of the year until the end. And that final separation, he could see now had been part of growing up, painful at the time but inevitable. No-one other than him expected it to last.

But with this, even though he could see how foolish it was, he didn't seem to be listening. *'Cloth ears'* his nan would have said. Wilful and driven and heading for a fall. That about summed it up. But he couldn't stop himself.

He fantasised about her, that's how crazy it was.

When he'd missed the last conservation activity because he was working that weekend, he'd sat down at the computer and gone onto their website. There was the report and photographs, showing how they had repaired and creosoted some fencing on a restricted byway. And there was the group, dishevelled, overalled and smiling away, holding their brushes and tools high in the air but no sign of Fran. That was the second one she'd missed.

He wasn't sure what to make of that. There might be nothing *to* make of it. She was probably getting on with her social life or on holiday. There was no way he could know. He made up his mind to go to the next one, anyway. He'd be doing something useful at least and it was nice to be part of a group. So he told himself.

*

Jack stood, looking at the rows upon rows of books. He needed to take his time. He wasn't sure what he was looking for but it was important to get it right. His first decent wage packet and he wanted to repay some debts. Well, not exactly debts. That wasn't it really. He wanted to show his dad how glad he was to have him back in one piece.

When you're young you think your parents are going to last forever, he thought – they'll always just be there. Then you wake up to a nightmare and you're never quite the same again. You become cautious; you start to think that however good life is, however well it's all going, there's something waiting to floor you, something obscure, an ominous cloud on the horizon. No way can you avoid it heading your way. And however Jack tried not to think about what life would have been like without his father, there were moments when it struck him with a shuddering fear.

The scare had put him on his guard.

But for now he concentrated on the task in hand and he took his time. Book shops always had an odd effect on him – the atmosphere, studied and quiet seemed to insist he walk slowly, browsing as though he must consider all the volumes on the stacked shelves so as not to miss anything. He moved between sections, examining the spines of the books, hardly recognising one author. He'd never been a great reader, had rarely spent time searching for something specific as he was doing now. He reached the Crime Section and slowed down even more. He knew his dad liked Michael Connelly and Ian Rankin (he'd looked through the stack of books on the shelves in the dining room) but wasn't sure which ones he'd already got. He'd just have to take a chance and buy the latest ones. Wasn't there someone around with a bit of inside knowledge about best sellers who could make recommendations? He looked along to the Biography Section where an assistant was emptying a trolley, so intent on the job she didn't notice him. So he turned again to consider the options. OK, one Rankin, one Deon Meyer – even *he* fancied that one after reading the back cover – and hoped they'd fit the bill.

He left the shop and crossed at the zebra, past McDonald's with its smell of fried food seeping into the street as a family pushed open the door. The only thing he'd ever liked in there were the skinny chips and tomato sauce in a carton, far better than eating them off a plate. It wasn't till he'd got in his car and headed out of town that he thought he should have bought something for his mother. Flowers perhaps, or chocolates. Not exactly inspiring but as Nan would say, '*It's the thought that counts!*'

Well, at the moment he didn't believe the thoughts he was having were the sort Nan had in mind. He didn't feel generous. He felt… no, not resentment, almost indifference. And part of this was because the job at Parsons had been going really well, it was certainly building up his self-esteem. He was valued on the floor and praised for learning fast and his good relationship with the customers. So the fact that his mother didn't rate his efforts, didn't matter so much.

But there's always a catch, he thought. Yes, he might be appreciated, trusted but at a cost. Something had come up, unforeseen and unsought, which had left him in a difficult moral position. Not just difficult – bloody unpleasant. A real double-edged sword.

It was last week when he'd had an appraisal. He hadn't expected anything like that until the six months' probation was up, but Steve had come to the main desk one morning and asked Jack to go upstairs with him to his office. For the first few minutes, Jack felt uneasy and sat wondering whether he'd made some mistake, upset a customer. It was like when you're driving and you see a police car in your mirror – you're doing absolutely nothing wrong but immediately you're nervous. You *must* be guilty of something.

But Steve settled himself in his chair and smiled at him. 'Now, Jack, don't look so worried. This is an informal chat. And I know you're the sort of lad who can keep certain matters to yourself. When necessary…'

What the hell was this about?

Steve coughed and rubbed the palm of his hand over his forehead. 'Can I trust you to keep this to yourself?' This time a question. Jack nodded, uncertain now. Was he being transferred to the store in Oldham? He hoped not, it'd take him forever to get there.

'We've had some… pilfering. Well, it's more than that. Products have gone missing and there's no corresponding payments, so stuff is leaving the store and not being paid for. Or products are not being registered properly and the money the customer is handing over is not reaching the tills.'

Jack hadn't been ready for this. 'You don't think…'

'No, no, no! We know you've got nothing to do with this. But we need someone who's new, who isn't so chummy with the other staff members, someone we believe will take a responsible view of this. It can't go on.'

Jack wanted to ask what Steve expected him to do but instead he just stared ahead of him. 'Have you an idea who it is?'

'We have. Some of the CCTV cameras have picked up pictures that could be incriminating. But not enough.'

Jack couldn't think of what to say.

Steve looked at him, an embarrassed expression on his face. 'If I say you seem to have made a friend of him on the shop floor, do I need to say more?'

Gary! Surely not. Of all people… he was such a hard worker. Lazy Martin, perhaps, but not Gary.

'We want you to keep your eyes open. Nothing too obvious but your feedback would help us enormously. I'll leave it up to you.'

He didn't answer, just nodded, unable to commit himself to what it meant… spying. As he went back down the stairs to the shop floor, he had mixed emotions. He'd thought he was in trouble, then found the trouble was of a totally different kind. He was being asked to snitch.

*

The relationship between himself and his mother hadn't improved much since that awkward meal. He hated atmospheres but he didn't know how to smooth things over. And was it really up to him? If she felt he was such a failure, then what could he do to change that? Well, nothing in a matter of weeks! He'd already offered to pay rent when he joined Parsons. At last he had enough in his wage packet to contribute to the household budget and that was something of a relief. She'd smiled and said she thought it a good idea so that was something. And he'd made a point of helping out more around the house and when he could, at the stables. But things were still strained. Even his dad seemed to be staying out of the firing range, preferring to read or go for walks on his own. *Surely it couldn't go on much longer. She must be as uncomfortable as we are.*

On a day off he'd walked down to the yard and helped Steph with a few regular jobs, while his mother was occupied fitting a new saddle on a horse owned by one of the liveries. He stood in the barn by the large feed bins while Steph scooped the coarse mix into bowls that he held out for her. She seemed unusually quiet, Jack thought. Had his mother had a go at her too? Everyone seemed at odds these days. He didn't know what to say, but after five minutes, he decided to pitch in. 'Why do these people need new saddles every six months? They're always changing them. It seems an awful waste.'

Steph had a resigned expression on her face. 'Well, they have the money to do it. Years ago, never mind new saddles, you put the same one on any pony that came onto the farm. Real leather saddles that had 'give' in them, not these synthetic ones with all the inserts and flaps.'

He laughed. 'You sound like an old codger when you say that!' He mimicked her. '*In my day, horses lived on fresh air, not these fancy feeds.*'

She managed a laugh then. 'OK, that sounded a bit like my grandad.' She kept ladling the feed. 'Don't you just love the smell in here? Even when the horses aren't in. I never know whether it's the haylage, or the saddle soap or the molasses.'

Jack could tell she was using diversionary tactics, saying anything but what was on her mind. This wasn't Steph at all.

'Is there something I'm missing here?' He put the bowls down to make her stop and look directly at him. 'You're talking like someone out of "My Friend Flicka".'

She did laugh properly then. 'Well, I am in trouble then.'

'So, is it something I can help with?

'No, I don't think it is, Jack.' But she held his gaze. She wanted to talk about it, he thought, so he waited.

Steph looked round as though making sure no-one was listening. It had to be his mother and he felt uneasy before he heard anything. He was the last person who could sort anything out in that direction.

'You're not to say anything.'

He nodded.

'Not to your father, either.'

'I won't say anything to anyone.'

'Well,' she wiped her hands on her jeans, 'it's that bloke who stables his horse here. David. The one with the little dark-haired girl. Your mother's giving her lessons. She's helping anyway, although Sarah's still doing most of it.'

'Yes, I get the picture,' said Jack, uneasy now. 'I know who you mean.'

Where on earth was this going?

'He's taking over.'

Jack frowned. 'How do you mean? He just keeps two horses here. How can he take over?'

'Oh, not really in that sense. He's… I think he's manipulating your mother. He insists on taking up her time, he seems to have a lot of days off so he's here much more than he was at the beginning. And now, I know it isn't really any of my business, but she was asking me the other day if I'd cover for her while he takes her to Brampton — you know, the one-day event. They're going to be guests of some big firm that hires machinery…'

She stopped and a guilty look crossed her face, her cheeks red patches and her eyes watering. 'I shouldn't be saying any of this, not to you I know that, but there's something about the man. Something I don't trust. He's the sort who gets his own way no matter about anyone else.'

Jack didn't know what to say. What could he say? He couldn't imagine his mother being 'manipulated' by anyone. But Steph had worked for them a long time, she knew his mother so well and she wasn't the sort to be scared for nothing. She was certainly serious about this. But he was hardly in a position to do anything about it. And if he couldn't tell his father, and obviously he couldn't, he didn't know what he could do.

'Has she said anything to you about him?'

Steph began scooping the feed up again, digging into the mix as though it deserved a beating. 'At the beginning. When he first came. He annoyed her as much as he did me. She thought like I did – that he was arrogant, pushy, used to getting his own way. But then when he persuaded her to start teaching the little girl, they seemed to be getting along. Really well. I know I'm not the only one who's noticed.'

Jack began emptying the bowls into the rubber troughs lined up on the floor, ready to be hung over the stable doors. 'Look, Steph, there's not much I can do about it. What on earth would I say?'

She nodded, then shook her head. 'Sorry, Jack, I shouldn't have gone on about it. There's nothing *any* of us can do. I just needed to tell someone and perhaps I should have kept my mouth shut. Forget I said anything. I'm probably overreacting.' And off she went to finish her jobs, her usually bright expression clouded and unhappy.

'Forget I said anything,' thought Jack. Easier said than done. This was getting to be like a spy thriller and he was hunting the mole, watching everyone… his mother… Gary. Christ, who next? His father?

*

He'd psyched himself up for the party, dressed in a blue shirt and jeans and his best Jacamo black boots, bought a bottle of Prosecco because he didn't know whether to take white or red and arrived at Rachel's flat late. Better to go in when there was a crowd and he could get lost in it. He was driving which meant he couldn't drink, so he'd need to find an extra dose of bravado from somewhere. At least being in his own car meant he could make his escape if it was a disaster.

The flat was on the second floor and he didn't need to ring any bell to enter, the door was open and the music, the chattering voices, the laughter, the clink of bottles, the fug in the air told him the party was in full swing. Good, he thought. Clutching his bottle of wine, he sidled his way through the guests who were already having to shout at each other to make themselves heard. He finally reached the kitchen where the table was strewn with glasses and bowls of crisps and nuts and plates of cheese. And bottles. And more bottles. Obviously not the sort of party where food was a priority. As he lifted a jug of orange juice, Rachel let out a shriek. 'You came, brother Jack. *So* pleased you came! Come and meet Florrie, I've told her about you. I knew you'd come on your own!' And with that she whisked him into the main room, her arm round his shoulders, staggering a bit and talking ten to the dozen. Everyone seemed drunk and it wasn't even nine o'clock.

Florrie turned out to be a kind enough girl with no sense of humour and the ability to tell a rambling tale about her cat that was so boring, Jack had to blink hard to concentrate. She seemed to be closer to his age than the others, pretty with a permanent smile on her face, probably what might be called a good match, looking on. But it didn't really matter what anyone else thought. *If you don't connect, it's useless,* he thought. *There has to be some chemistry… or whatever… Without that, forget it.* He tried his best to put on an interesting expression, but it was no good.

And then he saw her. She was standing talking to three people in a corner of the room, animated and smiling, her hand gestures accompanying some story. Her hair was pinned back off her face by a gold clip, her dress, pale blue in some silken material that looked expensive. It took his breath away. She was everything he'd dreamed of. Everything he wanted. No good saying this wasn't real.

Lucy waved at him from the side near the bookcase and he waved back over Florrie's head. He excused himself and made his way towards her.

'Why didn't you bring someone?' she asked, balancing her wine glass rather loosely between her fingers.

'You're going to spill that,' he said. 'You look as though you're well away already.'

'Oh, God, Jack, go away if you're going to be a pain. I'm enjoying myself so don't rain on my parade.' She moved into the room and put her arm round a man in a bright red waistcoat and bow tie and kissed him on the cheek. Turning her head towards Jack, she laughed. 'Let your hair down, kiddo. You're only young once.'

So he found himself, without quite realising it, on the edge of Fran's group, their backs turned on him. He didn't know whether to move away or not and for a moment he stood, hoping she'd see him, hoping she'd just draw him in to her circle. Which, amazingly, she did. 'Jack, nice to see you.' She looked at the others. 'Jack's joined a conservation group I'm in and usually we're covered in mud and slime. But we clean up nicely.'

He was grateful she'd made it easy. He looked at the couple opposite.

'This is Harriet and Tony.' They nodded, smiling.

'And this,' she motioned to the man standing by her side, tall, dark and good looking, 'this is Paul.' And she tucked her arm through his and looked up into his face with such a loving expression, Jack felt a wave of nausea hit his stomach. He could barely stand there, pretending to be interested when she went on. 'It's a wonder he isn't worn out.' She turned to Jack. 'He's driven miles to get here for this party. So we'd all better have a good time.'

And that was exactly what Jack *didn't* have.

One hour later, he was sitting in his car on the dark empty street, staring through the windscreen as drops of rain beat a steady rhythm on the glass. In minutes, the heavens had opened, rivers of water running down the window, wiping out his vision, closing him in.

Chapter 24

Sunday. Ten o'clock. Fran was looking forward to a lazy day. No smart clothes, no make-up, no phone calls. Just three-quarter-length trousers and a cotton top. No shoes either and it felt good to feel the cool tiles under her bare feet. She opened the back door to let in some air and in walked the black and white cat from two doors down that seemed to have adopted her. He looked up at her and made a guttural sound which meant he wanted some milk pouring into his dish.

She filled a glass with orange juice, picked up the newspaper from the hall mat and went back to the kitchen to settle down for half an hour. The bells were chiming for the start of Sunday service, she could hear someone mowing their lawn and there was the steady drone of a plane high up in the sky. She was absorbed in an article on hospital trusts when some sound made her look up. Head on one side, she listened, puzzled.

There it was again. A faint knocking. Unmistakable this time.

Frowning, she put the paper down and got up.

She turned the key in the lock and pulled the heavy door open.

It took her a minute to take it all in. A taxi, engine running waited in the road, a hand-wave signalling it to go and then he was standing in front of her, his expression anxious and apologetic and hopeful. All there in his eyes.

She couldn't believe it. This was the last thing she'd expected.

'Oh Alex, this is such a bad idea.'

He nodded.

She crossed her arms and took a minute to steady herself. Just seeing him there brought it all back – a rush of emotions she'd been only too glad to leave behind. She should have expected this after the barbecue, even though so many weeks had passed. She should have known he'd come eventually. But all she could think about was how it had ended and she didn't want to be reminded of any of it – the disruption, the waiting, the hurt. And yet… now… looking at his sad eyes, that familiar face far too thin, dark hair in need of a cut curling against his collar, the uneasy way he held himself, all she wanted to do was comfort him. Even after everything, she couldn't just stand there and be his judge.

You can't play the blame game because you've suffered heartbreak. We lived for those precious moments, we broke the rules and sometimes you pay. There are always consequences one way or another.

She took a step backwards. 'You'd better come in before you fall down.'

He forced a smile then. A mere ghost of his old smile but somehow it re-established some connection that perhaps had never really been broken. She led the way into the kitchen, her nerves on edge, and gathered up the newspaper that was spread over the table. She had to keep her distance, appear unfazed, so she tried to hold on to some composure.

'Just about to enjoy a quiet Sunday catching up on jobs and reading my book… looking forward to a bit of peace… and you turn up.' She knew this sounded all wrong. The situation needed to be taken seriously but she didn't know how to deal with it.

'Like a bad penny!' She could see he felt as awkward as she did. He looked round the kitchen, anywhere but at her. 'Good thing you hadn't moved. The taxi driver would've had to take me straight back.' He hesitated a moment, then pulled out a chair and sat down. He hardly needed to be polite and wait to be asked, she thought. That would have been too ridiculous. How many times had he sat at that table drinking coffee, drinking wine, talking into the night? She tried not to think about it. She didn't want to go over the past — she'd done that too often when everything had fallen apart.

But this was now. Too many questions needed answers, too much had happened that needed discussing, understanding. It wasn't just from seeing him at the barbecue. It was the accident, the effects of the coma, the fact he'd nearly died. And it was natural to want some light thrown on why he'd come, what he wanted.

But he didn't seem in a hurry to begin.

She sat down on the opposite side of the table, noticing how he clasped his hands in front of him to keep them still. It was obvious from everything about him — the way he looked, the way he spoke, the way he tried to hide behind an affected nonchalance that didn't convince her for a minute — that he was still shaky, still coming to terms with what had happened, something so traumatic it had damaged him.

He seemed hollowed out.

'How are you?' she managed at last.

'Compared with the last few months, I'm great. I suppose you heard what happened from Lucy. Well, I don't know how much I can add.' He pulled a face, weary and sardonic at the same time. 'I've made a miraculous recovery. Lucky to be alive.'

She shook her head, annoyed. 'Never mind trying to be funny. How are you *really*?'

He shifted in his chair and looked thoughtful. 'I'm getting there. It takes time. The headaches have gone and so mostly, have the nightmares. I exercise but I'm easily tired. The arm's mended and my head has healed, pretty much. Both ache like hell at times. Good job for the moment I'm not allowed to drive. Or drink.'

'And what else?' Perhaps she shouldn't be asking, but she had to push, otherwise he wouldn't open up. He might have done years ago, but not now.

He hesitated. 'My memory is... a bit out of sync. Inevitable, I suppose. At first I couldn't remember anything about the accident or the weeks before it. The days just after were gone too. Yet it was odd, coming out of the coma, my mind seemed to take off on its own. Sounds bizarre, I know. But I had a heightened awareness of everything going on around me. Strange because I wasn't able to speak or open my eyes. I could hear, though, I could sense things, even though it seemed to be behind a... well, a screen.' He was gazing past her, searching for the right words. 'I was out of it at times completely, but then I'd be there, lying in that bed, thinking so clearly and remembering...'

'Remembering?'

'A place, an image and a feeling of despair. For something lost. Something I'd never get back.' He looked at her directly then and she could have wept. It was all too painful for both of them and there were things she should tell him that would make it worse. But this wasn't the moment.

'I think my brain was working hard to rewire itself...' he began and then stopped and gave a half-hearted shrug as though he'd said enough.

They fell silent.

'And when did you realise what had happened?'

'Not straight away. I had to work it out. You wait for it all to fit together and there are gaps. Even the doctors can't tell you how things are going to pan out. It's quite common for head wounds to cause amnesia.' His eyes reflected the confusion, all the doubts. He wasn't making a drama out of it, but even so, she felt sick imagining how scared he must have been. 'Do you know the first *real* memory that came back to me after weeks of... pretty well nothing? It was when I first caught sight of you at the barbecue. Standing by the French windows in that white dress, looking across at me, all those people separating us. It was like being struck by lightning – my face must have been a picture. And the same look was on your face when you realised whose house it was…'

She put up a hand to stop him. 'Alex, I'd only just met Lucy. Her surname was Todd. I had no idea, even though you lived in this area back then…'

'Of course you hadn't. I could tell you were as shocked as I was.' He paused for a moment. 'How *did* you meet her?'

'Zumba.'

'What on earth's that?'

Fran only just kept a straight face. 'An exercise class. Never mind. I stopped going when I'd learned you were recovering. It seemed best to make a break.'

He nodded. 'Well, the rest of that evening's never come back to me. I suppose we managed to avoid each other, didn't we?'

'We did. It was awful.'

'Anyway the only person I could ask to fill in the details was my brother Joe. He described how it had gone, the people there, who he'd talked to, what we'd done – painting a picture for me really. But what he couldn't tell me, of course was…'

She finished it for him. 'Whether you were on your way to see me two days later.'

'Yes. It took me a while to realise I'd crashed too close to Whitegate for it to be a coincidence. But…' He blinked slowly. 'Did I ever reach you? That's what I don't know.'

He looked so sad, she ached for him and forgetting about her own frustrations for the moment, leaned across the table and put both her hands over his. 'No, you never reached me. You must have been on your way. But you didn't reach me.'

She stood up suddenly, turning away. 'Shall I make us a bacon sandwich? You look as though you need feeding up.'

He grinned at last. 'You sound like my mother.'

'Well, I'll bet you haven't had breakfast.'

'No. I didn't feel like eating. To be honest, I was plucking up courage.'

She had already turned on the grill, needing to be occupied and facing away from him when she asked the next question. 'Does Carrie know you're out and about?'

His voice had changed when he answered, stilted and unnatural. 'No. No-one's at home. She's gone to a horse trials thing. And my son's working.' He bent down to stroke the cat that had wound itself round his leg. 'I didn't know you liked cats. You always wanted a dog.'

'He's a visitor.'

'And you used to own this place with your brother.'

'I did. When he moved away with his job, I bought him out.'

There's something about the smell of bacon that always makes you hungry, she thought – comfort food. It reminded her of weekend breakfasts when she was a kid.

She waited until the bacon was crisp, made sandwiches wedged together with brown sauce and put them on plates. Then she brewed the tea. Watching him as he ate took her back to the first time he'd knocked on her door, months after he'd left Liverpool and she'd never imagined he would call. She'd given him her address and phone number, but it's the sort of thing you did, wasn't it? A casual *if you're passing...* It didn't really amount to an invitation.

He'd stood on her doorstep then, very like this morning, but even more unsure of himself, eyebrows raised, a quizzical expression on his face and carrying something in a cardboard box.

'Hope you don't mind. I didn't want to phone. But you said "any time" so as I was driving this way...'

She let him struggle on, so surprised to see him again. So *pleased* to see him again.

Her brother called from upstairs. 'Is it for me?'

And she shouted back. 'No, you're OK.' And she invited Alex in. He handed her the box, packed with hams and sausages and egg boxes and tomatoes.

'I was passing a farm shop and thought you might like these. Got some for myself.' She didn't even ask herself why he'd come. It was enough that he was there. That he'd wanted to see her. And they'd sat and talked at this very kitchen table, ate Welsh cakes she'd just baked and shared their experiences since Liverpool.

'In charge of three sites in this area,' he'd said. 'Nothing big, but I'm not making too many mistakes. What about you?'

And she'd explained how bored she'd become with her job and was looking around for something different. That she'd planned a holiday with Explore to Borneo because she'd always wanted to see the orangutans and needed to do it before she spent any more of her savings.

They'd chatted about books and films and pretended this visit was the most normal thing in the world. But as he got up to leave, she was determined to ask what she should have asked when he came. 'How's your family?'

He flushed. 'They're fine. Both taking exams this year and the lad's struggling. But... they're fine.'

They were both aware of the omission. He didn't mention his wife.

Then he was gone.

And now? So much water under the bridge it was difficult to fathom where they were now.

They finished eating, empty plates and mugs of tea on the table in front of them, Fran knowing she couldn't sit there any longer without finding out what else he remembered.

'Alex, after you'd seen me at the barbecue, you set out that night to come here. Was it to tell me to keep away? To ask why I was there? To talk? You must have had a reason.'

He rubbed his forehead and screwed up his eyes, almost as though that would help restore his memory. 'I can't give you an honest answer. It wasn't to warn you off, I'm sure of that. Did I see you and everything we had together came back? Did it wake me up to what I'd lost? Perhaps. I'll never know...' His whole body had tensed.

'All right. That's understandable.' She tried to keep any challenge out of her voice. 'But you're in a different place now. You're thinking clearly. Why are you here *now*?'

He didn't answer. Just looked at her with such a wistful expression it was hard for her to remain detached. 'Fran, you know why I'm here. It's because...' he paused, 'because after all this time, and you might not believe me, I know, but I still feel the same. Christ, nothing's changed. And after seeing you again, I couldn't stay away. I don't know how I've lasted so long when I've known you were only an hour away. I used to look up at the night sky and imagine you doing the same thing at the same moment – as though there was some sort of sixth sense that kept us close.' He gave a harsh laugh. 'Does that answer your question?'

She was so angry, it was as though the breath had been knocked out of her. *Oh God, don't start all this again.* 'Alex, *you* were the one who finished it! With a fucking letter! A letter! No warning, no proper explanation. Just sorry, something's happened at home, don't call me.' She wasn't just angry, she was furious. 'I think you might remember that!'

'Of course I do...'

'And have you thought that I might have moved on, married, had children? Left you way behind? Have you thought about that when you sit there saying all the things that are like salt in the wound? Fuck you!' She was having trouble forming the words. Had he expected her to just wait around in case there was a second act?

'And have you?' he said.

'Have I what?

223

'Got married, had children? Found someone else.'

She glared at him. 'No, I haven't got married or had children. But I might have done. I've certainly had relationships. One that very nearly ended up in something permanent. Seven years is a long time to wear black and mourn. That was never me.'

He nodded then. 'No, it wasn't. You were always much more positive than me.' He didn't seem to know how to go on. 'And what's your job now?'

She sighed. She could see the strain on his face and she had to simmer down. 'I have my own agency, F.R. Recruitment – an office in a new block in Liverpool. It's doing well, quite small but growing. I got fed up with working for other people.'

'I always thought you'd do well. You're bright.'

'Not bright enough obviously. Or I'd have seen where we were heading,' she said scornfully. 'You have no idea what it was like when that letter came. When I knew it was over between us.'

'Of course I do. Bloody painful. Like a wound that won't heal. Struggling to get through the days.' His voice broke. 'But there was no other choice I could have made. And if I'd seen you to explain... told you face to face... I'd never have left. I did what I did then for a good reason...'

'Don't say any more! I don't want to hear it.' She fought back tears, from anger and despair and an overwhelming sense of fear. 'Just go! My life is fine. I'm comfortable with it. I'm seeing someone really nice who's got no ties and I'm happy – well, *was* until you came today. Please, Alex, go away. Nothing's changed for you, you have your wife and family, I've seen that and I'm not going down that road ever again.'

He got up slowly and she kept sitting, her knuckles pressed against her mouth. He put his hand on her shoulder as he passed, making for the door, walking slowly up the hall. She kept her back to him and closed her eyes, not wanting to watch him go. There were so many conflicting emotions in her, she wanted to scream but in the end, she couldn't bear it any longer. She called after him and he turned, a wary expression on his face, ready for more home truths he knew he deserved for digging up the past.

But she came close and put her arms round him, buried her face in his shirt and held him – and kept holding him until he gently hugged her back and laid his cheek against her hair.

'Oh Fran,' was all he said, but there was such suffering in those two words, it sounded like a prayer.

They stood for a long time, almost holding each other up, an old embrace remembered. It was enough in so many ways, leaving nothing to say. What more could be said anyway? Words had lost their currency. When they finally moved apart, they just looked at one another, solemn, forgiving.

'We can't go anywhere with this,' she said. 'Not again.'

'No.'

'I'm older and a bit wiser now – I've learned the hard way that what you want and what you can have are two different things. But that doesn't mean I don't care, Alex. I care.'

'I know.' He tried a smile. 'And I shouldn't have come.'

'Yes, you should. There were too many unanswered questions, I understand that. I'm not sorry you came.'

'Neither am I. And don't worry about me. I'm going to be fine. Back to work soon and I'll…'

She pulled away from him suddenly and picked up a pen from the hall table, writing her mobile number on the back of his hand. 'Don't start being heroic!' She couldn't quite keep her voice steady. 'If ever you need me, if ever you're in real trouble, ring me. Promise!'

He kissed her forehead. 'I promise.'

She phoned for a taxi and they waited, close together but held back by some tacit agreement, an agreed red line, making small talk which had little meaning. In a way, it was a relief to see him go. She sat on the sofa and cuddled the cat to her, its warmth and steady breathing a comfort. She'd let the chance go, hadn't she? She should have been honest with him.

She should have said, 'Alex, I've something to tell you.'

But what was the point now? He didn't need to know about Jack. That his son had got the wrong idea about her – that he'd fancied her. It would have been too awkward to bring up – for all of them. And anyway, she'd done what she could to kill the whole embarrassing situation- stayed away from the conservation group and dealt the final and deliberate blow at Rachel's party – and that had been cruel. Surely that had finished off any idea in his head that she was 'available' or interested in him.

He wasn't to know the full story – that she'd deliberately set it up.

That Paul was her brother.

Chapter 25

I enter the empty house feeling like a soldier who's gone AWOL and made it back safely, guilty at the subterfuge and thankful not to be found out. I'm exhausted. Probably because I've been running on adrenalin and it's running out. Sam shuffles out of the kitchen to greet me, tail wagging and I find a treat for him then open the back door to the garden. He decides he'd rather stay and have my company and flops himself against the fridge.

'OK,' I say to him. 'Be awkward. I know you. In five minutes, you'll be mithering to go out.' He stares up at me with what looks like a smile on his face and pants in agreement.

God, I shouldn't feel good, but I do. Just to know she still cares for me. Isn't that what I'd selfishly hoped for all these years? I suppose because she stayed in my mind, a constant presence long after it was over – things we did together, places we went to, what we talked about. Is that what nostalgia is? A longing to keep hold of the past when you know with such certainty that you were happy. I think so.

And the amazing thing was she hadn't changed! Perhaps more sure of herself, stronger somehow, which is inevitable but other than that, she hadn't changed at all. There was the same warmth and humour, interested in everything, a quickness to understand. Christ, it's impossible to explain why you're drawn to certain people, why you instantly like them, why you have an uncanny flash of recognition. And a complete mystery how you're aware they see something similar in you.

It just happens.

So even though guilt and a sense of betrayal should overshadow it all, I feel good. Contented. I have no right to be. But for the moment, I allow myself this indulgence, quite aware that it'll be short-lived. I even spend some minutes staring at the smudged ink numbers on the back of my hand. This is not the behaviour of a sensible adult. I know that. But it certainly beats the despondency of the last few months.

I've got hours to myself before anyone comes back and I know at some point in the afternoon, I must go across to the yard to see if Steph needs anything. She's been left in charge and is more than capable of running the place but I've promised to check. And I'd said I'd walk down to the cricket club later and meet up with Colin. He keeps telling me to get out and enjoy life.

I don't think he meant in the way I've spent the day.

I go outside and wander round the garden which one of the local lads, Timmy, has been keeping under control, but now it's doing its own thing, roses beginning to outgrow their strength, bushes spreading over the borders, red berries dotting the grass where the birds have dropped them. Adrian has asked me to go back to work at the start of next month, two days a week, a driver will pick me up so I'm looking forward to that. I think. Just a couple of my old sites to look after for now and some estimating in the main office – all without much pressure. It'll do me good to concentrate on problems I can solve! And I've missed the company. What I've always liked about our industry is the lack of formality, first names only, particularly on site, whatever your status. No-one ever calls me anything but Alex. It's always struck me as healthy. You're in it together – everyone contributes towards the final outcome. Well, perhaps in one way it's not as democratic as all that. When it comes to who's responsible if there's a cock-up, it's me who carries the can.

I stroll back to the patio where we sat on Friday night, some candle holders and a ceramic pot with its array of small purple flowers still on the table. It was a long evening, mostly because I find Meryl, and particularly Bill, hard to take. It's not just that we have very little in common. We have a totally different way of looking at the world. I knew I had to keep off politics – anything to do with education, taxing the wealthy and asylum seekers makes him go very red in the face – still, there's only so long you can discuss the local news, sport, television programmes and holidays before you slip up.

They arrived for, as Meryl put it, *a little supper,* her voice full of consideration, *to see how well you are doing.* She handed Carrie a large bowl of trifle as her contribution to the evening. She headed my way with a sympathetic look on her face and gave me a careful hug, barely touching me in case I broke in half. And when Bill shook his head at me and said, 'You're a lucky man from what I hear!' I could only smile like a robot that's programmed to respond in the only way it can. Blandly.

They'd come formally dressed. Meryl, blonde and pale in a flowing outfit, Bill in a bespoke hacking jacket and wearing a tie, for God's sake. I caught a look from Carrie which was like a warning shot – *Be nice, be civilised, be a good host.* So I did my best.

But my best didn't prove to be quite enough.

The food Carrie had prepared was wonderful. Smoked salmon pate, chicken Caesar salad, tiny roasted potatoes, crusty bread. And a bottle of Sancerre – well, two bottles because I was allowed to join in and have one glass, like a child at a grown-ups' party. And after about an hour, I was wishing they'd send me to bed early! Perhaps it was the mood I was in but everything about them set my teeth on edge.

They're pretentious in the way that most people in this village aren't. They'd moved from the south when Bill's factory relocated to Merseyside years ago and they still seemed determined to make it clear that they were in a class above. Above what, I'm not sure, but even their way of speaking made them sound as though they were auditioning for the Royal Shakespeare Company. Forced and just a bit too loud and it irritates.

We'd heard all about their holiday in Sardinia before we'd got to the main course (and to be fair, they remembered we'd had to cancel ours), how they'd booked through a local travel agent – tailor-made, five star, private beach – the couple they'd met who they were going to spend Christmas with, the excursions… Carrie was bringing out the food and pouring the wine for much of this, so I was their audience. I nodded, made appreciative sounds, pulled appropriate expressions. Then perhaps they realised they were talking about themselves too much and just as I was about to enjoy my glass of wine, they wanted to know what progress I was making, how I was feeling, was I receiving all the help I needed. How the accident had *affected* me.

Carrie wasn't going to have *this* conversation again. 'I think Alex has had enough of going over it all, Bill,' she said, handing round the basket of bread. 'He's back at work at the end of the month and the physiotherapy sessions are not as frequent now. He's doing fine. Do you want butter…?'

So thank heaven, that was the end of that.

Things improved a bit as the time went on, more to-and-fro, and discussion about the village fete meant we were on safe ground, as were the complaints about the poorly placed signposts at the crossroads and the bin collections. We could all agree on those – parochial concerns that didn't ruffle any feathers. I almost relaxed. It might be boring but there was nothing contentious about any of it.

So we were doing OK until Meryl put down her napkin and turned to me, actually placing her hand around my wrist. 'We were talking the other night and came up with a really good idea.' She paused and with a look which smacked of conspiracy, nodded at Bill. 'We think you should join the golf club.' She made it sound like an announcement. 'It'll get you out in the fresh air, you'll pick it up in no time and the social life is really good. Carrie would love that.'

She could see I looked uncertain; the truth is I felt cornered.

'To be honest, I never fancied golf…'

Bill cut me off. 'Well, you'd need time to build yourself up after what's happened. But it's one of those games that becomes addictive once you've started. Even when you begin late like I did. It's not physical strength that counts, it's the mind that's important – controlling your nerves.'

I could see they'd already got me on the first tee. I waited and looked over at Carrie who was sitting back drinking her wine, her eyes on me. Whose side was she on?

'I'd be glad to put your name forward,' Bill said full of enthusiasm, for some reason eager to recruit me. A breeze had risen up, blowing gently across the garden which lifted the front of his immaculately combed hair off his forehead. He smoothed it down. 'They're a decent bunch of blokes on the committee. You'd have no trouble being accepted.'

That's good to hear. I'm obviously the type they want in their ranks. No riff raff to lower the tone.

Then Carrie joined in. Such a mistake! 'It's worth thinking about, Alex. All you seem to do is work and read books. Once your arm is strong enough, I'm sure you'd enjoy it.'

'He would.'

How I hate people deciding what I'd like. You can't speak for someone else. It's bloody presumptuous! And I'm not as compliant these days as I used to be when I'd shrug and think – anything for a quiet life. Must be down to the bang on the head.

I could feel my chest tightening, never a good sign. 'My grandfather played golf,' I began. 'He was a bit of an addict, Bill. And on a few occasions, Christmas and Easter, special holidays, we'd be invited to the club for a meal. A special treat. My mother would dress us up, Joe and me, warn us to be on our best behaviour and off we'd all go to be fussed over by the adults before we'd go along to the dining room and listen to a welcoming speech and eat this meal, always served by waitresses in black outfits and white aprons. Funny what you remember. But what sticks most in my mind is that when we arrived, my grandfather was always having a drink at the bar and had to be fetched. But it was a Men Only bar – my mother explained that she couldn't cross the threshold, even if she'd been there without us. It just wasn't done. And you know the other thing that amazed me, even as a kid? The women members weren't allowed on the course on Sunday mornings. They were meant to be at home cooking the family dinner which was obviously expected of the right sort of wife.'

They all stared at me. But I hadn't finished.

'So you see, I realised early on that it wasn't the sort of place where I'd ever want to spend my time. It's as simple as that. It wasn't for me then and it isn't for me now.'

Bill spluttered a bit and Meryl tried to disagree. Carrie looked daggers. No-one was bothering to eat anymore.

'It's nothing like that now,' Bill said when he'd caught his breath. 'It's very… egalitarian. There's no sexism in our club. Meryl wouldn't be a member if there was.'

But the discussion died after that and the evening ended on a rather desultory note.

The last words Carrie uttered as she let them out and shut the door behind them was what I expected.

'You shit!'

*

I walk over to the stables and find Steph filling a hay net and humming to herself, totally absorbed in the task. She always seems to be at peace with herself and I envy that – she certainly doesn't have an easy life, I've seen how farming can wear you down. If it isn't the weather, it's the crop yield or the low price of milk and it's hard manual work for most of the year. But she never shows any sign of discontent.

She waves me away when I ask if I can do anything.

'It's been a quiet day,' she says. 'Apart from Splinter in there who we've had to keep in because he's got a pulled tendon. He keeps kicking at the door, which isn't doing him any good... or my head.' She hangs the net up on a hook and smiles at me. 'Good to see you around again, Alex. We missed you.'

'Thanks. It's good to be back.'

I set off down the road to the cricket club. I'd sent a text to Colin to say I'd be there about a quarter to five, so he's already bought me a soft drink which stands on our usual table by the windows. We sit there because it looks over the pitch and we can be commentators and critics without having to stir. It's an odd room really, well an odd building. The upstairs is the social part, all pale wood and pale walls and the room has too much space to be cosy. I liked the old building much better, a bit more like a shed with lots of character and history about it and it *looked* like a cricket pavilion rather than a venue for a cabaret. It fitted in with the village in the way this didn't. But someone must have thought it needed modernising – probably as the cricket team improved its performance and more people started to follow its progress.

I sit in the vacant chair beside Colin and opposite Ken, another long-standing supporter – both are already into the usual bandying of jokes and insults – and I shake my head as I lift my glass. 'No-one would ever take you two for best friends,' I say.

'Ah, we're the best of enemies,' says Ken. 'And you know what they say. *Keep your friends close and your enemies closer.*'

I have to laugh. 'I'm not sure I understand that. Over the years, this place is becoming more like Alice in Wonderland. Not a lot makes sense.'

'It's a cover,' Colin joins in. 'We pretend to be what we're not. That way we get away with anything.'

And so it goes on – silly, funny, affectionate. And I'm glad to be here. These old men wrap you up in their world where the ambition and the one-upmanship have long gone.

They're comfortable to be with.

Until that is, Colin says, 'Saw you going off in a taxi this morning, Alex. Pleased you're getting out and about. But if you ever want a lift anywhere,' he pauses and gives me a look, kindly, direct, which I can't meet, 'give me a call. I'll be happy to take you while you're not allowed to drive.'

My heart rate has gone up. Does he sense my disquiet? I have no idea, but I don't stay long, I finish my drink and go over to the bar, buy a packet of crisps and head for home.

Has anyone else seen me leave in a taxi, someone who might mention it casually to Jack or Carrie? I can't do anything about it now anyway. It's done. Over.

And when I get back to the house and after I've set the table for dinner, I sit on the couch waiting for the evening to come, shadows forming in the corners of the room because although it's only five thirty, the clouds have gathered outside and the sky has turned grey and I wonder what's actually over. Do I really mean just today, a final moment, an end to it all?

I don't think I can answer that. She's in my mind – it's filled with the sight of her, the touch of her, the sound of her voice. The longing for her. What's the bloody good of telling myself to forget her? She's part of me and has been for a long time. My mind with its stored memories like photo shots in an album doesn't let me forget.

I'm not sure I can do it – leave it just like that, this lifeline dangling just beyond my reach, like a kite string about to be torn away by the wind. I know I should put her wishes first, I know it's a betrayal of every other relationship I have and yet… it's so hard to let go.

Today, standing at her door conjured up the same emotions I had the second time I called on her after I'd left Liverpool. The first time was easy, casual – I'd passed a farm shop near her house and bought a boxful of stuff as a sort of friendly gesture and I'd convinced myself that's what it was. But the second time, I couldn't pretend this was just because I was 'passing by.' I'd been constantly thinking of her as I'd driven between jobs, the car seeming to have a will of its own, directing itself towards that village where I'd no right to be. *Christ! Come on,* I'd tell myself, *this is crazy.* And then I'd tune into a local radio station only to hear love songs that echoed everything I was feeling.

I'd been driving on the outskirts of Runcorn, in a traffic jam actually, and when I'd seen an advert on a billboard for The Brindley, I guessed it was an arts centre rather than a cinema, but it was having a week showing retro films, *Double Indemnity, Psycho,* and on Wednesday, *Casablanca.* And that did it. It might be one of those films that crops up on TV every so often, but to sit in a cinema and see it on a big screen… it was too good to miss.

I knew it was only a chance, but I phoned the centre and made the booking. On the next Wednesday, armed with my two tickets for the eight o'clock showing, I again knocked on Fran's door. She'd obviously only just got in from work and when I'd told her my idea, she just looked at me. It was as though she was reading my thoughts.

'Alex, you're married.' She still held the door open. I wasn't being invited in this time. 'You have a family.'

'Yes.'

'I really don't know what to say.' She lowered her head, as though she was trying to work something out. 'I should tell you to go away, this is something I don't want to start…' She was silent for so long, her gaze steady and sad. But there was something in her expression I was sure matched my own.

'It *has* started…for me.'

And there it was at last.

So we sat through *Casablanca,* holding hands in the dark, me remembering all the best bits before they hit the screen – Dooley

Wilson singing *As Time Goes By*, Bogart drinking away to kill the pain, the sardonic humour, the brilliant ending. And Fran loved it as I knew she would. On the way back to Whitegate, we repeated the lines to one another, not always getting them right – *Of all the gin joints in all the world... our problems don't amount to a hill of beans... we'll always have Paris* and making up new ones that might have fitted into the screenplay. It was fun. It was such fun.

By the time we'd reached her house that night we were happily and foolishly falling into something neither of us had intended. Or that's what I told myself. I'm not sure I was ever completely honest about any of it.

The memory takes me back so completely that I can see it all in my mind's eye and I'm lost in it all, almost speaking the silly phrases out loud. Then I hear the front door opening and come to my senses in a rush, getting up and switching the lights on.

It's better if I don't think, don't daydream, don't wish for anything.

It's all too dangerous.

Chapter 26

The taxi had dropped them off near the entrance and they made their way through a tree-lined avenue towards the gate, two officials on guard checking tickets. People filtered through carrying picnic baskets and rugs, haversacks, many with dogs on leads, some struggling with pushchairs in a bid to get in early and make a day of it. With a light breeze and firm ground, the conditions would suit both horses and riders and Carrie was glad it didn't pose extra dangers on the cross-country course. Experience had taught her what a hazardous sport this was.

David guided her over the uneven grass past the trade stands, indicating to bear right towards a low white picket fence. As he walked, he looped his membership badge through the button hole on his jacket, then handed Carrie hers which she tucked through the belt of her suede waistcoat. She'd spent some time deciding what to wear. It might be a formal do but the clothes needed to be practical. Eventually, she'd chosen a white linen shirt, navy trousers and this soft blue waistcoat, which matched the stone in the pendant round her neck. As she'd climbed into the car that morning, David holding the door for her, she realised it was quite a while since she'd looked forward to a day out quite as much as this. Something different, a break from all the worries of the past months. She settled back, smiling to herself.

When David turned towards her, eyebrows raised and said, 'You look wonderful, Carrie,' she was taken by surprise.

Quite lost for words, she could only manage, 'I scrub up well.' How pat and unoriginal! The look on his face told her she should have taken the compliment as it was intended so quickly added, 'You look pretty smart yourself.' which was true. He certainly knew how to dress.

Now, leaving the crowds behind them, they stood at the entrance to the private enclosure, ready to be guided along its boardwalk up to the hospitality area.

David took her arm. 'Come on, time to meet Freddie Baxter, our host. He'll fill us in on the form for the day. He knows more about horses than you and I put together.' He took long strides which Carrie had trouble keeping up with. 'Champagne breakfast first, then the dressage. Best part for me. I find I learn quite a lot by just watching – try to put some of it into practice. Not quite at this level, of course.'

They passed the first two open-fronted marquees and stopped at the third one. People were already standing round, tall glasses in their hands, tables set with white cloths and carafes of water. She was led through the gathering – men in beautifully tailored blazers and Harris Tweed jackets and women, tanned, hair styled, their outfits simple and expensive.

At the drinks table, a young waiter handed David two flutes of champagne and he passed one to her. She took a sip which tasted acrid and gassy; she'd never understood what made it so special. But she was a guest, lucky to be invited so she pretended to enjoy it and listened in to the talk going on around her. What she heard and saw in the first ten minutes convinced her that half of them didn't know one end of a horse from the other. The chat was about holidays, the theatre, houses and share prices. This was the world of corporate business and these were the executives receiving the benefits due to position and status. They were here for the perks rather than a love of the sport. The irony of the whole situation amused her. A young Carrie had been on the other side of the white picket fence – working in one of the trade stands, earning a living by selling horse feed. But that was a long time ago. And here she was, drinking champagne. All very fancy but not as congenial.

It was clear though, David was in his element. He might not be quite one of them but this kind of society embraced the urbane, the confident, and that was the type of man he was. She could see how well he fitted in. He looked the part. He had that polished surface that impressed people. But she'd seen another side from her dealings with him over the past few months. Beneath the charming exterior was something much darker – a certain drive, a selfishness, a ruthless streak. Capable of getting what he wanted, never mind the cost. It put Carrie on her guard. She'd be a fool not to be. But in spite of those misgivings, there was something attractive about such self-assurance, such… audacity. He just took charge. And for once that was OK. It was a welcome change to be looked after, not having to make the decisions all the time.

A small, heavily built man, white-haired with strong features and supporting himself with a walking stick came towards them and David introduced Carrie with a flourish. 'Now Freddie,' he said. 'This is the woman I've been telling you about. It's all down to her that Jodie's doing so well now. She's done an amazing job.'

Freddie put out his left hand, catching hold of Carrie's in a strong grip. 'So pleased to meet you. It's nice to see this man happy again. He was worrying the little girl might be losing interest, but you've changed all that.'

Carrie didn't want to take too much of the credit. 'To be fair, I've done very little. It just took some time, that's all. And patience.'

'I'm sure that's false modesty,' he said. 'You actually own the livery yard, I believe. David's told me all about it. Sounds a nice little place you've got. I know he's pleased he moved from Wilmslow.' Someone shouted his name. 'Well, must circulate and make sure everyone's catered for. Hope you enjoy your day.'

He moved off to shake hands with other guests, some already helping themselves to the lavish breakfast laid out on a long side table

– smoked salmon, miniature beef wellingtons, egg mayonnaise salad and Melba toast. Freddie certainly knew how to entertain. Carrie wondered what his relationship was with David but now wasn't the time to ask. Other guests were moving out of the marquee to watch the dressage that had just begun in the arena. Some only managed to follow four or five competitors before giving up and wandering back under cover. Not surprising really. Carrie knew it could seem repetitive if you didn't understand the scoring or what comprised a good test.

David fetched two chairs from the marquee so they could sit outside, then brought out plates of food which they balanced on their laps and two more glasses of champagne. For a while they sat, their attention focussed on each performance, saying very little except for the odd comment.

'I suppose you come to this kind of thing quite often,' he said at last.

She hadn't meant to laugh. 'Well, not exactly like this! I'm more likely to be roughing it, trudging round in my wellies in the rain, grabbing a cheeseburger then staying in a scruffy B and B if it's a three-day event. Today, I'm going up in the world.'

'Well, it's good to have your company. Someone with the same outlook.' He glanced across at her as he put his empty plate under the chair. She had the odd feeling that he was weighing her up, passing some sort of judgement on her. 'This,' he waved his hand towards the ring, 'is so far beyond what I can do. But I'll bet you could have been good enough to compete here.'

'No, I was never anywhere near good enough. Reached Medium Level, but you know how it is, things get in the way.'

'Like what?'

'Life, work, circumstances.' She was quiet for a few minutes, relaxed in familiar surroundings – the concentration of the spectators, the soft sounds of hooves on the grass, the balmy day. No doubt the champagne helped. 'It's ironic, really. This was where I worked when I was eighteen. Oh, not in the hospitality tents. Out there on the grounds. For three years, my job was standing in a trailer belonging to big feed merchants, promoting their products, trying to sell new lines, giving advice on nutrition. Most of the time was spent in the office, but as soon as the season started, we'd go round all the big events – Badminton, Chatsworth, Burghley. It didn't pay too well but I so enjoyed it, the company was good, lively, you know... we were all young, a bit hare-brained...'

As she sat there, remembering how happy she'd been, remembering herself young, it was as though there was no audience to hear her. David wasn't there, he wasn't listening, no-one was listening. She was just talking aloud. And for some reason, or for many reasons, she felt at peace with herself. She'd needed this. She'd grown tired of trying to hold everything together, of being strong, reining in any emotion that might topple her carefully structured life. Or was it her carefully structured marriage? Usually she didn't open up to anyone – talking about oneself like this always seemed a kind of weakness. But perhaps the last few months had taken their toll. She needed... what? ...Some sort of release.

She turned her head, suddenly conscious he was watching her. Eventually he said, 'And then? What happened when you were twenty-one?' His voice was quiet, different from his usual combative tone – not badgering or calling the shots. He sounded genuinely interested when she'd often thought he was too self-absorbed to care about anyone else, other than Jodie.

She shrugged. 'I met Alex again, I fell pregnant with Lucy. It's not the sort of job you can do easily when you find yourself... tied down.' Those weren't the words she should have chosen, but they were out before she could stop them.

'You met Alex again?'

'Yes, the first time was when we were seventeen, still at school –

not the same one but we didn't live far from each other. I was riding along this country road on quite a high-spirited horse and knocked him off his bike.' Thinking about his behaviour on Friday night, how he'd ruined the evening, she wished now she'd left him in the ditch. She closed her eyes briefly then sensing David was expecting more, she carried on. 'He'd been away at university and had just come back home. We were both filling our cars up at a petrol station and it went from there. I suppose my crowd were the Cheshire set, going round Wilmslow and Prestbury, pub crawling, parties – we were all from fairly well-off families, had our own cars, money to spend and most didn't take work too seriously... or anything seriously. Looking back, I suppose it had got a bit wild. And Alex wasn't like the others. He certainly wasn't drawn in by my crowd and I liked that about him. He didn't put on an act. A good head on his shoulders, my father used to say. He approved.'

'That was important to you.'

'Yes, very. Well, he approved until I found I was pregnant. That didn't go down too well.' She stopped then, realising she'd given away more than she'd intended. 'God, you've got me telling you my life story!'

'And that upsets you, for some reason.' He frowned and picked up his drink, finishing it in one go. 'D'you know, I have the feeling you don't quite trust me, Carrie.'

She hesitated. 'It's not that. 'It's... well, I don't really know you, David. I don't really know anything *about* you.'

'Well, how about I sum up my life for you?' She could tell by the way he was clipping his words that he didn't really want to reveal anything too personal. 'I'm forty-three years old, one sister, private education in York, a director in the family business. Recently divorced. One child. That's about it.'

Carrie shook her head. He always had to be contrary. 'That's the full version, is it?'

'The details won't tell you much more.' He turned away, eyes back on the ring.

She felt they were sparring, playing some sort of game, which was so unnecessary. 'Perhaps they'd give me a better idea of who you are. You ask all these questions of me but you don't really give anything away about yourself.' She looked over at him, in a way challenging him to open up. But he didn't respond. 'You're not easy to work out, David, d'you know that? One minute you can be easy company, considerate, *sociable*, the next... well, evasive, short-tempered. Difficult. You're unpredictable, I suppose.'

He raised his eyebrows and she thought she'd gone too far. 'That doesn't sound too good.'

'It unnerves people, makes them back off. You come across as someone who's ready for a fight.'

He blew out his breath in a long soft whistle. 'Do I indeed?' He didn't sound annoyed. He sounded intrigued.

Carrie felt perhaps she'd overstepped the mark. 'Sorry, it's just an impression, David. I'm being hard on you. There's a really nice side to you and I've seen that. Not a lot but...'

He shook his head and began to laugh and she joined in, conscious that this exchange had become delicate, too intimate, stripped of all the conventions of good manners. It didn't sit right. The shift made Carrie uncomfortable and she felt the need to restore a healthy distance between them, so deliberately turned her attention back to the ring. 'That grey just did a perfect transition. Were you watching?'

He sat back and folded his arms with no intention of answering. There was no way she was going to win with him. Or understand what made him tick. But one thing she *did* know – he wasn't someone to be taken lightly.

At lunch, they found spare seats at an empty table and were soon joined by two other guests, a man and a woman who asked if they could sit with them.

'I'm Laurence.' The man stretched out his hand. 'And this is Tanya, my business partner. Doesn't Freddie put on a good show! Wonderful food. And we've got the jumping and the cross country to come.'

And when David made their introductions, it was in such a way that no-one would be able to work out their connection to each other.

'Carrie and David,' he said.

It was as though they were a couple.

As long as they were in company, Carrie was prepared to let it go. But in the afternoon, as they followed the crowds over the parkland alongside the roped-off cross-country course she decided to be cool, to send the sort of signal that said, 'Enough.' They were standing at the water jump, waiting for the next rider to canter down the bank to take the fence into the lake when he turned to her. 'What's annoyed you, Carrie? You're spoiling the afternoon.'

She looked at him in amazement. 'Really? I thought I was being the perfect companion.'

He laughed softly then, as though to himself, 'Don't be sarcastic. You know what I mean.' He had that knowing, supercilious look on his face that could be so irritating. As though he enjoyed winding her up. 'Have it your own way.'

She shook her head. This man was impossible to put down. Nothing she said was going to dent his ego. But she wasn't going to give in. 'You take over at times, David, as though you know what's best for everyone else... and I suppose I'm not used to that.'

'You mean I'm not like Alex, who's obviously kind and easy going and...'

She glared at him. 'No, you're not like Alex. But that's not the point. You don't see things from anyone else's point of view. Or consider how they feel. And that doesn't work with me.'

He suddenly looked contrite and Carrie had to wonder whether this was genuine. 'No, it doesn't. That's what I like about you. You're strong, independent. No-one would disagree with that.'

How do you deal with someone like this? Carrie thought.

It was when they were leaving and thanking Freddie for his hospitality that she began to understand something of what was going on. The old man made a point of making small talk until the marquee was nearly empty.

'David was telling me your livery yard is one of the best in the area,' he said. 'Efficiently run, well organised. You know a great deal about equine management.'

'Well, I've been around horses since I could walk. So experience is a good teacher.' She wanted to finish the goodbyes but Freddie seemed unwilling to let her go.

'You haven't thought of expanding your business? Making it a much bigger enterprise? I gather you have plenty of land, if you wanted to.'

What is this? she thought, starting to feel suspicious. *A proposition? What's David been saying to this man?*

'Yes, there's land. But I haven't thought about expanding. I like to have my hands on the reins — sorry, that wasn't meant to be funny — and I'm able to do that with the number of liveries I have.'

'Well, if you ever change your mind, I'd invest — really put your yard on the map. And I know David would give you his support. Think about it.'

She stared at Freddie, full of bonhomie with his bright eyes and genial manner and began to feel concern for the way this conversation was going, determined to give nothing away, not to him and certainly not to David. Even if the idea *did* appeal to her, she was far too circumspect to let them know.

'It's nice when people see potential in you,' she said, smiling. 'If I ever consider it, I'll let you know.'

245

*

It was getting dark and much later than she'd expected when she let herself into the house. She could hear Alex and Jack talking in the kitchen and from the smell of cooking, she knew they were having dinner. She heard laughter and was saddened by the fact that she had no part of it; if she joined them at the table, that easy camaraderie would be gone. *They're drifting away from me, and I'm not doing anything about it.*

Passing the kitchen door without them seeing her, she slipped upstairs to change, realising with not much pleasure that she'd been much more comfortable in the last twelve hours than she was in her own home.

It was a sobering thought.

Chapter 27

We walk side by side and I can't believe she's here with me. She has something to tell me but not yet. It's the middle of the afternoon and we're in no hurry. I can smell the grass and the earth is dry and brown on my shoes. It's odd that there's almost no sound — just the faint whisper of wind as we move higher. Not sure where we're heading but it doesn't matter. Fran is with me and it's everything I've wanted and I'm happy to wait and hear what she's going to say. As we climb further up the hill, her hair is blown across her face and she brushes it away. She isn't smiling but I feel that I am and so everything is all right. There's a moment when we become still and she turns to me, puts out her arms and enfolds me so tenderly, wrapping me in warmth and I am crying quietly. The sky is huge above us and she doesn't speak even though I wait. Then a cold rush of air and she pushes me backwards with all her strength and I stagger, arms flailing, clutching wildly, falling...

Jack woke with a start so sudden, it was as though he'd been thrown onto the bed from a height, his whole body in such a state of agitation, heartbeats pounding his chest so fast like drum beats he thought he must be having a heart attack. Lying on his back, bedclothes tossed aside, he struggled to come to his senses. God! He'd thought it was real. It *seemed* real. Certain that what he'd experienced was actually happening because he could see and hear and feel. When really, it was all just strange kaleidoscopic images. Pictures on the brain that usually faded so fast they were gone when you woke up. But not this time.

How can dreams put you in a state like this where you wake up trembling, in such a panic? he thought. As though your mind is full of trouble and this is the only way it can express itself. Is it about what you desire or what you fear? All the fragments you dig up from everything you keep buried, the worries you try to overcome without fully realising in your waking state that they exist.

Jack rubbed his face with both hands and sat up, breathing more regularly now. He looked at the bedside clock, 6.30, too early to get ready for work, but he had to move himself, have a shower, have a few minutes outside and make something to eat. No-one up. He could go down and let Sam out into the garden while the house was quiet.

But he couldn't get up yet. He looked round the bedroom in the half-light, his clothes tossed on the floor from the night before, the CD player on the bookcase, a mug on the dressing table beside a card with a photo of a dog – '*They make our lives whole*' it said – which someone had sent him. This is reality, mate, he reminded himself. Get it into your head that this ordinary, mundane life, getting up, going to work, sleeping alone after a night watching the television is your lot. And she isn't part of it.

Wasn't the humiliation at Rachel's place enough?

He winced at the memory of it. He'd come face to face with the true picture. And he'd seen how absurd he was being. A fool thinking he'd got a chance with a woman like Fran, older, sophisticated in his eyes, beautiful. '*Out of his league*' had been right. And there she'd been with her boyfriend, of *course* she would have had a boyfriend. Hadn't Lucy suggested that? They were a pair. It had all the familiarity of a long-established relationship, how close they'd stood, the eye contact, the familiar touching. They were just easy with one another. He'd looked nice, this Paul, older than Fran, tall and, Jack had to admit, handsome… an open friendly expression on his face. Jack had hovered for a moment at the edge of the group but the last thing he wanted was to stand there like a spare part, a spectator, so he backed off, making some lame comment that only he could hear. Well, he certainly couldn't stand there and chat away. So he tried to look purposeful as he headed for the kitchen, on his way bumping into

Rachel who put her arm round his shoulders and kept asking him if he was having 'a good time.'

*No, this is **not** my idea of having a good time!* he wanted to say. *This is my idea of hell!*

'Yes… thanks Rachel. Really good party. Just going to get another Coke.'

He'd had to endure a torturous hour of pretending to enjoy himself, not even able to have a drink, pretending it all didn't matter and he was fine. Knowing he must get out of there and give up on the whole hopeless idea.

And now here he was, dreaming in full technicolour of some moment with her on a hillside in a charade that didn't make sense (the whole thing like a bizarre foreign film with no subtitles) causing him to wake to a crazy mixture of longing and pain. A hopeless case. He couldn't fathom why thoughts of Fran still preoccupied him. Why couldn't he accept the brutal truth of it all?

Yet he knew the answer. He just wished it could be that easy.

Once he'd had a shower he felt better. He let Sam into the garden and filled the dog bowl with special biscuits and some ham. Might as well give the old boy a treat, never mind the diet he was supposed to be on.

As he drove to work, slowed down by a tractor piled high with round hay bales going at fifteen miles an hour, the downside of living around farms at harvest time, he turned his thoughts to Steve's 'request'. He wished he hadn't been asked to check up on a mate. Difficult to know how to deal with a situation like this, even harder when you were the new boy. It wasn't in Jack's nature to act as an informer, even though he could see the pilfering couldn't go on unchecked. Anyway, he liked Gary which made it even worse. He'd shown Jack the ropes when he'd started, offered to take him climbing, they'd shared lunch breaks and a Chinese takeaway, talked endlessly about football. Jack would have been friends with him even if they hadn't worked together.

He pulled into the staff car park and saw Lazy Martin slowly getting out of his four-by-four and ambling across to the back entrance. *Wish it had been him who was knocking stuff off,* Jack thought. But even then, whoever it was doing the filching, Steve had put him in an awkward position. Why didn't the bosses just look at the cameras a bit more closely, or mark bank notes, or question everyone, rather than be underhand about the whole thing? It was as dishonest as the stealing in a way.

As it happened, he was directed to the storage unit at the side of the shop, checking incoming boxes of goods and marking up prices and Gary had obviously been given the same orders. He was already moaning that this wasn't part of the job description when he'd become a Parson's employee. 'You're expected to cover everything at a moment's notice,' he said, as he lifted a heavy carton off the ramp. 'This'll do my back in. I notice they haven't sent Lindsay down to help. Sexist, I call it.'

'Softie.' Jack straightened up for a minute, wondering whether they'd been chosen to work together on purpose. 'Some heavy lifting'll do you good.'

'Ha! Are you saying I'm not fit?'

Jack looked over at him and grinned. Surely Gary wouldn't be such an idiot as to take money straight out of the tills when he was serving. Or was there another way of defrauding a company of its profits? Taking goods home under your coat? Suppose if you really wanted to, it probably wasn't hard to pull a scam like that.

The job they'd been given wouldn't last longer than twenty or thirty minutes, so he knew his opportunity for sorting things out *his* way was limited. If he was going to say anything, it would have to be now.

It was too early for anyone else to be around in storage and whatever Jack said, he couldn't afford to be overheard so this was his chance. He bent down to lift a lawn mower from its casing and with his head lowered found it easier to sound casual. 'Do you know anything about the rumour going round? Someone's stealing apparently.' It was better not to look at Gary's face. 'They're checking the tills and the stock lists. Makes you feel a bit uneasy.'

Gary rested his hands on a pile of rubber matting, his body still for a moment. 'Blimey, no, haven't heard a thing.' He slowly brushed some packing chips off his trousers. 'Who d'you hear that from?'

'Well, no-one's told me directly. Didn't really mean to be listening, but Lazy Martin and I think it was Dom talking. It must have come from higher up, but they didn't say who. There's those cameras, the ones behind the tills that keep an eagle eye on us. I mean we're handling money all day so they're bound to keep a check… Anyway, it makes you nervous, doesn't it? Even when you're doing everything right.' He felt he'd gone on a bit and hoped he wasn't being too obvious. Hoped as well that Gary didn't check this out with any of the others.

'Well,' Gary pushed a bird pedestal stand into a space, 'I'll keep my eyes and ears open. Let's hope it isn't Martin – he'd never get another job. I'll let you know if I hear anything.'

Jack suddenly saw how this could escalate if he wasn't careful. 'I wouldn't say anything on the shop floor. It could be any of the departments and it's just better to keep our heads down. Until it's public knowledge anyway.'

'Right, mate. I won't say anything.' And Gary clapped him on the shoulder and they finished the unpacking talking about the match that was on TV later. Safe, no hidden agenda. When Gary had gone back upstairs, Jack breathed a sigh of relief. He wasn't sure whether he'd done the right thing or the wrong thing, but his conscience felt healthier.

At least now, Gary knew the consequences, had a second chance. *Everyone does things they'd think better of later on*, he thought. *There's no way*

I could rat on him. I'm pretty sure Dad would have done the same in the circumstances.

*

At the end of a winding drive lay The Manor House Country Hotel, so old and well established it didn't need the plaque saying 1802 over the entrance to give it authenticity. The brickwork was darkened with age and covered with ivy and the door was panelled with brass fittings and painted grey.

They'd arrived almost at the same time as Lucy. 'I'm not late, please note,' she'd said, manoeuvring her body out of the low driving seat. 'But it's not all good news. I think I was speeding when I passed the camera on the bypass. Let's hope it wasn't working.'

So they'd approached the entrance, the family get-together off to a good start. Jack hoped it would stay that way, but there was never a guarantee. Sometimes good intentions veered off course. It had been Carrie's idea – a way of celebrating Alex's recovery, and doing what normal families did all the time, going out for a meal, enjoying each other's company. That was the hope, anyway, and Jack wanted it to be a good night for his dad's sake.

When Carrie gave the receptionist her name, they were directed straight into the dining room where the head waiter, graciously bowing his head, led them to their table. He made a fuss of moving some cutlery and repositioning the wine glasses a fraction, which Jack thought was overdoing it. But this was The Manor House Country Hotel, renowned for its extensive fish menu and expensive wines, so all the rest was part of the package. They'd only been twice before, a family New Year's Eve dinner dance and for Jack's 21st and although the food was something else, he found it all a bit over-the-top. But his mother liked the place. She used to come here with her father years ago and he supposed it must have had good memories for her.

The dining hall made Jack think of something out of an old story book on castles; heavy wooden tables, pink and green wallpaper, dark portraits on the walls and velvet-backed chairs, plush carpets your feet sank into. You just hoped you didn't clatter your knife and fork and disturb the dignified hush of the well-mannered diners around you.

They were left to study the menu and try to remember the 'specials' that had been reeled off by the head waiter, Alex frowning, saying, 'Why don't they just write it all down? It'd be much easier!' and trying to decide between the spinach soufflé and mozzarella risotto balls as a starter.

And so it began. The usual banter, the catching up, discussing what was in the news…

'How's the job going, Lucy?' his dad asked, once he'd chosen what he wanted to eat. 'How's the annoying woman you hoped would hand her notice in?'

'She's on her first warning.' Lucy picked up a breadstick and waved it about. 'It's so hard to get rid of anyone these days, even when they're totally inefficient.'

Then his mother was telling them about her day out at the horse event, leaving them a bit behind with some of the more technical details of the competition. 'Real VIP treatment and some big names doing amazing times in the cross country. But the guests of this man Freddie were full of themselves and it was money talking. Interesting though.'

And later, his dad relating an amusing story about a sewage treatment site with a flourishing side business in growing and selling tomatoes – 'Something about the soil being rich which must add to the flavour.'

Before the main course, they'd lifted their glasses in a toast to his health.

Jack sat there, happy to listen but with nothing he could think of to offer. Nothing interesting or amusing that would have added to the enjoyment of the evening. It worked as every family gathering worked on one level – there were a few old memories raked up and argued over who was remembering the correct version, talk of Joe and his children, there was some conversation about items in the local news, of problems with the internet, the forthcoming election. And his mother seemed to be making a special effort to include him in all that. As though everything had been forgotten. Which was good in a way. No point in holding on to grievances.

And he was feeling OK.

But still…

Ten o'clock and they went out into the cool night air, lamps lit along the wall by the cars, the cows in the field opposite, large misshapen shadows lying under the spread of an oak tree. A cat skittered across the cobbles in front of them. As his parents walked on ahead, Jack found himself beside Lucy who to his surprise turned to hug him.

'Isn't it great to have Dad back to his old self!' she said, emotion making her voice catch in her throat. 'Made my night to hear him joking and looking so… full of life.'

Jack nodded in the dark. 'Yes. Really great. And reading again. I bought him two books when I was in town and he's finished them already. You know what he's like for reading, or he was, and now he's getting it all back.'

They moved on slowly towards Lucy's car. 'Well, it was a good night. The Taylor family on the up again.' She glanced over at him, pausing slightly before she said, 'Was going to ask – Rachel's party… you disappeared rather early, didn't you?'

'Yeah, I was tired. And I didn't really know anyone. Felt a bit like a fish out of water to be honest.' He didn't know how much more he could say.

'There weren't many I knew, either. But a few drinks and I was away.' Again, a pause. Lucy was giving him one of her shrewd looks. 'Saw you talking to Fran early on. I hadn't met Paul before but he seemed a nice bloke.'

What could he say to that? Perhaps nothing was best. But like a masochist who's determined to subject himself to pain, he had to know.

'How long's she been going out with him?'

Lucy had clicked the fob to open the car door when she turned and stared at him. 'Jack... he's not her boyfriend. He's her brother. He'd come up for the weekend and obviously she'd brought him along. Didn't she introduce him?'

'Yes, of course, but only by name. I just assumed...'

His dad was calling him. 'Jack, hurry up. You can talk to your sister anytime.'

'Coming,' he called back and hurried over, climbing in the back seat, not sure what he was feeling, a mixture of surprise and confusion. He'd got it all wrong and that made it all right. He smiled to himself at the contradiction.

It would take some time to sink in.

Chapter 28

It had begun to get dark in the evenings by 7.30 now and Fran was almost glad summer was over. She liked autumn, the sharp air, the mists, the fine rain and wet leaves covering the ground. And the warmth from a log-burning stove. She could never have lived in a country where there were no changes of season. Ten days in Italy last summer had seemed like one energy-sapping day after another, waking up to a merciless sun beating down, not a cloud in the sky. It had made her thankful when it was cocktail hour.

She decided she needed to prepare an updated information sheet for new clients before tomorrow so she climbed the stairs to the front bedroom, which she'd made into a study when Paul had left. She turned on the computer and leafed through her notes. An hour should do it.

Her house was small enough to be cosy in every room and once she'd pulled down the blind and switched the angle lamp on, she was comfortably warm, ready to start devising the document's layout, the form and tone. She'd check it through with Jill before it was finalised.

And she began well, concentrating, reading it aloud to herself after each section. But before she'd finished, she started to lose focus. Her mind kept coming back to Alex. She couldn't quite get over the fact that after all this time, he'd turned up at her door. After so many years of nothing. Not a phone call, a letter, an e-mail. Seeing him at the barbecue had been enough of a shock. At least there, they hadn't come near one another, they hadn't spoken. It was a large garden, there were plenty of people to keep them apart. She'd been able to handle that, although with difficulty. But things changed when she'd heard he was in a coma. She seemed to be part of his life again, desperate for details of how he was doing from Lucy at the exercise class, desperate enough to pray for him to survive. Even though their lives were separate now and she was convinced she'd never see him again, she couldn't bear the thought of him not being there.

So that visit had shaken her – his physical presence, seeing him up close, hearing his voice, sitting in her kitchen eating a bacon sandwich... God, it had thrown up all the old emotions and that wasn't doing her any good. It hadn't helped that he'd seemed so sad and lost. It was painful to see.

She was torn between genuine fondness for him and anger that he'd had the nerve to show up. He was the one who'd left her, with no warning, no explanation, and left her heartbroken. However dramatic that sounded, it was true. It had been a loss she wouldn't like to experience again. And wasn't going to. At least she'd learned something and it had been a comfort – *How selfish we all are*, she thought – she'd learned that all the anguish she'd gone through he'd shared. It was something she'd always wondered about. Whether he'd found the ending as hard as she had. It shouldn't have made her feel better, but it did.

Come on, she thought, *that was the past.*

Surely it was all behind her...

Of course, it was inevitable that seeing him again would upset her. She'd be fooling herself if she'd expected anything else. Even though she was older and a damned sight wiser than that girl of twenty-four who'd been blind enough to fall headlong and not think seriously about the consequences, she couldn't deny she still had feelings for him. Even so, she had no intention of defining them. Or acting on them. That time was long gone.

And however painful it might be at this minute, she'd have to live with it.

But his being here again revived memories. Of course it did. And you always remember the good bits she thought, because that's what made the whole thing so special. Even with all the difficulties, the emotional ups and downs… they'd had some wonderful times.

Some days she remembered as vividly as though it was now. The night they'd gone to see *Casablanca* – how he'd booked two tickets without even asking her and she'd ignored the red warning lights and gone anyway. It was one of those moments when they'd stepped over the line never to turn back, when they had to acknowledge this was more than just friendship. Before then, she thought, it was as though they'd been hiding their feelings in plain sight. Knowing and not knowing. They hadn't allowed themselves to recognise where it was heading. That evening they opened their eyes.

It just seemed right. Which of course, it wasn't, not right in any moral sense. There was no getting away from that.

As they'd sat in the dark auditorium, elbows touching, she was acutely aware of their closeness, her senses on high alert. Then he'd reached out and caught her hand in his. They never took their eyes off the screen, pretending nothing was happening. Like a pair of teenagers making tentative steps. And that was just how she'd felt. Young, unsure. By the time they came out of the building, there was a sense of anticipation, a nervousness that was palpable.

They drove back to her house in a giddy mood, exchanging half-remembered lines from the film, misquoting and competing with each other. As they sat at a red light, Alex couldn't resist repeating in a fair imitation of Bogart's lisp, 'We'll always have Paris,' and they sang '*As Time Goes By*', only the first verse because they couldn't remember the rest. Fran had been touched by the story, sad and romantic, even though the settings were phoney and it was in black and white, for heaven's sake! It wasn't something that would usually appeal to her. But she was sold.

When the car had pulled up in Whitegate, there was a moment when she was unsure what should come next. Did she just get out, wave goodnight or invite him in? Paul was home but he always went to bed early when he was leaving for work at six in the morning.

She pulled on the car door handle and made her decision. Impossible to ignore the obvious now. 'Do you want to come in?' she asked. 'My brother's home but he'll have gone up.'

He looked across at her with such an engaging smile she was glad she'd asked.

'I'd love to.'

So they'd gone into the kitchen and she'd had to clear the table where Paul had set out the cereal packets and bowls for the morning. She'd made hot chocolate and found some little Italian almond cakes in the cupboard, brought back from her holiday. It was odd but the mood suddenly wasn't light-hearted any more. And Fran stalled and wanted to return to something that kept them on familiar ground.

So she took a step back, teasing him to ease the tension.

'This is your idea of an education, then is it?' she said. 'First you introduce me to Stephen King – you're right, I've read a few of his now and you can't put them down – and now it's old war films!'

He nodded, pulling a face as he swallowed a cake. 'I'm giving you a chance to appreciate the best. Now it's your turn to pay me back with some of *your* favourites.'

'No, I'm not as confident as you are that the stuff I like is worth recommending.'

'What you're trying to say politely is that I'm old enough to know good from mediocre.'

'Well, there's that!' she laughed. 'How old are you anyway?'

'Thirty-nine.' He rubbed his mouth. 'Those cakes have a very odd taste. How long have they been in your cupboard?'

'Too long, obviously. They're past their sell-by-date. Sorry.' She gathered up the package and put it in the bin. 'I've no complaints about tonight. The film was good. I really enjoyed it. Thanks for taking me.' She suddenly had the urge to lean over and put her hand over his, to feel his fingers wrap round hers, capture what they'd had in the darkness of the cinema. She hoped the look in her eyes didn't give her away. The thought that he might be able to read her mind made her flush so she hurried on. 'Though I'm not sure the ending was what I'd hoped for.'

'Well, they didn't *have* an ending till the last minute. There were so many script writers on the set, no-one could agree.'

'How do you know that?'

'There was a book about how it was made, *The Usual Suspects* – forget who wrote it now but it was full of fascinating information – like how they filmed the plane in the last scene when Rick makes Ilsa leave him. It was only a model and a poor one at that, so they used the fog as a cover-up.'

She blew out a breath. 'It still wasn't too convincing when it took off.'

'Fran, it was 1942. They hadn't invented CGI then.'

'Anyway, he didn't have to give her up. She was the love of his life, he'd been miserable without her and he made this incredible sacrifice…'

'But he had to. He knew she must get on that plane with Laszlo, she'd regret it later if she didn't. He was being noble in the end.'

'That wasn't noble. He was throwing it all away.'

They looked at one another, not quite sure what they were arguing about – if it was arguing they were doing – and they were suddenly still, facing each other across the table, something like an understanding, wordless, expectant passing between them.

Alex spoke first. 'Fran, look at me like that and I have to be honest, I'm out of my depth.' He put his elbows on the table and clasped his hands together. 'But this has got to be up to you.'

She should have been prepared. She was only too aware that in a moment everything could change, everything depended on what she said next. There were such huge implications. 'Alex…'

He turned away slightly. 'I'm so out of order here and you've every right to put a stop to this.' It was as though he was already anticipating that was exactly what she'd made her mind up to do. 'I just need to tell you... this sort of behaviour is not like me. I've never...'

She held up her hand for him to stop. 'I know that. I think I'm a pretty good judge of character. You're not the type who'd find it OK to play around. If you had been, you wouldn't have got through the door.'

She could see he was struggling to find the right words, ones that wouldn't completely destroy what they already had. She hesitated for exactly the same reason. But they were on the brink of committing to something that was not only taboo but a dangerous gamble. Tightrope walking with a horrible drop beneath. It was more than enough to make her think twice.

'This is all new to me, Fran. I can tell you it's been causing me sleepless nights recently and I know it shouldn't. Every bone in my body's telling me to stop seeing you, stop calling round but I don't listen. I can't get you out of my mind.' He paused, his eyes never leaving her face. 'I'm sorry if you don't want to hear this.'

She shook her head. 'I'm... it's just such a leap in the dark. This is anything but straight forward. And let's be honest, we don't really know each other that well, do we?'

'Perhaps not in the conventional sense, I agree. If you count the number of times we've seen one another. But there's something, some understanding that cuts through all that. On some level, we *do* know each other. Christ, I'm a philosopher now. But what I'm trying to say is you can be with someone for years without feeling this close. It isn't ordinary, Fran. It's... exceptional.' He smiled in a resigned sort of way. 'I think so anyway.'

'So there's some predestined bond between us. Like ESP.'

'I can't be flippant about it, Fran. I'm serious.'

'So am I – but more important, there are things we need to be serious *about*.'

'I know. You're young, so much younger than me...'

'That's not the problem Alex. I'm 24, going on 25 and I've had enough experiences to know what's what. I'm not a naïve teenager who's bowled over by your mature charms.' She could hear her tone becoming exasperated. 'Sorry, but you're treating me with kid gloves and it's not necessary. It really isn't.'

'OK. I asked for that.'

He waited. They sat at either side of the table, not moving, eyes locked together, stillness filling the room. The moment seemed to last a long time after all the talk just circling the issue. She knew, of course she did, what was going to happen.

So in the end, she stood up and held out her hand.

'Come with me.'

She led him into the sitting room and moved over to the couch without turning on the light, all pretence gone. They sat, half facing one another, quiet and certain. He cupped her face in his hands and kissed her.

'If this isn't love...' he began.

She put her arms round him. 'It just might be.' *Never mind 'might,'* she thought. *This is like nothing I've ever felt before.* 'Alex, you're the nicest man I've ever known.'

'That sounds horribly dull.'

'Believe me, it's not.' She began to undo the buttons on his shirt and she could sense him hesitating.

'I haven't got any...'

She nodded in the half-light. 'Paul has. He keeps them in the bathroom. Give me a minute.'

She crept up the stairs, praying the boards wouldn't creak, and back down again, closing the living room door as softly as she could.

'I feel like a burglar in my own house. How ridiculous is this!'

He was stifling a laugh. 'I'll bet Rick didn't have this problem.'

'They probably didn't even do it.'

'Are you kidding?'

And that set them off, giggling like children and trying to suppress the sound, but the more they tried, the more it set them off again. Once they'd calmed down, all the tension had disappeared.

'Well, that's a good start,' she said. 'Romance has gone out the window.'

'Don't you believe it,' he said, pulling her gently towards him. 'Just don't laugh for the next half hour and we'll be fine.'

*

Remembering it all now, she could still smile. He'd been such easy company – thoughtful, perceptive, funny. Different from anyone else she'd been with, no ego, more concerned with her needs than his. She'd just hoped after that first night that he'd felt as strongly as she did.

But his situation wasn't like hers.

For him, there were complications. Responsibilities that overshadowed it all in the cold light of day. He was married, two teenagers still at home, a life she really knew very little about. He'd always avoided details. She knew his wife was called Carrie and he had a brother, Joe, who he was close to and that his parents lived nearby. But nothing about what he did when he wasn't with her. He didn't offer to tell her and she could understand why. It was human nature to hide unpalatable truths and it was also human nature for her to be curious.

It was some weeks later and they'd arranged to meet in a wine bar in Northwich – he'd found it on an app on his phone and thought it sounded the sort of place Fran would like. Northwich wasn't a town either of them knew well but the distances for both seemed doable and *Henry's*, as it was called, had *'an award-winning menu'* and looked easy to find. It turned out to be an odd choice!

She'd left work early to give herself plenty of time. The satnav had done its job but then she'd spent twenty minutes trying to find a parking space, so she was running as she hurried down the street, relieved when she spotted the name on the fascia board. She could see Alex waiting for her as she pushed her way in. It was all slate and glass and silver, with high swivel chairs in black leather and jars of tall lilies on the tables. And lights. God, it was bright. But mostly empty at five thirty.

As soon as he saw her, he rose to his feet and gave her a hug. 'This place isn't quite what I expected. Too bloody shiny. We'll have to put it down to experience. Perhaps I just wanted to see how the young and upwardly mobile live.' He smiled at her, knowing she'd share his wry take on the world. 'I've got you a Prosecco. You can have one drink, can't you?'

She was glad to be here, whatever the place was like. It didn't matter. It was enough to have a couple of hours together – 'stolen hours' came into her mind and she tried not to think of it in that way. But it wasn't easy. She could imagine how her friends would react if they knew…

'Married? Nearly forty? Are you crazy?'

Yes, probably. But you don't know him.

She took a sip of her drink and hoped she didn't look too windblown after the run down the street.

'They do tapas. Wasn't sure what half the things on the menu meant but I've ordered a selection of… God knows what.'

'Sounds positively delicious,' she said. 'Don't worry. It'll be fine.'

He looked round at the empty tables. 'This place is like something out of the space age. Bet it's got robots cooking the food.'

'As long as they're not mixing the drinks, we'll be OK.'

They grinned at one another. Stupidly happy. What made him so attractive, she thought then, was the way his face came alive when he spoke, the way you could sense a mind that was quick, sense the warmth of him. She had no idea what he saw in *her*.

The food arrived on oblong platters with spiked sticks and little shovels to eat with and they began swapping stories about their week and trying to work out exactly what they were eating.

'Sorry,' Alex said, poking at an olive coated in red sauce, 'had to guess what I was ordering. And the waiter wasn't much help.'

'It actually tastes pretty good.'

They finished their meal and ordered coffee. Time was running out. There was a long moment when their eyes met and they fell silent. Fran didn't want to think of him leaving and her expression must have been solemn because he said, 'What's up?'

She didn't answer straight away, unable to think of a way in. She wanted to ask him what it would be like when he got home, what he'd say, how he'd feel. Perhaps it was better not knowing. Perhaps this was better left alone for now. But she couldn't help herself. She couldn't just go on and on, wondering.

'Do you mind if I ask you something?' she began.

'That sounds loaded,' he said. 'But go ahead.'

'I want you to tell me about yourself – what you were like at eighteen, at university, how you met Carrie.' She could see the unease in his eyes. 'I'm bound to be curious, Alex.'

His expression was thoughtful as though he was working out what to say. 'Well... at eighteen I was a bit of a nerd, spent all my time studying. Then at university, fell in with the card-players, brag, poker, staying up all night, missing lectures – I was given a warning. So in the third year, I worked, kept my head down.'

'And you met Carrie.'

'Yes. I'd met her briefly before, then we bumped into one another again. We were twenty-one, our first serious relationship – and, well, we got careless... the usual result, Carrie found she was pregnant. You think you're so smart you can take risks and get away with it...'

He shook his head. 'Her father was furious and mine weren't too happy about it either... Anyway, living together wasn't an option. So we got married. Struggled for a few years, but we did OK. I'd got a fairly safe job straight out of university and hopefully, a career ahead of me and Carrie did some temporary bits and pieces to keep our heads above water. So it wasn't a disaster. Her father had money, but there was no way she was going to ask him for anything. We didn't dare admit failure.' He stopped, not knowing whether she wanted to hear more. When she didn't speak, he went on. 'I suppose having two children when you're young makes you grow up fast.'

'I'll bet.'

The coffee was brought to their table with the bill and that seemed to put an end to it. He'd obviously told her all he was going to. But there was still the question she most wanted to ask.

'What's Carrie like?'

'Strong, I suppose, an organiser. The opposite of me. I'm inclined to let things ride.'

Fran let it be but she was disappointed. It barely told her anything. Particularly about Carrie. It was merely an outline, a sketch with no detail, two-dimensional. Hardly a real person. Hardly a flesh-and-blood woman she could see in her mind's eye.

*

Now of course, after that barbecue, she *did* have a picture. She'd seen her, elegant in the way she dressed and moved, delicate features and confident smile, a woman in control. And there was an edge to her that told you – here is someone you wouldn't want to cross. It had sent a sliver of fear through Fran on that night. She'd stepped into a minefield and couldn't bear to think of what might have happened, just one mistake and... she didn't want to dwell on that prospect. At least she'd knocked the Zumba class on the head. She just hoped Lucy wouldn't try to get in touch.

Looking at the clock on the computer screen made her realise nearly an hour had passed and she wasn't any nearer completing the work she'd set herself.

Come on, stay in the present! That's got fewer problems.

So she believed until the phone call came.

Unexpected, disturbing her peace of mind.

Chapter 29

I make my way to where the foreman, Patrick, is standing surveying the foundations, fresh red mud clinging to the sides of the trenches which are filling up with sludge and water. The men are packing up for the day, climbing into their trucks and cars and heading home. Early finish because you can only do so much under lights and the days are shortening.

I slide through the squelch and come up behind him. He doesn't turn, just keeps looking over the site area, bleak now it's deserted, the heavy plant standing bulky and silent against the hoarding panels that fence us in.

He's worried. And he's a right to be but he isn't to blame for the cock-up and he shouldn't shoulder the responsibility alone. It's either the county surveyor or Ian Black who's fucked things up, so all we can do now is try to mitigate the damage and throw the extra cost back onto the developers... or ask for an extension while we do some major repair work.

I stand with Patrick and take a minute to figure out what can be done. Christ, it's a mess. I hadn't intended to come today, but the call from Adrian had been urgent – if initially he'd been concerned about my delicate health, he'd forgotten about that now. So I'd left the water treatment works by three thirty and managed to get here before everything closed up. I knew I was to take over from another of Ian's sites this week but no idea that it had already hit trouble.

'We'll use the pumps as a temporary measure, then work out the best way to deal with the water level. It's solvable, Patrick. No good worrying yourself to death. Lock up and go home. I know you worked all last weekend and you look bloody tired.'

Patrick is shaking his head. 'Ian's always on our backs but when it comes to problems, he doesn't want to know. You sort it out, he says – those were his parting words last week.' He still can't look at me. 'Thank God you've taken over. The men are sick to the back teeth. Thought two of them were about to quit.'

I'd never liked Ian Black. A good engineer, I'd always thought, a bit fussy over details, but efficient, got things done though he rankled the men on site, and the two women engineers avoided him like the plague. Philippa, who'd been doing the job longer, had said to me at a works do when she'd had a few, 'He's always right. He's a machine that doesn't think about who's doing all the hard work.' She'd put a finger to her lips. 'I keep my mouth shut and stay out of his way.'

Well, he'd certainly made a mess of this.

I can see that Patrick's going to worry himself sick if I don't come up with a more permanent plan. He doesn't seem to want to go home and my car's waiting. We can't stand here all night.

He starts to turn towards the hut, head down, walking slowly as though his boots are heavy.

'Look,' I say, 'we'll use the pumps, then we'll place interlocking sheet piling all around the site. That might mean we take a bit more time, but it'll work. I'll come back tomorrow and we can go through the logistics together.'

He's looking thoughtful and then a slow smile spreads across his face. 'Yes, that'll do it.'

'So forget about it till the morning. Nine o'clock?'

He nodded, making a gruff sound that was almost a laugh. 'I'll get the pumps going… and tell the men your head's on the block if it doesn't work.'

'You do that.'

I sit in the back seat on the drive home, glad to have lifted some of the worry off Patrick's shoulders. My job, after all. I'm thinking that, eventually, you can usually find the solutions to practical problems.

Not so easy with emotional ones. They're a minefield. I know the cool atmosphere at home is my fault. I don't wonder Carrie's becoming increasingly frustrated with me; we seem to be constantly engaged in some silent stand-off, nothing said, plenty going on under the surface. Can't blame the head injury anymore. I've just become perverse, must be her take on it. Well, perhaps that's true.

We leave the motorway at the slip road, the commuter traffic coming out of Manchester just a row of headlights heading our way at crawling pace, and dip into the unlit countryside, hedges lining the road, which winds along dark stretches until we near the village. I become anxious and tiredness fills my body. But I must appear good humoured, for Jack's sake at least. Don't want him worrying. He does enough of that.

John, the driver, drops me off and when I open the front door of the house, I'm cheered by the sound of voices coming from the kitchen. It's already just after six o'clock and I'm far later than usual on the three days I now work and even before I recognise Joe's voice, I have the feeling that perhaps life is getting back to normal. Whatever normal is. OK then, back to an existence where there's some order to it without the constant strain of trying to *manage* it.

They're sitting round the table and Joe is smiling at Jack who's talking away, telling some story about work with Carrie listening, a cup of tea in front of her. Good to see them all more relaxed with each other.

Jack turns when he hears me. 'Guess what Uncle Joe's brought you?'

I pull off my coat. 'I dread to think! Could be anything from a skateboard to a Zimmer frame!'

Carrie gets up to turn down the dial on the oven. Obviously, dinner is delayed.

Jack takes my arm and leads me towards the back door as though some ceremony is about to be performed. Which in a way, it is.

There, draped with a huge red ribbon is a bike propped against the wall. 'Da daaa!' says Jack with a theatrical gesture. 'Ready for the Tour de France.'

Joe comes up behind us and I turn, grinning, 'Well, you're as good as your word. I can see it's even got gears to get me up the hills.'

'It's not too complicated,' he says, stepping out into the garden to wheel it forward. 'Second hand, of course. I wasn't going to pay a fortune for you to crash first run out! But it'll do for a start.'

Carrie comes to stand in the doorway. 'I did remind him it was nearly November and you'd probably kill yourself before the end of winter. But... he's determined to get you fit.' And I can see she thinks it's a good idea really. I want to thank her for not making a fuss about it, finding objections or making Joe feel uncomfortable. But, hell, that's an awful indictment on our fragile marital state! Why wouldn't she see the positive in this, pleased that I'd be exercising, getting my strength back? I need to stop being so bloody defensive and give credit when it's due.

Today's been OK, I think as I climb into bed later. I read through the newspaper that I'd not had time for and set the alarm for the morning. Must make sure I'm not late for Patrick – see if he'd like to call a site meeting before getting started on the revised plan. And I drift off before I've finished reading because I'm tired out. This often happens now and it's a bit worrying that I've only done half what I could do before the accident. Getting there, though.

*

I'd been doing better; I felt I was coming to terms with life as it had to be, fewer thoughts about the past... fewer thoughts about Fran. Hoping her face would fade from my mind so that I could concentrate on the here and now. But then sometimes, when you're least expecting it, you find you're sitting bolt upright, paying attention...

I'm half watching the television when a programme is advertised for an up-and-coming documentary on Jersey in the 2nd World War. Black and white images from then, jack-booted German soldiers marching through narrow streets down to the harbour, watched by women in headscarves and hungry-eyed children. Then in colour, interviews with old inhabitants, survivors, their sons and daughters, stone houses and green fields behind them.

And I'm back. Walking along the wide sandy beach with my arm around her, beyond peaceful, in love with her, with life, with everything around me. A weekend of happiness I can feel again – as though I'm there, as though it's happening now. When I think about it, when I remember, perhaps there's only one word that sums it all up – it's as though I'm intoxicated. As I was then...

...It was late September and Adrian had arranged for me to meet this developer who refused to come over and discuss a project with us here, so I was to fly over to Jersey and suss out the feasibility of his idea. There was nothing set in concrete and it could have all turned out to be a waste of time, but anyway, meetings were planned for the Friday and Monday (this bloke liked his weekends free to go sailing, so we had to fit in), which meant there were two days for exploring the island and enjoying the late sun.

I was booked into this hotel on the beach away from any towns, somewhere Adrian had stayed years before. 'You'll love it – family business, full of character, wonderful food,' he told me. 'Make the most of it. You've deserved some payback.'

Not often you get those sorts of instructions!

On my own for two days that weekend sounded OK, but two days with Fran sounded too good to throw away. I asked her to come with me.

'I'm working,' she said. 'And you've cut it fine. That's the end of this week.' But I could see she was tempted. Still, if she couldn't get away, that was that.

I flew from Manchester Airport on the Friday morning and by

teatime, after a rather fruitless day going over the outlines of Geoff Denham's project, I climbed into the hire car and set off to find my hotel. I still had no idea whether his plan was viable. He wasn't the sort to gain your trust and I filled Adrian in on the progress we'd made so far which wasn't much. We'd spent a day talking and drinking coffee in his office in Saint Helier, discussing financial implications, a late lunch, with nothing decided.

I drove back along the road west, catching glimpses of the sea to my left as the car made its way through the warm evening, window down, the radio tuned to a music station. I felt carefree, looking forward to the evening ahead of me.

The hotel stood on the lip of a bay looking over the coast road to a beach and beyond, an expanse of sea that blended with the sky, the horizon barely visible. I pulled into the car park at the rear and gathered up my bag. There was a smell of cooking from one of the outlet vents in the side wall as I passed and it seemed like a welcome sign – here you'll eat well, we'll make you comfortable, look after you. I love hotels, perhaps because we never stayed in them when we were kids; holidays were in B & Bs or caravans, hotels always out of our reach. Anyway, The Breakers was everything I could have wanted – white stone frontage, pink flowers on the balconies, even a bronze fish on a plinth near the entrance. And a palm tree in the garden, its fronds blowing in the breeze.

I settled into my single room, all white and pale blue décor, fancy metal-frame bed, a bowl of fruit on a small round table and I couldn't resist opening up the sliding doors onto the balcony to breathe in the sea air. I just wished Fran could have been here. But I was soon downstairs, enjoying a drink at the bar, then dinner followed by coffee and brandy (I felt like a tycoon, all expenses paid) then up to bed, reading 'I am Pilgrim', such a good book, and falling asleep by ten o'clock.

I'd got up late, had breakfast and mulled over the newspapers that were on a desk in reception and was wandering out into the garden when I heard someone calling my name. Looking back, I saw her coming towards me from the hotel doorway, quickening her step, a smile a mile wide on her face. She reached me and I opened my arms, wrapping them round her, not wanting to move, holding her so close, so tightly, I could hardly breathe. *Thank you, whoever arranged this – the gods, fate, whoever – I owe you.*

'Fancy meeting you here,' I managed after I'd recovered.

'Caught the early plane, managed to wangle Monday off.' She was laughing, excited, I could see she was loving my surprised expression. 'And they've found me a room.'

I put my arm round her as we walked along the front of the hotel. 'Well you won't be spending much time in that!'

'I was being discreet. You're on business. Wouldn't do for people to talk.'

'Good thinking.' We looked at one another like conspirators. 'Have you had breakfast or did you arrive too late?'

'No, I haven't eaten and I'm starving. Been up since five.'

'OK. Apparently there's a café about 300 yards up the beach. I'll treat you.'

So we sat on wobbly wooden chairs under a canvas awning and I watched her as she finished scrambled eggs and coffee and we talked... talked about nothing really, just shared all the bits of our lives and our feelings that we didn't share with anyone else.

'I was really unsure,' she said, her face solemn and her eyes a darker blue as she recalled making the decision. 'I kept thinking I should have phoned you, sent you a text, let you know I was coming. What if I was making a real blunder here and you'd made arrangements with this client to spend the day on his yacht...'

'He doesn't have a yacht.'

'OK, but you might have been meeting him and his wife...'

'Shut up, Fran. Finish your breakfast. Don't want you fainting on me for lack of nourishment. I've got two days to show you how happy I am you're here. No, happy isn't enough. I'm on cloud nine if there is such a place. Anyway, I'm on it.'

We strolled back along the beach, arms round each other, keeping in step. It was as though we were the last people on the planet, just us, free to do whatever we liked. All around us, the vast expanse of sky and sea. A boat was crossing the bay, its engines chugging along, the steady beat reaching us across the water and seagulls were diving and squawking overhead.

Fran looked up. 'Why don't seagulls fly in a swarm like other birds?'

'Bees swarm,' I said, my head resting against hers for a minute.

'You know what I mean. Most birds fly in a group. Seagulls circle on their own, they keep separate. Look at them.'

'There's a scientific reason for that,' I said.

'Is there?'

'Yes. They fly singly because the bastards want to be the first to dive down and snatch the sandwich out of your hand. It's a competition – winner takes all.'

She laughed. 'Yes, OK. Every bird for itself. I get it.'

The dry sand was getting deeper and more difficult to walk on, filling our shoes, so Fran decided to go barefoot and paddle through the shallows, rolling up her jeans and jumping back when stronger waves swept over the shingle.

There are some memories that remain as moving pictures, sharp and distinct, choreographed, the sounds that should accompany them in the background faded to nothing. Her slim body arching as she swerved away from the incoming tide, raising her leg, one arm above her head, dark hair swept back, face wet and shining with spray. A free spirit, if only for a few minutes – part of the natural beauty of the place, the turquoise streaks in the sky, the tidal push of the ocean, the textured contours in the sand.

God, I loved her. What was the good of denying that! I could have wept knowing it. Wept for what I was feeling and for the sense of transience that made me acutely alive to what I was sure to lose. I wanted to stop time, just stay right there and hold onto something as damned near perfect as it could be. That's how hopelessly unrealistic I'd become.

We made our way back to the hotel, picked up my room key and climbed the stairs.

'Did you see the poster?' she said. 'Saturday night there's a pianist in the bar. Honestly, what a brilliant place. Everything you don't expect.'

We shut the door to my room and leant against it, my body warming hers, cold from the sea air and ocean spray, her face and hair encrusted with tiny flecks of salt. We didn't even bother to close the drapes, just undressed each other slowly, eyes intent on one another, our breathing rising and falling as though we were one. She was shivering so we crossed the room to the bed, climbed beneath the duvet and lay still for a minute.

'Are you still cold?'

'No, I'm fine.' Her voice a whisper. 'I'm fine now.'

It was so much more than sex, I thought afterwards as we lay, looking out through the window that led onto the balcony at the midday sky, her head tucked against my shoulder and her arms round me. It was warmth and giving and a yearning satisfied, a fulfilment I suppose, of something I didn't believe I'd deserved. Thankful for a closeness I'd been allowed to share.

You can't get luckier than that.

Christ, what do I sound like! This isn't what I could say out loud, even to Fran, but it's what I felt.

We drifted off for a while, drowsy, comfortably listless, not caring that the day, the time was moving on. But then Fran stirred and propped herself up on one elbow.

'Come on. We can't just stay in bed for two days.'

'We could.'

'No. We should explore. We'll walk until we get tired, then come back, have dinner and a bottle of wine and listen to the pianist.'

'Sounds good to me.'

So we left the hotel behind, our bolt-hole with its bronze fish and pink flowers and palm tree, setting off across the beach to the far end, heads close together, me tailoring my longer strides to let Fran keep pace.

We passed a man with a dog and a woman and child collecting shells and when we'd walked further on and there was only sand and sea, not another person ahead of us on the beach, I turned to her, drawing her close and kissed her. We stood still for quite a while, the only sound the rhythmic ebb and flow of waves on the shoreline and the cries of seagulls.

'I'm happier than I think I've ever been,' I said.

'Oh, Alex.' Her voice sounded husky. 'Me too.'

Sometimes life seems perfect and that weekend was the closest I've ever been – climbing over hilly paths, scrabbling along stony coastal tracks, visiting the zoo to see spectacled bears and lemurs, back to The Breakers for four-course meals and good wine, the pianist, a woman draped in a long black dress and swathes of beads, with braided hair and dramatic flourishes, playing songs from another era. And falling to sleep in each other's arms, lost to the world in my small room. You could never forget all that.

I ran her to the airport on Monday morning before my meeting with Geoff, walking with her up to the airport doors. I had to keep the farewell up-beat, not sure why now, but as I passed her bag over and hugged her goodbye, I felt hollow, scared somehow, and I didn't want her to see that.

'So, take care on the way home.'

'I will.' She looked at me searching for something more. 'I've so enjoyed this, Alex. It's been… wonderful.'

I could feel my chest tightening and a lump coming into my throat. This was so hard.

'Remember,' I tried to smile, to be reassuring, 'whatever happens, we'll always have Jersey.'

She shook her head but she understood. 'That's the worst impression I've ever heard. Were you trying to be, Tom Hardy?'

'OK, I've lost the lisp. But it'll come back.'

'Love you, Alex Taylor. I really do.'

I stood watching as she walked into the departure area, giving a small wave of her hand just before she disappeared...

At the time, I couldn't have imagined that six months later, it would all be over. And it would be me who walked away, deliberately, cruelly, and unable to give her any explanation.

Life has a way of throwing you a curveball.

And there's not a lot you can do about it.

Chapter 30

Carrie knew she was overdressed, but she needed to be. Meeting her mother was like going for an interview at an up-market lawyer's office. She would be judged, analysed, notes taken. And most probably, found wanting.

God, she didn't want to do this.

The air was damp as she made her way down Deansgate and onto King Street, spots of rain already darkening the shoulders of her suit. She just wished she hadn't agreed to this. Lunch was booked for twelve thirty, her mother had informed her and *'it wasn't the sort of place where you can come in jeans.'* As if! Perhaps she thought Carrie was still the tomboy she'd been at ten and couldn't even remember on the few occasions they'd seen each other, how she'd grown up a bit since then. And it *was* only a few occasions. As a child, Carrie hadn't questioned how a mother could leave her daughter like a piece of left luggage and not take any interest in her thereafter. And as her father never had any desire to discuss his wife's absence or the complete lack of contact, she didn't spare much time thinking about it or seeing it as so unusual. But when she became a mother herself, when Lucy and Jack were little, she began to wonder at the whole strangeness of it, how you could just walk out of one life into another and never look back. Leaving a husband was one thing, but leaving a young child…?

She glanced at herself in a shop window. Surely her mother couldn't find fault before she even sat down – and then realised how ridiculous this all was. Why did she care? If she hadn't got past the notion that anything her mother did could affect her, then she should have. But what was causing her some unease was not knowing what this meeting was all about; she wasn't in the mood for guessing games.

Her mother was rummaging in her handbag and didn't notice Carrie until she was standing by the table. She looked up, pulled off her glasses and focussed, tilting her head for an instant, inviting Carrie to sit as though bestowing a favour.

'You look very well,' was her first comment. Almost amicable! 'Menu's here. I've already chosen.'

Carrie studied the options while her mother fussed with the silk scarf round her neck, waiting to get started. Despite the greeting, there was a distinct chill in the air that didn't bode well for a pleasant reunion, but then neither expected this to be harmonious. Too much distrust.

It was never going to be easy.

'Once you've made up your mind, I'll call the waiter over. We'll have some of that non-alcoholic cordial and pretend we're drinking Chablis.'

'Fine,' said Carrie. It had been three years since the last phone call and five since they'd last met and when the menu had been put to one side, she took a long look at the woman who had in many ways shaped her. Well, the woman's *absence* had shaped her. Amanda Bannister, that was, now Mrs. George Clifford, had always worn well. At seventy-three, she was still slim and her hair dyed to a fairly natural auburn, good clothes, the posture of a younger woman and a way of moving that was still graceful. But now her face told a different story. The heavily made-up eyes were veined, her cheeks pouchy, the lines round her mouth deep and down-turned giving her a discontented look and she wore a thick layer of foundation that was too dark. She'd be in full armour when she was a hundred, thought Carrie, like some macabre doll. One thing was certain, she didn't look happy. There was something tragic about her that couldn't be hidden and it was unsettling to see.

'I presume the children are well. And Alex.' She sniffed, bringing out a tissue from her handbag. 'You look amazingly fit.' It didn't sound like a compliment. She lifted her hand to call for service and they put in their orders; no starters, just the main and Carrie wondered whether she'd even get through *that*. She wasn't the least bit hungry.

Carrie felt she had to ask, even though she could hear the edge in her voice. 'And how's George?'

Her mother pursed her lips and took a moment before she answered. 'He died. Twelve months ago.'

'Oh, sorry.'

'Heart attack. As sudden as that. I was bereft.'

Carrie waited. There was more to come and she was ready for anything. Did her mother need money? Did she want to get in touch with her grandchildren? Was she ill?

Why didn't she just come out with it!

'Let's enjoy our meal before we talk, Carrie. I spent hours with the solicitors yesterday and I'm quite worn out.'

And so they ate in near silence, Carrie loath to tell her about Alex and his accident so she glossed over it as though it was a trivial matter. And what was the point of telling her about Lucy's marriage? The woman didn't want to know, she was sure of that and she couldn't take the flak that was sure to come her way. What a situation this was! She wished she hadn't come.

Finally, her mother pressed the napkin to her lips and sat back.

'I'm sure you're wondering why I called.'

Carried straightened her back. 'I am, Mother. It must be something important.'

'Before I go into details, I want to put some matters straight which seem to have been misconstrued for too long.' She looked Carrie in the eye, defiant and commanding, as though she wasn't going to be stopped. 'I'm sure you'll find this of benefit in the end.'

Carrie had never noticed it before – her mother didn't ask questions. She made statements, gave commands, occasionally exclaimed in mock amazement, but never asked questions. She wasn't interested in anyone else, just herself. Vain, self-centred and not in any way likeable. Nothing had changed.

'I want to go back to when you were a child, Carrie.' She paused, waiting for an angry response but got nothing, just a stony stare. 'I want to tell you something of your father's behaviour back then which made it impossible for me to stay.'

'Oh, Christ, Mother. What are you on? A guilt trip? You left. for George I gather, wealthy, young and fascinating apparently, and you've had a good life with him. Sorry he's no longer here but sometimes you have to accept that things don't always work out to suit you…'

Her mother's face became a mask, eyes dark and still, impassive almost, yet not quite able to disguise the anger. 'You always were a difficult child, Carrie. Your father indulged you, made you into this fierce little tomboy without any grace or… well, you were feral and I couldn't do much about it. I see you haven't changed…'

'Feral?' Carrie had gritted her teeth so hard her jaw ached. 'Mother, you left when I was not quite eleven. No, I wasn't the daughter you wanted. I was never the sweet little thing in pretty dresses who liked to play with dolls, someone you could dress up to complement your outfits. OK, I could forgive you buggering off to be with your wealthy beau, but what I can't get over is that you never came back to see how I was doing, take me out, have a share in my growing up. That to me is the unnatural part. You wanted out, not just from Father, from both of us.' She had to force herself to keep her voice low. 'You didn't *like* what I was, you made it quite clear, and that to a child is the worst type of rejection. It was my father who gave me a sense of my own worth. So don't start calling him now.'

Her mother sat back in her seat with a dramatic sigh, as though the attack was so unwarranted only a monster would say such things. 'You only see one side of it. Of course you do. Your father was always good at rewriting history. I'm well aware you thought the sun shone out of him, but there was another side that only a wife would see. However, if you don't want to know…'

'I *don't* want to know.' Carrie placed her hands flat on the table. 'It's thirty five years too late. Now,' she paused, 'what's this all about? Why did you want to see me today – surely not to whitewash the past? Are you in trouble?'

For once, her mother looked almost sheepish. 'Not exactly trouble. But things in the last year have been difficult. Since George died…' Her eyes became moist and Carrie had the awful thought that she might be acting. 'Well, it's come to light that he'd got us into rather a lot of debt.' She was rushing on now. 'All right, I should have realised we were living beyond our means but when you're used to living well, it's easy to let things slide…'

Carrie wasn't going to help her out.

'…And time and taxes have a way of eating away at anything you have. After nearly forty years… it just goes.'

A moment of protracted silence.

'I've been trying to sort through all the paperwork with the solicitors and the truth of the matter is, I'm not going to be able to pay all the creditors.'

The sound of a glass breaking on the far side of the dining room sounded unnaturally loud.

'Look,' she went on, eyes filled with unshed tears yet crafty, Carrie thought, at the same time, 'your father left you everything. He left me nothing. It wouldn't be out of the way to let me have some share of your inheritance. I was married to him for fourteen years, after all. I think I have a right to be considered now.'

Carrie almost wished her father could be here to listen to this tale of woe. He'd been such a *gentleman* about the whole business, that's how she'd seen it and this dreadful woman was trying to make out she'd been forced to leave because... of what? She took a long hard look at her mother and could see nothing honest or sincere in that doleful expression, the drooping eyes and turned down mouth. *I've been naïve*, she thought, *I should have known this would be about money. Certainly not about wanting time with her grandchildren or offering an apology, heaven forbid. She wouldn't know how to spell reconciliation.*

'Well, don't keep me waiting.' Her mother had an imperious look on her face now. The second act. This was her right, she was implying, there was no way it was begging. Let's be *fair*!

Carrie kept her face as expressionless as she could, inscrutable, no anger, no frustration. She knew she was stalling for time but couldn't resist playing the game by her mother's rules. She spoke slowly, 'If I've always been such a disappointment to you and you never expected me to turn out half-civilised, how do you think I'll respond to your suggestion?'

'I have no idea.'

'How much money are you short to pay your debts?'

Her mother looked down briefly then lifted her head, deciding it was worth the gamble. 'Twenty-five thousand.'

'Twenty-five thousand?'

'Yes, take or leave a few hundred. I'm sure you could afford to help if you wanted to. Your father must have left you plenty, the house was worth a fortune, so that's not too much to ask for...'

'I invested in a business. Bought a home, bought land. I put the money into something for my whole family.' Carrie could hear her voice turning into a hiss of fury. 'How much capital do you think I have left after all that?'

Her mother shrugged.

Carrie pushed back her chair and stood. She looked down at this vain, selfish woman, the mother who'd all but abandoned her and was ready to walk out, a stinging farewell retort the only thing she was prepared to offer. But at the last minute, what she saw was a sad, lonely figure, slightly hunched, trying to keep up appearances yet having to swallow her pride. She was shocked to realise how small her mother had become in every sense.

'Ten thousand,' Carrie said. 'That should go some way to help. Send me your bank details.' And even now, she couldn't quite resist the bitterness in the next remark. 'It is, of course, Lucy and Jack's money you'll be taking. But I'm sure they'd want to be generous. You are their grandmother after all.'

And she turned on her heel and hurried out into King Street, walking quickly as though a wind was behind her. She was sure the next time she heard anything about her mother would be a letter from a funeral director and she bit her lip at how barren this relationship had always been. Nothing to be done about it now, she thought, no good regretting any of it. But what a waste.

*

Carrie arrived back at the house earlier than she'd anticipated, so she changed into her work clothes and walked down to the stables with an hour to spare before she needed to bring the horses in. It was one of Alex's work days so she took Sam with her, bribing him with treats to get him moving. Steph had left for the day, but she could see two of the girls brushing their horses ready to go into the school, so she called to them, 'Everything all right?' and they waved at her.

She walked on to check the ones still out in the fields; by now they were already standing at the gates ready for their evening feed but they'd have to wait a while. This wasn't her favourite time of year, the long winter ahead, no goodness in the grass and the mud churned up at every gate. And since the clocks had gone back, the days were grey by four with the chance of the rain turning to sleet, chilling you to the bone. But for Carrie, it was all worth it when finally the horses were bedded down for the night, the straw banked high in the stables and she could hear the rhythmic chomping of the haylage being eaten. It gave her a sense of calm. Which had not been her state of mind recently.

She leant against a stable door and thought about the lunch. It had left her feeling sick and resentful. At least, she consoled herself, she'd taken after her father. She'd loved it when people said that about her. She desperately wanted to be like him, because to be told she had some of her mother's traits would have filled her with horror. She supposed she'd painted a picture of a woman who didn't have one redeeming feature. And worst of all, Carrie had always felt unloved. It's hard, she thought, to be such a disappointment to a parent. It erodes any self-confidence you might have had.

It was then that a terrible thought struck her. If she'd known what a let-down she was for *her* mother, that she didn't match up to expectations, that she wasn't *accepted* for who she was – how must Jack feel when he knew only too well that he was a failure in *her* eyes? After all Jack had been through as a kid, why hadn't she seen what damage she'd done since then with her pushing, expecting, comparing… thinking she was doing it all for the best when really, she'd been destroying any faith he had in himself? How could she have been so blind? Usually so perceptive, she'd always thought, so *right* – yet she'd been unable to see her own failings.

Well somehow, she'd have to make amends. But just talking it through might not be enough. She just hoped she could find a way of repairing the damage. Before it was too late.

The wind had got up, blowing bits of straw and fallen leaves against her back. Better get on with the jobs she'd come out to do. She noticed now what she hadn't seen before – David's car parked alongside one of the trailers. So he must be either in the barn or in his horse's stable. Odd that he hadn't come across to talk to her first.

She was surprised when she found him standing at the work place in the corner at Steph's desk; she couldn't quite take it in. Surprised and slightly alarmed. What was he doing? The office area wasn't exactly private but he shouldn't be there.

'David, can I help you with something?' She moved in close to make him step away from the desk and turned the top sheets over. 'Why didn't you come over the yard if you wanted to ask me something?'

He smiled, that self-assured, winning smile. 'Ah, Carrie. I would have but I didn't see you around. I really wanted to ask Steph about the food she's been giving the pony. Bertie seems to be playing up again and I wondered whether the mix she was giving him is too rich.'

'He's getting low protein, no molasses and fibre plus, the correct amounts measured out for his size and work load. And two slices of haylage. Can't be much wrong with that.'

'No.' David looked thoughtful. *Is he playing a game here,* thought Carrie, *trying to stir things up, looking into the set-up here, or is he really concerned about the pony? God only knows.* 'Just need to be sure she knows what she's doing.'

'Well, yes, she certainly does. Anyway, you know she doesn't work in the afternoons unless she's covering for me, so you'll have to wait to have a word with her. If you want to organise your own feeding regime, then fine, we can adjust the costs but you'll have to fetch the bags yourself.'

He nodded and didn't respond.

'Is there something else that's worrying you?' she said, raising her eyebrows. 'I thought you were happy with all the arrangements. Say if you're not.'

He stood looking at her as though he expected her to read his thoughts. 'You know what we discussed the other day.'

'What did we discuss?'

'Expanding the livery, giving this place a name, making it the best in the county.'

Carrie stared at him. He seemed to assume this was something that was a possibility rather than a probability and she could hear warning bells. He was too enthusiastic, too adamant, too... presumptuous! And he had a habit of always standing up close, invading her space, suggesting some intimacy that didn't exist. She had a sense of being overwhelmed. *'Drop this,'* she wanted to say, but her business acumen told her to be more diplomatic. He wasn't in a position to suggest taking over, after all.

'Look, David,' she began, trying to sound firm, trying to distance herself from him in every sense. 'I'm not saying I haven't considered it at times, but I'm not ready to go down that road at the moment. Perhaps in a year or two, I might think differently. But I like running things on my own. And if people start investing money...'

He humphed and looked offended. 'I'm not people.'

'OK, but this would apply whoever it was. I don't think any sort of partnership would work, if that's what you have in mind. Forget about it for now. I'm sure you've got enough to occupy you with your work as it is at present.' She started walking out of the barn and hoped he'd just follow. 'Must see to these horses. Help if you want.'

Surely, she thought, *that's the end of it.* He must have got the message, she'd been clear enough.

He sauntered after her and pulled a lead tope off a hook by the door. 'Glad to help Carrie. Anything for you.'

And when she glanced back at him, he didn't look offended. He had a self-satisfied look on his face as though he was enjoying all this.

Bloody man! thought Carrie. *He doesn't know when to stop.*

Chapter 31

'Time, please!' and they finally managed to close up and bolt the door. The last two regulars had taken forever to finish their pints and struggle into their coats which meant with an hour spent clearing up, Jack and Leo wouldn't be home till midnight. They turned off the lights in the seating area and left the ones on over the bar; it created an eerie effect, half gloom and half snug.

'Don't you get tired, Jack, working in the day then doing a shift here?'

'I do but I wouldn't want to give this up completely. I like it, totally different from what I do at Parsons.' Jack carried on washing glasses and stacking them on the drainers. 'Couldn't leave you in the lurch, now, could I?'

'Oh, I'd be lost without you helping me get through the night,' said Leo. 'Especially when the customers get difficult. I'm no good as a bouncer.'

Jack laughed. 'Well, neither of us has the build for it. Good job we never have any trouble.'

They worked away, cleaning the bar top, collecting debris from the tables, putting chairs back in position, chatting away. And wondering whether Benny, who'd gone down with a heavy cold, would be back tomorrow. 'We get as much done without him,' said Leo. 'Certainly do things faster.' He filled up the ice tray and slammed the fridge door shut. 'And how's your love life, young Jack? Getting anywhere?'

Jack pretended not to understand. 'Like with who?'

'The one in the white dress. From the party. You've been very quiet about it.'

'Nothing to tell you,' he mumbled but he'd flushed. He wished he could cover up his feelings better. Twenty-two and still giving away every emotion he'd rather keep hidden.

'Must be something,' said Leo, straightening up the bottles of spirits. 'You're a funny shade of red.'

Jack sighed, put down his cloth and leaned on the bar. He trusted Leo not to say anything and it helped to be able to talk about it. 'Actually, it's all been a bit tricky.'

'How come?'

'Well, I've joined this group she's a member of – they meet once a month and clean up the countryside… and I've been a few times, but… she's kind and sits with me to eat lunch sometimes and I think she likes me… but not like that.'

'Not in a romantic way, you mean.' Leo stopped working too and took a seat on a bar stool, cloth in hand, listening.

'Yes,' Jack frowned. 'It's difficult to tell. She probably thinks of me as some daft kid with a crush, and that might be what this is. I don't know. I went to a party where she was with a bloke I thought was her boyfriend. Turned out it was her brother but I could see the age difference would matter. Or I think it might.' He shook his head. 'Perhaps I should just give up before I make even more of a fool of myself.'

Leo's expression had all the wisdom of a canny elf. 'You know what they say? *Faint heart never won fair lady.* Or something like that. Why don't you just ask her? Then you'd know and if it isn't any good, you can stop hoping for what can't be and making yourself miserable.'

Jack didn't answer. But there was some sense in the advice – if he just had the nerve. He wasn't sure he had.

*

Jack was in two minds whether to bother turning up. It wasn't ideal weather for being outdoors. The forecast wasn't good, strong winds and the possibility of sleet, the remnants of a storm coming in from the Atlantic. After all, it was November, what did he expect? But it wasn't just the weather that was making him hesitate. It was facing up to reality, hearing a truth he didn't want to hear, punching a hole in his dreams.

In the end he plucked up courage and headed for Macclesfield where the group was clearing a local stream blocked with fallen branches and leaves. Now or never, he thought, and if it was obviously going to be awkward and embarrassing, then he'd finally come to his senses and accept she wasn't for him.

He pulled up on a dirt path off a road-side layby as instructed on the website and looked to see which cars were already parked there. Just two – Trish and Rob. But as he sat there, still undecided whether to get moving and join them, Tom arrived and Jack could see that his passenger was Fran, a hood covering her hair and a scarf wrapped round her neck. She was looking over at him so he forced himself to climb out of his car, a flurry of cold wind and icy rain hitting his face, making him flinch. He was glad he'd put on a thick fleece and found some old gloves in the hall cupboard and managed to get his feet into some old waterproof boots. He didn't fancy being cold *and* wet. However warmly dressed he was, the wind was biting and he began to question what the hell he was doing here.

Tom took a saw, some cutters and secateurs out of the boot and waited for Fran to join him as he headed down the path. But she motioned him to go ahead while she walked purposefully across to Jack, a solemn look on her face. He attempted a smile but couldn't quite make it and braced himself to be ready for anything.

'Would you mind giving me a lift home later?' she said. 'There's something I'd like to talk to you about. And here isn't the right place.'

'Course,' he said, locking the car doors and instead of being pleased at the suggestion, he felt anxious. He watched as she set off through the trees to follow Tom, annoyed with himself for caring too much.

It was a long morning. Fran said not a word to him as they all worked away, pulling fallen branches onto the banks of the stream, sawing the biggest limbs in half and digging out the debris that was obstructing the water flow. It wasn't so much the work that was wearing Jack down. It was the thought of the conversation that would follow. He didn't want to drive Fran home now because he was pretty sure of the outcome. But he couldn't duck out of it.

In the end, Tom decided they should pack up before lunch and get home or they'd all freeze to death. And so, on the journey to Whitegate, Jack found himself sitting nervously beside Fran, wanting the whole thing to be over and not in any mood to make trivial conversation. They were both wet through and cold so he turned the heater up high, steaming up the windows and struggling to see the road ahead.

At last they reached her house and he waited for her to start. Whatever she had to say, well OK, he could take it.

She turned in her seat and looked at him. 'Not the best day to be messing about in water,' she said, pulling down her hood and shivering a little despite the fug in the car. 'But I haven't been able to make the last two so I thought it was a bit lily-livered to cry off.' She paused. 'And I was hoping, if you were there, we could... clear something up.'

Jack nodded slowly, on the face of it composed and quiet. But his heart was thumping in his chest and he didn't trust himself to speak without his voice giving him away. This was going to be awful, he just knew it.

'Jack, if I've got this wrong then I'm truly sorry. I'll be embarrassed and you'll quite rightly be offended.' Her eyes were sad and she let out a long sigh. 'And I know you've had a rough time lately... with your father... but this needed saying.' She stopped and the atmosphere in the car was strained – more than strained – it felt to Jack as though every moment that passed made it harder to breathe. 'If you thought… if you think there could be anything of a romantic nature between us, then I have to be straight with you and say… that's just not going to happen.'

Jack looked down and briefly closed his eyes. What could he say?

'It's not the age thing, I don't think that always matters. And it's not because I don't like you. I do, very much. You're such a nice bloke, you're kind and thoughtful and… easy to talk to. But… you're not for me.'

Jack found his voice. 'I was beginning to realise I had the wrong idea. Sorry if it's made you uncomfortable.'

'I'm flattered, I really am. And I don't want you to feel that you've upset me in any way. But whatever it is that attracts one person to another, well, it's not there for me. And I don't want you to go on wasting your time thinking otherwise. That wouldn't be fair.'

He wanted to curl up, desperate to end this whole conversation and forget the whole embarrassing episode. He wanted to disappear. What an idiot he'd been. Not enough sense to realise much earlier that she'd just been kind to him. Nothing more.

'Please say something, Jack. I feel awful having to spell this out but I'm right, aren't I? You did have those sort of thoughts about me.'

He murmured a 'yes' which she had to bend her head towards him to hear.

'This is between you and me,' she said. 'No-one else needs to know any of it, Jack, not Lucy or Rachel or… anyone here. It's between you and me. And I hope you'll still come to work with the group and not be put off….'

He didn't want to hear any more. It was too painful. 'Thanks, Fran. And I'm glad you've said it all. It was honest and I think I knew it was hopeless. I feel I've made a fool of myself…'

'No, you haven't. You haven't. And I know for sure you'll find someone who'll be right for you, appreciate all that you are. Don't let this knock you back.'

They exchanged smiles then, relieved, at last able to look at one another, experiencing different emotions but at least there was honesty at last.

She went to open the car door and stopped. 'Don't let this put you off helping.'

'No, I won't.'

But he knew there was no way he'd carry on.

She climbed out of the car and walked quickly to her front door.

Jack turned on the ignition and set off down the road, away from anything that reminded him of how naïve he'd been. But after driving further on round a few bends, he pulled into a gateway and got out of the car, needing a moment to himself to let everything that had been said sink in. It wasn't the end of the world, he thought. At least she'd done it as kindly as she could and perhaps it was his pride that was hurt most. Take a bit of time to mend, that was all. But he could feel the old sense of failure, of falling short again when he'd just determined he was handling his life with much more confidence lately.

The sky was leaden above him, the clouds so low it was obvious the day wasn't going to brighten up. He hugged his body to warm himself, both hands clapping his arms to get the circulation going. But he still stood there. A flock of geese, making their usual din, flew overhead in a V formation, circling and swirling down to some expanse of water out of sight behind the trees. Once the cackling had died away, a silence fell over the wet countryside except for the sound of the rain falling from branches to the sodden earth.

A fitting end, he thought. Like something out of a film. Well, he'd tell Leo that his advice had been sound but the '*fair lady*' wouldn't be won at any cost. Sometimes, you just had to give up.

It was still early and he wasn't ready to return home. He didn't want to be asked questions – where he'd been or what he intended doing with the rest of the day. He didn't want to be under any sort of scrutiny. And there was only one place he could go where he could just walk in, fit into a family group without anyone expecting anything from him and feel comfortable. Uncle Joe's house.

He climbed back into the car and drove on towards the motorway, his mind occupied, determined to leave it all behind him…

Then he saw it. A billboard at the side of the road:

Expressway Bridge Replacement.

Start date 2021.

He'd braked without looking in his rear-view mirror and pulled onto the grass, backing up to read the smaller lettering.

Combining the Chester Road to Runcorn over the M56

motorway.

And it all made sense to him at last. His dad's car had crashed near here, somewhere near anyway, and this is where he must have been going that night. He'd obviously driven over to look at the proposed site to see if it could be a job for his firm, to be ahead of the game. Or to look at the competition.

Of course! Jack couldn't believe that, quite by accident, he'd solved the mystery. He'd wait for a good time to tell his dad and at least that might jog his memory. Something good had come out of the day anyway.

Although the light wasn't good, he lifted his phone from where it lay on the passenger seat and took a few photos of the board, then started up the car, pulled out and drove along the road with a sense of satisfaction that he might be able to put his dad's mind at rest.

He turned on the radio and sang along to *Star Boy*, drumming his fingers against the steering wheel and shaking his head at the surprise of it all. He'd keep it to himself until he'd sounded out his dad who'd see the logic of it all, even if the actual memory didn't come back. It certainly explained a lot.

*

The moment Jack entered through the garden gate at his uncle's and opened the door into the bustle and noise of the kitchen, he relaxed. Usually, the mayhem of the house got too much for him after a while but today he found it to be welcome. A big pan of soup bubbled away on the hob, the kettle was whistling, plates and bowls stood ready on a tray. And Aaron was throwing toast from the grill to land in a bread basket at the side of the sink, some missing the mark and some just making it to his whoops of delight and Stella's shouts of annoyance.

Their mother, Anna, tea towel in hand was shaking her head. 'Aaron, there's no need to throw them. It's not basketball. If you can't do your job, I'll find you another.'

Aaron was grinning. 'I *can* do it, Mum. I don't miss many.'

'It won't be fit to eat,' Stella grumbled. 'And there are crumbs all over the floor. Aaron, just *hand* me my piece.'

Anna looked up and put her arms out to give Jack a hug. 'Jack, my favourite nephew, come and have some lunch. Or have you already eaten?'

'You only *have* one nephew,' said Aaron, hugging Jack on his other side. 'You'll have some of my toast, won't you? You can put butter on yourself…'

'Give him a chance to take his coat off and sit down, son,' said Anna. 'He's wet through.'

She pulled up a chair and put a can of Coca-Cola in front of him as Joe and Jemma, who at fourteen didn't say much but sighed a lot, came to sit down at the table. Joe patted Jack on the shoulder and tousled his wet hair, saying in a mild voice and obviously not expecting an answer, 'What's all the racket about then?' And everyone was talking over one another which to Jack, this morning, sounded the way meals should be – chaotic and funny and disorganised. He was glad he'd come.

'Aren't there any scrambled eggs, Anna?' Joe said. 'This boy looks like a drowned rat. He needs something besides soup.'

'I was just going to ask him.' Anna was about to get up but Joe put out his hand.

'I'll make it. I'll do my favourite recipe, some cream in it and hot pepper. Give me five minutes.' Aaron clapped his hands and began jumping up and down. Joe calmed him. 'You can help me. Get five eggs out of the fridge. And be careful not to drop them.'

Anna, elbows on the table and chin in her hands, looked at Jack. 'How did you get so wet? Were you doing the horses?'

'No,' he sat back in his chair. 'I was going to help with this conservation job on a blocked up stream, but the conditions were pretty awful...'

'Quite right. Not the weather to be doing anything outside,' said Anna. 'We're not even sending Joe out to fix the drainpipe that's coming off the wall.'

Joe turned from the stove. 'I wasn't intending to do it anyway. Hope that wasn't a serious suggestion.'

'We'll let you off. You can do it tomorrow evening in the dark.' She gave Jack a sideways glance to include him in the teasing. 'We'll give him permission to go and watch that documentary series on Netflix, the one with lots of cases of unsolved murders in America that fascinates him so.'

'Yeah,' said Jack. 'I like those, too.'

'And is your dad still chipper?' Joe asked as he let the butter melt in the pan.

'Yes, good. Working more. He can drive the car next week which'll make things much easier for him. You haven't been out on your bikes yet, have you?'

'No, not exactly ideal conditions for that. But we'll get round to it.'

By the time he'd finished eating – the vegetable soup, toast, Joe's special scrambled eggs and a flapjack – he was barely able to move, and helped Stella fix a glitch on her iPad and played a card game with Aaron.

He felt ready to head home. Perhaps he could persuade his dad to walk down to the pub later on. Benny was sure to have lit a fire and it seemed ages since they'd done something together, other than drive to doctor's appointments and attend the hospital for physio.

Oddly, he felt easier; his life had become less complicated, less hopeful perhaps but now at least he knew the score with Fran. And he could live with it.

*

He found his dad reading the Sunday supplements in the sitting room, the pages scattered around his chair. And because he wasn't paying enough attention to what was underfoot, he nearly fell over Sam who lay sprawled on his side, legs twitching as he slept.

His dad put the magazine section down. 'That dog'll be the death of someone. Probably me. He always lies in the doorway.' He cocked his head on one side. 'Thought you were out for the day.'

'Rain stopped play,' Jack said. 'On my way back, I popped in to see Uncle Joe and they fed me.'

'Bet that was lively!'

'Yes, that's one word for it. But they always make you feel so welcome, you don't like to leave too quickly. Even though it's a mad house.'

'Yes, your grandmother always wants to tidy up when she goes there, but she doesn't in case it'd hurt Anna's feelings. Quite right too. They're a lovely lot.'

Jack couldn't keep it to himself any longer and began smiling. 'Guess what?'

'Surprise me.'

'I think I've found where you were going on the night of the crash.'

The expression on his father's face was frightening, as though he'd gone into shock and it was so unexpected, Jack put his hand out as though to pull him out of it. There was a terrible silence that needed filling.

'Hey Dad, it's only a guess, but it all makes sense.' Jack rushed on. 'Near where you crashed, they're planning some sort of Bridge Reconstruction over the M56, a big job by the looks of it, starting next year. There's a billboard on the side of the road announcing it. I'll bet that was where you were heading, to look at what was going on, what the job was. Hey, don't look so serious. I thought you'd be pleased that there's a possible answer.'

A weary shake of his head and a deep breath. 'Yes, yes.' He looked at Jack, his eyes dark and worried. 'What were you doing out there? It's not where you usually hang out.'

'Conservation work. They go all over and it's often in some remote spot. I just happened on it as I was heading home and I couldn't believe it. I thought you'd be relieved. Aren't you?'

A long pause, but colour was coming back into his dad's face. 'Yes, I suppose I am. It's just... it reminds me... of how much I don't remember. What I can't picture. Nothing seems to bring it back.'

Jack looked out at the rain running down the windows. He wanted to leave the whole subject behind now and the last thing he'd thought was how upset his dad would be at hearing something *he'd* thought would help. 'Tell you what I fancy – going down to the pub, sitting by the fire and being waited on. Make a change from being on the other side of the bar. Are you up for that?'

'Sounds like a good idea.'

'We can drive down if you want.'

'No, let's walk. It'll do me good. I'll just go up and get a jumper.

Won't be a minute.'

But he was more than a minute. Jack waited in the hall, not even bothering to undo his coat. He began to worry and finally ran up the stairs and pushed the bedroom door open. His dad was searching through the pockets of a jacket draped over the bedside chair.

'Have you seen my phone?' he said, frowning as he straightened up. 'I'm sure I put it… well, I'm certain it's in this room somewhere.'

Jack shook his head. 'No, I saw Mum with it this morning. She must have picked it up from where you left it. Have you looked in the kitchen?'

'Are you sure… that Mum had *my* phone, not her own.'

'Dad, I bought it for you. I know one phone from another. It was definitely yours.'

Jack turned to go, saying over his shoulder. 'I'll find it for you.' But not before he saw the look of alarm on his dad's face which he couldn't make sense of. What on earth was the problem? He'd find the phone. Everything seemed to send his dad into a blue funk for no reason today.

He searched the kitchen, sweeping his hand over surfaces, under the pads on the chairs, looking behind the microwave in case it had slipped behind that and eventually, there it was, on top of the fridge. Obviously where his mother had put it out of harm's way. So he yelled to his dad who was just coming into the room.

'There,' Jack said. 'It's not been smashed on the floor or fallen down the toilet. Stop panicking.'

'I'm not. Just annoyed with myself for losing it.'

But Jack felt there was an overreaction here; it couldn't be that important, unless he'd thought he'd missed some appointment at the hospital or an SOS from work. He watched his dad press the home button and flick through some screens before he put it in his pocket. There seemed to be a jumpiness about him, thought Jack, as though he could go off the rails at any minute..

'OK. No harm done. Let's get going.'

They pulled on coats and walked down the road together, sheltering under a large umbrella. By the time they reached the Fox and Hounds, the rain had soaked their trousers below the knees and their shoes were sodden. Jack pushed open the door to the main bar and looked towards the end of the room where the fire was going strong.

'Come on. Good thing it's early. There's a bench right by the hearth. You grab it while I get us something to drink. At least we'll have a chance to dry out before we have to climb back home.'

'Here Jack,' his dad said, shoving a couple of notes into his hand. 'Get me some beef sandwiches and crisps. I haven't eaten.' His voice had steadied now and he looked calm, Jack was thankful to see. 'And, sod it, I'll have a whiskey. Don't say it's against doctors' orders. It's medicinal.'

They sat in the warmth while his dad ate his sandwiches, surrounded by the usual local Sunday drinkers and for Jack, it felt, for now, nearly like old times.

Chapter 32

Twenty minutes and she'd be out of the office and on her way. The theatre, a real treat, even if she'd never heard of any of the cast and she wasn't sure it was a good idea to go out on a date with a client. Even though she'd known him, sort of, for a year.

Rhys ran a medium-sized advertising agency on the outskirts of Liverpool and had needed a temporary 'Friday Girl' who could be flexible and use her initiative. Fran had sent Olivia along who'd eventually been taken on full-time. She'd left, pregnant, a month ago and Fran had been trying to find a replacement without much luck since then. There'd been quite a number of telephone calls back and forth recently, mostly from Rhys, who'd also twice made some excuse to come by her office, which made Jill raise her eyebrows and Fran had realised this wasn't all business.

So the invitation hadn't come completely out of the blue.

She liked him. He'd worked hard to build something from scratch and she admired that. He was interesting and a bit shy and loved musicals, she'd learned, so when he asked her if she'd fancy going to the theatre with him, she didn't hesitate for long. She needed to get out there, see people, find new friends – and the show was *Chicago* which had got good crits, so it was an evening she was looking forward to.

'Go and spruce yourself up,' was Jill's order at quarter past five. 'You want to look your best.'

'Do I?' Fran loved winding her up. 'Thought I'd go without brushing my hair or changing my shoes. Won't that do?'

Jill laughed and went on filing a CV in the cabinet. 'He's nice, Fran. A really nice clean-cut young man, as my grandmother would say. And he's keen. Just enjoy the evening.'

'Yes, of course I will.' But she stood for a moment staring at nothing. 'But…'

'But what?'

'Well, I don't really feel anything… you know… there's no spark, I suppose.'

'It doesn't always happen like that though, does it, straight away?' said Jill, shutting the drawer and turning towards her. 'Sometimes it takes time, the attraction grows. It isn't always instant.'

No, Fran thought, *it isn't. But deep down you know when it could be the start of something. You might kid yourself at first, ignore all the signs. But already your instincts are on the alert and they're not usually wrong.*

She took a deep breath and straightened her shoulders. 'Good advice. I shall "do myself up", as you suggest. You've missed your forte, you should have worked for a dating agency.'

And when Fran saw Rhys standing outside the theatre, topcoat collar pulled high against the cold, his eyes lighting up when he saw her, she softened and was determined to make the evening as pleasant as she could. It wasn't *his* fault she didn't feel any rush of emotion that might mean this was going somewhere.

He took her arm and led her into the warm foyer, people circling around them looking at their tickets, searching for the right stairs or the right doorway to reach their seats. Rhys suggested they order their drinks for the interval so they threaded their way up to the bar, then headed for the auditorium.

The evening should have gone smoothly. There should have been no surprises. But just after the interval when they'd settled down for the second half to begin, Fran heard her mobile buzz quietly in her handbag. She'd put it on 'Silent' but you get used to the sound the vibration makes, and she was curious to see if it was important. So she took a quick look at the screen and her heart seemed to do a drum roll in her chest.

Alex. Alex had phoned her a minute earlier.

She couldn't just sit there for another hour in a state of pure anxiety. She'd told him to ring if ever he needed her and that need might be urgent. She excused herself, telling Rhys she'd be back in two minutes and rather clumsily managed to navigate past the knees of the other people sitting in her row, trying not to notice their exasperated expressions. By the time she'd reached the Ladies', she was breathless.

As she pulled her phone out of her bag, it buzzed again and she quickly touched the screen to answer.

'Fran.'

'Yes, I'm here now. I'm at the theatre, so couldn't... what's the matter? Are you all right?'

There was no response straight away. All she could hear was faint music in the background. Was he ringing from home?

'Sorry to spoil your evening.'

'Don't be silly. Just tell me what's wrong.'

'I know I said I wouldn't phone but I need to see you.'

'OK. Tonight's difficult but I can take tomorrow afternoon off. Will that do?'

'Yes, that would be... thank you.'

Fran became fraught with worries and questions and horrible imaginings. What the hell was the matter? Was he ill? Had the doctors given him bad news?

Then another thought struck her. Had Jack confided in him about the whole sorry story of his misguided attraction and her rejection? He wouldn't understand why she'd kept it all secret, why she hadn't just told him about it.

Well, she had to return to her seat and get through the evening. Behave as normally as possible. There was nothing else she would do but wait.

Rhys accepted the line that she had to be up early, work next day, so no going for a nightcap or on to a supper bar. Of course they must do this again, she'd had a lovely evening and so enjoyed the musical. But she could see he was disappointed and she felt guilty that she couldn't like him more. She didn't even need a lift because her own car was in a nearby carpark, so they parted on the street and as she looked back, he was watching her, with a hopeful look on his face – surely not waiting for her to change her mind! It made her feel even worse. Ungrateful. He deserved better than a brush-off.

Why did Alex always have to be so *present*... even when he wasn't?

*

Two o'clock and Fran was already so wound up she was unable to think clearly. No good trying to second-guess what he was going to say, but whatever it was, she had a feeling it didn't mean good news. The most she could hope for was that he hadn't had some sort of relapse. She could cope with anything if it wasn't that. Even if she couldn't be part of his life, she wanted him well.

So when she opened the door and took a long look at him, she was so relieved to see that he was like the old Alex. On the surface anyway. He'd put on weight, he had colour in his face, his hair was still a bit too long and fell over his forehead but at least it hid the scar, so to all intents and purposes he was mended. She wasn't to know what his mental state was but he certainly didn't seem depressed. A little anxious; then so was she.

'At least you look OK, Alex,' she said as she let him into the hallway. 'I was so worried you were having some sort of setback. But I can see you're... well... almost normal.'

He smiled. 'That sounds reassuring.'

'You know what I mean. You look like your old self. I was scared you'd had some sort of setback.'

'No. I'm feeling pretty good, considering.'

She put her hands on both his arms so he had to face her. 'I'm not making you a cup of coffee or making bacon sandwiches until you

305

put me out of my misery and tell me what this is all about. Once I've calmed down, then I might forgive you enough to be pleasant.'

He looked at her with such fondness she had to let her hands drop to her sides.

'Oh, Fran, have I missed you!' he said. 'Let me just take my coat off. I got too warm in this new car, couldn't work out how to turn down the heater. Then we'll talk.'

She led him into the front room. 'You're allowed to drive now?'

'Yes, from three days ago. And it's a different model from my old car. I'm still getting used to it. The instrument panel's designed for a cockpit, I'm sure – so complicated it takes some getting used to.' He sat down on the couch and she sat beside him.

'Come on, what's the problem?'

He rubbed his fingers against his temple and pursed his lips. 'I bought a new mobile phone, mine was lost when I crashed the car, and I put certain contacts in. One of them was yours. Just the initials F.R.'

Fran began to tense, waiting for the rest of it. 'That wasn't too clever.'

'It wasn't. I was worried I'd rub the ink off my hand where you'd written it, so I… I entered the number to keep it safe.'

'But it hasn't been safe, has it?' She was watching his expression, solemn, worried. Her own must have matched his.

'No. It was a stupid thing to do. And I'm fairly certain Carrie's been looking through my messages. Nearly all of them are from work so there's nothing for her to find there.' He paused and looked at her as though he didn't want to go on. 'But she'll have gone through the contacts list.'

'And she'd do that, why?'

'Because she's still trying to figure out where I was going that night, why I wasn't where I said I'd be. I'm a complete blank and can't give her any answers – well, I *couldn't* before – so she's going to find out any way she can. And she's bound to be suspicious, Fran. All I know is, I'm absolutely certain I didn't leave my phone just lying about, certainly not in the kitchen where it turned up.'

A tremor of fear ran through Fran's body. They'd both been so careful seven years ago, determined to leave no trace, no connection between them, and now it could all blow up in their faces. But she tried to stay calm and at least be rational. 'Are you being paranoid about this? You don't *know* she's going to make anything of two initials. I could be anyone.'

'But what if she rang you? Bloody awkward if you answered and she recognised your voice, your name, whatever and remembered that you're Lucy's friend who came with her to the party.' He watched her face, trying to gauge her reaction. 'God, it's like a maze trying to think this through. Two days after that bloody barbecue I crash my car on some mysterious errand…'

She put her hand over his, warm under her fingers, so familiar still. Then she tightened her grip, as though telling him to slow down, to stop dramatizing this. 'Look. If anyone rings, I'm F.R. Recruitment. And that's how I'll answer if the call comes from your phone or from a number I don't recognise.' She nodded to herself. 'Think about it. It's part of your job to find workers, so that makes sense of the entry in your contacts list. The business can be looked up on the internet if she wants to go that far. That solves it, doesn't it?'

'But it's a mobile number.'

'So? Lots of firms use mobiles as well as landlines, especially if that number is given to the executives and HR managers who do the hiring.' She shrugged. 'That makes sense, doesn't it?'

He relaxed his shoulders, relief on his face. 'Yes, it does. God, I panicked, sorry. I've brought you enough trouble in my time. I couldn't face the thought of giving you any more through being bloody careless.'

They sat looking at each other, hesitant, the moment so emotionally charged it was as though it had a life of its own. And when Alex reached out and pushed back a strand of hair from her forehead, she found she was shivering, a reflex she was unable to control.

He spoke first, his voice quiet. 'You're always on my mind and I don't seem to be able to do anything about it. Oh, Fran, it just doesn't go away. Perhaps I'm not trying hard enough.'

There was nothing she could say. If she told him how she felt, they were in deep water again. And what then?

She sat back and folded her arms, doing her best to gain some distance in every sense. They'd sorted out one worry and she'd no wish to hear anything else about his life or rake over the past. Just go, she wanted to tell him, that's best. Just go.

But she stayed silent.

And he hadn't finished. 'The night of the accident, I'm pretty sure I was coming to explain something to you. Something I should have had the guts to face up to years ago. Instead I sent a letter. Then… seeing you again left me shattered. I think I didn't want you to spend the rest of your life not understanding why I ended it… and how it had nothing to do with how I felt…'

'Oh, Alex, it's a bit too late for this.'

'I know. It's *way* too late, but when you understand why I had to make a clean break, what I was facing at the time, you might be able to forgive me. I sent the letter because I knew if I saw you, I'd weaken. And I couldn't afford to do that.'

The more he spoke the more furious she felt. This all reminded her of the anguish she'd suffered in the months after he'd left and she wanted to shake him, to hurt him back, to show him how selfish he'd been.

'Well, to me it smacks of cowardice, Alex. No good writing "*Darling*" and ending the bloody thing with "*Please don't phone.*" It was… brutal.'

He bent his head and couldn't look at her. 'It was.'

'Go on, then. Enlighten me. What was it that made you do it?'

He seemed to be gathering his thoughts. And perhaps his courage as well. 'I'd been with you. That Tuesday, you remember. I hadn't answered any calls. None from home, anyway. I'd ignored them all. And when I arrived back at eight o'clock there was Carrie waiting for me, crying – God was she crying – and I couldn't make any sense of what was going on. I knew it was something awful but I couldn't get anything coherent out of her. She made me sit down and eventually I managed to make sense of what had happened. It was Jack. They'd called from the school, they'd found him cowering in the toilets, wouldn't go into lessons. He'd lashed out at another boy and wouldn't speak to anyone, not the staff or Carrie. He just shook and cried. And things didn't get any better. The next night he ran away. He was found by a dog walker in a dreadful state, beyond reasoning with, camping out near a wood and then the police got involved. He had counselling for a time… he'd just lost it.' Alex took a deep breath and his words were coming so fast Fran needed to concentrate to take it all in. 'You don't think at fifteen, things can get that bad. Or that other kids can be so cruel. Don't they realise the damage they can do…?'

'What? What had they done?'

'Jack's a sensitive lad, you know? He takes things to heart and he's always measured himself against his sister. And we hadn't done enough to bolster him up so we can't shirk that. Even though I know teenagers hide problems, we should have been more… vigilant. Taken more care. Anyway, it all came out then. Not just failing in his subjects, he'd been the target of bullying on a scale I'd never have imagined, not just at school and outside the school gates, but cyberbullying – that's what they call it – bombarded with messages and texts and God knows what. And he'd said nothing to anyone, just crumbled, I suppose until it all got too much and he'd gone under.'

'How awful,' said Fran, beginning to understand more about the Jack she'd met – the naïve lad with so little confidence who'd just seemed to want affection, who was trusting to the point where he could easily be hurt. She didn't dare say any more. God, where was this going?

'On the day he was allowed home I went up to his bedroom. He just smiled at me, so sorry for any trouble, wished he'd told us. I can't explain the look in his eyes when I told him how sorry *I* was for not being there for him, for not seeing how unhappy he was. Then it all came out how he'd been missing school and going to hide in Steph's barn for the day... And you can imagine what went through my mind... it wasn't only that I'd let him down so badly. Carrie was right when she said how I was never home, that I hadn't been taking any interest in her or the children for months, that I'd removed myself from all of them. There was truth in all that.' Fran could see the memory had brought him to the edge of tears. 'I'd let Jack down. The blame fell at my door. Do you see? I *had* to make a clean break. I had to let you go. There wasn't a choice to be made. It was made *for* me.'

He bent forward and rested his head on her shoulder and she put her arms round him, holding him gently, rubbing her hands over his back in an attempt to soothe him. Her mind trying to absorb all the implications of this. She could never, ever tell him about Jack's infatuation with her. He would never, ever do anything to hurt his son. Or be the cause of something that would mean separation from him, an estrangement neither could get over.

How ironic. Their affair had been doomed from the start, even though they hadn't known it. Lucy's birthday party had been their undoing, second time around. Meeting Jack had offered a prescient warning which she had no way of recognising.

They were both silent for some time, absorbed in their own

thoughts. She thanked heaven Alex had no way of knowing where hers were heading. He sat back and held her gaze.

'I am so sorry, Fran.'

'Don't be. You did the only thing possible.' She tried to keep her tone positive. 'I met Jack at the barbecue and he seemed a nice lad. Making sure all the guests were looked after. So I'm sure in the end you helped him get his confidence back.'

Alex shrugged. 'I don't think it was all down to me. He met a girl... Grace, really nice... and she did wonders for him. That is until she went off to university. I thought she seemed just right for him but it didn't work out. He drifted for a while after that. Still, he's got a new job now and... he's OK. It's just... once someone's had a bad experience, you worry about them, hope they've got the strength to face life when things get difficult again.'

It's odd, Fran thought, something that should make you sceptical and dismissive, like listening to a long-awaited excuse, has the opposite effect. The whole story endeared Alex to her more than she could explain to herself. She loved him more for caring so much about his son even if it had meant losing her. How could she not see his dilemma? She didn't have children but she could understand a bond that you won't break whatever the circumstances. Some relationships are too precious to jeopardise.

'Alex, come on,' she said. 'Let's go for a walk and put this behind us for a while. An hour of peace before you go.'

'It's miserable out there!'

'Well,' she managed to laugh, 'I think we'll survive.'

They wrapped up and headed out, the odd car coming down the road with its headlights already turned on as the light faded. Fran led them to a right-of-way that formed a circular route round the edge of a cornfield and back to the village where she knew there was likely to be no-one out at this time of day. They reached the furthest end and stopped by a large oak tree, branches denuded now of leaves and its bark glistening in the wet.

Alex put his arms round her and kissed her on the forehead.

'I will never be able to forget you, Fran. Doesn't matter what happens, you're here with me. I hope you find someone who deserves you…'

She put her hand over his mouth. 'Don't say anything else. We'll be crying next. Let's pretend for once.'

When they reached his car, he paused. 'Will you do one last thing for me?'

She waited, afraid to even nod.

'It's nearly Christmas. I want to buy you a present. Will you meet me in Chester like we did before and we'll have one last day…'

She knew what her answer should have been, that the sensible thing to do was to end this here. But it was no good. She couldn't refuse, not standing there so close to him, his gaze steady and such a hopeful expression on his face. 'Yes,' she said. 'It might be a crazy idea but yes, I'll meet you. Just let me know when and I'll be there.'

As she watched him drive away, she wondered whether this might be their undoing, one more risk that shouldn't be taken.

But she couldn't let go. Not just yet.

Chapter 33

Being back at work full-time (well, almost) stops me thinking too much, throws me into a life that can be demanding and pressured but it's what I'm used to. When I was young and hard up and read stories of lottery winners in the newspapers, I'd think how all that money would be the answer to everything, imagining it'd be great to spend your days doing just what you wanted, when you wanted. Free to do nothing. But it doesn't work that way. Too many months of sitting idle has taught me that. It's not good for me. I've become restless, unable to concentrate on finishing a book or a film, impatient, lying awake at night thinking through problems that don't have a solution and some that are non-existent. I'm conditioned, obviously, to keep going. Well, perhaps that's how most people are.

The company has just won a new contract against the odds, a major road plan, large and potentially very profitable so there's a healthy optimism all round in head office. And we're waiting to see who's going to be put in charge. I could be bottom of the list, of course – they're bound to wait for the company doctor's report on how fit I am. But it's in our area and we've just handed over the NPG Treatment site to the client, so you never know.

We're in Adrian's office going over some general stuff and I'm trying to be casual. Not ask any questions about whether he knows who's in the running for the road contract. And he's keeping his cards close to his chest. You can tell he's pleased though about getting the job. 'Was a bit uneasy when the tender went in,' he says. 'Thought we were too high. But there you are. Reputation helps every time.'

He sits back in his chair and clasps his hands together, giving me a long look.

'Are you feeling up to scratch?' he asks.

'I am. I was beginning to think I'd never get there, but the last four or so weeks have been good. I've stopped thinking about it all. Work's helped. And I was given quite a grilling from the company doctor, Stevenson. He seemed happy with me at the end of it.'

'I haven't seen the report yet. Takes a while,' Adrian says, then pretends to pick up some papers from his desk. 'You know Ian Black and Chalmers are keen to get the road extension.' It isn't a question. Well it is in a way, but it's baited. He wants to see my reaction.

I pull a noncommittal face and shrug slightly. 'Look, I know how important this is and I'm not saying I wouldn't love to do it. But if I'm considered a risk, I understand...'

He gives a lopsided grin. 'Let's see what the health report comes back with. Then it'll be up to the MD to make the decision. But you'll have my backing. You've worked hard enough for it.'

I left his office with that odd mixture of elation and nerves. I'm always fairly confident when I'm about to take on a new job, then when I'm faced with the reality of what's involved and the difficulties it will probably bring, I wonder why I was so convinced I could do it. Usually, thank God, it's worked out. You learn as you go along.

Better to keep everything to myself until there's something definite. I'm just hoping no-one suggests a stint behind a desk; my eighteen months in the Drawing Office early on was so bloody tedious I certainly don't want to repeat it. But surely that's unlikely.

It's not an easy journey as I drive home on the motorway – dark winter weather, convoys of lorries and SLOW DOWN signs, and even darker when I hit the countryside, water running off the fields onto the road forming deep pools which send up huge sprays as I pass through them. Pulling into the driveway, I turn off the engine and don't do the automatic thing of getting out. I pause and I'm not sure why. Perhaps it's because my world is split in two – of my own making, this – and it's a mental effort to adjust. I've always thought of myself as kind, within reason, that I treat people pretty well. But that doesn't hold with who I am now, does it? Someone's always bound to get hurt when you flout the rules, however much you justify your actions. So let that just be me who ends up wounded… or I'll be living with regrets the rest of my life.

*

I shut the front door behind me just as the house phone is ringing and Carrie shouts, 'Get that, will you?'

So before I take off my coat, I pick up the receiver and a breathless voice says, 'Dad.' Lucy, sounding as though she's run a marathon. 'Good job it's you. Can you talk?'

'Yes. What's the problem?'

'No problem. It's just…. well Christmas…'

I listen, no idea where this is going.

'I know how Mum likes us all round over the two days and I'll certainly be there for New Year but…'

'Lucy, stop stalling. What is it that's bothering you?

'I've been given the chance to go skiing in Austria with friends – someone's dropped out – but they're leaving on Christmas Eve and I have to get the same flight…'

I smile to myself. 'Fine, go, enjoy yourself. I think we can manage without you. As long as you buy us all decent presents.'

She laughs then. 'Thanks. You're a star! All you have to do now is break it to Mum. Will you do that?' She doesn't wait for an answer. 'See you in a few days.'

I replace the receiver and shake my head. There's a problem I *can* solve. We go from the sublime to the ridiculous in minutes. You can't stay lost in your own world for long, the ordinary everyday gets in the way. Not such a bad thing.

So the evening is filled with the meal, taking Sam for a quick walk (in the winter, a black dog is a hazard on country roads), quick catch-up with the paper and then, usually sitting down to watch TV, news first then a film on Netflix or Sky Atlantic.

But tonight, Carrie doesn't turn on the TV. She holds the remote in her hand and waits for me to join her.

'You haven't asked me about my mother,' she says.

'Well, you didn't seem keen to go into any details so I assumed you just wanted to forget about her.'

Carrie sighs. 'I *do* want to forget about her. But I'd like to have your opinion.'

She has my attention. It's not like her to want my opinion on any matters regarding her family. She's always made clear they're her business, always have been and off limits to any interference on my part. Particularly when her father was alive.

'OK, go on.' I settle back, knowing she's already made her mind up about what to do but never mind. That mother's a lot to answer for.

'Well,' Carrie clasps a cushion to her chest as though she needs to hold onto something, 'to start with, she just did her usual. Kept me waiting as we ploughed through this meal I didn't want to eat. It was strained but she was determined to keep a good face on. I can't explain how she manages to poison the whole atmosphere just by sitting there. I'm always ready to put up the barriers, defend myself. How's that for a grown woman! Pretty pathetic.'

'No,' I say. 'What's done in childhood stays with you a lifetime. She certainly didn't have any maternal instincts.'

'She didn't. And then she expects to waltz back into my life every so often and expect… God knows what. A grateful daughter!'

I nod. 'So what was the lunch for?'

'She's broke. No… she's in debt. The lovely George died and left her in the shit, twenty thousand pounds of it.' Carrie doesn't go on for a while, just looks thoughtful and a bit lost. So unlike her. Only her mother has ever been able to get through the armour that usually protects her.

'And she's asked you to pay off the debt?'

'Yes. That's what she honestly expected. I'd had my inheritance from my father – a fortune, she thinks, and now it's time to share and share alike.'

I watch her, moved by her struggle to come to terms with what's due, what's fair, and what is deserved. 'So what have you decided to do?'

'I've offered her ten thousand. To help. Not to sort her out. Not sure what would be the right amount, but how does that sound to you?'

'Well,' I begin, 'you had to do something. And I think that's probably enough. She must have been left a property to sell. George was hardly without means. Did she say whether the house was sold in Gloucestershire?'

'No, I didn't ask. Should have.'

For a while we don't speak, just sit in the half-light until we hear the front door slam and Jack shouting, 'Hi.'

Carrie starts and gets up, immediately reverting to the capable, self-sufficient woman who never worries or doubts herself. I rather liked the one who puzzled over a difficult decision and showed concern about doing 'the right thing', a side of her she rarely allowed anyone to see.

'Give me ten minutes to brew the coffee. I'd like to watch the new series of *The Crown*,' she says. 'You liked the last one, didn't you?'

I try not to groan too loudly. 'I like the political parts. Not the soap opera.'

'Well, you can go to sleep through those bits.'

And she goes into the kitchen to see if Jack wants some supper.

*

I'm pulling my life back into some sort of shape, that's what I tell myself. An acceptance of reality for how things must be. But my thoughts can't get past the inevitable – the last time I'll see Fran, the last time I'll have a memory of her to store away. There's no help for it. We'll be separate, leading our separate lives, getting older, having experiences we'll never share, going places where I'll say to myself, *Wouldn't she have loved this!* – where I'll see someone across a room and think, *That smile's so like hers!* And although this might fade as time passes and I'm caught up in the everyday, it will always be there, perhaps coming back to me at longer intervals, but there. Like moments in childhood you lose for a while but never forget, moments when you first know what rejection is or experience fear or joy – emotional highs and lows so deep-seated they have their own momentum, suddenly flooding back, unbidden.

I remember a December when Joe was sick, he was about five, I think – it was chicken pox but I didn't know the name for it then – and he was confined to the bedroom with its drawn curtains and smell of antiseptic for what seemed like days. I was told to keep out of his room. In fact my mother had a sign on his door which read DO NOT ENTER, which was a bit over-the-top. But I was convinced he was going to die. No-one told me anything. When I asked, my dad said to be a good lad and stay out of the way. One late afternoon when the only lights on in the house were downstairs, I crept into Joe's room with a torch in my hand and took a good look at him. I kept the beam low and I couldn't really see much other than he was fast asleep, breathing heavily and his face was odd, blotchy and covered in white patches (calamine lotion, I know now). He didn't look like my brother. He was beyond help. It was a terrifying moment.

And what always amazes me, other than the fact that I didn't catch chicken pox or measles, whatever it was, myself, is that I can see it all in my mind in every last detail. I suppose because the terror was so great, it will always be there, the shockwave, the echo, hard-wired.

Of course there are other memories that surface like that one. Like on a reel of film. There's the moment I plucked up the courage to dive into the outdoor swimming pool at the deep end – it was like flying... or forgetting my lines in the school play, Noah and the Ark... or fetching our new puppy from the farm, a collie called Rocky who cried all the way home... or opening the letter that told me I had a place at university. Perhaps everyone has these involuntary flashbacks. Don't they? Or is remembering so vividly an odd trait? Like recalling dreams in colour or remembering phrases word for word from an early picture book.

It's difficult to know. They aren't the subject of normal conversation.

But I'm sure that's how it'll be with Fran. Moments and songs and words, place names, a laugh, a feeling... they'll bring her back. Will always bring her back.

I don't know whether that's comforting or sad...

A sudden banging on the back door halts all these thoughts and makes me jump. It's early evening and anyone calling usually rings the bell at the front.

Jack comes up behind me as I make my way through the hall into the kitchen. 'Hurry up, Dad. Turn the outside light on.'

We open up, trying to adjust our eyes to the dimness outside. I'm surprised to see Steph standing there, woollen hat jammed on her head, waterproof coat buttoned tight, wellies splattered with mud and eyes full of anxiety.

'Is one of the horses in trouble, Steph? Did you get called to give a hand?'

Jack is already heading for the coat stand to pull on his anorak but he stops when she says, 'No. Nothing like that. I just thought Carrie might be back by now. Wanted a word.'

It's after five, long past her usual shift, except Carrie has gone to collect some jumping poles in the trailer and probably asked her to check back to make sure all the horses were in, the barn doors shut and the gate locked.

'She shouldn't be long,' I say, worried by the way she's shivering with cold, despite all the protective clothing. 'Come inside and wait. Have a cup of tea and warm up. You look frozen. You haven't been waiting outside in the yard, have you?'

'For a while.' She still stands there, looking uncertain, glancing from me to Jack. I didn't know whether to push it or not. Then she looks round as though someone might be behind her. 'No, I'll go. I can see Carrie in the morning. Don't mention I came back. It's nothing really. It'll wait.'

And she's gone, hurrying down the path to the yard, small and somehow vulnerable. We both sense it. This isn't how Steph usually strikes you. She always has this pragmatic attitude to life, doesn't flap or overdramatise.

We sit down at the kitchen table eyeing each other, curious and uneasy.

'Something's up,' says Jack. 'Steph's never put out. She usually copes with anything.'

'I know. I feel I should go after her but it's probably nothing I could deal with if it's to do with the stables. Can't be a horse or she would have said.'

Jack gets up and brews some tea, two mugs in place on the table.

'I've got a horrible feeling it's to do with that bloke, David, who's got Mum teaching his kid. You know, the one who took her to that horse thing last month. He's dodgy,' he says, pulling a face.

'Why d'you say that?'

'Because the man's a bully. He criticises everything Steph does, the type of haylage she buys, the way she sets the horses up, how she puts the orders in – totally rubbishing the fantastic job she does. It's bound to upset her. She's worked for Mum so long and then he comes along and well, seems to want to take over. He interferes, always got the best vet, the best blacksmith and he wants his say in everything. When it isn't his business.'

'Your mother's never said anything.' I realise I haven't asked Carrie about the business for ages. I haven't been interested enough, that's the honest truth and I feel guilty. Jack knows a bloody sight more than I do.

'Can't think of anything else that would get her so upset.' Jack stands up because he's too angry to sit. 'It wouldn't be one of the liveries, they all think she's great. Which she is.' He looks fierce which is not just unusual, it's an eye-opener. 'Bastard. He'd like to take over, that's what he'd like. And Mum just doesn't seem to see it. He's all charm and chat.'

'I don't know what to say other than let's wait till your mother comes home and get her view of this. But it's awkward. Steph's asked us not to say anything.' I shake my head. 'Don't overreact yet, Jack when we don't know the full story. We might be barking up the wrong tree. Wait.'

So we end up talking about everything under the sun to pass the time until Jack looks at me with the beginnings of a smile and I have a fairly good idea he's going to tell me something important. Something personal. He has that sort of open face that doesn't hide much and we've been through enough in the past for him to feel comfortable unburdening himself when we're alone.

'Go on,' I say before he even starts. 'What is it?'

'Well,' he twists his empty mug round on the table top and doesn't look directly at me, 'I've heard from Grace.'

I don't react. I don't want to stop him.

'She's got a job in a school in Stockport, primary school, been there since September. I went for a coffee with her and a friend, oh, months ago now. Didn't know what to make of it. But she must have got my number off Terry…'

'And…?'

'Well she wants to meet up. But I don't know. It didn't end too well, did it?'

'Jack you're a good four years older now. People grow up and change their minds. I always liked her. Good sense of humour.'

'The trouble is I'm not sure what I feel for her anymore. And I've had a confusing time lately – I know I haven't said anything but I got myself into a tricky situation recently. I had a real crush on someone who didn't feel the same way about me, I should have seen it coming. So I'm not sure I'm ready to put my head on the block again.'

'Sounds a bit grim.' I try to keep all this in perspective, but he probably thinks I'm being dismissive. 'How do you know this girl didn't feel the same way. Did you ask her?'

'I didn't have the nerve. And then when I'd made a fool of myself, she told me… very nicely… that I had no chance.'

'Where did you meet her?' I'm curious. Jack's social life is hardly hectic.

He's quiet. He seems about to tell me, then changes his mind. 'Doesn't matter now. It's in the past. But she seemed perfect for a while. That's what worries me – my choices haven't been too clever. And I don't want to be the loser again'

God, you're so young, I think. *So hard on yourself. And I love you for being so honest when it's not easy to be, when you admit to being vulnerable without pride getting in the way. I could learn a lot.*

I get up and lightly touch his shoulder. 'Let it ride then. If Grace wants to see you, she'll find you. Come on, let's go and watch the news and get depressed by hopeless politicians and climate change deniers. That should cheer us up!'

He looks sheepish and smiles at last. 'Good idea!'

When Carrie comes home, we say nothing about Steph. It seems right to let her deal with whatever the situation is, in her own way.

Chapter 34

Carrie threw the saddle over Merlin's back and bent low to fasten the girth, the horse's nose inches from her arm, his warning not to tighten up too quickly. She checked the noseband and led him out of the stable. There was a lot to think about and she needed to digest what had being going on without her realising. Not just what was going on but the seriousness of it.

Heading out along the road towards the bridle path she met little traffic, just one motorbike which slowed down to a steady thrum as it passed. She lifted her hand to signal thanks and cut away onto the track which would take her down the side of Black Wood.

Being in the saddle always felt like the place she should be, no need to even adjust her balance – it was all there, instinctive, long practised. Like driving a car when you've done it for years, leaving you time to mull over things. Work out what you're going to do. And Merlin knew the way, he'd done it enough times so he turned without being directed and went into trot where he always did. It helped her relax in a way that nothing else did at the moment.

Saturday, nine o'clock. She needed time to think but she hadn't got long. She wanted to be back in the yard to see David when he arrived. Confront him with what she'd found out and make some pointed remarks. It was time to clear the air... or not, if he wasn't going to listen. And Steph needed to hear what she had to say. So it was a sort of summit meeting and like the recent lunch with her mother, this wasn't going to be pleasant.

Sometimes you miss what's right under your nose.

Earlier, she'd left Alex and Jack in their beds and quietly closed the back door, barely able to see outside but the lights were shining in the yard; Steph was already letting the horses out. And as soon as Carrie joined her to help, she could see how upset the woman was. More than that. It was clear from the strain on Steph's face that she'd been fretting enough to give her a sleepless night or two. She looked small and grey and worn out.

'I need to talk to you, Carrie,' she'd said, 'before anyone gets here.' And even though the yard was empty, they moved into the privacy of the office area of the barn. Steph stood, apologetic, uncertain, her back against the desk. Eventually, she began. 'You know me, I don't usually let people get me down. I don't usually let *much* get me down but it's come to the point where I don't know what to do.'

'OK, go on, Steph. It's serious, I can see. We've been together too long not to be frank with one another. We can sort anything out, whatever it is.'

Steph slowly took off her gloves and her eyes filled with tears. 'It's David. I know you like him but he's making my life unbearable and I can't understand why he has such a down on me. I do my very best...'

'Of course you do,' said Carrie, uneasy at what was coming and angry at the same time. 'What on earth's he been up to?'

'I'm not sure where to start. He disapproves of everything I do. He interferes all the time, gives me orders, they aren't suggestions any more – I'm giving cheap feed to the horses, I don't bank up the straw enough in the stables, I should bring Jodie's pony in first before the others when it's getting dark... Oh, it goes on and on.' She took a tissue out of her pocket. 'And usually, I can reason with owners who think they know best, there've been enough of them in the past and usually they're fine after a while and accept that we know what we're doing. But he's... hard to deal with.' She bit her lip, as though trying to keep her emotions in check. 'And... worse than that... he's dropping hints that he's going to be running the place with you soon and there'll be no job for me if he's got anything to do with it... That was last week when he got in a temper...' She blinked her eyes rapidly.

'Christ, what a bloody nerve! Arrogant sod. He's talking out of his hat!' Carrie couldn't quite grasp how he'd come to get so far ahead of himself. She'd known, of course, that he could be forceful, someone who liked to take charge. She had to admit that lately he'd behaved as if he'd the right to take matters in his own hands, matters that weren't his business. He'd become... what was the word? ...Proprietorial. She should never have given him any leeway, never have gone to that event with him, never have let him think for a minute he could play a part in any development he'd obviously been cooking up. She'd lowered her guard when she should have kept things totally professional. Well, this was the outcome. Had she been flattered? Perhaps. Or had she just wanted someone to give her some support, show some interest in her life, give her the attention that had been lacking from Alex.

Well, she wasn't going to make excuses for herself. She'd allowed the situation to get out of hand and it was her job to fix it. She was annoyed with herself. David was *her* problem and she'd deal with him once and for all.

She'd looked at Steph, strong, reliable Steph and wished she'd noticed how it was all building up. One thing was certain, she wasn't going to let someone else suffer...

She set Merlin off at a canter over the muddy track, ducking her head to avoid overhanging branches and by the time she reached the far gate, three fields on, she was out of breath. The horse didn't understand the meaning of 'Steady'. On the way home, she thought again about how she'd handle it. She could only stay cool and calm for so long. She might manage the haughty self-control with her mother but this might not be so easy.

Riding through the yard entrance, she could see David's car parked in its usual place. He'd be in one of the stables, probably

---

feeding Jodie's pony. At least the little girl wasn't there this weekend to witness a row which Carrie was pretty sure would be the end result. David wouldn't take criticism with a good grace. Or back down.

By the time she'd taken Merlin's tack off and put a sweat rug on him, Steph was standing at the stable door, waiting just as Carrie had asked her to. 'We'll approach him together,' she'd told Steph earlier. 'Make our point clear and then listen to what he has to say. Not sure how he'll react however we do it.'

They looked at each other now, a tacit understanding passing between them and moved together into the open.

David was coming out of the far stable block, dusting straw off his jodhpurs. When he saw them, he stopped, waiting for them to approach.

'Could we have a word in the barn, David? There's something we need to sort out.'

He gave his most charming smile and bowed his head slightly but he kept his eyes on Carrie's face. There was something formidable about him that was hard to explain, but it had to do with his bearing, his look of authority, his self-assurance.

God, this wasn't going to be fun! But he has to be told.

He followed them to the small office area walking deliberately slowly, eyebrows raised.

'Is there a problem?'

Hostility conveyed in just four words, she thought. *Oh, to hell with him. He's not going to bully me.*

'Yes, David. I'm afraid there is.' She watched his face which gave away nothing. 'Go back a few months. You came to us, you said, because we had a good reputation, impressed by how much preparation and hard work we put into looking after the horses. Now though… you seem dissatisfied. You want to override everything we've put in place. For a start, if you had complaints you should have come to me.' She paused. 'What you don't seem to realise is that Steph and I are a team, have been for many years. We've worked out how to run things together, know about feeding, buying, which horses make good field companions…'

'Ah, but you don't *own* my horses.'

'No, we don't. Some people like to do most of the looking after themselves and that's fine. We come to some mutual agreement, we can accommodate that. What causes problems is when owners want to dictate, challenge everything we do and as a consequence, make us unhappy by unreasonable demands and a badgering attitude.'

David didn't speak straight away. He crossed his arms and sighed. 'And you're saying my attitude is the problem.' His gaze travelled from one to the other. 'I'm not sure I understand. I've made some *suggestions* to Steph. Surely that isn't a punishable offence, is it?'

Carrie could feel her jaw tightening. 'David, you've picked on her constantly and made her miserable. You've overstepped the mark here. I've never seen her so upset and I'm not having it.'

She heard someone come into the barn but no-one turned, just remained in their fixed position, three unmoving figures obviously in a serious conversation. Not to be disturbed. Whoever it was hurried out again, letting in a gust of cold air before the door closed.

David shook his head wearily, as though it was all nonsense and he couldn't understand what the fuss was about. 'Look, this is not how I see it at all. Carrie, can I talk to you alone?'

'No.'

'OK. I'll give it to you straight. You think Steph is a good worker. She probably is… with cows and sheep at her farm.' Carrie's eyes widened in disbelief. 'But I know about horses. Believe me, I do. And if Steph is so sensitive, so averse to criticism, she shouldn't be working in a competitive business like horse management.'

'That's insulting and you know it. You're being deliberately provocative. But I think there's another agenda here. Tell me if I'm wrong, but you implied that when *you* were running this place, she'd be out on her ear. Now what gave you the impression you'd ever be in that position?'

'You. You did.' He was frowning as though she was an idiot. 'At Brampton. When we were talking with Freddie Baxter. You certainly considered expanding the place and bringing me in on it.'

'Oh, David, that was all your idea. I never agreed to any such thing. And even if I had been considering it, I wouldn't dream of it now. Certainly not with you. Your idea of how the world works isn't for me. It's bullish and unkind and... you'd ruin the set-up we have here.'

'Oh, would I?' he said, eyes cold and narrowed, his smile predatory. 'So that's how it is, is it? Do you realise I could wreck your set up in a day with a few well-chosen words among some of my friends. Be careful...'

Carrie's fury matched his then. 'No, *you* be careful,' she said, ice in her voice. 'I don't think you belong here anymore, David. You just don't fit. So *I* have a suggestion – it just might suit you. By the end of the month, I want you out of here. Find somewhere else for your horses and if you can go sooner, that would make me even happier.'

He stepped towards her then, tall and threatening, looking down on her. 'I don't think so. I'm not going to be kicked out, I can assure you of that...'

A voice behind them, decisive and measured, cut him off.

'You heard what my mother said. You're to be out of here by the end of the month. Otherwise, we'll take legal action. And the right's on our side.'

They turned and there was Jack, fists clenched, eyes steely and determined and with only one focus. David. 'How you've behaved to Steph is... unforgiveable.'

In the silence that followed, it was as though they were waiting for the hammer blow to fall, waiting for the inevitable clash of wills that might erupt into something nastier at any moment.

But nothing happened.

David took them all in with a malevolent stare. Then, making a disgruntled sound in his throat, he brushed past Carrie and Steph, strode past Jack and wrenching open the door of the barn as though to pull it off its hinges, left. The sound of his car engine starting up and then revving as he sped away had them looking at each other, not quite believing he'd gone. After all his bravado, he'd just gone.

Steph broke the silence. 'Well, that told him, Jack.' She even managed a smile. 'You frightened him away. Good lad!'

It was then that the tension in the air dissolved into nervous laughter. Carrie was the most surprised. *Not how I thought it would turn out. Not at all.*

But she couldn't help feeling uneasy. He wasn't the sort to give in without a fight. 'He's not going to take this lying down,' she said. 'We'll have to handle it very carefully.' She looked at Jack who was nodding. 'You were great, you really were. You came in just at the right moment. Brilliant. How much did you hear?'

'Most of it,' he said, flushing at the praise. 'Just glad he left when he did. Don't think I'd be any match for him in a fight. He'd slaughter me.'

'Well, we don't know whether he'll pack up and go yet. Hope there isn't a stand-off.'

Steph pulled her coat round her tightly as though warming herself up. 'I think you'll be all right,' she said. 'He's the sort who won't want it to look as though you've asked him to leave. He'll go as though it's his idea and slag you off afterwards. That's my bet.'

'Perhaps.' It was no good worrying what *might* be, Carrie thought. They'd won the first round at least. 'Let's go into the house and get something to warm us up. We deserve a ten-minute break. Come on.'

They walked up the path through the garden and as Jack opened the door to let Steph through first, she turned to them both. 'Thank you for standing up for me.' She was on the verge of tears. 'I was so worried. I hadn't said much to Will to start with but then he kept on at me to tell you sooner, Carrie, but I thought… I thought things would settle down, not get worse. David was so difficult to handle.'

'I never liked him,' Jack said. 'Too full of his own importance.'

Carrie said nothing. She'd seen two sides to him and been fooled; no good saying now how charming he could be when it suited him. He was clever, playing people to get the upper hand and it was a devious trait she should have recognised. So much for being a sound judge of character!

*

She was quiet that evening. Thoughts going round in her head, not just about the row with David, but wondering whether she'd dealt with anything right lately. She looked across the room at Alex who was watching a TV documentary on the Kennedys, totally absorbed and unaware of her eyes on him. He seemed so well now, eating properly, balance steady. Mended, she supposed, certainly on the outside… But… there was still this gap between them. Something sensed rather than identified. And she'd begun to question whether she'd given him the sort of support he'd really needed. Not just the practical stuff – she was good at that. Competent. Efficient. But not much on the emotional side. For too long she'd valued self-sufficiency, keeping your feelings private, *'soldiering on'*, and perhaps those qualities she'd considered so important weren't enough. Everyone wasn't the same. That shouldn't be a surprise. Just as some valued human life over any other sort, she could weep for an animal that had been injured or harmed but not for people. She'd always felt most could look after themselves. Not children, of course, they were vulnerable, but adults… it was the essence of what her father had tried to teach her, having *'backbone'*, he called it.

But there was something missing in all that. There'd been something missing in her childhood, she supposed – a warmth, a soft voice, comforting arms. No, there'd been none of that. She'd managed very well without it. But Alex wasn't her.

So had she been blind to the differences and allowed a chasm to open up and get wider until it became just a part of their lives? How often had she heard couples say, '*We're like chalk and cheese. Not important, that's the way we are,*' and laugh. Well, perhaps they were kidding themselves. Perhaps in some cases, one of them wasn't happy with this at all.

Was that Alex? Was he so separate from her now that she couldn't reach him anymore? She began to accept she hadn't tried hard enough, she'd just let any closeness they'd once had slip away. And now it might be too late.

When you start analysing and looking at your own behaviour, she thought, you see all sorts of things you don't want to see.

That lunch with her mother. Had she done the right thing there? Begrudgingly perhaps, given what was asked for, the money, but no warmth in the gesture, certainly no forgiveness. She didn't have to *like* the woman to show some kindness.

And finally there was Jack. Exasperating, irresponsible Jack, whose whole character was her polar opposite, who irritated her with his lackadaisical attitude, his absence of ambition, his *weakness*, she'd always thought. Especially after that awful business when he was fifteen, so frightening to see him go under. Threatened by other kids. So vulnerable he was always going to get hurt and couldn't seem to toughen up to save himself. She'd felt the need then to do the toughening up herself, make him strong enough to survive in a world where you had to stand on your own feet. Well, she'd not succeeded there. She'd just turned him away.

Yet today, there he was, quite able to fight back when something really mattered to him. He'd certainly shown her what he was capable of, standing by her, speaking out with a resolve and a strength she'd not expected. It took courage for someone like him to confront a man twice his age. Courage and determination. And she hadn't appreciated him. Just as, in exactly the same way, her own mother hadn't appreciated *her*, not seen the good, always the flaws. It was like a hereditary curse.

Well, she could change all that. Make amends.

It wasn't too late. Jack had all the kindness *she* should have shown over the years; he'd needed understanding instead of the constant pushing to be something he could never be.

From now on, she would accept him for what he was, a gentle soul who didn't have a nasty bone in his body. And the way she was feeling tonight, that was more than she could say about herself.

Chapter 35

The pub was busy and now it was only Jack and Leo doing the serving; Ernst had moved on after the summer to pastures new. So they were under pressure. No good hurrying the chef though, the food would be ready when it was ready. That was Leo's philosophy anyway. The punters would just have to wait. But the atmosphere was genial enough, the comments mostly good-natured, mostly edged with sarcasm, like, '*Had to go to the North Sea to catch the cod, did you?*' and, '*We'll settle for a bag of crisps!*' But it was warm in the pub and freezing outside so they were content to sit patiently and take their turn. Benny, as usual, wasn't much help, spending too much time chatting to the regulars at the bar to bother about the food orders.

The day was icy enough to turn faces red and fingers stiff under your gloves, but Jack liked the crisp cleanness of it all. The sun was bright even when it shone low in the sky, just above the horizon by mid-afternoon. And he loved this month because it meant there was Christmas at the end of it to look forward to. He'd never quite grown up, he decided as he'd walked down the road earlier to start his shift, pleased that so many houses had been decorated already, brightening up the village. Lights flickered in the trees and shone in windows and when he reached the pub, coloured ones framed the door and lined the pub sign. Best of all though was the large Christmas tree that stood in the centre of the green, its branches holding hundreds of tiny bulbs, sharp pin-pricks against the evening sky.

He hummed to himself as he moved around the bar and snug, placing small candles in the centre of each table while Leo used bellows to keep the fire going in the grate.

'You going to dress up as Santa then, Leo?' said old Jerry, nursing his pint which he'd do all night until Benny suggested perhaps he should buy another.

'Oh yes. And I'm thinking Jack could be an elf!'

'We just need the reindeer now,' said the old man, chortling away. 'And free drinks!'

Jack smiled to himself. It wasn't just the time of year that was putting him in good spirits – well, perhaps more on tenterhooks if he was being honest. Anticipating something positive and fearing the opposite. But he tried to curb any feeling of optimism.

By the end of the evening, he'd know.

The text message had been quite a surprise. Chatty, not really telling him anything new, just a sort of reaching out. Lots of exclamation marks as though she was trying to make it all light-hearted and casual. How was he, did he have any spare time, end of term soon and the last few weeks meant less marking and more nativity play rehearsals... perhaps they could meet up. She didn't actually write *for old times' sake* but that's how it came across. Well, their *old times* weren't so old and they'd parted in a way which had left a bitter taste in his mouth so he wasn't sure how this would go. Meeting Grace by chance with Sylvie in a café was one thing. Meeting her alone was another. He wasn't sure how he'd answer.

Then after two days, he'd sent a text back. Yes, they could meet up but he was working flat out in the day and the shifts at the pub were busy so he didn't have much time to spare. Which was true and anyway he didn't want to appear too interested. He was learning.

Then she'd phoned him. He was just about to get in his car after leaving Parsons.

'Hi, how's things?' She sounded upbeat. Or nervous, Jack couldn't tell.

'Fine... just heading home.'

'From your text, I gather you don't have much time for socialising.'

'Well, not a great deal. No.'

He thought the line had gone dead, but then, 'Jack, what d'you say to a drink one evening? If you don't want to, that's fine but…'

'No, it isn't that. It's just… how about you come down to the pub when I'm doing my shift? Later, say nine o'clock and all the meals have finished. Then I can get you a toasted sandwich or something and finish early… You know where it is?'

'Of course. The Fox and Hounds.' Again, a long pause but he knew she was still on the line. 'Thanks. I feel I've a lot of apologising to do…' And then she rang off.

Well, tonight was the night. And he wasn't sure what to expect. Perhaps just a 'Sorry' and that'd be fine because he didn't want to be emotionally messed up again. He'd had to tell Leo, who'd be working twice as hard to cover his back, so he was getting knowing looks which he was determined to ignore. And of course, Leo couldn't resist the odd comment.

'So, Romeo, who's this new one?' he said out of the corner of his mouth as he passed Jack, carrying a dish of scampi. 'You're a fast worker.'

'An old friend, that's all. From school.'

And as they waited in the kitchen to pick up the meals, 'What happened to the girl in the white dress? I thought you weren't going to be "faint-hearted".'

'I wasn't. I did as you said and met with a polite put-down. Anyway, this time Grace, that's who it is, approached *me*. So I thought the best idea would be for her to come here, keep it casual. Which it won't be if you start making dodgy remarks and embarrassing me.'

'Who, me?' Leo grinned, looking more like a wicked old gnome than usual. 'I'd never do that to a friend. But I'll be watching your technique and giving you some tips later.'

'Leo…' Jack said in a tone he hoped would warn him off.

'Ah, don't you worry. I'll say nothing and keep my fingers crossed. You deserve some luck.' And he grabbed two meals off the hotplate and whisked through the doors into the bar.

Nine o'clock.

He wasn't going to be watching the door, not so anyone would notice. But of course, he knew immediately when she came in. She paused for a moment, pushing back the hood of her raincoat, and looked round for a spare seat. He wished he'd put a *Reserved* notice on the small table in the corner. Too late now. He moved over to where she was standing and suggested she sit at the bar for a while until the last diners had left.

'I'll get you a drink,' he said, refusing to look at Leo. He suddenly felt awkward, realising this could be a mistake and wishing they'd met somewhere else and at some other time. In the day might have been better. He was wary of her and couldn't pretend otherwise even though she was the one who'd wanted to meet up. She'd have her reasons but he wasn't sure he wanted to hear them. In those last few weeks before she'd gone away to college, she'd said some pretty hurtful things and he'd had enough of brush-offs lately. There had to be some sort of declared truce before he let his guard down.

She perched on the bar stool and placed her wet gloves on the counter, rubbing her hands together to warm them up. Her cheeks were flushed from the cold outside and her damp hair stuck to her face in spikes. Jack placed a small glass of white wine in front of her with a bag of peanuts and went back to serving.

She began to sip her drink and look round the room, cupping her chin in her hand. Even in a strange environment, Grace was always at ease, he thought. Nothing's changed. At seventeen, she'd been the one who'd led the way in every sense – she'd seemed much older than he was, more adventurous, more sure of where she was going, determined to leave home, get to college, to teach. To *experience life*, she'd said which struck him as affected at the time but he understood a bit more now. And he'd been such an introvert, withdrawn, only slowly recovering from that low ebb, that time when he'd been beaten down by fears that she could barely imagine. But somehow, gradually, sharing some classes together she'd been drawn to him, really liked his company, encouraged him and without really trying, restored his self-esteem. *I must have been hard work,* he thought now. *A wonder, really, that we lasted as long as we did.*

It was nearly half an hour before he could join her at the bar, sitting beside her with a half pint of Black Sheep and leaving Leo to do all the work. Benny had done his usual 'early night' departure with a *'You can lock up, lads!'* as though he was bestowing a favour. But this made it easier for Jack to concentrate on the conversation he guessed was going to be dicey.

'You've eaten all the peanuts,' he said.

'So I have.' She turned on her stool so that she was facing him. 'You look pretty good, Jack. I've heard how you were doing from time to time. Terry fills me in on all the home news.'

'Yes, he comes back quite often. Everyone must be missing the old place.'

'It's strange, isn't it! Desperate to get away, then we keep coming back.' She seemed to be studying his expression and he was determined to keep it neutral. He wasn't about to jump in and go down the wrong track. Or any track at the moment.

Start with something safe. 'Job going well?'

Her face lit up. 'Really well. The kids are lovely, mostly – now they've got used to me. I don't mind the naughty ones 'cos they soon get the message. What I don't like are the ones who lie and think they can get away with it. I don't go easy on them.'

'I bet you don't,' he said, grinning. 'I remember you at school when Janice Stevenson copied your Biology notes. God, you had her terrified.'

'She deserved it. She's working in a bank now. Hope she's learned her lesson.'

They looked at each other, suddenly aware of the drinkers in the room, aware that what they had to say might be overheard. Jack moved away slightly as though sending a signal to her that she shouldn't start delving any further into the past. Not *their* past, anyway. This was his place, his refuge, and he didn't want it spoiled.

But Grace had never been one to equivocate. 'I've missed home, Jack, in a way I never thought I would. What I thought was going to be my grand adventure wasn't quite what I thought it would be. Funny, I was talking to Terry about this and he understood completely. We're a bit disappointed in ourselves. The course was fine although some of it was boring. I made friends, some really good ones, but... well, in my second year, I started going with this engineering student who turned out to be an absolute shit...' There was a hard edge to her voice and he could tell there was pain behind it. 'He didn't just cheat on me, he was into some weird stuff that was a real eye-opener... I won't go into detail but I realised before it ended that I'd landed myself in an unholy mess. Not just in falling for him... but more that, when I looked back...' She fiddled with the stem of her wine glass. 'I started to make comparisons. You were always so kind, really caring... and we *liked* one another, didn't we? I realised then that certain things I'd *thought* were important, in the end weren't. Not when it comes down to it.'

Jack didn't dare speak.

'I hadn't the nerve to find you and tell you. I was such a crass idiot before I went away and you don't have to remind me of some of the things I said.' She closed her eyes briefly as though wanting to forget. 'I was awful. And seeing you in the shopping centre that day, I so wanted to say sorry and I could tell you were ready to run a mile...'

'I was,' he said. 'Especially with Sylvie there. It was awkward.'

'I know.' She was nodding and seemed to be searching for what to say next. 'I'd like us to be friends again, I really would.' Again, she hesitated. 'How do you feel about that?'

'OK... I feel OK,' he said, taking his time to digest all this. *And what does 'friends' mean exactly?* 'Of course, that's fine. I'm happy with that.'

She leaned over and kissed his cheek. 'Thank you. I can enjoy my wine now.' She clinked his glass with hers. 'Here's to Christmas. And to our reunion.'

And when Jack looked round he caught sight of Leo smiling away and doing a little dance as he carried the empty glasses to the sink. It had turned out to be quite a night.

*

Going to work in the dark and driving home on full headlights was depressing for some of them at Parsons, they didn't half go on about it, but Jack didn't mind it at all. It was good to be earning which meant he could afford to buy everyone presents this year. Decent ones. And he liked being busy all day. The journey took about twenty minutes and while he was driving, he listened to the local radio station which was playing Christmas music on a loop, mostly the same old pop songs over and over again – George Michael, Slade, Band Aid. Even '*Jingle Bell Rock*', which he managed to sing along to because he could remember all the words. Not quite his thing though. And even with sleet hitting the windscreen – the icy rain had been falling for days now with no let-up – coming home and seeing the tiny star-shaped lights his mother always attached to the ivy round the porch, cheered him up. It made the house seem warm and alive.

Of course he knew it wasn't just the time of year that was making him feel upbeat. The other evening had something to do with it. It had been unexpected and he was still mulling over everything that'd been said. He wasn't sure what to make of it. Since Grace had left for college – and in such a way that he never even considered she'd ever think of him again – he'd wanted to push her and their whole relationship into some dark recess of his mind. It had ended on such an acrimonious note. She'd become more and more impatient with him, she was ready to leave... and he wasn't ready for anything different. She'd been contemptuous about his lack of adventure, that he had no goals. Even her parents had told her, she informed him, how she was wasting her time with someone who'd hold her back. He certainly didn't want to be reminded of all that.

But inevitably some things stick and he remembered every word of the most stinging comment of them all: *'You'll be fifty, still living with your mum and dad, having done nothing, been nowhere, your idea of a good night out sitting in old Bernard's seat in The Fox and Hounds, grumbling over your pint.'*

It had been inclined to haunt him.

But now? Was Grace coming back to him because she was on the rebound? Was he just being used as a stop-gap until she met someone else? Someone more dynamic, more *worldly?*

His dad put him on the spot a few nights after the pub get-together. He'd been asking about Steph and the upset caused by David as they cleared away the dinner plates.

'So,' he'd said. 'Is this bloke leaving as he's been told to do? He's surely not going to challenge it.'

'Difficult to know. He's got a few more days yet, then I'm not sure what Mum can do. She's got the right to kick him out, legally, but that could take time. Just hope he leaves without causing any more trouble. Steph's happier now, but she's obviously still on edge. I would be too.'

His dad was quiet. 'Your mother's talking about having cameras put in the yard which is a good idea.' He threw a scrap of meat to Sam, who snatched it as though no-one ever fed him, then stood for a minute, frowning. 'I should have been there. It shouldn't have been you.' He put a hand on Jack's shoulder. 'Sorry about that. I'll deal with it if he doesn't shift. He's not going to take on all three of us... well, four.' He leant against the sink, wiping his hands on a tea towel.

'It's not what you expect, is it? There's never been any trouble like this before. Poor Steph, being ordered about by the bullying prick. No wonder she was upset. Good job you were there when your mum faced him.'

Jack flushed. 'I didn't do anything really. Just backed up Mum and he hadn't much option other than to walk away. He was bloody annoyed but at least he left. For now, anyway. But you never know with people like that.'

'What d'you mean?'

'Well, he doesn't like being told what to do. He doesn't like losing an argument. There's something about him that's... sort of threatening.' Jack had been hoping David would have gone by the weekend but his horse and Jodie's pony were still in their stables. He felt sorry for the kid though; it wasn't her fault they were having to shift again. And he could understand Steph was nervous about the whole thing, in the yard on her own most of the time but there wasn't a lot he could do, working all day and she was only there till lunchtime. At least his mother was on watch and she wouldn't take any hassle without a fight.

And then when he thought they'd ended any further discussion, his dad said, out of the blue, 'And Grace? Have you heard any more from her?'

'I...' Jack didn't know what to say... or how much.

'Sorry, I shouldn't have asked. It's your business...'

Jack shrugged and went to the back of the kitchen to kick off his shoes. Stalling, he supposed, but then he thought he might as well open up. 'As a matter of fact she came to the pub the other night when I was on my shift. It was OK actually. We talked. She wanted us to be "friends".'

His dad looked at him in surprise. 'What does that mean?'

'Exactly. I haven't a clue. I'm being... inscrutable. Is that the right word?'

'Yes. I'd stay that way. Keeps you safe.'

And that was it. He liked the way his father never really gave him advice. Or probed too deeply. He listened and understood. It was Jack's life and his choice. There was this element of trust between them which he recognised now. He supposed he'd always felt it but valued it much more since those awful days when he'd thought he'd lost him. An involuntary shiver went through him at the memory of the fear, the helplessness, time held in abeyance.

He should put this aside, he told himself, and just be grateful.

But all he could think of right now was how horribly empty life would have been if his dad hadn't made it.

Chapter 36

The train rattled across a countryside shrouded in white mist which hovered inches above the fields. It created an eerie landscape, Fran thought as she looked out, the whole world silent and unmoving beyond the window. Solitary trees, spectral and thin, could just be seen through the haze, bare branches forming black lace-like structures, ethereal and strange.

She imagined someone watching from a distance as the train threaded its way through the mist, only visible for a few seconds before it was swallowed up again, speeding onwards along the track, disappearing so quickly only the faint sound of the engines told you it had passed through. She sat back wondering whether she'd done the right thing, agreeing to meet up – it certainly wasn't the wisest decision she'd ever made. But sometimes wisdom only comes as an afterthought.

It had been nine thirty-five when Fran boarded the train at Runcorn East, only twenty-two minutes to Chester. She'd timed it carefully, for some reason wanting to arrive after Alex so that he'd be waiting for her on the station concourse. Funny, seven years ago at the same time of year, just before Christmas, she couldn't have imagined their affair ever having an ending. This time, she had no illusions. There was a certain symmetry about it all. The second time around without a happy ending. Well, she wasn't going to be sad about it or have regrets. It was inevitable.

He was waiting for her by the newspaper stand, winter coat buttoned up, a smile spreading over his face when he saw her coming through the automatic doors with the other passengers, a smile that was warm and familiar and dear. She'd come against her better judgement. She'd come because she so wanted to see him for one last time, wanted this final short day to be a memory she could keep when they'd gone their separate ways. A weakness of resolve, she admitted to herself but after all, she was only human.

When she reached him, he hugged her, holding her tightly to him as though he wanted the moment to last. Finally he said, 'Do you want us to get a taxi to the centre or are we walking?'

'Walking. It's not far. And at least the sun's coming out. All the way here, we were going through such a thick mist, I was glad we'd decided to come by train rather than drive.'

'I thought it was because we wanted to have a drink. No good having a Christmas lunch without a bottle of wine.'

'Agreed.'

They made their way along City Road to Foregate Street, Fran doing most of the talking but eventually falling silent, just happy to be there, her arm linked through his, anticipating the day. It was enough. It was how she'd always felt when she was with him, knowing she'd be happy, that she'd be in good company, that she'd want nothing else. Some people just make you feel better about yourself, a gift that they aren't even aware of but you recognise it instantly. And that was Alex.

'Where are we going?' she asked, stopping in front of a small bookshop window, tucked under the black and white timbered galleries that towered above it. 'I hope you've planned this with your usual care.'

He gave her a look which acknowledged the sarcasm. 'You'd be amazed how much research I've done. I've got the whole day worked out. Coffee first though and then I'll lead you to our first venue.'

She looked at him with a doubtful expression on her face. 'Don't tell me we're exploring the medieval castle and climbing ramparts. I'm not dressed for that.'

'No, but it's sort of an adventure.'

'I just hope you're kidding.' She'd stopped and turned to face him, placing her hand against his cheek, chilled by the cold air. 'I might do a lot for you but I'm not going on any expedition.'

For a minute he just stood still gazing at her, then covered her hand with his. 'It might be corny but you'll love it. Trust me.' The minute became so long, a woman shopper had to sidestep round them, tutting as she did so; they didn't even notice. Drawing closer together, Fran felt the roughness of his coat collar as he drew her to him. 'Anyway, you need to build up an appetite for lunch.'

She could sense this feeling of longing, this emotion which made her catch her breath was pulling her in too deep, making it all too serious again, too difficult to break away from and she didn't want the day to become like some tragic tryst. This hadn't got to be sad! So she drew back a little and said, 'Well, I'm pleased there's one part of the schedule I'm going to enjoy. Eating.'

After wandering past brightly lit windows crammed with tempting displays of chocolates, art works, party dresses and knick-knacks, they settled for a small café with sickly cakes in rows behind the glass counter and coffee that came out of a machine already tepid, customers settling with bags round their feet and talking too loudly.

But none of that mattered.

Later, they headed out into a street already crowded with shoppers.

'Now, are you ready?' Alex said. 'We need to head for the river.'

'The river? It's December. We're not going out on a boat, are we?'

'You'll see,' he said, walking a little ahead of her and shouldering through the people coming towards them – people with concentrated looks on their faces, hurrying as though there would never be enough time to fit everything in before the days leading up to Christmas were used up, whereas Fran had no wish to look ahead, no wish to race towards an ending. Time for her must be slowed, the day put on hold. Alex looked back at her. 'Come on. You don't want to miss anything. There's an added attraction.'

'Santa?'

'Nearly right.'

They were laughing now. It was suddenly just the two of them on some holiday outing and Fran felt young and silly. It was allowed because none of this was going to last. She might as well enjoy it while she could.

They reached the riverside walk with Alex seeming to know where he was going. He caught hold of her hand and began to quicken his pace. 'Nearly eleven thirty. Come on. We'll make it.'

'We're going on a boat trip? It's freezing! Are you mad?'

'It's a special boat trip. Spiced punch and mince pies. Lots of Christmas music!' Alex pulled the tickets out of his pocket. 'It's all booked, but we have to get a move on or they'll be sailing without us.' He looked like an excited teenager, she thought, and it might be corny but she loved the idea. She loved the fact that he'd gone to the trouble of planning the day, wanting to see her happy, wanting it to be something they'd remember with a smile, with affection.

They were out of breath when they reached the boat which to Fran looked like an old-fashioned steamer, painted white and decorated with coloured lights and wreaths of holly wound round the uprights. It swayed up and down as they climbed the gangplank, lurching unsteadily as they crossed the deck and found a space to sit on a bench, hemmed in by the boat's side and another couple. The 'captain' came round with the punch on a tray and some mince pies, the boat's propellers churned in the water and they were off.

They sat side by side, crammed together by strangers, sipping their warm drinks from plastic cups and listening to Christmas songs, Alex amused as some of the passengers sang along. At times as the boat chugged its way up the river, Fran caught his eye and smiled, his answering smile so full of love and meaning it made her throat tighten. *Don't you dare cry,* she told herself. *Don't you dare.* And as he watched the young couple in front of them pointing out landmarks on the bank, she found herself studying his profile just as she'd done in Jersey, remembering lying beside him in the night, light filtering through the curtains from some beacon on the shoreline. Nothing to disturb the peace of their just being together, the whole night ahead of them, the only sounds their breathing and occasional footsteps in the corridor beyond their room. He'd looked contented, lying on his back, his arm thrown out and she'd propped herself up on one elbow and gazed at him sleeping, taking in every detail – the straight nose, the dark lashes, the curve of his mouth, the face that could change expression in a second, so alive when he spoke, so intent when he listened, the way his smile made his eyes light up... how funny he could be.

Nothing's changed, she thought, as she looked at him now on a crowded boat in the middle of winter. *Nothing's changed. How I wish I'd met him years ago when we could have had a life together. How I wish he was mine.*

A few snowflakes were falling as they were herded back onto the quayside, holding each other up and happy to be one of the crowd. The atmosphere buoyed them along as the sky grew darker. They passed families pulling up hoods and cramming woolly hats on their heads; two small girls were pushing each other, laughing, parents calling them away from the water's edge with alarmed instructions; a seller of chestnuts was standing by a brazier, shouting something Fran couldn't even begin to understand.

It felt like Christmas.

*

Alex led the way and wouldn't give her any hints about what was next. But by one o'clock, they were sitting at their table, ordering lunch and lifting wine glasses in a silent toast that made them both smile.

'Not sure what you say in these circumstances,' he said, raising his eyebrows as though asking a question that had no answer. 'To us.' He hesitated. 'Even if we're not going anywhere.'

She held out her glass. 'To us. For what we've had. How's that?'

'Better.'

The restaurant around them started to fill up, groups hurrying in out of the cold, closing the doors quickly behind them to keep in the warmth, casting off coats and looking round expectantly for the girl at the desk who was checking the bookings. Fran liked the atmosphere. The ceilings were low and the lights covered in decorative red gauze which made the room seem to enclose them into a world that wasn't quite real.

Alex was watching her face waiting for her full attention. They'd ordered, but could see that nothing would be hurried. Too many customers all arriving at once. She was glad of that. It wasn't a day to be hurried.

'We haven't bought each other presents,' he said. 'We were going to.'

'No. Let's not.' She took the serviette off the table and smoothed it over her lap. 'That would be too ordinary somehow.' She laughed despite being serious. 'We're past that, aren't we?'

'Perhaps we are.' He shifted in his seat as someone pushed through the space between the tables. 'Are we allowed questions? Or is it too late to expect answers.'

Fran tensed. It was as though she'd always known he'd ask. And this, finally, would throw it all into some sour mix of wrong emotions and hurt pride and ruin everything she'd tried to hold together. Even to the last. She was certain that Jack, so close to his father, must have confided in him, told him about the whole misguided infatuation, how he'd believed he was in love, oblivious, of course, of their relationship. And Alex would see it as a betrayal on her part, or at the very least a distasteful mess. Would he have waited all day to bring this up? Surely not. She was being paranoid. But if this was the burning question, she wouldn't be able to find the words to make it all sound as innocent and as coincidental as it had been.

She kept her gaze steady and hoped the expression on her face was open, nothing to hide. 'Questions are allowed. Although I can't promise you'll be satisfied with my take on things. What do you want to know?'

'Well...' He put down his glass, hesitating slightly. 'There's something I've wanted to ask you and I've no right to. But I'm curious.'

'Go on.' Her heart was beating uncomfortably fast.

'Haven't you ever met someone you wanted to live with... or marry, at least fallen in love with, since us? Don't tell me you haven't been asked.'

She nodded and looked thoughtful, letting out a long breath and touching the chain at her neck. OK, she could manage that, although she couldn't make up her mind how much of the story she wanted to tell when it had long since ceased to matter. But it was a reasonable question. Perhaps he needed to know even though she'd asked nothing about his years between. She took a sip of water. 'I was engaged once, very nearly married him. Kieron. It would have been a huge mistake.' She shrugged her shoulders and stopped.

'I thought *I* was the mistake.'

'You? No. You were never that.' She put down her glass and reached out to clasp his fingers, entwining them in hers.

'Why didn't it work out?'

'I should have known from the start. Paul really didn't take to him, even though he didn't see much of him because he was working away a lot of the time. He said he'd never grown up.'

'That doesn't sound too hopeful.'

'I should have listened. I suppose he was nice-looking in a conventional sort of way, entertaining, good company. Didn't take himself too seriously and he had a lively group of friends. He was my age but seemed much younger in many ways. Self-centred, I suppose, but you get carried along by the whole thing and try and convince yourself it'll work.' She closed her eyes briefly. 'I was lonely after you, Alex. I wanted someone to go places with, to share my weekends, and, well… in the future, to have children with, I suppose.

'And…?'

'I'd met him in at a dinner party and we got on. Superficially anyway. But – of course there's a "but" – he wanted everything his way. He didn't like being crossed and could sulk when things didn't suit him. My dad was pleased when we got engaged, Paul kept silent, my friends thought I'd found "the one", romantic idiots, and I put my doubts behind me, fooled myself really.'

'Something happened then… to end it all.'

'Yes. I got pleurisy and was in a lot of pain this Saturday. We were meant to be going to a party and I couldn't face moving, never mind socialising. He was annoyed. I'll never forget the look on his face as he left me sitting in the house, hardly able to breathe. Do you know what his parting words were? "*You're no fun anymore.*" And I sat there when he'd gone, calling him every name under the sun and remembering how you'd been when I'd had flu.'

Alex frowned trying to think back seven years but shook his head.

'You came one evening when I was feeling awful. You got me to bed with a hot water bottle, made me tea and toast and sat with me, not saying much, just being there. Then tidied up the kitchen and wouldn't leave until you were sure I was going to sleep. You were so… loving…' Her eyes filled with tears… 'Those kind of moments you don't forget.'

'Oh, Fran…'

'He wasn't you, Alex. He wasn't you… and I couldn't go on with it.' She shook her head. 'Then, he wouldn't take no for an answer. Badgering me at work. Kept trying to persuade me I was being silly, that I was blowing it all up out of all proportion. Thought if he apologised for being a selfish git that night, it'd be OK again, but… I knew that underneath, the only person he cared about was himself. I was glad when it was over. No more pretence.'

Alex said nothing, just allowing his silence to show he understood, to show he felt for her. Disappointment and sadness shared.

The waiter came over, changing the mood by placing dishes of Thai prawns carefully in front of them with a cheery, 'Enjoy.' Laughter erupted from a corner table and they watched a group of twenty-somethings opening presents and putting coloured triangular hats on their heads.

'My turn,' she said. She broke off a small piece of brown roll and thought for a moment. 'I suppose I want to know how you'll be, where you'll go from here, what it'll be like for you. But then perhaps that's too hard to imagine.'

'Fran, no-one could give you an answer to that. We don't know what we're going to face. You just have to keep going, a bit like navigating a river that's carrying you along at the rate of knots and hoping for the best. You don't have as much control as you think.' He put down his fork and stared into the distance. 'I'm sure of one thing – there'll be a longing that might not go away. On the surface, I'll cope OK, looking after the family, doing my job as well as I can, seeing friends. But I can't say what I'll *feel* like in five years' time. I might not even *be* here, knowing my tendency to drive like an idiot.' He tried for a smile but there was a soulful look on his face. 'I believe memories of all the really important moments in your life stay with you. When you're quiet or feeling low and they comfort you, warm your heart. Make you thankful, somehow, that you had something wonderful for a time.' She could see he was suddenly overcome with an emotion that stopped him talking until he could regain his composure. 'I'll remember you for the rest of my life. That's the only thing I'm certain of... will that do?'

'Yes. That'll do.'

*

It was dark on the quayside when they left the restaurant, the boats, mid-river, brightly lit and full of another charter of revellers with their Christmas spirit, music and boisterous shouts reaching the land. Further up approaching the bridge, it grew quieter, more dimly lit, and Fran felt their mood becoming sombre. She could hear the river lapping gently against the wharf as they walked slowly along, hugging each other partly to keep out the cold. As they reached one of the main streets, the haunting tune of *Have Yourself a Merry Little Christmas* was being played on a saxophone by a street musician who stood beside a sound box on some stone steps, surrounded by a small group of people.

'A sax always sounds so sad when there's no accompaniment,' she said. 'It needs to cheer up.'

Alex tightened his arm round her shoulders and bent his head towards hers. He couldn't find any words of comfort, she knew. An hour left and then everything worth having would be in the past. That's how she saw it. That's how she'd seen it all those years before, yet she'd survived. No good being dramatic about it. Staying together would have meant disaster on so many levels, at least this way the hurt was theirs alone.

As they stood on the station platform waiting for her train, an amused look crossed his face..

'What?'

'I was thinking about that film, black and white, old as the hills, but it's on every Christmas, a couple meeting on a platform like this, a station café really, and they have to say goodbye. Trevor Howard, but I can't think of the woman.'

'Must be before my time.'

'Christ, it's before *my* time. But it's emotional, it really gets to you. You want to say to the woman, don't go back to that boring husband and spend the rest of your time having regrets.'

'And I suppose that's what she does.'

'Yes, it's the forties, I think, when Duty had a capital D.'

'Things don't change that much, do they?'

'No, perhaps not. Perhaps doing the right thing is how you live with yourself.'

'You think too much,' she said. She could hear the train approaching along the line, the other travellers moving forward to the edge of the platform. 'Make sure you take care of yourself, Alex. Promise me.' How trite that sounded.

'I will... physically, anyway. Can't vouch for my mental state.'

There was a moment of hesitation, poignant, so much unfinished. She wanted the last few seconds to mean something more, something for both of them to hold on to. So trying to keep her voice steady, she said, 'Whatever happens, whatever's coming, I'll always be glad we met...' Then she turned quickly away. 'Don't wait. I won't be looking out.'

And the day was over.

The train trundled out of the station and she sat, facing forward, in an odd mood of acceptance of the inevitable. When she thought about it all, with hindsight, the irony of the situation was obvious. It could never have been.

Fate had taken a hand from the beginning.

It was Jack of course, who, unaware and unintentionally was the reason. The first time when Alex broke it off to care for his son, she understood now, he had no choice. The boy needed all his help and support and Alex chose him before her. And the second time around? Well, circumstances they couldn't have predicted meant *she* had to protect them both by pulling away. She didn't have a choice either. Even if she and Alex had made the commitment, even if he'd made the break, left Carrie, left his family, he'd have been faced with Jack's horror at finding out that the woman he'd fallen for, the woman he'd thought was available, had been his father's mistress. What other word was there for it? He would never have been able to forgive his father, wouldn't have been able to look him in the eye. And Alex would have been devastated. No way could he have lived with that. It was one thing leaving your family behind. It was quite another if the break was so disastrous it meant the son you loved so dearly never spoke to you again.

Twenty-two minutes later, she left the train and walked quickly to the taxi rank. When she got home, she'd have a gin and tonic and remove Alex's mobile number from her phone. Then she'd do some work for the next day. She'd make the effort anyway.

Chapter 37

It's December 23rd. The Christmas preparations are underway – Carrie in charge – the ones that have been established year after year since the children were little. These have always seemed as important as the day itself and can't be changed, even down to the same shabby fairy that has to sit on top of the Christmas tree, the weird cane rabbit that stands in the porch and the ancient pot ornament of a child on an old-fashioned sled that's always placed on the hall table. *'This is going to be a real celebration,'* Carrie tells me (even though Lucy's not here and the news of her timing to go on a skiing holiday hasn't gone down too well). But anyway, this year it's all going to be quite something, with Carrie at the height of organisational fervour. It's even started to snow which makes Sam scuffle round the garden in a rare display of excitement until he flops down exhausted and has to be dragged into the kitchen to dry off.

'He forgets how old he is.' I make excuses for him as I rub him with towels and hope he stops panting.

There's a normality in all this that pulls me along and I'm grateful for it. At least a part of me is. The rituals hold the house together and move us through the days, like an evolutionary clock ticking away the minutes and hours towards the end of the year, with a strange mix of dogged optimism and lack of vision. I'm sitting back and being carried along as perhaps I've always been. Allowing Carrie to call the tune. And anyway, the others will appreciate all the festivities and I'm glad – Jack and my parents and Joe's lot deserve a break. They've all had enough of the whole scary business that I brought down on their heads. And Carrie is making it all happen with the right motives, cheerful, positive, hopeful.

355

God, I wish I could feel the same way. How I wish that.

I'd been slow with my planning when I could see everyone else had already got in the spirit – the shops ready in October as they always are, and the advertising companies and TV pundits looking ahead in August! Jack's been talking about Christmas menus at The Fox and Hounds for weeks, even bought me home a sample one evening, and the build-up at the farm shop has meant some long hours for him. Of course, I hadn't ventured into town this autumn which was one benefit of not driving. It was only earlier in the month that I'd started buying presents over the internet, a lazy way of doing it I know, and then I get stuck... What on earth do my parents really want after all these years? We've exhausted all the ideas and it's become a real guessing game. Jack's always easy, always broke so needs boots or tyres for his car or clothes and I'll give Lucy something towards her skiing holiday. Joe's kids put in requests, a Wish List which I think is a really good thing, so they're soon sorted.

And Carrie? Haven't a clue. One evening, eight o'clock, I sit at my desk in our office and wait for inspiration. Shutters down, glass of red wine next to the mouse pad and I've had enough, bored with scrolling through websites and not getting far. Years ago, when your money's gone on the mortgage or the kids' shoes and there's not much left, there's always something you really want, but now... you buy what you need as you go along. Kids love it because they get indulged. We're past that – we just indulge ourselves in too much food and too much booze.

Am I beginning to sound like Scrooge, needing a Ghost of Christmas Past? *Change your ways before it's too late...* OK. I promise. I am doing.

Eventually, I end up buying Carrie a waterproof riding coat with every possible buckle and flap that makes it worth a hundred and eighty pounds and sit back in my chair as though I've succeeded in solving some difficult engineering problem. My conscience, what's left of it, is mollified.

I start looking round at my desk, which is always a bit of a mess, most of the papers and invoices needing to be thrown out, so I start to sort through and chuck stuff in the waste bin at my feet. It's not that I hoard, I just don't tidy up like Carrie. Her side of the room is uncluttered, a sense of order to the shelves at the side of the computer desk. She doesn't allow herself to be distracted. It sums us up, I think now. We're so bloody different and I don't know whether I believe that the myth of '*Opposites attract*!' creates a healthy balance and it all works out in the end. Sometimes, it's as though you're up against a shredder that's tearing strips off you and you want to wrench yourself away. You don't want to make compromises all the time. You want to be free.

Then I begin to think of the children we've brought up, who I'm more conscious than ever we're responsible for, particularly Jack who's struggling still to find his way… this boy I love so, who can't quite find his feet but is getting there, this odd mix of doubt and hope and kindness… of vulnerability. Sometimes you can see the pain written on his face. When he and Lucy were young I always thought, well, once kids are eighteen they're on their own, they won't need you anymore. But I didn't know anything about being a parent. You realise it's long-term. The whole weight and joy of it.

Christ, I'm sure all that sitting around recovering my senses has left me with profound thoughts from some ethereal plane. And they aren't particularly comforting. I shake myself, literally, and leave my untidy desk just as it is. *Sod it! Let things be! There's always time to tidy up. Take your drink and go and watch 'Spiral' – that should numb your mind.*

But it isn't always so easy getting back to 'normal'.

You'd think I was almost there. I've had the week off – we always close down for the days leading up to Christmas, usually because conditions are poor – and although I've purposely missed all the drinks parties, I've tried to be sociable when I've been on site. Off any medication weeks ago and it's six months before my next hospital check-up. I'm mending physically pretty well... but 'normal' it isn't.

It's as though I'm waiting for my mind to catch up with my body. To synchronise. There's a light-headedness that comes at odd times and I drift. And my dreams can still throw me, the ones that lock me down, where I have to force myself to wake up. Strange that you can be asleep and still aware of the struggle! And I have moments of despair.

Perhaps it's just something I have to come to terms with. Something I just have to live with.

*

Two days to go now, lunchtime. I stand for a minute at the bedroom window and look across to the stables which you can just about see with the leaves on the trees not blocking the view. Although the snow is turning to sleet, everywhere remains clean and fresh, the roofs of the farm buildings still thickly covered and all is muffled and quiet. There's no noise of traffic coming up from the village, and the fields are empty of horses. They must have been brought in early.

I'd come up to the bedroom to put on an extra layer of clothing and then stopped, trying to see if the problem with David had been resolved, whether his horse box was still in the yard or whether he'd done as he'd been told. Taken his horses and disappeared. But so far, no. It's still there. Steph is acting like the Praetorian Guard ready for battle; she says he's been but ignored her and left pretty quickly. I need to join them in a show of strength if it all gets difficult, and if Carrie agrees, but I think we're all getting uptight a bit soon. Surely he hasn't much choice. Carrie sees the biggest difficulty in where we go from here if he just stays put. I know she doesn't want solicitors' letters and court orders and hope for her sake it doesn't come to that. But he seems a stubborn bastard and if he's waiting for the bad weather to let up, he's cutting it fine to leave before the end of the month.

Suddenly a shout comes from downstairs. 'Phone, Alex! Hurry up, it's Adrian.'

I get moving, knowing this phone call could go either way. I'd learned that the company doctor had been conferring with the directors on my fitness and they've probably made their decision now whether I could manage a larger load – in other words, the road job, and I was still ambitious enough to want the challenge. So my hand is sweating a bit as I lift the receiver off the table.

I make my voice sound as neutral as I can when I answer.

'Sorry, Adrian. I'd put my mobile down somewhere. What can I do for you?'

'Christmas cheer, my friend.' He sounds as though he's been drinking, which he probably has. 'They've given you the green light and I've fought for you to take on the road construction job. So there it is and I'm delighted about that. Get ready for some bloody hard work from January 4th.'

I can't help smiling. 'That's really good news. Thanks for letting me know. See you in a couple of weeks.'

'Come straight to the Planning Office on that Monday. We've a lot to do. All the best to Carrie. Happy Christmas!'

And as he rings off, I'm aware of Carrie leaning against the kitchen door, listening and waiting.

'They've given me the major road works, so they must trust that I can handle it.'

She comes over and kisses me on the cheek. 'Of course you can. Well done. Let's celebrate by cutting into the Christmas cake. Should be saving it but what the hell...'

And there's an air of light-heartedness that's good to feel instead of the tension and unspoken worries that seem to have filled every corner of this house for so many months.

Carrie leads the way and reaches under the kitchen units, pulling out a bottle of Chablis from the rack. 'No time to chill it but it'll go nicely with the cake.' And she cuts two huge wedges of rich fruit cake and pours the wine into two glasses, holding hers up to take a swig before she sits opposite me at the table.

'It's good to see you smile, Alex. I've missed that.'

'I'll try and do it more often.' I suddenly feel the danger of an in-depth talk coming up and I don't want the atmosphere to be spoiled. *Keep it light, Carrie, before we slip back into our old defensive positions.*

Then in a flash of reproach, I hate myself. Who's to blame here, for God's sake? Me! And it's up to me to put things right, to make a bloody effort, to make up for... what? ...not feeling the right emotions? ...Is that it? Or for not understanding where my priorities lie? Funny how you always hear that parental voice when you know you're in the wrong – *Come on, Alex... make an effort... stop feeling sorry for yourself... there's always someone worse off...* It's the mental equivalent of the lash.

Carrie looks thoughtful as she finishes eating. Then resting her chin on her hand, she says, 'I never told you what that detective asked when you were in hospital.'

I wait. 'No, you didn't. He was an odd little man.'

'Yes, he was. Quite sensitive, really. He wanted to know if you might have been intending to wipe yourself out. Driving deliberately fast to kill yourself.'

I nod. 'He asked me the same thing.'

Carrie is hardly listening; she is focussed on remembering the conversation from those weeks after the accident when everything was so tense. 'I said no, never. It wasn't in your nature to give up. I told him that some years ago we'd gone through a very difficult time with one of our children, we hadn't known where to turn, but you carried us through. In fact, I used the term – you *soldiered on*. Which I suppose was an odd phrase for me to use.'

I smile. 'Not so odd. It was one of your father's phrases. Used to drive me mad.'

She lowered her head. 'It did. There was a lot about him that drove you mad. He didn't bend, did he? But he was wonderful to me. He made me tough and you need that, I've realised, more and more.'

'Yes, you do,' I say. 'It can't have been easy for him bringing you up on his own when your mother left. He made you a survivor, Carrie, and that's not a bad thing.'

We sit for a moment, somehow on an even keel, both aware of a kind of truce between us, letting the other be themselves. No questions and no answers expected.

'Do you remember the time we had to go and fetch Jack from the police station?' Carrie says, back in another part of our past. 'We'd been frantic when he'd disappeared and some dog walker had found him crouched in the wood in a makeshift tent... God, that was an awful time.'

'It was.' The memory was still raw. 'It was a long time ago. I really think he's doing OK now. That job's given him confidence and he's doing well at it. I'd have been lost without him over the past few months. He's been such a support.'

'Yes, he has. And trying to help Steph and me... and how he stood up to that bloody David...'

'Yes, don't go worrying about Jack. He's doing fine.'

She's looking at me as though there's something else she wants to hear. When I tilt my head and stay silent, she says, 'I know I've been much too impatient with him...'

'Oh, Carrie, none of us gets it right all the time. Being a parent's bloody difficult. You learn as you go along.'

She nods and I can tell she hasn't finished. She's going to make the most of the first real talk we've had for a long time and needs to get everything off her chest.

'There's something else, Alex,' she says.

I tense, afraid of what's coming, though I've no idea what's on her mind. Guilt has a terrible way of making you hypersensitive, as though you're waiting for the bombshell you're sure will come at the most unexpected moment. I decide to give no encouragement.

'It was yesterday,' she said. 'Jack told me about the billboard he happened to pass near where you had the accident. It was advertising a bridge over the M56 and he was convinced you'd gone that night to find out more about it. He said he told you and it didn't jog any memories...' She waited for me to say something. 'Why didn't you tell me about it? Especially when it makes sense of the whole thing. Why didn't you mention it?'

I couldn't answer straight away. Whatever I said would be a lie, but I wasn't going to add to my sins by pretending that this scenario provided a solution to my whereabouts on that night. So I chose the lie that let me off the hook. Always the coward.

'I didn't think there was much point. I still can't remember what happened so it's no good guessing, going over it all again and again. Nothing comes back to me and I want to forget the whole thing. Selfishly. I don't want to think about it anymore.'

That much is true. I shrug and look away.

Carrie's voice is full of sympathy, understanding me when I don't deserve it. 'OK, but it's the likeliest reason.'

I'm desperate to change the subject, so I say, 'Have you heard from your mother?'

'Yes, a text. She'd like to come for Christmas Day.'

I pull a face and we both laugh. 'That'd be an interesting mix!' I wait for her to go on. 'What did you say?'

She sighs and runs her hands through her hair, already wild and curling out in a sort of ragged halo. 'I said no. There are some things you can't forgive. Going off is one thing. Leaving us behind and creating a new life without even a thought for us is another. It was betrayal. And I don't want to look her in the eye ever again. So she's had it.'

She stands up and goes to the back door to pull on her wellies and a waterproof coat, nudging Sam to get up and keep her company. 'He's had enough of the snow, Carrie,' I say. 'I know you want to keep him going but he's daft enough to lie down in the ice and make his arthritis ten times worse. Leave him with me.'

She lifts her hand as she goes out the door, never one to be contradicted but she's letting it go, seeing that's best. Perhaps after all, there's a way of meeting in the middle, I think, of coming to some sort of mutual respect that hasn't been fostered for a long time. If ever. Time stops you noticing. Or caring. We've been too busy going our own way not noticing the gaps.

I sit in the kitchen with the winter light fading outside even though it's only afternoon and I fall into a bit of a doze. Something about the mood I'm in makes me think about the time I was helping Lucy with the novel she was studying for GCSE, '*To Kill a Mocking Bird*'. We'd come to the part where Atticus is explaining to Scout that to really understand someone you have to '*stand in their shoes.*' Or was it '*walk around in their skin?*' Same concept. It's such a wonderful lesson to learn, particularly for a teenager but the trouble is whatever age you are, it's so hard to do. You try and see things from someone else's point of view, but your own outlook gets in the way. The only one who I think comes near it is Joe. And it's Aaron who's been the teacher. You have to adapt to another way of looking at the world without words being either a help or a hindrance. Trying to understand where Aaron is coming from, you have to work out what's going on inside his head. And because he doesn't quite fit normal expectations, you're feeling your way. What's amazing is you soon realise his other qualities – an amazing intuition, a joy of simple things, that loving nature without a hint of nastiness. Perhaps you don't always succeed in standing in his shoes but you damn well keep trying. Not just for his sake but for yours as well.

Something makes Sam start suddenly and look alert. Then, the moment gone, he lowers his head onto the mat, one bright eye now fixed on me, hoping for a Bonio if it's just the two of us. He's another one you have to learn what the signs mean.

And it's two-way. He can read me like a book.

Later, when Jack comes in from work, we all eat together in the warm kitchen and he never stops talking; the day had been hectic, customers needing advice on presents for their family, how some of the temporary staff are too slow. I tell him about my job and he smiles congratulations. He's anxious he's bought everyone enough presents and I keep saying, it doesn't matter. As long as he's bought one for Sam! Anyway, it's good to hear him rattle on and his mother listens without asking too many questions. Of course eventually he wants to know about David removing his horses.

'He's been to feed them the other morning,' Carrie says. 'Steph was wary, naturally, but he ignored her and was gone when she looked round. Haven't seen anything of Jodie, poor kid. Anyway, I don't think he's going to cause trouble – well, only by slagging me off. I can take that.'

Jack nods as he shovels in more spaghetti carbonara and lets it go. Then, as he finishes his meal, he surprises us with news that Grace is joining him at the pub tomorrow night, Christmas Eve, for a bit of a party.

Carrie and I look at one another and say nothing. We let it ride and keep our fingers crossed.

*

And Fran? With my family round me, work keeping me occupied, a Christmas gathering of everybody I hold dear? My body healthy and a new year to look forward to?

Don't I think about her?

You might as well ask – don't I breathe?

Of course I think about her – at every quiet moment in the day, when something I'm watching on TV triggers a memory, when I sip a drink, before I fall asleep. Like a comfort blanket for a small child, I can't let go. Not in my head. She's as much a part of me now as my appendix scar, my weakened right arm, my memories of childhood. The image of her – what a photo captures in a fleeting second: the dark hair curving round her face, the expressive eyes, the sarcastic lift of one eyebrow, the way she'd laugh – that might fade is it did before. That's inevitable. But her *being* won't fade. How she made me feel, made me smile, the sense of being loved.

You only have one chance at that sort of perfect.

Yet of course you know life's always more complicated than that. Perhaps you wish it wasn't and the 'one chance' could last forever. But there are always other things to consider, other commitments, other pulls, other debts to pay. No matter what, relationships in your life can be wildly different but the word '*love*' still comes into the mix somewhere. So many interpretations that can't be bound up in a word too small to cope with all the vagaries of living.

So Fran did the right thing in so many ways. We weren't to be. Face it. And get on with making things work.

Too many years ahead for us to sit feeling sorry for ourselves.

Whenever as a kid I felt hard done by and decided to sulk, my mother would say, '*Now young man, you can just get that look off your face.*' Even though I was never quite sure how to do it. I got the gist.

Chapter 38

Jack had got up before it was light. He felt pretty good considering he'd only had four hours' sleep. But he'd always loved Christmas Day. It was as though he was still six years old waiting to find a pillow case with all his presents left at the end of the bed. He loved having all the family here, particularly Joe's lot, and Colin and their neighbour Mary had been invited to join them, so there was plenty of company. Everyone would be arriving at eleven for the usual snacks: crostini and sausages and blinis, and there was always the hope that the dinner would be on time, not the hour late as it inevitably always was. Even with his mother's sheet of instructions in place next to the oven, the meal was never quite ready; there was too much toasting with glasses of Prosecco and opening of presents and getting distracted. The morning went by before they realised, everything taking longer than planned. Every year, the whole day always ran late.

He'd padded down to the kitchen in his pyjamas and made himself a cup of tea and toasted a muffin. The house was quiet, everyone, even Sam still sleeping. So he sat for a minute, tired after a hectic rush at work the day before and then the party at the pub which went on into the early hours of the morning. He felt in a good place as though this was the beginning of something, not sure quite what, but he supposed part of that was Grace. He had no idea whether this fledging relationship in its latest form was moving towards something more serious or not... but that wasn't what mattered. It was just nice to have her company, to find that they still had a lot in common. It secured him to something he didn't have to work at from scratch.

Two o'clock in the morning, they'd sat on the stone seats outside the pub door waiting for Grace's taxi to arrive in the freezing cold

('*No chance before three, mate! It's Christmas Eve!*'), half-asleep, keeping an eye on the road beyond the green in case they missed it and were left there till morning. 'We'd be statues by then,' Grace had said, rubbing her arms in her padded jacket to try and keep the blood circulating. 'Christ, it's cold.'

'The night was fun though.' Jack moved closer to give her some body warmth. 'Didn't know Leo could play the violin. He's full of surprises.'

He could sense her amused expression in the dark. 'It *was* fun. Really enjoyed it. There's something about a village. Everyone knows one other and they aren't bothered about letting their hair down.'

'Well, that's not what you said before you upped and left.' Jack couldn't help himself. 'How did it go? It was claustrophobic, no-one getting out into the world, any ambition stifled.'

She shrugged. 'Ah well. You're allowed to change your mind.'

'Yeah! Right!' He wasn't going to carry on with that. No point going over old ground. 'So your first term's over and it sounds as though they like you. They're bound to give you a permanent job at the end of the year, aren't they?'

'Hope so. I've got really fond of the kids but not so sure about what we're made to teach – it just isn't going the right way. No-one's allowed to explore anymore.' She sighed, her breath white as it hit the frosty air. 'I'm going to bore you now, but you did ask.' She looked over at him to make sure he was listening. 'If it's meant to be about the children first which is what the government always says, then they're concentrating on the wrong things. All this structure, all these rules that you can't deviate from, it just kills any enjoyment. They've cut all the imaginative stuff, the music and art and they're exhausting the teachers with all these forms and assessments which take them away from the classroom. It's stress all round...'

'Hey, I thought you were nearly asleep.'

'I am. But it's nice to have an audience. And nice to tell someone who knows how bloody dull it can all be. You weren't the most engaged at school…'

'Well no…'

'All I'm saying is, it's ten times worse now. Most of these politicians have never been inside an ordinary primary school or a comp…' She jerks her hat down over her ears. 'Sorry. I'm going on and it's the holidays and I should shut up. But I just hope it all goes in a full circle and we get someone leading who knows how things should be run.'

He caught hold of her gloved hand and squeezed it. 'It's good someone is taking up the fight. I'll bet you make a difference for some little underachiever like I was.'

'Hope so.'

They watch as car headlights move slowly along the road, wheels ploughing through slush as it drives on, up through the village and, seeing it isn't stopping, they sink back to wait a bit longer.

'What's your news this week then?' she said. 'Bet you've been run off your feet at Parsons.'

'Yes, enjoyed it though. I'm treated like an old hand now. It's working out.' He paused, looking up at a sky so bright with stars it looked unreal. 'The less light coming from your patch of earth, the more you can see the stars. Did you know that?'

'Everybody knows that.'

And they chuckled at it all – sitting together again, sharing their thoughts, comfortable with each other, even in the almost unbearable cold.

'Had some trouble at the farm last week. Or was it this week? I'm losing track of time.'

'What, an accident?'

'No.' He wondered whether he should say anything about the business but he'd started now and it was Grace he was talking to. 'A bloke has been stabling his horse and his kid's pony with us for a few months. I hadn't taken much notice of him. They're always coming and going, the liveries, and it was only when I saw how anxious Steph was that I started to worry. You know what she's always been like – a rock, so steady, loves the horses and does more of the work than my mother. Anyway, she told me this bloke was starting to take over, trying to anyway…'

'From your mother?' Grace's voice rose in surprise. 'He'd have to be something to manage that.'

'Well, he was a difficult type to deal with, all charm one minute, demanding the next and I think, well, I think my mother was sort of flattered. He had her teaching his kid, took her to a fancy horse event and then began talking about expanding the business. He wanted a piece of it, Steph reckoned, and he had no time for her because he must have felt she was on to him.'

'Go on. This is like a film.'

'Anyway, it all blew up when he'd upset Steph so much with his criticising and bullying it was time to tell him to go and of course, he got nasty. It all got nasty and I was in the yard when my mother ordered him out.'

'What did you do?'

'I told him to go, otherwise there'd be legal consequences. I didn't think he'd take any notice and I can't remember actually what I said – I was bluffing really – but he began backing off. I'd butted in not knowing what would happen, but nothing did. Not really. He just… backed off.'

'That was brave. Well done.'

'It was only after I began to think about it, it all began to add up… He was a typical bully, you know, and bullies always go for what they see as weakness or fear, for people who aren't going to fight back. They have to keep control and they get used to being top dog because no-one wants to take them on. We're all too ready to avoid confrontation.' Grace was looking straight ahead towards the road, but he sensed she was listening intently, not wanting to interrupt until she'd heard what he'd made of it.

'What I've learned, I think, is that bullies are really the ones who are scared. They make a lot of noise and show because there's something lacking in themselves and they don't want to face that. They have to bluster. Once you stand up to them, they... deflate! Does that make sense?'

Grace pulled him to her and kissed his frozen mouth. 'Jack, you're a wonder. Why on earth didn't you work that out when you were having all that awful hassle with those Gordon brothers? They weren't even much older than you. But they needed a punch bag and you were it. We all heard later that you'd been made ill by it all but it was *much* later, so there was nothing we could do to help by then.' She kept her face very close to his. 'God, it's good to hear. You *have* grown up. And thank goodness for that.'

He grinned. 'Yes, thank goodness. It's taken a few years...'

'Never mind. You haven't needed to study Psychology. Far better to think it out for yourself.'

A car tooted from the road as the wind blew icy shards into their eyes, obscuring the near distance.

'Quick, Grace.' He pulled her up. 'Don't lose him whatever you do.'

And he watched as she ran across the green towards the taxi, its engine idling, two beams of light picking up the flurry of falling sleet. He waved but couldn't make out whether she waved back. He thought about lifting his tired body off the bench, knowing it would only take him five minutes to reach home but he felt too comfortable, his legs a bit wobbly and not yet ready to hold him up. So he sat there, cold but quite content, listening to the sounds of drunken shouting and laughter echoing through the night from the village.

He leaned his head back and found he was looking up at the black sky and the bright pinpricks of light with a sense of how vast it all was, how small he was in the whole scheme of things. And how incredible it was, him sitting here looking up from his bit of world, that he knew barely anything about the universe, about what life was really about, what future had in store for him. You were in the hands of something so much bigger than yourself and he didn't understand any of it. There'd been news coverage over the last two days about two incidents of stabbing in different parts of London – lads younger than him – and old photos of them as kids. And he'd looked at the grainy pictures and thought, Imagine, fifteen years old and you'd never see the sky again, the trees, the fields. No more family or friends... no more years ahead. No sense of... anything. You're wiped out in an instant by one single blow. It could be any one of us – we're too fragile. Just a pity whoever made us didn't provide some steel coating for a bit more protection, like a shark's skin or give us speed, like a cheetah. We're too vulnerable. Arms and legs that can snap, skulls that aren't thick enough, body parts that go horribly wrong; then we create wars to make things even more hazardous. It's a wonder there's a human race left at all.

He shifted on the hard bench and still couldn't quite get up the energy to head home.

So Dad was lucky. A blow to the head could have been the end. And not just for him. It would have been the end for us. What on earth would life have been like if he'd never recovered from that coma, if he'd been absent from our lives, if we hadn't had a chance to let him know how much we loved him?

He could feel himself sobering up at the thought of that ICU room in the hospital and those desperate days when it was touch and go. The filtered air, the artificial light, the sounds of breathing through those tubes and the unbearable waiting, waiting for some sign. For the first flicker of an eyelid, the first sound or movement. It wasn't something he ever wanted to go through again.

It wasn't something he would ever forget...

...How all he could think of doing was talk and talk – anything to reconnect, bring his dad back into a world he'd recognise. What a moment when he'd felt him grip his hand! Not wanting to call anyone and raise false alarms. But then he'd opened his eyes – just for a second and it was enough to feel hopeful. You could see it was such hard work and he had to take his own time, you couldn't push him. You were holding your breath. It was like watching a kid with building blocks that needed such care fitting them together and you had to be patient. The painful struggle to form words... the evening when he made a sound like one he'd made before but this **time it was** a word – 'Sorry,' he'd said. Sorry for what? Sorry for crashing his car? For frightening us all?

And why say that to me?

His leg suddenly cramped and he jerked up, banging his head against the stone wall behind him. He realised he'd half dozed off and he'd better move before his body froze and they found him in the morning glued to the bench. He stood up and hobbled a few steps, trying to get his legs to work. Tiredness really hit him now, he'd never felt more ready for a warm bed and a good few hours' sleep.

He pushed himself on. Five minutes and he'd be home. It had been quite a night...

So why he'd got up so early after so little sleep he didn't know. Except it was Christmas Day. He sat at the kitchen table now, cupping his hands round his mug of tea and deciding to light the wood-burning stove before he got dressed. His first good deed of the day. He heard the bathroom door opening and closing upstairs.

Time to get going.

*

They all seemed determined to have a good time and it was great to have the house filled with noise, as though the whole place was loosening up again, Jack thought. He stood at the door, taking coats and shaking hands, hugging Aaron who was wearing a cowboy hat and carrying a large model aeroplane. The last to arrive was Mary, dressed as though she was going to church, insisting she'd have been perfectly all right on her own. Colin had come early with a pot plant for Carrie, getting soil all over his shoes as he took it into the kitchen. But Jack saw how pleased she was, making sure the old man had a beer rather than wine which was much more to his liking.

Aaron was high as a kite, a bundle of enthusiasm about everything and they all let him be; Joe's girls were prepared to be bored and his grandparents were full of fuss and chatter and smiles. Christmases, Jack thought, in good years, follow the same pattern – snacks, present giving, a turkey dinner, too many glasses of wine, a determination to be good humoured and stamina to make it to the end of the day. And this was no different. It had its usual clamour and humour as the hours passed...

...Grandad asleep amid all the noise, a yellow paper crown still on this head... Aaron lying on the floor playing with the dog. Joe's girls on their iPhones, fighting over the Quality Street... *Does anyone want a turkey sandwich yet? ...A chorus of, 'Nooooo...'* Gran tidying up... *Sit down for Heaven's sake! ...Remember Frozen's on at six...* His mother and Anna in deep conversation by the window, sharing something intimate... *Someone put a log on the fire! ...Don't, it's like an oven in here...* Mary, confused, turning her head from one group to another... *That bike hasn't been used yet... As soon as the roads are clear...* Colin, eyes half-closed like an old sheep dog, aware of everything around him. *Lucy hasn't rung, has she? 'Articulate... you promised we'd play... As long as I'm not with Grandad... Another drink, anyone?*

By nine o'clock, Jack's head was spinning. The front door had finally shut and everyone had gone home. And although the house was turned upside down, at last there was calm. He was meant to ring Grace and he would in a minute but for now it was good to sit there, surrounded by empty plates, discarded wrapping paper and stacks of books and games, with boxes of chocolates piled up against the wall. His dad was dozing in front of a muted TV, his mother lay full-length on the couch with a tumbler half full of whiskey balanced on her stomach and Jack could feel the drink he'd consumed through the day adding to last night's, all that over-indulgence catching up on him.

'Dad, are you asleep?'

'Well, I was.' He gave a yawn.

'I'll make us some coffee.'

'Good idea. Just for us, Jack. Your mother's asleep.'

Just as he said that, she jumped suddenly, half sitting up and spilling her drink onto her shirt. 'Blast! Wasted a glass of good whiskey there,' she said and yawned. 'OK, I've had it, I'm off to bed.' She pushed herself onto her feet and made her way up the stairs, calling back, 'Don't drop off in that chair, Alex.'

In the kitchen, Jack put the coffee in the percolator and rang Grace on his mobile. The call was short and easy and he took a deep breath of relief. Perhaps things were working out. Life could turn on a sixpence, he thought, one minute crap, the next positively hopeful. Perhaps you have to experience highs and lows as you grow older to realise that usually, neither lasts. It's like riding a roller coaster and you hope you can grip hard enough and hold on as you go down the steep bits.

So when he went back into the lounge, he wasn't quite prepared for what he saw, what he only caught a glimpse of – such a forlorn expression on his dad's face, a sadness in his eyes, as though he was thinking of something miles away. Lost in thought that made him heavy-hearted. It was one of those private moments Jack was sure he wasn't meant to see. As soon as his dad heard him, the expression was gone in a flash and he smiled as he took hold of the mug.

'Great. Need this to stay awake.'

'You're allowed to go to bed if you want.' Jack wasn't sure how to go on, how to pretend he hadn't noticed, how to lift the mood. 'What did you think of the book I bought you? Clever choice? I really went to town on the research.'

'Yes. I thought '*The Dead Zone*' couldn't be a coincidence.'

Jack squatted on the floor beside his dad's chair. 'You've read it before, haven't you?'

'Years ago when I was a teenager. One of the first Stephen King I bought – lent it to someone though and didn't get it back.' He looked better already as he talked, Jack thought. Good. 'I've forgotten quite a lot of the detail so it's about time I read it again.'

'I looked up the blurb on Amazon and thought, hey, this is Dad – a bloke out for the count in a coma then when he recovers he can see what's about to happen. He touches people and gets vibes from them. You could become famous.'

'What an imagination you've got. I certainly can't see what's coming and I couldn't think of anything more frightening.'

'He also can tell what someone's done in the past.'

'Even worse.' He ruffled Jack's hair. 'Let's just be glad I'm well.'

'I really am.' Jack looked up at his dad with a serious face, sobered suddenly. 'You've no idea how much.'

There was a moment when something deeper passed between them, too delicate to be spoken out loud, perhaps because it wasn't part of their established relationship. Jack flushed, feeling awkward until his dad brought them back onto safe ground. 'Anyway,' he said, 'thanks for going to all that trouble. It was thoughtful. Which you always are, Jack.'

They nodded at one another and decided against turning the news on, too depressing, and began watching an old episode of 'Fawlty Towers', just as they'd done when he was a kid.

The two of them sitting in the half dark. Neither wanting to see the future.

Or look back into the past.

After all, they couldn't change any of it even if they wanted to.

ABOUT THE AUTHOR

The author has spent her working life in journalism and education. Originally from Manchester, she now lives in County Durham with her husband, a collie called Murphy and an ex-racehorse, Bertie. She has an MA in Creative Writing.

Printed in Great Britain
by Amazon